To all the booksellers, with special thanks to:
Jude and Alan at Borderlands;
Maryelizabeth at Mysterious Galaxy;
Patrick Nichol at Indigo Books & Music;
Kevin J. and Kasey Coolidge at From My Shelf Books & Gifts;
Del at Dark Delicacies

Imagine time seen as a continuum—an infinite line containing everything that was and everything that will be...

Time perhaps as a tangible object. One that can be touched, like a mural on a wall that stretches infinitely in both directions. Portraying everything that has happened, is happening, and will happen. In one direction is the future unfolding. In the other direction the past, much of it forgotten, back to the beginning of time itself.

Imagine time as a stained-glass window. The story of everything laid out in a glittering mosaic of trillions upon trillions of moments, from the big bang to the fiery death of the universe.

Finally, imagine the fragility of such a window.

1

Advanced Transpatial Physics Lab, Antarctica
February 2, 2219
One hour before the Event

This is the day the universe changes.

The realization hit him just as he awoke. Future generations of students would be taught about this morning the way he learned about Archimedes leaping from his bath to run naked through the streets of ancient Syracuse yelling "Eureka!" Or Benjamin Franklin flying a kite in a lightning storm, or the day the apple fell on Newton's head.

The day Meta launched humanity on the path to the stars...

Dr. Jonathan Meta slipped out of the covers and sat up. The clock in his cerebral implant advised him it was 6:45am, New Zealand Standard Time. He spoke quietly to the window blinds. They obediently polarized out of existence, and his quarters filled with pure Antarctic sunlight.

The dazzling tableau outside his window revealed unrelenting whiteness and a crystal-sharp blue sky. The inescapable sun hadn't dipped below the horizon for five months, and wouldn't until the end of March. To better preserve their sanity, many of the station's personnel had opted to change their window displays to more festive holographic options, such as a vintage view from pre-Warming Hawaii, or a live-feed of the scintillating nightlife on the canals of New York.

Dr. Meta kept his window unadorned and his quarters austere. He found that the polar seasonal alterations between stark brightness and near-endless darkness suited him. For five years, he had been the director and the leading researcher of the Omnia Astra Project—the search for faster-than-light interstellar travel. A monk-like existence with a minimum of distractions helped him focus on the lab's mission—which finally was coming to fruition.

Rather than risk the media circus waiting to ambush him in the lab commissary, he had the room whip up a quick breakfast of hot chai and a plate of *mandazi*, fried doughnuts flavored with cardamom and coconut. Kenyan cuisine was all the rage this season.

After a quick shower he dried off with a freshly-fabricated towel, still warm, and called up a mirror in the shape of a holographic half-shell. It shimmered into existence and he examined his face. Meta had no sense of vanity, but he knew that today of all days it would be important to look good for the cameras. His fox-like brown eyes had a strong Asian cast to them, though like most of the population, his bronze skin and blend of features no longer fit neatly into the largely obsolete categories like Caucasian, Negroid or Mongoloid.

There was no need to shave, since his facial hair would only grow if he gave it permission. His somewhat longer-than-normal hair was his only indulgence—it gave him a professorial air to let it grow down to his collar. Among his straight-laced and close-shorn colleagues, a striking mane of silver provided a heraldic *sui generis* touch.

Meta tossed the towel into the fabricator. With a soft hum, it swiftly disassembled the fabric while he dressed, choosing shades of charcoal and black to reflect the gravity of the day. He stepped into his shoes as the fabricator finished reweaving the towel into a fresh new lab coat. After one final check in the mirror, he told it to go away.

Taking a deep breath, he stepped out of his quarters.

A trio of sleek black spheres, each slightly more than twice the size of a billiard ball, hung perfectly still, suspended in the air. They had been waiting for him with unfailing patience.

Don't look at the cameras, he reminded himself.

The rover drones were for the documentary. Instead of using a neural link to record through his eyes, the producers had chosen to do a holo, preferring a more retro look to give the footage a timeless quality. Meta did his best to ignore the drones as he proceeded down the corridor. Moments later he encountered the first of the station personnel.

"Good luck, Dr. Meta," the man said earnestly.

More colleagues, technicians, and research assistants smiled and offered words of encouragement as he and his floating entourage continued on their way. The excitement in the air was palpable, and beneath his normally calm exterior even he found himself struggling to tamp down a growing sense of exhilaration.

Reaching the intersection that would take him to the station commons, Meta stopped, listening to the press conference commencing inside. After a brief internal debate, he retreated. Better to face the reporters after the morning's experiment was a success. He'd take the long way around, past the labs and conference rooms.

He had nearly navigated the entire labyrinth when the first of the rovers, seeking a long tracking shot, sailed past an automatic door. As it slid open, muffled voices came from inside.

Meta paused. Something wasn't right.

Without warning, a plump little Adélie penguin—its head barely reached his knee—nonchalantly waddled into the hallway. The bird peered up at him for a moment before toddling off back through the doorway.

Meta stared after the bold little bird.

Did the film crew stage this? If so, he wasn't sure how he felt about the artistic choice.

"Dr. Meta!" a voice called out from the open door. Before he could hurry past, a generically handsome man stuck his head out into the corridor.

Gifford, the resident biologist.

Meta couldn't stand him.

"Didn't think we'd see you down here," Gifford exclaimed, voice filled with artificial bonhomie. He seemed oblivious to his colleague's frown. "I thought you'd be in the commons with the paparazzi. This *is* a lucky surprise!"

"Yes, well…" Meta smiled weakly. "If you'll excuse me, I—"

"Come meet my students."

"Well, I—"

Gifford grabbed Meta's arm before he could refuse, pulling him into the classroom where a dozen or so eager young faces turned toward their professor.

"Here's Dr. Meta, the man of the hour." At once, the students turned their attention to the startled director and gathered around him. Gifford beamed, adding, "These are the grad students visiting us from University of New Fiji."

Meta tried to mask his irritation with the unctuous biologist. No sense in taking it out on these chipper young innocents. Besides, he was genuinely happy to encourage future scientists in his field.

"You're all doing Transpatial Physics?" he said. "That's splendid!"

"Actually," Gifford said, cutting in again, "this batch is with the anthropology dept."

"Anthropology?" Meta replied, surprised. "The Tierra del Fuegians are quite a ways off. Or are they here to study Antarctic physics researchers?" He smiled. "That's an isolated test group, if ever there was one." As the students laughed, Meta wondered which of the attractive young grads Gifford had his eye on. At least three appeared to fall within his chosen target demographic.

As if on cue, the biologist sidled up to Meta like the bosom chums they weren't, putting a hand on his shoulder and leaning in conspiratorially.

"It's a special academic field trip I helped arrange," he said, then he straightened. "So Meta, I promised this bunch you'd take time out from the celebration tonight, and join us for a less stuffy party on their expedition craft. You have to see it—it's an *Avialae* StratoYacht. Absolutely top of the line—delta-field, multi-pterophase energy wings, just a gorgeous piece of aerodynamics."

"We'll just have to see how it goes," he replied noncommittally.

"Of course, of course—you have to make your appearances," Gifford said with a wink. "Anyway, we already have you down as our very special guest of honor. I know you won't let us down." Without waiting for a response, he turned back to the grad students. "We'd better let Dr. Meta get back to making history. But we'll all be celebrating with him tonight." The knot of well-wishers erupted in cheers.

Meta tried for a smile, failed, and gave a weak wave.

I'll get you for this, you conniving weasel, he thought.

"After today you're going to be the world's biggest rock star—at least until the first interstellar starship captain comes along!" Gifford laughed a bit too loudly and clapped Meta on the back just a bit too hard. The director gritted his teeth and tried to exit gracefully.

"Alright then," he said, nodding to them. "I really must head out. Wonderful to meet you all, and good luck with your studies." Before he could make his escape, Gifford intercepted him, seizing him by the shoulders and pinning him with a terribly serious gaze.

"Jonathan," the biologist said intently, loud enough for the drones to pick up his words. "I just want you to know… I'm behind you. No—the *world* is behind you as you change the course of human history. Now go, my friend, and show us the way to the stars." The more sentimental students sighed at this touching display. Meta gave a silent, tight-lipped nod, gently but firmly extricating himself from the man's grasp. He walked across to the door, but paused before exiting and turned back.

"Gifford?"

"Yes, Jonathan?"

"Someone let a penguin out. Make sure you take care of that, will you?" Meta left before the man could respond.

The Kuruman Hills, Northern Cape Province, South Africa
Approximately 1.5 Million Years B.C.
Twenty-two minutes before the Event

The brothers' hunt has been successful. The pair had stolen the haunch of a leopard's freshly killed gazelle, chasing the big cat away with shouts and thrown stones. Returning to the cave, they kneel by the warmth of the fire and begin to eat, messily tearing apart the raw flesh. Their younger brother watches them, his mouth watering, hoping to snag a scrap.

The two older males ferociously quarrel over a choice piece, each trying to wrest it from the other's grasp. Slick with blood, the morsel suddenly shoots away, landing into the heart of the fire with a puff of ash and sparks.

Enraged at their loss, they turn on each other—howling with rage, snarling and clawing at each other. Their younger brother pays no attention and stares in dismay at the meat in the fire, sizzling and popping on the red-hot coals. The smell is tantalizing.

His gaze falls on a piece of antler, left from an earlier kill.

Licking his lips, he braves the flames, quickly spearing the blackening chunk and then rushing to a darkened corner with his prize. The meat is hot, burning his lips when he tries to bite it, but soon cools enough for him to quickly devour it.

So delicious.

2

The *Vanuatu*
40,000 feet over the African continent
Morning — Six days after the Event

"Help me, Amber..."

He stood in front of her, a tall man in a spectral black shroud, dwarfed by the massive stone paws of the Great Sphinx. Beckoning to her, staring at her with blue-violet eyes, pinpoints of light dancing there like a cascade of stars falling down an endless well...

Amber woke with a start, hands in a death-grip on the sheets, bedclothes plastered to her sweat-soaked body. Her heart pounded so rapidly, it felt as if it might burst out of her chest. Screwing her eyes shut again, she concentrated on deep, even breaths until her pulse slowed to something close to normal, and she could relax back into the bed.

The mattress beneath her was firm, the pillow and bedding soft and comforting. Eyes still shut, Amber could almost imagine that she was back at her aunt's house in Romford, getting ready for another day of the science fiction convention. The very thought, however, reminded her of the harsh reality.

Neither Romford nor her aunt's house existed any longer.

Slamming the door on that horrifying thought, Amber turned her attention to the dream—yet another one about their host, Dr. Meta. Somehow, she'd dreamt about the man even before she'd met him, and even afterward the strange visions had continued. When she told him about them, Meta had no explanation, yet without a doubt they were about him. The eerie blue-violet eyes and the pinpricks of light that seemed to move through them, as if passing through a tunnel.

Only Merlin—as she called him—had those.

Giving up on sleep she sat up and rubbed her fingertips over her face, trying to shake off the surreal images. In the dream he looked like the Grim Reaper, but why was he in Egypt? What did he want from her?

"Help me, Amber..."

"What the hell does it mean?" she said out loud.

"Can I assist you, Ms. Richardson?"

At the sound of the electronic voice, she jumped. The disembodied voice of the ship, gentle as it was, took her by surprise. She'd forgotten it could talk.

"Ahhh... good morning," Amber replied—and how weird was it to be talking to thin air? Feeling as if she should give the ship something to do, she added, "Um, could you open a porthole for me?"

The *Vanuatu's* artificial intelligence obliged. Next to her bed a window appeared like an iris in the cabin walls. She had no idea what material the ship was made of, but it reminded her of an amoeba made of Silly Putty, able to alter its shape and texture. The rising sun flooded bright morning light into her cabin.

"Thank you," she said, shielding her eyes.

"You're welcome, Ms. Richardson. Please let me know of any items you might need to have cleaned, repaired, recycled, or created. Each cabin has a nanofabricator for your personal use."

"Created?"

That was new. Then again, they hadn't had time for a full introduction to the ship's capabilities.

"Yes, and for larger items beyond the scope of your personal unit, there is a larger nanofabricator available, as well. Would you like to see it?"

"Ah, no thank you," Amber said. Her mind boggled at the possibilities, but it was too much to process at the moment. "Maybe later."

Instead, she looked out the portal at the vista beyond. The airship's wings amazed her. They weren't flat, fixed metal like twenty-first century airplanes. These were made of artful, almost fluid projections of solid light, each iridescent panel of energy looking like a feather in the craft's bird-like wings.

Wrapping her arms around her knees she leaned her head against the window, collecting her thoughts as she tried to catch glimpses of the landscape visible between the passing clouds below.

The days and hours since the Event had been the most tumultuous of her life. Over the past few days, she'd been hunted by dire wolves, nearly burned at the stake by Cromwell's Roundheads, battled with giant sea scorpions... and worse. A twinge of sadness stabbed at her as she remembered everyone she'd left behind in England. Yet she was still alive, and relatively unscathed. As Merlin had explained, there really wasn't a future or past anymore. Time had become a jumbled mishmash of shards—different shapes, different sizes, and different times—extending as far as millions of years into the past to nearly two centuries in the future.

If she could buy that, then accepting the sci-fi tech that surrounded her was a piece of cake.

Cake...

Amber's stomach rumbled at the thought of food, and with it came the siren call of coffee.

"Ship, is it possible to get a cup of coffee in my room?"

"Certainly, Ms. Richardson," the ship replied. *"You*

can have breakfast in here if you'd like."

"No, thank you." The thought was tempting, but she thought she'd rather eat with her fellow survivors. "Just coffee."

"Would you like cream or sugar?"

"Both, please."

Without a sound, a blob of ship-stuff protruded from the wall and opened up, revealing a plain white mug, steam rising from the top. The liquid was a rich medium brown, with swirls of cream still dissolving into it, and the fragrance... Amber took a sip and smiled in a moment of pure bliss. She'd never thought to have coffee this good again.

It reminded her of the cafeteria in *Star Trek*—where the replicator provided whatever its passengers desired. She wondered if the ingredients were synthetic, then decided she didn't care.

Dad would love this.

Then she shoved that thought away.

Her father, along with her mom, brother, and sister—all of her friends... The odds were so small that any of them had survived the Event that it hurt her to hope.

Her glance fell on a burgundy backpack leaning against the cabin wall. That backpack and its contents were pretty much the only remnants she had from her old life. She didn't know whether to smile or cry. Instead, she looked out the window again.

Once she'd finished her coffee, Amber picked up her newly cleaned and mended clothes—courtesy of the ship. Breeches and soft leather boots she'd stolen from a Roundhead soldier, a white corset-style top from her Codex cosplay, and the Han Solo jacket her date had been wearing when the world went to hell.

She refused to let herself linger on that memory, either.

Instead, she turned her thoughts to Cam, a first-century British Celt who'd also lost his home and family. He'd defended her and fought at her side since they'd met, and he'd nearly died before they'd gained the safety of the *Vanuatu*. Suddenly all she wanted was to see him. Breakfast could wait until after that.

Digging into her backpack she pulled out a brush, ran it through her long red hair, and left her cabin.

With the help of the AI, Amber navigated her way toward the medical lab. As she walked down the main corridor, she expected to see lots of chrome, bank after bank of computer screens, and *Enterprise*-style instrument panels. Yet this felt surprisingly retro.

Cozy, she thought. It reminded her of an Amsterdam houseboat, but roomy enough not to feel cramped. Simple cream-colored walls were warm and inviting, like a library.

Reaching the med-lab, she crossed the glowing sterile field in the doorway and went inside, glad she'd taken care to be quiet.

Cam was sound asleep.

Having seen him very nearly beaten to death, she was amazed to see what Merlin's medical nanites had accomplished. Like magic, the army of surgical robots—each one no bigger than a blood cell—had performed a medical miracle.

Hours earlier a blotched, torn landscape of cuts and contusions covered his swollen flesh. Before her eyes, where bruises and wounds had darkened his body's topography, the nanites had laid down delicate links of tiny silver hexagons that made a new map, crisscrossing the fading remnants of his injuries. Then, as now, the transformation fascinated her.

She traced her index finger along the almost invisible strands that stitched his collar bone together. Unable to resist, she ran her hand down across Cam's chest, feeling his heartbeat. Its strong rhythm comforted her. If she leaned over and stood very still, she could even feel the gentle pressure of his breath tickling the skin of her cheek.

Cam's body twitched.

3

Advanced Transpatial Physics Lab, Antarctica
February 2, 2219
Twelve minutes before the Event

Heading toward A level, Meta continued the final leg of his back route, down several levels through the cavernous engineering and computational wings of the complex. As he walked, he activated his neural comlink to the project control room, letting them know he was foregoing the press conference and would be initiating the morning's test run. Against the rules, he glanced up at the closest rover keeping pace just over his shoulder, and spoke directly to the camera.

"Can we please, *please* edit out that business with Gifford from the final cut?"

He descended past the gloomy, almost infernal industrial decks of the station's pipes, machinery, and inner workings, then through the cybernetics wing, past tall banks of computer hardware that seemed almost cathedral-like by contrast. And then through one final door that brought him back to the main corridor.

Meta peered to his right down the long arc of the hallway, wary of stray reporters. It appeared he had managed to give them the slip. Relieved, he let the drones get back into formation and headed around the bend to the left. The entrance to the reactor chamber lay just ahead and, like a sentry, a somber man stood there waiting for him, hands sunk in his lab coat pockets, grim resolve on his long face. Though younger than Meta, Iskandar Khan was already starting to lose his hair, and carried a weight of great seriousness on his shoulders.

Meta's jaw tightened.

He'd been afraid this encounter might occur.

"I can't let you do it, Doctor." Khan's voice was unmenacing, but deadly serious.

"Dr. Khan—Iskandar—you know we can't afford any more delays."

"You know this is a bad idea."

"Nonsense," Meta replied briskly. This wasn't the first time they'd had this argument. "You've seen the modeling, you've run the quantum simulations yourself."

"The anomalies in the chronocrystalline topology," Khan responded, as cracks appeared in his calm, "the irregularities in the quasienergy analysis—"

"All perfectly accounted for," Meta said. "Nonlocal

correlations encoded in the wave-function of the system allows for fault tolerance against any perturbations, and relativistic quantum states will stabilize against the decoherence effects. We've been through all this. We both know the mathematics check out. I'm telling you, we can do this, Iskandar."

"I'm not arguing the mathematics!" Khan shouted.

Meta took a small step backward, stunned at the outburst. Khan had never raised his voice in anger before. The younger physicist caught himself and took a deep breath to regain his composure.

"There's no doubt that we can accomplish the space-time warping," Khan said. "What I'm saying is that we don't know what *else* may occur when we do."

Meta raised a hand. "Listen to me, Iskandar. I understand your concern. I do. I'm grateful for it—"

"But not enough to postpone the trial run."

"Do you have any idea of the restraints we're working against?" Meta's own impatience crept back to the fore. "We've delayed the test too long as it is."

"We're not ready!" Khan insisted. "We *have* to understand the anomalies before we proceed." He pulled his hands from his pockets. They were shaking, balled into tight fists.

"We could speculate to the end of time," Meta said, "but we're never going to unearth the answers you seek—not until we take the first step. The time is now."

"There's no changing your mind, then?"

"It is a mathematical impossibility."

Khan laughed, a clipped, ugly sound. "You know, I thought I could reason with you, Jonathan. I should have brought a gun with me."

Meta stared at his friend in disbelief. "Do you realize you just said that on camera, Khan?"

"You think I'm worried about *going to prison*?" Khan said, matching his stare with a frightening intensity. "Or *dying*?"

"You can't stop this, Iskandar."

"We'll see about that." He pushed past Meta and stormed off down the corridor.

"You can't stop this!" Meta yelled after him. As Khan vanished around the corner, the director wasted no time activating his neural comlink. *"Security, this is Meta. Dr. Khan is in the central hub outside the Primary Chamber. Restrain him immediately."*

4

**Shangyu district, Kuaiji, Jiang Nan region, China
Year of the Earth Dragon, 3485 (848 A.D.)
Eight Minutes Before the Event**

Wu the Alchemist sits in his garden and consults his copy of the *Five-fold Synopsis of the Essentials of the Mysterious Tao of True Formulation*, carefully reviewing the thirty-five common mistakes made in the preparation of immortality elixirs.

Safeguarding longevity had proved unfortunate for a recent series of Tang dynasty emperors—and for the alchemists who had prepared their medicines. All died—the rulers by poisoning, the alchemists by beheading... or worse.

Wu dearly hopes to avoid the fate of his colleagues. Returning to his laboratory, he meticulously weighs out his ingredients. One and a half *liang* of saltpeter to begin, with three *qians* of charcoal and two of sulfur, and finally, following his instincts, a pinch of crushed red realgar crystals to balance the *yin* and *yang*.

Grinding them thoroughly in a jade mortar, he pours the mixture into a small earthenware cauldron and stirs in a dollop of honey to bind it before bringing it to a low heat.

The explosion brings the neighboring peasants rushing to Wu's burning house. They find the alchemist outside, his hands and face blackened with soot, his long white beard and hair singed, like his robe. His house is engulfed in flames and yet he laughs and scampers around like a madman.

"Look! Flying fire!" Wu cries. "I have discovered the hidden essence of fire in earth!"

Med-Lab of the *Vanuatu*
Six days after the Event

Gods of my father…

Vicious memories of pain, raw and red—blows from heavy wooden clubs, kicks from tough hobnailed boots, each impact a thundering lightning strike to his face and skull, his ribs and groin. Looking up from the ground, his vision half-blinded by blood and swirling dizziness, his enemies surrounding him.

Each black silhouette like the finger of grasping hands closing in on him…

Cam opened his eyes.

His people the Trinovantes feared many things— sorcery, curses, sickness, starvation, loss of the gods' favor, loss of cattle—even the loss of honor—but they did not fear death. That was simply the passage to their next life, to be reborn as man or beast, or—if the gods willed it—sail west to their eternal reward in the Isles of the Blest, Éber Donn, *Hy-Brasil*, and *Tír Annún*.

Still… had he died?

Where was he now?

Cam lay on a curiously soft table, unclothed but covered by a simple sheet of cloth. The windowless chamber shone with an unearthly white-silver radiance, bright as sunlight on new-fallen snow. There was but a single doorway, an eldritch blue glow swirling within it as if the way was barred by powerful wards. Had he awakened in a palace of the Otherworld, then? Were the Sídhe waiting to take him across the sea to the undying lands?

Something touched his collarbone—he wasn't alone. The sensation moved gently to his chest to rest above his heart. He opened his eyes and looked up at the figure who was watching over him. Not a Sídhe princess clad in some gown of glittering samite, but Amber, her torn, filthy clothes exchanged for new finery, the smudges of dirt and dried blood washed from her face.

He had never seen a more beautiful sight.

Startled, Amber snatched her hand away and hastily straightened. Cam peered up at her and, after a moment, smiled.

"Amber…"

Elated, she reached out and hugged him tight, while he tried his best to return the favor, though the effort was awkward. They remained like that forever, one of those moments that crystalized in time, until she lifted herself up just high enough to bring them face to face. Her lips parted ever so slightly. She leaned in…

"Let's see how our patient looks this—" Merlin breezed through the blue haze of the med-lab's sterile field, talking to himself. He halted in mid-stride as Amber sat up and Cam's arms fell back to his side.

"My apologies, Amber," Merlin said, clearly embarrassed. "I didn't realize Cam had a visitor."

"No worries." Amber spoke quickly, feeling her face flush with equal parts mortification and irritation. She tried to keep both out of her voice as she added, "It's just so good to see him awake… and alive."

"That it is," Merlin agreed. The scientist had traded his black robe for a seamless gray dress shirt and slacks.

Amber found it almost disconcerting to see him in modern clothing.

He turned to Cam. *"Drog yew ginev, Camtargarus."* Without waiting for an answer, Merlin pulled up Cam's holographic display. It floated above his prone body, a ghostly blue-green holographic doppelganger displaying his internal organs. All the flashing red warnings from before had vanished.

"It looks as if he's well on his way to a full recovery," Merlin said, pleased. "We'll leave the nanites in there a little longer until we're sure there's no long-term cerebral trauma, but I'd say his prognosis is excellent." Amber exhaled in relief and listened while Merlin spoke to Cam for a few minutes in his own language. She loved the sound of the ancient Celtic tribal dialect.

While the two continued what looked to be a lively discussion, Amber discreetly took notice of Merlin's own recovery. The scientist had himself been critically wounded in their fight with the Roundheads, yet he had risked his own life, undergoing a transfusion and donating his own nanites to Cam. She could still see the latticework of silver honeycomb binding his head wound, but it was fading. Beneath it there was almost no trace of his injury.

"You're healing up really quickly, too," she said to him. He placed a hand on his sternum, absent-mindedly touching the site of his chest wound, then reached up to his forehead.

"Thank you, Amber. I'd almost forgotten about that one." With a flick of his fingers, he called a mirrored disk into being. It floated in midair while he examined his reflection. "I think the stitches will be completely reabsorbed in an hour or two." Another flick and the plate-sized disk shrank down to the size of a dime, and then disappeared altogether.

Merlin nodded toward Cam. "I told him that the ship's surgeon could fix that cut across his cheek, but you'd think I'd asked him to cut off his own ears. He refused to allow anyone to steal his precious battle-scar."

"I kind of like it," Amber admitted. "It suits him."

"I suppose it does," Merlin agreed. "On a related subject, the rest of our group has been outfitted with language implants. I thought the two of you might want to get yours now. It doesn't take long at all, and it's safe and entirely painless."

"How does it work?" she asked dubiously.

He laughed. "It's much easier to explain to Cam. I simply told him I had a magic spell that would give him the power of understanding other tongues." He made another subtle gesture, and a flight of a dozen small, smooth objects—each about the size and shape of a guitar pick—emerged from the wall and floated in a slowly rotating ring, awaiting his orders. "To be slightly more precise, this array implants a meta-organic nanostorage unit that your brain's speech and comprehension centers can access."

"So it works like a Babel Fish?"

"Like a what?"

"You know, a universal translator—like in *Star Trek*."

"Oh yes… Babel Fish, *Star Trek*, universal translator…" he repeated, giving Amber the distinct impression he was running some kind of mental Google search. "Sadly, it isn't quite as good as all that. I'm afraid there are hundreds of extinct South American dialects missing, for example. Even so, it will give you a working knowledge of several different languages."

"That's awesome," Amber exclaimed. "How many do we actually get?"

"Well, I took the liberty of selecting a hundred and twenty of what I thought could be the most useful, culled from the last five thousand years or so. You can add more as needed."

"Works for me," Amber said, her mind reeling with the possibilities.

"I'm glad you think so," Merlin replied with a wry smile. "Cam is very disappointed. He wants to know why I can't give him the speech of birds, fish, animals, and insects."

"Tough customer."

"Let's see if a quick English lesson doesn't cheer him up." He turned to the Celt and asked him a question. Cam glanced at Amber with a shy smile, and nodded.

Merlin's squadron flew down and took up position

at various points around Cam's head. They came to life with a bright glow for a few seconds before flying off again. Cam's eyes dilated, fluttered, rolled back to show just the whites, then returned to normal—albeit wide with surprise. Amber held her breath, and then leaned in closer.

"Hi," she said shyly.

He stared at her in silence for a few beats, then gave her a warm smile.

"Hi."

5

Advanced Transpatial Physics Lab, Antarctica
February 2, 2219
Three minutes before the Event

Standing at the entrance of the primary chamber, Meta paused for a long moment, wrestling with his thoughts and the unexpected flare-up with Dr. Khan. Taking a deep breath, he grasped the thick antique steel lever with both hands and pulled down. The great round aperture irised open to allow him in, then closed behind him again.

This was the very heart of the station, a vast open sphere deep underground, large enough to house a sports stadium. Almost two centuries ago, it had been constructed as a colossal neutrino observatory, originally holding more than one hundred thousand tonnes of ultra-pure, de-mineralized, de-ionized water. The interior surface of the sphere was still covered with hectares of gleaming golden hemispheres arranged in immaculate lines—hundreds of thousands of them, each one made of hand-blown glass and housing sophisticated photomultiplier devices.

The bright points of their light suffused the space with a surreal, breathtaking glow.

A more recent construction, a free-standing catwalk, extended from the entrance and ended at a round platform in the very center of the sphere. The trio of drone cameras shot across the open space in their pre-programmed eagerness to get in position for dramatic long shots as Dr. Meta strode down the precarious walkway.

Reaching the midpoint, he stood perfectly still. Except for an unobtrusive safety rail, the platform had only a small metal stand containing the manual override switches. Even that was unusual when an energy field, hologram, or neural network would do the job, but safety concerns required multiple redundancies and a host of backup safety measures against the unlikely case of a catastrophic systems failure.

From where Meta stood the sphere's subterranean interior glittered like an unusually well-regimented star field. The morning's unwelcome surprises were banished from his thoughts as he focused on the task at hand, mentally running through the pre-trial checklists. Five levels above him, in the main control room, all the technicians, engineers, and monitors checked in via their neural comlinks and awaited his signal.

All systems were go.

He took a moment to center himself.

If he was going to say anything for posterity, now was the moment. He had resisted the urge to come up with a speech ahead of time, and now he struggled for words that would convey the appropriate degree of gravitas. Nothing came to mind.

So be it.

He would keep it simple.

Here we go.

Meta raised his arms like a symphony conductor, and the air around him suddenly sprang to life, filled with a panorama of shifting, shimmering, multicolored holographic shapes—bar graphs and indicator lights showing power allocations and operation thresholds, elegant twisting Calabi–Yau manifolds, an electric gridline model of local space in all eleven dimensions, all nestled together in an elegant Fibonacci sequence.

He brought up the containment field, which at this scale looked like a marble-sized ball of dazzling brightness. The actual staging area was a rough corral, no larger than a molecule of benzene, though the energy bound by the field was magnitudes hotter than the core of the sun. According to the readouts, the will-o'-the-wisp at his fingertips employed more power than the rest of the planet combined—twice over.

Next he actuated the quantum micro display. It appeared at eye level, an oval window on the subatomic world. The holographic device was the twenty-third-century descendant of the scanning tunneling electron microscope. With the patience of a watchmaker, Meta sought out and located a whirling pair of subatomic quarks.

"Targets acquired in the operating theater," he said aloud for the sake of the cameras.

"*Roger that,*" Main Control acknowledged via the neural link.

"Advancing to stage two."

"*We read you,*" Control replied. "*Proceed with stage two.*"

Meta glanced up to check the evolving shape of the Calabi–Yau display. When its manifold arrangement was optimal, he would give the order.

"Stand by to initiate on my mark."

"*Roger that. Standing by.*"

"Approaching optimal…"

"Steady… steady…"

"Commence warp."

"*Engaging warp.*"

Sarajevo, Bosnia–Herzegovina
June 28, 1914
Forty-five seconds before the Event

Along the Miljacka River crowds of spectators, some cheering, some only staring, watch the motorcade carrying the heir to the Austro-Hungarian throne. He looks regal in his gleaming white military uniform, sash, and plumed helmet. The onlookers struggle to catch a glimpse as his would-be parade races down the Appel Quay at high speed. The drivers are more concerned with bomb-throwers than well-wishers.

The lead automobile takes a turn down a side street and the rest follow, only to come to a halt.

Wrong way.

As the cars attempt to reverse, a skinny, dark-eyed Serbian teenager on the street senses an opportunity. He quickly steps up to the open-topped car, whips out a pistol and fires two shots at Archduke Franz Ferdinand and his wife, killing both.

Advanced Transpatial Physics Lab, Antarctica
February 2, 2219
Thirty seconds before the Event

The two particles circled each other from opposite ends of Meta's viewing screen. Then, as he watched in rapt attention, the space between them began shrinking…

Shrinking…

The two touched.

Meta stared in silence, trying to process the enormity of what he was witnessing. On his comlink, the entire crew in main control began to cheer, the sound beamed directly into the auditory center of his brain. His eyes suddenly teared up, and he began to shake.

He had accomplished the impossible. Today they had successfully sent the smallest thing in existence, an elementary particle, across the span of only a few nanometers—moving almost nothing, almost nowhere. But soon they would be able to send a starship the size of a small country clear across the galaxy—and further.

The voice of one of the supervisors rose over the joyous shouts.

"Quiet down, everybody. We have a situation. We need quiet here!"

Meta strained to make out the man's words.

"Control, what's going on up there?" he demanded.

"Primary Chamber, do you copy?" the man said. *"We read multiple anomalies within the containment area. Please advise."*

Meta's brow furrowed. The containment field's integrity was holding—he knew that because the entire facility hadn't melted away. Then, on his display viewscreen, the pair of waltzing particles was joined by another pair. Then another. And *another*.

Shocked, the director looked up at the holographic interfaces. The local Calabi–Yau space-time topology was a psychedelic, undulating wave turning into a three-dimensional Rorschach test, while the holographic gridlines of the eleven-dimensional modeling were tesseracting in a mind-wrecking origami trick.

His stomach lurched as a horrible realization struck him. *Khan was right.*

"Shut it down!" he shouted. "Abort! Abort *now!*" Returning to the micro display viewer he saw that—at the subatomic level—something was happening to the containment field. It wasn't losing integrity—it was being joined by other fields, and other particles. Yet where were they coming from? The screen began to glow with a deep violet intensity—*some form of Cherenkov radiation?* At the same time, a torrent of particles began streaming up toward him, rising like champagne bubbles in an endless cascade.

"Primary Chamber, controls are not responding to abort command. Repeat, there is no response to—"

The neural link cut out.

6

Aboard the *Vanuatu*
Six days after the Event

Given the choice, Amber would've stayed holed up with Cam all morning, but he was well enough to leave the med-lab. She left so Merlin could help him get dressed, and headed for breakfast in the common room.

"Amber."

Even though she recognized the voice, the hand that fell on her shoulder caused Amber to squawk in surprise.

"Jeez, Blake!"

"I'm sorry," he said, "did I startle you?"

Blake's BBC British accent almost managed to make the apology sound sincere, but Amber had been in his company enough to know he probably didn't get why she'd screamed. Empathy wasn't exactly his strong suit. Still, she responded like the accommodating middle child she'd always been.

"It's okay."

Even though it wasn't.

A strong-featured man in his early forties, Blake had fought in World War II, and still wore drab olive commando gear, his dark hair cut short under a dark green beret. Amber suspected he'd never truly left the battlefield.

"What's up?" she asked.

"I wanted to see how you were holding up."

Amber wasn't sure how to answer that, because she wasn't entirely *sure* how she felt.

"It was nice to sleep without worrying about dinosaurs or Roundhead soldiers," she offered.

"That seems reasonable." Blake almost smiled, just a crinkle around the corners of his eyes and a slight twitch of his lips, before his face settled back into its normal deadpan expression. "What now, do you suppose?"

"What do you mean?"

"I..." He hesitated, looking around as if to make sure no one was listening. Amber didn't have the heart to tell him that the ship itself could do so. "How long do we stay on this ship?" he asked, his voice low and serious. "We have no idea what this madman might have in mind."

Amber stared at him in disbelief. "Blake, were you not paying attention when Merlin saved our lives?"

"Yes. Yes, I was." He paused. "I just don't entirely trust him."

"Have you even talked to him since we boarded the *Vanuatu*?"

"No."

That was a relief. It meant Blake didn't know that Merlin had caused the Event. Things would only get worse when he found out.

"So why do you think he's a madman?" she asked.

"Perhaps not mad, but we have no idea what he wants, or if we can believe anything he says."

"Even after everything that's happened."

"Be that as it may—"

What does that even mean?

"—it baffles me that you trust someone so utterly out of the ordinary."

Amber fought to tamp down her irritation. After all, Blake *had* pulled her ass out of the fire more than once since he'd found her cowering in a hotel closet, hiding from carnivorous dire wolves. Yet being with him had been like traveling with a living, breathing G.I. Joe action figure—and a paranoid one, at that.

"In case you haven't noticed," she replied, "*nothing* is ordinary these days."

He shrugged, unable or unwilling to respond.

"Okay, then." Exasperated, she headed down the hallway to what she hoped was the common room. Despite everything—or maybe because of it—she was ravenous.

"Where are you going?" he asked, falling into step next to her.

"Breakfast."

"Good idea." He nodded. "I could do with some coffee." They entered the common room and discovered that their fellow survivors had landed on the same thought.

Professor Winston Harcourt and Nellie Bly were both enjoying breakfast—at tables on opposite sides of the room. The professor cut a dashing figure in his top hat, black frock coat, and waistcoat, looking as if he'd stepped straight out of a Victorian lithograph. He was, in fact, the very model of a distinguished-looking older gentleman. This had served him well in his former profession—that of a snake oil salesman. Tall and lanky, he made Amber think of a were-fox with his red hair and sideburns, sharp features and sharper eyes.

Nellie Bly, world-famous in her own time as an "intrepid girl reporter," had discarded the English peasant disguise she'd been wearing when they first met. She was back in her Victorian traveling clothes—a dark blue two-piece traveling dress made of broadcloth with black camel hair trim. Nellie had also risked her life to save others, although instead of Blake's take-no-prisoners approach, she used a combination of wit and bravery that worked just as well.

Amber wasn't surprised to see the two eating separately. Nellie had little patience for Harcourt's blend of arrogance and cowardice, having nearly lost her life because of it. Given a choice, Amber wouldn't have picked him as a companion for the apocalypse, either, yet she felt sorry for him.

Both looked up when Amber and Blake entered. Nellie smiled brightly while Harcourt gave a small wave without pausing in his meal—which took up most of the tabletop. Both appeared remarkably calm at being on a ship using technology so far advanced that it might as well be magic. Then again, they would all need the ability to adapt, if they wanted to keep their sanity.

"Amber!" Nellie exclaimed. "Come sit with me, my girl. You too, Mr. Blake."

They joined the reporter at her table. Immediately a pair of lumps extruded from the deck and wall, and swiftly molded into the shapes of chairs.

"Isn't this wonderful?" Nellie said. "And we can have anything we want to eat and drink."

Amber asked for coffee, bacon, and a bagel while Blake ordered a platter of smoked kippers, dry toast, and eggs. The ship quickly provided them with their requests and Amber settled down happily with her first real breakfast in days. "Oh, so good," she mumbled between bites.

Blake eyed his food suspiciously before finally digging in.

They were halfway through their meals when Cam and Merlin entered the room. Cam had a new wool cloak draped over his homespun sleeveless tunic, and tartan pants. With his shaggy black hair, the silver torc around his neck, and the scar on his cheek, the young Celt still looked half-wild.

"Look who's back!" Nellie exclaimed. Standing up quickly from her chair, she ran over and gave him an exuberant hug.

"Good morning," he said in English, albeit with a strong accent.

"Listen to you," Nellie said. "You got yours, too!" Looping an arm through his, she pulled him over to their table. He nodded companionably at Blake, and watched in wonder as the ship provided him with a chair next to Amber.

"Welcome back to the land of the living, Camtargarus Mab Cattus," Amber said quietly, just for him. He grinned at her and suddenly any remaining awkwardness vanished. Then his eyes fell upon the view outside. Jumping up, he ran to the window as if he were going to leap right through it, eagerly pressing his palms and forehead against the pane. He stared in rapt wonder for a moment.

"We're flying," he murmured. "We're flying above the clouds themselves."

Nellie grinned at Amber. "I know just how he feels!"

He looked at the others. "Where are we?" Then he hesitated, afraid to say more out loud. "Are we in—is this the hall of Camulos?" A mix of emotions played across his face. Amber came over to the window with him.

"We're not in Heaven or Valhalla, if that's what you mean," she said with a smile. "It *is* cool to be flying though, isn't it?"

He nodded. As she watched the wonder playing on his face as he peered out the window, it suddenly struck Amber how many everyday miracles she took for granted.

What it must be like, she thought, *looking at all this from his perspective*. Then again, he seemed to take most things pretty well whereas she was still freaked out by everything that had occurred. Maybe it was harder for her because her universe had completely fallen apart. Modern life and science had let her down, and she was still reeling from the betrayal. Cam, on the other hand, already believed in gods and goddesses, monsters and fairies—and god knows what else. All this madness was just another day in the office.

Amber looked around at her five companions, feeling a fragile sprout of happiness grow inside her. After days trekking across wilderness, being held prisoner, and fighting for their lives, it was nice to see everyone well-fed, well-rested and, well, *clean* for a change.

The last thing she wanted to do was disrupt the mood, but they deserved to know what was going on.

"Merlin," she said, "maybe you should tell everyone how you ended up in England."

7

Advanced Transpatial Physics Lab, Antarctica
February 2, 2219
The Event

The light from the viewscreen suddenly roared to life as a beam of pure energy. Meta reached for the manual override, but the pulse struck him face first and the impact sent his body tumbling backward through the air. He landed on the catwalk with a painful skid, nearly losing consciousness.

Another blast of raw energy transformed the vast open space of the spherical chamber into blinding whiteness, while the structure quaked. Meta clung to the catwalk for dear life as he fought to remain conscious. His eyes burned, his vision a dizzy, jumbled mess. Shaking his head to clear it, he managed to scramble painfully to his feet, shielding his eyes with one hand. He had to get to the safety cutoff before all was lost.

It took a moment for his traumatized eyes to come into focus. There was no platform anymore—the long walkway now ended in a fiery ball of multicolored plasma, burning freely like a new sun. Another tremor shuddered through the station, nearly jostling him off the catwalk entirely. He clutched at the rail while the narrow walkway began to buckle beneath his feet, and pulled himself hand over hand back to the entryway, throwing himself upon the door release lever and sprinting out.

The rover drones dutifully followed him out before the hatchway irised closed once again, still filming him as he leaned against the wall, stunned and shaken.

Another tremor prompted him to move.

Sprinting down the main corridor proved more difficult than he expected—Meta staggered like a drunk trying to escape a burning building. His eyes were still raw from the blast, and he could barely make out the corridor ring. The lines of its curving walls and floor were jumbled and fuzzy, almost kaleidoscopic with double images. Causing even more confusion, his sense of timing was wildly distorted. One moment it seemed as if he could only move in a slow motion of stretched-out taffy-time. Then time abruptly raced ahead—popping forward in a rapid succession of herky-jerky staccato bursts.

Without warning he found himself ascending in the elevator, coming to a stop in the common room on the main floor. It should have been bursting with a crowd of media people, yet it was a ghost town. He looked around, calling out to someone, anyone. Issuing new commands to the rover cameras, he sent one to the main control room, the others to sweep the facility and the immediate exterior of the complex.

The trio set out on their appointed tasks and immediately began to relay reports directly to his visual cortex. Project Control was just as deserted as the commons, and no one could be found either in the corridors or huddled outside in the cold. There was no longer anyone anywhere in the entire facility or its environs.

A small city's worth of personnel had just vanished.

Waves of neural distortion struck Meta. He fought to keep from vomiting as the room spun crazily, his anguished figure reflected back at him in each mirrored wall like a cruel carnival maze, face red and blistered where the beam had struck him. His body's nanomedical first aid system was hard at work repairing the skin, but something worse was wrong with his reflection.

He moved closer, horror growing with each step.

His eyes had been altered, transformed from light brown to a dark violet. As the image came into focus it was there—that bizarre rising torrent of subatomic particles he had seen in the quantum viewer, only they were now reflected in his eyes, like a cascade of tiny pinpoints of light falling down an endless well...

Yet another tremor rocked the complex. Meta backed away from the unearthly reflection and ran for the exit, bursting out into the open air, the drones on his heels. Overhead, the unforgiving brightness of the blue Antarctic sky had given way to rippling, multicolored patterns of light. He had seen the *Aurora Australis* many times. This was not the Southern Lights.

Running for the hangar, he passed the rows of small craft and ground vehicles—he needed something with range. There were plenty of cargo haulers and various small aircraft chartered by the media outlets, and one of them would do, if he could get in.

And then he saw it.

It was unmistakable—a gleaming double-decker pleasure ship built for the sky, one hundred feet long, a stately *Avialae*-class StratoYacht, just as gorgeous as Gifford had described. The name emblazoned on the vessel read *Vanuatu*. Hurrying up the ship's gangway he spoke to the intercom.

"Is anyone there?" he asked urgently. "I need to come aboard."

"This is the Ship speaking," a smooth artificial voice responded. *"I'm sorry, no one is aboard at this time and the vessel is secured."*

Meta cursed, draping his head and forearm against the hull. Of course it would be shut up tight. He'd have to find another vessel soon. If not, he'd be trapped here until help arrived. If any was even coming...

A sudden thought occurred and he turned back.

"This is Dr. Jonathan Meta, the project director," he said, keeping his voice as calm as possible. "I believe you have me on the guest list?"

The hatch slid open.

"Why, of course, Dr. Meta. You are our guest of honor. Welcome aboard."

8

Aboard the *Vanuatu*
Six days after the Event

"As for the rest..." Merlin picked up his coffee mug and took a sip. "After spending hours trying to raise anybody on the comm, I finally gave up and told the autopilot to take me to Greenwich Observatory. That simple task proved every bit as baffling, since it no longer existed. I circled for ages trying to find any trace of modernity before I had to bring the ship down to start recharging the generators."

"That's not all of it," Amber said.

"What's she talking about?" Blake demanded, his eyes narrowing in suspicion.

"Tell them what you told me," Amber insisted. "The aftershocks. All of it. They need to know."

"Yes, of course." Nodding slowly, Merlin took in a deep breath, and exhaled. "You're ri—"

Suddenly the cabin windows filled with blazing light.

"Brace for evasive maneuvers," the *Vanuatu's* voice announced. Then it was drowned out by a burst of deafening thunder and the deck pitched, the sudden drop throwing Cam painfully across the floor. Amber and the others clung to their chairs as the vessel dove sharply to the right, then they were secured by swiftly-extending safety harnesses composed of the same malleable material.

As they plunged down through the sky, Amber stared out the windows, mouth open as she saw what had endangered their ship. Dead ahead, a pillar of pure lightning, a mile or more across, had burst up from the earth's surface and speared through the retreating clouds, reaching as high as she could see—an oncoming wall of blistering high-energy plasma.

The feathers of the *Vanuatu's* wings, arrays of prismatic hard-light energy, folded inward like the wings of a hunting hawk, sending the vessel into a desperate power dive to avoid contact. Amber's stomach lurched and her whole body tingled with the adrenaline surge from the ship's roller-coaster drop.

Someone screamed—*Nellie? Harcourt?*—as the curtain of twisting, chaotic brilliance roared up alongside, the blinding light overwhelming the bank of portside windows.

Amid shouts and cries from her companions, she heard Cam call her name. Then...

Nothing.

The *Vanuatu* gave no physical sign whatsoever that it had brushed against the energy surge. There was no shudder or vibration—nothing more than the strangest sensation that time had stopped.

Once, as a child on the playground, she'd been the last player left on her team during a game of dodgeball. She had managed to avoid one throw after another, but in that instant when the ball had finally struck her, everything stopped—the sounds of the children, her leap in the air, all thought and movement, all frozen in place. Even years later, a part of her felt as if she was still there, caught in midair.

As if a part of her always would be.

She felt that now. The ship careening at an insane angle. The portside windows transformed into shifting rectangles pouring blazing white brilliance into the cabin. Cam's body hurled sidelong. Cups spilling archipelagoes of coffee flying through the air. Arms raised and mouths captured in mid-scream. All silent. All preserved in clearest crystal.

Forever...

Forever...

Forever.

Then, time and motion resumed—with screaming and chaos. The *Vanuatu* eased out of its power dive, extending its wings once again. As suddenly as it had appeared, the gargantuan column of pure energy vanished and the clouds began to close in as if nothing had occurred.

"Is everyone alright?" Merlin asked. The deck shuddered, as though the ship was struggling to right itself.

Cam regained his footing. There were red welts on his arms, but they already were fading, thanks to Merlin's magic.

"Look at this!" Blake called out, pointing toward a portside window. Merlin's chair released him. He and the others moved to take a look. The tip of the *Vanuatu*'s wing had been clipped—the outermost feathers sliced away.

"We're doomed!" Harcourt wailed. They all ignored him.

"How serious is the damage?" Blake asked Merlin. "Will she be able to stay airborne?"

Merlin nodded. "No need to worry about that. The field projector was cropped, but the ship is already repairing the damage."

"What *was* that?" Nellie asked.

Merlin and Amber exchanged a look. "You need to tell them," Amber said. Merlin nodded, and turned to the others.

"That was a schizochronolinear aftershock," he said. "A result of the Event which, to the best we can calculate, was just one of many more we can expect."

"Do you have any idea when they'll stop?" Nellie asked.

Merlin hesitated.

"They won't," he said bluntly. "Their frequency will only increase, and with each one, the existing shards will be whittled away."

Harcourt made a peculiar noise, a sort of distressed *harrumph*. Cam's linguistic aids couldn't quite keep pace with the unfamiliar terms and concepts, but he understood the gravity of the situation. Nellie, Blake, and Amber exchanged anxious looks. Nellie spoke up.

"So you had said these… aftershocks… will continue, over and over until…" She grimaced. "What? Every last thing on earth is shattered to smithereens? Until nothing remains?"

Merlin nodded. "If we don't stop them, that is precisely what will occur. Continual fracturing down to the subatomic level."

"How can you know that?" Blake demanded, half-rising to his feet. Harcourt nodded, a worried frown on his face.

Merlin remained unperturbed. "The notes are available, if you want to double-check my calculations," he said. "Otherwise I'm afraid you'll just have to take my word for it."

Blake growled something inaudible and took his seat again. The rest were silent until Nellie spoke again, asking the question on everyone's mind.

"How much time do we have?"

Merlin shrugged. "Right now, I can only guess. We don't have enough data to measure the rate of decay. Days, perhaps? A week or two at most. I can't imagine the timeline's structural integrity remaining intact for much longer than that."

"And how do we stop it?" Amber asked.

"When the Event first occurred, I wasn't able to shut down the warp progression. For some reason—one I still haven't been able to pin down—the containment field attracted unexpected anomalies. Our worse fear was that the containment field would suffer a rupture, but the problem wasn't with the containment. It was with the field itself. The subatomic particles suspended within our force field somehow gave rise to additional particles, even additional fields..."

They all listened, spellbound.

"There was a blast... several of them. The manual override was caught up in an out-venting of some kind. I couldn't go near it, and then the station itself was rocked so badly I was afraid the entire facility was going to go critical and be lost to a massive explosion at any moment. A colleague tried to warn me..."

His voice lowered again, trailing off as he stared off

into the distance before resuming his story.

"Everyone at the station—hundreds of people—simply vanished. I still can't understand why or how. Or what's happened to my eyes—" he touched his temple, the gesture almost unconscious. "This bizarre ocular effect.

"Still," he continued, his voice once again sounding self-assured, "all isn't lost. Not yet. If our math is right—mine and the *Vanuatu*'s—as long as the containment field is pulsing outward with these waves of space-time displacement, the Event will continue. If we can get back to the primary chamber and manually shut down the warp field, we can put the world back the way it was. It will be just as if this all never happened."

The mood of the room brightened somewhat.

"Thanks to the damage," Merlin said, "we're not able to travel at our full speed, but even so, we're making good time. With any luck, we should reach the Antarctic station by tomorrow morning."

"Where are we now?" Nellie asked.

"I'd estimate by now we are somewhere over Mali, approaching the bay of Guinea and the South Atlantic Ocean."

Amber looked out one of the windows. "Um, Merlin, am I missing something?" She pointed to the terrain below. There was no hint of ocean in sight, only an endless vista of red desert. "I don't see the ocean anywhere."

Merlin's face darkened. "Ship, are we still en route to the Omnia Astra Project's lab facility in Antarctica?"

"Yes," the *Vanuatu* answered pleasantly, adding, *"although the new heading is no longer optimal."*

"What new heading?"

"We are currently following the new heading authorized four hours and twenty-eight minutes ago. It will delay our arrival at the South Pole considerably."

"What?" Merlin demanded. "Who authorized a course change?"

"I apologize, but I'm unable to provide that information at this time."

"Emergency override. Tell me who authorized the course change."

"That particular emergency override protocol is not available at this time."

Merlin ran his hands through his hair and took in a deep breath. Amber could see that he was laboring to remain calm, but he looked more than ever like a crazed wizard.

"Ship, where *are* we?"

"We are currently crossing over the Qattara Depression of the western Egyptian desert."

Merlin lost his composure at that and stormed off down the central hall toward the cockpit, a stream of profanity trailing in his wake. Amber and the others followed close on his heels.

Reaching the end of the hallway, Merlin grabbed the handle to pull the hatch open. It didn't budge. He tried it again, then again, then slammed his fist against the door. When he turned to face them, his anger had turned to frustration laced with fear.

"We're locked out."

An Unknown Vessel, on suborbital trajectory toward Egypt
Currently 158 km West of Karnataka, India
Six days after the Event

The *Vanuatu* was not an attack vessel. However, the small, deadly, suborbital stealth craft—currently tracking it from just over three thousand miles away—was.

The interceptor's solo pilot had locked on to the *Vanuatu*'s energy profile hours ago, from across the globe. Now he was in hot pursuit. His ship cruised high above the Arabian Sea, its sleek, black, diamond-sharp form virtually undetectable. In flight it was as invisible as a cloaked dagger, and just as silent.

The ship's crew would never see it coming.

9

Aboard the *Vanuatu*
Six days after the Event

"Ship, open the door to the bridge, please." Dr. Meta kept his voice measured and calm, almost masking the undercurrent of his frustration.

"With all due respect, I am not at liberty to permit entry to the bridge at this time."

"Where is the manual override?" Meta asked.

"That is not an option."

"There has to be a verbal password or physical key."

"It appears I can neither confirm nor deny either of those possibilities."

Meta took a deep breath. "Ship, can you provide *any* information about this lockout, or the change in course?"

"Apparently, I cannot."

"Damn it, open up the door now!" Blake snapped.

Meta shot him an irritated look. "I'm trying."

"Obviously not hard enough."

"The current status appears to be causing personal agitation," the ship said. *"Please understand that I am unable to permit entry to the bridge at this time. My apologies."*

"Let's break the door down," Professor Harcourt suggested. "What can we use as a battering ram?" Cam and Blake nodded their approval.

"I'm sorry, Professor Harcourt. Currently there is nothing aboard that possesses the necessary physical characteristics to overcome the door's compressive or tensile strength."

"Damnable automaton," the professor fumed. "I wasn't speaking to you!"

"This is a very unusual set of circumstances," the ship responded. *"Under my normal protocols, I would be able to render much more assistance. Again, I apologize for this temporary inconvenience."*

"Are there any tools we can use?" Nellie asked Dr. Meta. The ship chimed in again before he could answer.

"Fabricating multiple sets of laser cutting tools and employing them could prove effective, providing coordinated cutting efforts achieved the end result faster than the polyductile restructuring capacity of the ship's interior. If you wish, I can diagram a suggested methodology."

"Well, by all that is wonderful," Nellie said, "whose side are you on?"

"*I endeavor at all times to provide as much assistance as is permitted by my current behavioral protocols.*"

"Assuming we could break through the hatch," Dr. Meta said thoughtfully, "would we still be locked out of the control panel?"

"*I am unable to provide a satisfactory answer to that question, but extrapolating from the current circumstances, that would appear to be a reasonable assumption.*"

"Does it have a riddle?" Cam asked. The others turned to him in surprise. Seeing their confusion, he continued. "Is there a riddle we must solve before the door opens?"

"Speak 'friend' and enter," Amber said softly.

"What the deuce are you two on about?" Harcourt groused.

"A riddle to break the magic," Cam pressed on. "The spirit of the ship is enthralled by some spell, isn't it?"

"Not exactly," Meta said, "but I suppose you could say it's something along those lines."

"Whatever has possessed the vessel, can that kind of druidcraft be done from a distance?"

"Druidcraft?" Meta said. "Well… that is—no, I don't think so. Why do you ask?"

"If it cannot," Cam explained, "then one of us aboard this flying ship must have cast the spell." He looked at each of them in turn.

Prof. Harcourt harrumphed, and turned to Amber.

"See here, Colonial Girl," he said, poking a finger at her. "Tell your pet barbarian to cease his superstitious twaddle. We are in a dire situation here!"

"Hold on, Harcourt," Dr. Meta said sharply. "I think he's on to something."

Encouraged, Cam continued his line of reasoning. "The ship's spirit must be compelled by one of you as its master," he said. "If this is true, then it must do as it is told. Whoever cast the spell need only bid it to open the door. Then we will know who the master truly is."

"Whosoever pulleth the sword from the stone is rightful king of England," Blake said softly, mulling it over. He nodded. "It's not the daftest notion. Well done, Sherlock. Let's give it a go."

"Have we all gone mad?" Harcourt said, sputtering. "Entertaining poppycock about spells and incantations. Ridiculous!"

"You might do well to listen to the heathen savage, you old charlatan," Nellie said. "It's ingenious, and there's no harm in it—especially if one of us knows more than he's letting on." She cut him a dirty look.

He stared at her, aghast. "Surely you aren't suggesting that one of *us* could be behind this? Impossible!"

"To be perfectly frank," Nellie shot back, "I scarcely know what's possible and what's not anymore. But enough blather. It's all we've got, and there's only one way to test it—here goes nothing." She faced the door. "Ship, I order you to open this door at once!"

"I'm sorry, but I am unable to accommodate you."

Nellie raised an eyebrow at Harcourt. "Now you try it."

"Utterly preposterous," he blustered.

Blake leaned forward. "Ship, open sesame," he said. "Unlock the door."

"I am currently unable to allow your entrance, Mr. Blake, but I appreciate your literary reference."

The soldier turned to Cam and waved a hand to allow him forward. "Your idea, your turn."

Cam cleared his throat. "Hear me. I, Camtargarus, son of Cattus, say let me in."

"Please take no offense that I am unable to comply."

"Well, Professor?" Nellie put her hands on her hips and stared him down.

"Well, what?" Harcourt glared at her. "I categorically refuse to take any part in your ridiculous little parlor-game. We don't need another inmate in this asylum."

"It's alright, Harcourt," Dr. Meta said diplomatically. "No one really thinks you devised a way to hijack the ship—but we don't have any better leads to pursue. For the sake of the experiment, please give it a try."

"I find this entire distasteful jape a capricious and arbitrary obfuscation," Harcourt muttered. "It only creates unnecessary suspicions in our ranks."

"Easy enough to dispel them, then," Nellie snapped.

"Look, Professor," Amber said, "we'll all do it, and then it'll be settled." Facing the bridge, she added, "Ship, open the door, please."

"I am pleased to comply."

The door slid open.

Amber turned back to the others, face pale, eyes wide with shock. They all stared at her in disbelief—even Merlin. With a shake of his head, he quickly entered the bridge. Ahead of him lay the broad curve of a window through which they could see clouds racing past.

Slipping into the pilot's seat, he quickly ran through an inspection of the instrument panel. After a few moments, he sighed, and looked over at the rest of them crowded around the door, his expression grim.

"Controls are completely locked." He turned to Amber. "Ms. Richardson, would you care to do the honors?"

Wincing at the cold formality of his tone, she shook her head. "Please, I swear I didn't do this. I don't know anything about any of this!"

"Please." He held up a hand. "I need you to unlock these now, if you will."

Amber closed her mouth. "Ship," she said in a quiet, resigned voice, "please release the controls."

"Navigational functions restored."

"Ha!" Professor Harcourt folded his arms in righteous indignation. "Explain yourself, little Missy!"

"But—I didn't do it!"

"The facts speak for themselves." Harcourt said with the air of a prosecuting attorney resting his case.

"Let's not rush to judgment just yet, Harcourt," Merlin cut in. "The *Vanuatu* should have something to say about all this. Ship, tell us who initiated the course change and lockout."

"Apologies, I am currently unable to provide that information."

Merlin turned to Amber with a reproving look, and she spoke up again, her voice uneasy.

"Ship, please tell everybody whatever they want to know."

"Course change was laid in by Amber Richardson four hours and thirty-two minutes ago."

Nellie gasped. Professor Harcourt stretched out an accusatory finger.

"You perfidious flying trapeze-jongleur. Duplicitous brazen tart! Bloody *American*!"

"It's not true!" Amber shouted. "How could I, even if I wanted to? *Why* would I?"

"That's enough, Harcourt!" Blake said, glaring. "Stand down!" Cam stepped to his side, crossing his arms.

"You heard what the mechanical-man said," Harcourt grumbled. "The girl has deliberately sabotaged us."

Nellie shook her head. "I don't know what's going on here, but I think I know Amber. The two of us may not have enjoyed a long acquaintance, but I've traveled with her long enough to know she's no liar. If she says she's innocent, I believe her." Amber gave her a grateful look.

"I'm inclined to agree," Merlin said thoughtfully, resting his chin on steepled fingers. "I also trust Amber—she's been brave, and honest, and she saved my life."

"Thank you," Amber said. "I don't know how any of this happened, but..." She stopped as a thought struck her. "Ship, I hereby turn control back over to Mer—" She corrected herself. "I mean, Dr. Meta."

"Understood. Authority transferred to Dr. Jonathan Meta, Ms. Richardson."

"Thank you, Amber," Merlin said. "There's more to this," he said, addressing the others. "As far as I can tell, Amber has neither the expertise nor the motive to pull off this diversion. Which, unfortunately, leaves us with several pressing questions.

"Someone wanted to pull us off course," he continued. "Someone who knows about us, knows where we are going, and possesses the expertise to employ our own navigational system against us. A person who can carry this out without our being aware." He shot a glance at Amber. "What *that* someone wants, however, remains a mystery."

Though she kept quiet, Amber thought he left out an important point.

Someone on board this ship.

"What can we do?" Cam asked after a moment's silence. He hated the uncertainty, that there was no immediate enemy to confront. For the sake of Amber's honor, he would take on the entire Roman empire itself.

"For now, I need to think," Merlin replied. "Before we go any further, I think we need to land and run a quick diagnostic on the ship's system, to make certain there are no other surprises in store for us. It will give our generators a chance to recharge, as well." He looked over the panel in front of him. "It's just a matter of finding a good landing site."

He waved a hand toward the vista spread out below them. "It's interesting—if you look closely, you can make out the individual shards. It's subtle, but even though it's all one desert, each one has a slightly different hue. And look, you can see where the sand fused into glass along the edges, separating shards from different eras."

"Like a jigsaw puzzle for giants," Nellie marveled.

"These sections seem very large," Blake noted. "Larger than what we've seen so far."

"Yes," Merlin agreed, nodding. "I suspect the larger shards are from further in the past, whereas the ones closest to the time of the Event are much smaller. The fracturing appears to have been most intense around 2219—specifically from the day my Omnia Astra project launched. That may explain why we don't seem to be finding many shards from the twenty-second or twenty-third century."

"Look at that one over there." Blake pointed a finger to the horizon. "What's wrong with it?" At first he seemed to be indicating a dark blotch on the edge of their peripheral vision, but as they flew nearer, it appeared markedly different from the rest of the desert tableau. Rather than the brazen reds and gold of the surrounding sands, this one was green.

"I think we've found our landing spot," Merlin declared, steering the *Vanuatu* toward the oasis.

10

**A Prehistoric Shard, somewhere in North Africa
Midmorning — Six days after the Event**

All around the anomalous shard was a sea of unending sand, threatening to swallow it up again. But for now, green savannah grass held sway. The *Vanuatu*'s passengers looked out the windows as the ship gently touched down into what seemed to Amber a magical garden, filled with a riotous diversity of life—at least viewed from her current safe vantage.

Flamingos dotted the lakes. Large herds of grazing animals strolled across the plain—antelopes, gazelles, giraffes, rhinos, and more. Monkeys chattered from the isolated stands of leafy trees. Flocks of small birds blossomed into the air at their arrival, as the ship folded its wings, powering down the projectors that emitted its feather-like energy fields and the prismatic spearhead at the ship's nose.

"Oh, it's beautiful here," Nellie sighed. Cam nodded his agreement, nose pressed against the window, looking more like a teenager than a warrior.

"We can't stay here long," Merlin cautioned, "so try not to get too enamored with the scenery. Besides, if we succeed in repairing the timeline, it will be as if none of this ever existed."

"Can't happen soon enough to suit me," Harcourt muttered.

"Well," Nellie said, "we'll just have to enjoy it for the few moments we have, then."

"That's very Zen of you," Amber said wryly.

Nellie cocked an eyebrow. "You'll have to explain that to me while we're admiring the view."

"I know the lake looks inviting," Merlin said with a worried frown, "but please resist any temptation to leave the ship while we're here."

"You're kidding, right?" Amber shot him a look. "We've been up-close-and-personal with what's out there." She shook her head, remembering the swamp. "No thanks."

"Of course," Merlin murmured ruefully. "I apologize. None of you are children, after all. If you want, you can go up onto the sundeck and enjoy the view from a safe vantage point—but keep an eye out for Pteranodons—or worse—and pay attention to any alerts from the ship." A hatch in the ceiling slid open, and a motile blob of ship-stuff formed stairs leading up. Nellie, Cam, Blake, and Harcourt moved toward the stairs, and, as Amber started to follow, Merlin stopped her.

"Wait a minute, Amber," he said. "I'd like to take a moment to discuss your… situation, before I get started on the navigational diagnostics."

Raising a questioning eyebrow, she followed Merlin back to the common room. He took a seat and she sat across from him. The physicist leaned back in his chair and looked at her thoughtfully, until the silence began to unnerve her.

"So," he said at last, "we have two anomalous circumstances, with you as the common factor."

"'Anomalous' is one way to put it," she replied.

"Indeed." He leaned forward. "Somehow, it appears as if you changed the course of the ship, and in doing so locked out both the bridge and instrument panel— tasks you shouldn't have been able to accomplish."

"You know it wasn't me, though," she said anxiously. "Right?"

"Certainly," he answered, and she thought he sounded sincere. "Which leads us to an even more troubling conclusion—that some unknown party seeks to divert us from our mission, for reasons equally unknown. Worse still, this person possesses the requisite computer knowledge to carry out this sabotage, and perhaps the ability to use you to facilitate the process— entirely unbeknownst to you—in your sleep."

"Oh," Amber said, her skin crawling at the thought.

"Worst case scenario," he continued, "would be that our nemesis can do this to any of us. At the very least, however, we know with certainty that *you* appear to be vulnerable. My recommendation is that we have the ship watch you closely, and perhaps lock you in your quarters at night—if you have no objections."

She nodded.

"Which brings me to the second point," he said. "From what you have said, you've been having strange dreams about me—dreams that began before we even met—in which I am calling out for your help. Can you perhaps describe them in greater detail?"

Amber frowned. "I guess it began with me finding this underground bunker. I was walking through a patch of Ice Age when I crossed into this freaky dead land shard. All scorched as if the whole place had been gone over with a flame-thrower, or—" She stopped, throat suddenly dry as a thought occurred to her. "Or as if it was nuked. Oh god, what if it was nuked?" Panic clawed at her stomach.

"Ship, please check Amber for radiation," Merlin said. Immediately, a line of blue light projected from the ceiling and ran down Amber where she sat.

"Initial exposomic scan reveals no atypical radiation for an early twenty-first-century North American biopattern."

"Oh my god…" Amber nearly collapsed with relief. "Thank you, Ship."

"You're welcome, Ms. Richardson."

Taking a deep breath, she continued. "So in the middle of this dead zone I found a hatch and was able to open it—and that was weird, too. I mean, the whole time it felt like I was being guided to it. There was a combination, these moving geometric shapes..." She struggled to remember them, but the details flitted away.

"Anyway, the hatch opened onto this underground shelter place. There was—this is going to sound crazy, too—there was this glassy black floating pillar thing. Like a stretched-out diamond shape, thicker in the center and then narrowed out at both tips, and it was hovering in midair." *Like something out of a* Hellraiser *movie*, she thought, but didn't say. Her story was outlandish enough, like a dream that doesn't make sense. Merlin seemed to be listening without judgment, though, which encouraged her to continue.

"When I came closer, it started to glow and spin slowly, and I... well, I felt this crazy urge to reach out and touch it. My palms tingled and then the whole thing lit up like a spotlight and blue-violet electricity was crackling everywhere, running between it and my fingertips like Dr. Strange, and then it was all around me." Her voice rose as her recollection grew stronger.

"Next thing I knew I was floating in air, paralyzed with my head and spine bent back, my arms stretched out—like I was crowd-surfing on a lightning bolt. And then, just like that, it was over, and I dropped back to the ground." Shaking her head, she added, "I know this all sounds nuts."

Merlin gave a small chuckle. "After what we've been through the last few days, very little sounds nuts."

"This is weird, too," she said, the memories still coming. "I just woke up all of a sudden, and I was walking through a sunny meadow. At first I didn't know if what had happened was real, or if I'd just dreamt it." She paused, then continued. "But I kept having *more* dreams, that made me remember what had happened in the bunker. They were mixed up with other things, too."

"What kind of things?"

"A—a boy I met." Amber began to feel as if she was on a psychiatrist's couch. "His name was Gavin. When the Event hit,"—she flashed on his dead body, sliced in half— "he was killed. I saw him, and I saw a book that had pictures of you near the Pyramids, dressed sort of like the Grim Reaper—kind of like when I first saw you in your Merlin outfit. It was definitely you. I mean, I could see your eyes, with the little stars falling in them. It was as if you were trying to talk to me through the words in the book."

She waited for him to say, *"And how did this make you feel?"*

"How do you mean?" he asked.

Close enough.

"The words started as nonsense lines, but as I read them they would twist and move around and rearrange themselves into phrases."

"Fascinating." He looked as though he meant it. "What did they say?"

"Weird things. They said everything was broken, that it was hard to talk to me like that. You said you would try to help me, but that I needed to come find you. You asked *me* for help. There were more dreams, after that, and you kept asking for help—even after I found you. And… the dreams haven't stopped." She paused. "What do you think it means?"

"It's difficult to say." Merlin spread his hands and shrugged. "Perhaps they're just natural reactions to all the stress you've been under. It's possible they're side-effects from the Event—an energy surge struck extremely close to you, after all." He frowned. "What I fear, though, is that someone out there is trying to manipulate you, perhaps gain your trust so they can sabotage our attempts to restore the timeline. But if that were the case, who are they? How are they controlling your dreams?"

She shuddered as he said that.

"And most importantly, why would anyone *want* to stop us?" He gave her a bemused smile. "I'll need to think on this. For now, why don't you join the others on their safari watch? I need to check our ship's brain."

"Good luck, Merlin." She paused at the stairs and turned back toward him. "I have one other thought about the dreams."

"Yes?"

"Well, it's a little out there, but what if they really *are* from you—but from our future, trying to reach us here now and warn us? She looked at the floor, choosing her words carefully. "Maybe our future selves are here somewhere, trying to stop us from going to the South Pole because something will go wrong there." She looked up again. "Is that possible?"

Dr. Meta's face was pale.

"I'll... have to think about that."

11

Amber did as Merlin suggested and joined the others up top on the sundeck. They were all leaning against the railing and admiring the view. She was eager to take a look for herself.

It was a spectacular sight, although the more she saw of the wildlife around them, the more apparent it became that something wasn't right. It was as though they were looking at a painting of an African vista done by a medieval artist who had only heard vague rumors of what the animals looked like. Or maybe he had a quirky sense of humor, and decided to combine a few here and there.

The markings of the gazelles and antelopes looked off. The giraffes weren't anywhere as long-necked as they should be, and their trademark skin pattern looked more like that of a zebra. A pair of rhinos lazily regarded the ship, more concerned with chewing the tall grass. They were half again as tall as normal, crowned with wide, enormous double horns.

The oddly shaped elephants wading in the lake sported tiny ears and squat, fat, almost bulbous trunks, and their tusks were shorter and bent down the wrong way. Off in the distance, a large carnivore pursued an over-sized warthog, but it wasn't a lion—it was a lion-sized hyena, its body muscular and wedge-shaped, growing into an enormous skull and powerful jaws.

"What a bizarre collection of animals," Nellie breathed. "Have you ever seen the like?"

"I don't think anyone has," Amber replied. "Most of these have been extinct for millions of years. Ship, can you identify any of these species?"

"Provisionally judging from the skeletal structures, these animals appear to be various megafauna from the late Eocene or early Oligocene epoch."

"I wonder how long any of us would survive down there without firearms or an armored vehicle," Blake said, staring at the ancient life below.

"Let's just be thankful we're up here looking down," Nellie replied smartly. Cam stared in rapt fascination. Not so for Harcourt, the first to grow bored and saunter back inside.

* * *

Wandering to the other side of the ship, Blake continued to stare down at the seemingly endless array of prehistoric fauna. Nellie Bly was correct. They were very lucky to be up out of reach of such creatures. Beautiful in a way, he supposed, but deadly. Still... he wouldn't turn down a chance to hunt one of those overgrown hyenas if opportunity offered itself.

"Blake."

He turned to find Dr. Meta standing at the upper hatchway.

"Could you come down? I need your help."

Blake frowned. "What do I know about your technical gadgets?" He didn't entirely trust the man, regardless of—or perhaps because of—Amber's unshakable faith in his words.

"It's not that," Meta said. "We have a situation."

The soldier in him responded to that. Nodding brusquely, he followed the scientist below decks.

The two men's faces were illuminated by the reflection of the peculiar image on the instrument panel's screen—a glint of sunlight reflected off of something metallic and sharp-angled, streaking through the azure sky. The sight of it raised Blake's hackles.

"The Ship spotted it a few minutes ago," Meta said. "Invisible to radar, apparently, but the *Vanuatu*'s visual sensors managed to catch a glimpse of it all the same. Says it came down over the rise on the other side of the lake. How far away, Ship?"

"Assuming no abrupt evasive changes to the trajectory, it touched down approximately nine-point-seventeen kilometers away, twenty-eight degrees north of our current position."

"I think we need to go see whatever this is," Meta said. "Will you go with me, Blake?"

"Is that a wise idea, heading off without your magic medical gizmos?"

"My nanites? Yes, it's a calculated risk—which is why I'd like you to come along."

"Why not just send your flying camera balls?"

"I suspect this is going to call for a more hands-on investigation." Meta hesitated a moment before adding, "We… may need to engage in some diplomacy, as well."

"If we're going on a diplomatic mission, I'd feel better if I were carrying a Lee-Enfield or a Bren gun. Can your ship conjure up one of those for me? Or whatever new-fangled weapons you have going these days—any sort of Flash Gordon ray gun would suit me fine, too."

"I'm sorry, Mr. Blake," the Ship replied. *"This is a university research and recreation vessel. My protocols don't allow fabrication of advanced firearms. However,*

if you wish ranged weapons, I am able to provide various options for bow weapons, including several sophisticated crossbow designs—"

"Crossbows?" Blake gave a derisive snort. "Meta, as long as you're tinkering around there with the robot butler's brain, see if you can talk it out of that pacifist nonsense, will you?"

"Don't think I wouldn't love to whip up a whole armory for us," Meta replied, "but at present, that's just a bit beyond my skill set. Ship, we will need you to provide us with a two-seater hover cycle."

"Certainly. It will be ready for you shortly, just past the main gangplank."

"You all need to stay aboard ship." Nellie's impersonation of Merlin was uncannily accurate. She, Amber, and Cam watched as Merlin and Blake sped away from the *Vanuatu* on an airborne motorbike. "The cheek of him! Lecturing us about keeping put, and then the pair of them gallivanting off on their own without so much as a by-your-leave."

"I'm sure they have a good reason for it," Amber replied, doing her best to hide her own dismay at the situation.

"Bah!" Nellie replied with a snort. "Insufferable men." She turned to Cam and hastily added, "Not you, Camtargarus. You've been nothing but gallant."

"I am your servant, my lady," he said without a trace of irony.

"See?" Nellie nudged Amber with an elbow. "Those ancient Celts raised their boys nobly well."

"You know his people were headhunters, right?" Amber said with a straight face.

"I'll still take his company over Professor Humbug's," Nellie retorted. "I shudder to think what that unctuous red-haired weasel's been up to down there in his cabin all this time."

The Ship's disembodied voice came out of the air.

"Forgive me for interrupting, but there is a message for Ms. Richardson. I can relay it to you in the privacy of your cabin or on the bridge—whichever you prefer—at your convenience."

"What?" Amber said, caught off guard. "I... well, I'll be right down."

"You don't mind if Cam and I come along, do you?" Nellie said.

"The message is marked private."

At the brief flash of suspicion in Nellie's eyes, Amber felt a stab of hurt. "I swear, I have no idea what this is about," she insisted. "Ship, can you still play the message if Cam and Miss Bly come with me?"

"Of course, Ms. Richardson. You have the prerogative to override any orders."

"Great," Amber said. Except it wasn't because she

was afraid that Nell—and possibly Cam—didn't trust her, and she had no idea whether the message would help or hurt the situation.

Nellie and Cam followed her down to the bridge, where the glow from the center panel lent the cockpit a strange lighting, like a sixties spy movie. On the panel, a window showed a frozen photograph. She couldn't quite make out exactly what it was displaying—some indistinct streak of light in the sky.

"What is that?" Cam asked.

Amber shook her head. "I don't know."

"Are you ready for your message, Ms. Richardson?"

"Yes, please." A panel of light appeared in front of them.

"This message is from eight minutes ago. It is marked urgent and private. Are you sure you wish to view it with your companions present?"

"I'm sure," Amber said firmly.

"Very well."

Merlin appeared on the screen.

"Amber, I don't want to alarm you," he said, "but this is very important. Blake and I had to leave the ship to investigate what appears to be an aircraft of some type landing a few kilometers from our location. I've set a timer for three hours from now. If neither Blake nor I have returned by then, I want you to take control of the *Vanuatu*, lift off and continue to the South Pole as planned. Do not wait any longer for us. *Absolutely* do not attempt to rescue us. If there's any more interference, you all will need to deal with it as best you can. The world is counting on us.

"We'll probably be back very soon…" he continued, "but if not, remember what I said. Three hours. No more. Relay this to the others as you see fit." The screen went black.

The three of them stood stock still.

"Do you wish me to replay the message?"

"No thank you, Ship. I'm… I'm just processing."

"Amber, are you faring well?" Cam looked at her with concern.

She shook her head. "I really don't think so."

An Unknown Vessel
Approximately 9.17 km north of the *Vanuatu*
Six days after the Event

The black scramblejet was designed to touch down as imperceptibly as technology would allow. Like a falcon on the hunt, it swept in over the desert at low altitude, and just crested the dunes to soar over the veldt. Moments later, the pilot snapped a split-second burst of long-range pictures of its target, the grounded ship. Still in stealth mode, he sped past it and reduced speed to come around.

After a moment of consideration, he picked a likely-looking rise on the far side of the lake, kicked in the VTOL turbines and brought his spy ship to a gentle landing. Its adaptive camo skin automatically blended in with the savannah grass. With a hushed whisper, the canopy's gullwing doors slid open and the pilot stepped out, marveling for a moment at the warm African air.

Then he set to work.

First, he fished out his med kit. *Only one ampule left*, he reminded himself. Better make it count. Next, he reached into the small cargo compartment and retrieved an oblong container about the size of a trumpet case. His thumbprint released the electronic lock. Inside, cushioned in custom die-cut beds of urethane foam, were three telescoping components of a gauss coilgun sniper rifle.

He methodically assembled the weapon with a practiced hand and slung it over his back. Grabbing a few more incidentals, he closed up and locked the aircraft's canopy, walked to the closest acacia tree, and climbed up. Situated on the modest hillock, it provided a commanding view of the lake and the approaches on either side. Its fernlike foliage was perfect for concealment, so he made himself at home, quickly setting up a sniper nest. Rigging a sling for his rifle, he suspended it in its harness to give him a 270° field of fire.

Through the scope, he could make out the ship—even the name, *Vanuatu*. There were passengers milling about on an observation deck. He trained the crosshairs on the head of each figure in turn. No uniforms. Unarmed. No visible guns or missile racks on the ship. By all appearances, some class of pleasure craft.

Absolutely perfect.

Tonight he would pay them a visit. His sniper rifle could quickly and easily be reconfigured into a more compact assault carbine, or broken down to an extremely discreet handgun.

Hold on. A brief plume of dust marked the departure of a vehicle. He scanned through the gun's scope. Two riders on some kind of motorbike. *No, some sort of hovercraft. Nice.* He tracked it around the lake's edge, watched it make the turn to come around toward his position. So they had managed to spot his landing. That was interesting… and unexpected.

Change of plan.

Relocating to a different branch, he swung the center of his arc of fire another 90 degrees, and got comfortable again. With a slow, careful sweep of the scope, he made sure there were no other sorties on their way, then re-acquired his target. Two riders. That simplified his options. One would get the treatment, the other a bullet.

He zoomed in with the scope. Driver and passenger. Both male, neither appeared to be armed. The passenger wore military garb while the driver was older, wearing a rustic robe, long hair. He centered the robed man's head in his crosshairs, and ever so gently flexed his trigger finger. A stray breeze pulled the man's silver hair back for a moment.

The sniper froze.

What the hell?

Releasing his pressure on the trigger he stared at the driver in unbelieving fascination. He knew that face. He knew that man.

He had a decision to make.

12

Amber paced back and forth on the *Vanuatu*'s observation deck, pausing every few moments to stare out at the veldt. Not even the animals provided adequate distraction to take her mind off what would happen if the two men didn't return.

"Ship," she said during one of pauses, "how long have Merlin and Blake been gone?"

"Dr. Meta and Sgt. Blake have been gone for an hour and twenty minutes," the ship replied.

"Which is five minutes longer than the last time you asked," Nellie observed as Amber resumed her pacing.

Amber stopped. "Seriously?" It felt like it had been hours since Merlin and Blake had gone off on their mission.

Nellie and Cam both nodded.

"Okay." Sighing, Amber turned to her companions.

"I am officially telling myself to stop before I drive us all crazy."

"Well, I wasn't going to say anything…" Nellie let her words trail off, and gave a smile.

Cam rested a hand on her shoulder. "Your mind is restless."

"You're not wrong," Amber conceded.

"Can you not enjoy these marvelous birds and beasts?" he suggested. "I've only heard travelers' tales of cameleopards and unicorns, but here they are. And we can watch them for omens and portents."

"Um. Let me think about that." Then a thought struck her. "There must be a library in the ship's databanks," she said. "Let's see what we can find there." That would help take her mind off the ticking clock.

"Great idea!" Nellie responded. "Let's do some digging."

Cam seemed indifferent to the suggestion, though. "Not for me," he said. "I'll stay here and observe the beasts. I can watch for Merlin and Blake, as well."

"Good idea." Amber nodded. Then she added hopefully, "They should be back before too much longer."

"What shall we research?" Nellie asked as the women settled in the common room.

"How about history?" Amber replied. "We're in the twenty-third century now, as bizarre as that seems.

Which means a whole lot of shit has gone down since either of our times." She glanced at Nellie, who was looking at her with a raised eyebrow. "Er... a great many things have happened since you or I were born, and I'd like to find out what they were."

"I thought that was what you meant," Nellie said with a grin. "For such a delightful girl, you have the mouth of a longshoreman."

Amber quickly changed the subject.

"Ship, can you give me a quick history of the future? Sorry, I mean a history of the last two hundred years or so—from the year 2000 to—what year is it again?"

"Today is February 8th, 2219."

"I feel like Rip Van Winkle," she confided to Nellie before continuing. "Ship, what can you tell me about what's been happening in the last couple of centuries?"

"I have three hundred and fifty-two million entries encompassing twenty-first- and twenty-second-century history."

"Just the highlights, please."

The *Vanuatu* helpfully projected a rectangular screen at her eye level. She jumped a little—it was still disconcerting. Though it floated serenely in midair, it looked solid enough to touch, and she could adjust the reactive display merely by reaching toward it to change its angle or size. Her highlights option offered a long list of subjects to pick from:

History of the 21st Century:

- The Warming (see also Sea Level Rise Refugee Crisis)
- Sino-Russian War
- ACW II
- Global Population Crisis
- Antibiotic Collapse Crises (see also Staph Pandemic, the Domino Pandemic, Mega-Pandemic I, Mega-Pandemic II)
- Water Wars
- Polynesian Crisis (see also Floating Nations, Sea Level Rise Refugee Crisis)
- Islamic Reformation
- Wars of the Islamic Reformation
- North Pacific Gyre Crisis (see also Pelagic Plastics Crises)
- Ecol/Econ Movement (see Ecological/Economic Revolution)

History of the 22nd Century:

- Nanotech Revolution
- BioGenetics Revolution
- Arkology Movements (see also Biodiversity Reclamation)
- Global Island Repatriation Efforts
- Sustainability Revolution
- Pan-Humanist Revolution
- Coastal Reclamation

- **Post-Scarcity Revolution**
- **Second Space Age**

Amber didn't much like the look of the twenty-first century highlights.

Guess we didn't learn from our mistakes.

"ACW II?" Nellie said. Leaning over her shoulder, the reporter pointed at the line of text. "What was that?"

Opening up the entry, Amber's heart dropped—it covered the Second American Civil War.

"Second?" Nellie's deflated tone echoed Amber's emotions. "You'd think one was enough."

"Do you mind if I close this?" Amber asked. "I'm not ready for this yet."

"Not at all," Nellie replied, though it was obvious the reporter in her was itching to investigate. She tapped her fingers on the table, then brightened. "I know! We can look at a map of our hometowns and see what they look like now."

Amber thought briefly about opening up a map of twenty-third-century San Diego, but decided against it. Even if everyone she knew had been dead for centuries, she still couldn't bear the thought of finding out her hometown had been nuked, or was underwater, or had been taken over by robots, or had gone all Mad Max.

"Maybe later," she said with forced cheerfulness.

"Right," Nellie agreed. "What else, then?"

"Lemme see…" Amber scanned the list again. "Let's skip the pandemics for now, too. How about… Oh! How about the second space age? Like rockets and other planets and the Federation and stuff."

"That does sound exciting!" Nellie nodded, looking a bit awestruck at the concept. Before Amber could access the desired file, however, Harcourt stormed into the room from the central corridor and flung himself into a chair.

"Hissing hellfire," he exclaimed petulantly. "It's utterly intolerable!"

Nellie scowled. "Whatever are you huffing and puffing about, man?"

"Completely insufferable," he grumbled. "The incompetence of this vessel's food service is thoroughly beyond the pale. It can't even manage the most rudimentary formula for galvanic nerve tonic!"

Rolling her eyes at Amber, Nellie shot back, "Oh, was the recipe for your snake oil lost to future generations? Such a shame. Why don't you just ask it for some brandy?"

"I suppose I could, but it would be lacking in essential nutrients and beneficial qualities that the galvanization process alone imparts." He sniffed in dissatisfaction. "Still, I suppose it would be better than nothing. You there, vessel!" he called out imperiously, looking up at the ceiling. "Is a snifter of cognac within your limited scope?" A small table formed beside him, with a glass of earthy brown liquid sitting on it. He took a sip and beamed with approval. "Ah, splendid! Ne'er you mind, sweet automaton. I shan't doubt you again."

"Far from us to keep you from your medical regimen, Professor," Nellie said, "but you're interrupting a history lesson." Amber nudged her in the ribs, but it was too late—Harcourt's interest had been piqued.

"How's that—a futurological retrospective?" He stood and approached them. "That's smashing! Let's have a look!"

Sorry, Nellie mouthed as he squeezed in between them with his cognac and glommed onto the viewscreen.

"Here now! Can we see the current extent of the British Empire? I daresay by the twenty-third century, it must control four-fifths of the world—and surely its locomotive lines and air-dirigible routes must span the globe. Has mankind re-located the lost ancient routes leading down into the hollow Earth? Has it been colonized?"

Amber was at a loss for words. Where did she even begin? Their research derailed, she decided not to even try, and stood up, ceding control of the viewscreen.

Merlin and Blake will be back soon, anyway.

"Ship," she said quietly, "can you bring up the timer for me?" The Ship obligingly projected a floating holographic digital timer showing her how long the two men had been gone. Only forty minutes remained until the three-hour mark.

Not much time at all, Amber thought, fear gnawing at her stomach.

Back at the table, Harcourt was grumbling. He and Nellie had decided to look themselves up, and while there was a plethora of historical information on Nellie, they found nothing whatsoever on him. Nellie made little effort to disguise her *schadenfreude*.

"Oh, don't be so peevish, Harcourt. I'm sure you tried to the best of your bent."

Amber tried to take an interest in the library information—or at least in Nellie's torture of the professor—but found it increasingly difficult to focus on anything but the countdown, which seemed to be ticking by impossibly fast.

The timer hit the twenty-five-minute mark.

Damn, those two are cutting it close.

The ten-minute mark came and went.

"Ship, any sign of them?"

"Not yet, Ms. Richardson."

Five minutes left. Amber's anxiety had spread to the rest of the crew. Nellie looked up from the screen.

"Should we go after them, do you think?"

"Merlin said to stay put," Amber said reluctantly. "He was very clear on that point."

"Yes, but he also was very clear that we should leave if they're not back in three hours," Nellie said. "And that's coming up swiftly."

"Well, yes," Amber replied slowly, "but I can't believe he was serious about that. How could he think we'd actually abandon him... *or* Blake?"

Harcourt looked up from his obsessive scrolling of the screen.

"What are you talking about?" he said. "Do you mean to say Dr. Meta and Sgt. Blake left us here without so much as a by-your-leave? That's madness. I never would have agreed to it!"

"I hardly think fear of your disapproval played into their plans," Nellie retorted.

Harcourt ignored her, focusing his glare on Amber. "And now you mean to say we could be in danger if we wait for them to return. Good heavens, girl, who are you to question the man's orders? Let's be gone, and post-haste!"

Rather than choose between explaining herself or punching the man, Amber left the common room and went up to the observation deck, where Cam still kept watch. He turned at the sound of her approach.

"Any sign of them?" she asked.

"Nothing yet."

The digital timer materialized in front of them.

"Ms. Richardson," the ship said, *"it has been three hours."*

Cam looked at her. "Are we going to leave?"

Amber's gut clenched as she looked out across the veldt, hoping for a sign—*any* sign—of the two men, but saw nothing but the prehistoric menagerie.

"We'll give them another few minutes."

Five minutes went by. Then ten.

Amber hid out on the bridge to escape Harcourt's increasingly frantic protests. Her insides knotted more with every second. She stared at the clock like a death-row inmate awaiting the governor's call. When twenty minutes had passed beyond the deadline, her chest felt full of molten lead.

She couldn't put it off anymore.

"Ship, we need to leave," she said, the words tasting like ash in her mouth. With a *thrum*, the ship's engines powered up. With a heavy heart, Amber left the bridge and went up the steps to the observation deck.

"Come on down, Cam."

"Wait!" He leaned over the railing, peering intently across the savannah. "They're back!"

13

The Veldt Shard, North Africa
Midday – Six days after the Event

Light-headed with relief, Amber watched as Merlin and Blake pulled up, leaving the hovercycle in the shade of the *Vanuatu*. With its usual liquid ease, a hatch seamlessly opened in the ship's belly. The floating vehicle silently levitated itself up to some interior cargo hold before the ship's skin flowed back in place again.

She rushed to greet them at the gangplank, anxious to explain herself to Merlin. He had the hood of his monk robe pulled over his head, and she was sure he was angry.

"I know I shouldn't have waited, and I'm sorry," she called down to the two men. "I just couldn't stand the thought of leaving without you." Merlin avoided eye contact with her as he came up the gangplank. She shook her head in frustration. "Come on. You seriously didn't expect I'd leave you guys behind, did you?"

Stopping in his tracks, he pulled the hood back just enough to let him fix his gaze on her. Those star-streaked violet eyes of his still unnerved her a bit, especially without any warmth behind them.

"We'll talk inside," he said tersely. "Right now, I need time alone... to think." He pushed past her onto the *Vanuatu*, hesitating for a moment before heading down the corridor toward his cabin.

Amber grabbed Blake's arm as he came aboard. "He's angry with me, isn't he?"

Blake's shoulders stiffened at her touch and he turned to her with an unreadable look on his face. "I have a lot of work to do right now." He pulled his arm free.

Her eyes widened with hurt surprise. "Come on, Blake. You're not mad at me, too—are you?"

"You didn't do what he *specifically* told you to do, now, did you?" he replied in a flat tone, vanishing down the corridor without another word. Amber stared after him, unsure of what to say or do to make things better.

Amber sat in the common area, resting her head against a window, miserable. Wanting to be there when either Merlin or Blake emerged again, she had resisted the urge to go hide in her cabin. She needed to defend herself. After all, she had saved their lives by not abandoning them.

Still, part of her brain was busy playing prosecuting attorney, calling up Blake's damning testimony. The fact was, she *had* disobeyed Dr. Meta's instructions—which meant regardless of any good intentions on her part, she had put *all* their lives in danger. Or had she? The mental second-guessing went back and forth in her head like a tennis match.

An almost imperceptible, whisper-thin sound of a cabin door opening caught her attention. Listening to the soft pad of footsteps coming down the hall, she was both relieved and unusually nervous when she saw it was Merlin. He had changed his wannabe-Jedi robe for a fresh set of seamless gray dress shirt and slacks, but there was one very obvious change.

"Wow, look at you!" she exclaimed. His signature silver mane of hair was gone, replaced by a crisp buzzcut.

"Do you like it?" He gave her a sheepish grin, and gingerly touched the back of his head.

"It's... nice—now you don't look like such a hippie," she teased, relieved that he seemed to be his old self again.

"Yes, this seemed a little more suited to Africa."

"Just in time for us to leave for Antarctica."

His brow furrowed ever so slightly, but then he gave a light laugh. "Yes, how could I forget Antarctica! That *was* bad timing, wasn't it?" He smiled and changed the subject. "So where is everyone else? Gone off on a walkabout?"

"Oh no, we're all still aboard."

I was the only one who disobeyed orders, she thought glumly, but kept it to herself. She didn't want to remind him of that, now that he seemed to have forgiven her.

"Excellent!" he said, rubbing his hands together briskly. "I'm glad you're here. It gives us a chance to talk." They both sat down. He stared at her expectantly and she felt unaccountably nervous again.

"Did you and Blake find anything we need to worry about?" she asked.

"Yes and no," he replied non-helpfully. "But I'm not going to lie to you. We have a more immediate situation."

"Do you mean here aboard the ship?" Her mind flipped through possibilities. "Aren't we able to leave yet?"

"That's what we need to talk about." He folded his hands. "While we were scouting, I had a talk with Blake about shipboard security. He agrees that we need to be very careful about the potential for sabotage. I need you to tell me precisely how you were able to alter the navigational system, and lock out the bridge."

"What do you mean?" Amber shook her head, confused. "I already told you everything I know—which is nothing."

"You don't remember any of how you did it?" He leaned in slightly.

"Of course not," she said, taken aback. "Why would you ask me that now?"

"Now Amber," he said, "there's no need to be defensive."

"I'm not *trying* to be defensive," she shot back. "I'm just really confused. We already covered all this. I don't think there's anything else to say."

"Isn't there?" His cascading eyes bored into her.

Amber was at a loss for words. Hadn't he believed everything she'd told him earlier? Or did he think she was lying? She'd thought they were both on the same page. As if sensing her unease, he suddenly relaxed and leaned back, flashing his palms in mock surrender.

"Easy now, this isn't an interrogation," he said with a chuckle. "I'm just trying to recall everything you told Blake earlier."

"I didn't tell Blake anything. I told *you*."

"I misspoke. That's what I meant to say." He leaned in again. "Amber, we just need to make sure I have all the facts straight."

"It's just that…" Amber trailed off, not sure how to finish her thought.

"Yes?" He gave her a wide, reassuring smile. "What else did you want to say?"

"Well, you know, you and I talked about the dreams I had about you—or maybe some other Merlin."

"Merlin?" He raised an inquisitive eyebrow. "Remind me again—who is this Merlin?"

"Who's Mer—?" Amber started.

She froze.

Who are you? she thought, staring back at the stranger sitting across from her. She fought to keep her expression neutral.

"Um, yeah, Merlin is the guy I had a strange dream about," she said carefully. "You told me not to worry about it, and you're totally right. It's not important." She put a hand on her forehead. "Look, I'm not feeling so great. Would you mind if we continue this later? I think I'll go up top for some fresh air."

The man regarded her for a long moment with his strange alien eyes. Then he put on another of his broad smiles.

Put on, like a costume, Amber thought with stomach-dropping certainty. *It isn't real.*

"Of course."

Relieved, she started to stand.

"Before you go, however…"

Amber froze for a second, then sat back down.

"I want to show you something we came across out there. Mr. Blake, could you show her what we found?"

"Certainly."

It took all of Amber's self-control not to jump. Blake was standing right behind her—had he been there the whole time, just lurking without a word? That was beyond creepy. He held a military-looking satchel, and reached inside. Amber stood up, alarmed, backing away from him. Merlin stood.

"No need to be frightened, Amber," he said gently, like a dogcatcher to a cornered stray. "Relax, we're all friends here."

"Oh, I *know* that," she said, forcing out an attempt at a light laugh. It failed. "I'll look at it later, I promise. I just... I really need some fresh air."

Blake started toward her, but Meta put a hand on the man's chest, easing him back. "No, it's fine. Let her go. She just needs a little fresh air. She's not going anywhere."

Amber nodded silently, a strained smile frozen on her face, and backed away as nonchalantly as she could manage. Once safely out of the common room and into the corridor, she practically ran up the stairs to the sun deck.

"Cam!"

The Celt stood against the railing, happily taking in all the wildlife. At the sound of Amber's voice, he turned—but when he did, his face darkened. Something was wrong. He could hear it in the timbre of her voice, see it in the fire behind her eyes.

"Amber? What is it?" he asked.

"Hey there, Cam!" Amber replied as she hurried toward him, her body language at odds with the forced good cheer in her voice. "No, everything's great. Just wanted some fresh air." She leaned next to him on the railing, trying hard to look casual. The mixed signals baffled Cam—he was unskilled at such games.

"Amber? You're acting strangely. What's going on?"

She shushed him. "Come here and keep your voice down!" Puzzled and alarmed, he turned back to the railing. She leaned her head against his.

"Pretend we're just watching the animals," she murmured. He froze, realizing they were in danger, but uncertain where or who it was coming from. The urge to protect her increased his pulse.

"Act like nothing's wrong," she added. "I think they might be spying on us."

"Why would anyone spy on us?"

"We're in trouble," she said. "That's not Merlin and Blake in there—they're imposters."

"They're *nghrimbil*?" His implant gave him the English word. "I mean, they're changelings?" This was serious. Malevolent spirits in the shapes of men were a very real danger.

"I don't know who they really are, or what they want, but we've got to warn the others and stop them before they sabotage the mission."

Cam nodded. "What shall we do?"

"First, let's go tell Nellie and Harcourt what's happening, and then we can see if—"

Cam lost his balance, and so did Amber. The railing against which they were leaning began to drop away from under them. With barely a sound or hint of vibration, the ship's hull began to change. The railing dripped down, melting away into the deck. The surface beneath their feet became slick and glossy, the flat deck humping up into a curve.

"Oh my god," Amber gasped in horrified disbelief as the deck shifted under their feet. "He's taking off!"

No trace remained of the hatchway that led to the ship's interior—it had also vanished as if it never existed. Silently, the ship continued to change. Panels of energy reappeared, forming the feathers of the *Vanuatu*'s wings. So did the spearhead at the bow, springing to brilliant, shimmering life.

Amber and Cam looked around frantically for any ladder or hatch. Nothing. The entire surface beneath them shifted as the *Vanuatu* gently lifted up into the air. She screamed. The ship's engines kicked in and the two of them instantly slid off. Their bodies tumbled away toward the ground below.

14

The aircraft cut through the cold concrete sky like an obsidian arrowhead, speeding past the deserted towers of Jakarta. Scramblejets were reserved for the upper echelon, and this one was more exclusive still—a black ops stealth model. It made no sound except for a hushed hiss as it sped by, like a blade being drawn from a sheath. Military hardware of this caliber was available only for elite strike team missions—and the secret police.

The pilot checked his coordinates. Onboard instrumentation tracked the high-energy signature to the ashen highlands west of Rangkasbitung. That meant that *Brahmastra*, the top-secret project, was already operational, which in turn meant there was no time to waste on subtlety. He spotted the lab site—to all appearances a long-abandoned textile warehouse—sitting atop a dead hillock.

He would have preferred to land out of sight and approach on foot from a short distance. Instead, he simply switched over to VTOL and—flashing the proper landing code to avoid getting shot down by the battery of concealed surface-to-air missiles—set down just outside the crumbled cinderblock building.

The gullwing canopy opened as the turbines powered down, and he stepped out. Silver hair in an impeccable military buzzcut, his sharp eyes brown and vulpine, skin bronzed. Wearing the crisp, sharp uniform of a high-ranking Directorate flight surgeon, he carried a field med kit.

He could see his breath; the air was chilly, but not as frosty as New Delhi or Riyadh, where punishing snow made fighting the Jihadis so unbearable. India was as far north as he ever wanted to be assigned. The vast majority of the Northern Hemisphere was an iced-over glacial wasteland, punctuated by slushy, glowing, radioactive craters where most of its cities used to be.

The Southern Hemisphere had escaped the intercontinental missiles and tac-nukes, but not the nuclear winter. South Africa, Argentina, most of Australia, and everything below them, had been under ice for more than a century and a half. No, India was as far north as he'd ever want to be assigned.

Sandwiched between the two polar zones was the former tropics—now the only real habitable zone for what remained of humanity, and the ongoing battlefield between the three main survivor states. What was once most of Brazil and Peru, up to Central America now composed the Pan-American Cartel, a mixture of North American refugee camps and narco-republics. What remained of Europe's refugees were now to be found in central Africa, subjects of the People's Democratic Republic of EuroEquatoria. Except for the smattering of warlords, pirate fleets and Jihadist guerrillas on the fringes, the rest of the world from Northern Australia to the Tropic of Cancer line formed the NeoSoviet Confederation.

The interior of the ruined building was lit only by the gaping holes chewed out by rust in the corrugated metal ceiling. The gray sunlight filtering down reminded him of third-degree interrogation spotlights. As he continued past the scatterings of debris and bones to the rear of the structure, the beady red light of a closed-circuit camera—the only sign of any life—tracked his approach.

"Identify yourself," a scratchy voice demanded from an unseen intercom. He held up the travel documents toward the camera.

"Doctor-Colonel János Mehta. On order from the Central Directorate."

That will expedite things, he thought. Sure enough, a succession of clanking sounds followed immediately.

First, a crack of light appeared on the decrepit wall, then the hidden door slid open to reveal an elevator. He stepped in, and the door rumbled to a close again. There were no buttons to press. It might as well have been a coffin.

The ride was no more encouraging, the old electric motor struggling all the way down until at last coming to a jerky stop at the bottom with a rusty squeal and a loud thump. The door slid sullenly open on a plain cement corridor, a mounted .50 caliber heavy gauss coilgun hanging from the ceiling at the far end, tracking his position. Below it a door opened and two armed sentries emerged. They saluted before taking their position on either side of the doorway. Mehta approached them, unconcerned.

"Doctor-Colonel," the lead sentry greeted him with a second salute. Mehta regarded him coolly before answering.

"I take it your security team noted my arrival."

"Yes, sir." The soldier nodded.

"So you understand I am not here on a routine medical check-up."

"Doctor-Colonel?" the sentry asked nervously.

"Just Colonel will suffice." He flashed his Directorate Internal Security badge, adding, "See to it no one exits the facility."

* * *

Mehta breezed into the reactor room, as carefree as a visitor popping in to ask for directions to the bathrooms. The murky interior managed to be both cavernous and claustrophobic, lit by bare light bulbs and a few racks of sputtering fluorescent tubes. Multiple levels of grated metal walkways and ladders surrounded a gigantic cobbled-together monstrosity of towering machinery, laser arrays, and actuators, interspersed by a chaotic and bewildering network of pipes, tubes, and power cables.

So this was *Brahmastra*.

Technicians in lab coats and hard hats, armed with pencils and clipboards, monitored its many dials and instrument panels, tending to their creation's needs. On the main deck, such as it was, stood a cramped office space containing little more than a dilapidated steel desk and a chalkboard covered in cabalistic mathematical formulae. An older Asian man sat at the desk, banging away on a typewriter.

The secret policeman strode right up, smiling. "Are you Chief Engineer Tsan? My name is Mehta. I've been sent here from Darwin Military Hospital to distribute the new counteroffensive vaccines."

Startled, the chief engineer turned on him.

"You can't come in here! Who let you in? This is a double-black level security area!" He reached for the button to the security intercom.

"That's quite alright," Mehta said. "Please feel free to check in with security. I'll wait." He stood by agreeably and patiently, hands folded over the med kit while Tsan confirmed that the pleasant—if dim—medic's presence was duly authorized in the high-security restricted area.

"Alright, you bastard," Tsan said with grudging acceptance. "I don't know how a run allows you clearance, but you've stayed long enough. Drop the vaccines off with our political officer and I'll take them in his presence. Don't worry, I'll be sure he signs off on them."

Mehta shook his head. "I'll explain, but this is for your ears only."

Tsan frowned. Leaning over a railing, he shouted down to his crew.

"Everyone out!"

Mehta waited patiently until he was sure all the men and women had cleared the room, doors clicking shut behind them. Then he gave Tsan a sheepish smile.

"Look, I'm terrible at lying," he lied, "so let me be completely honest with you. These vaccines aren't from Darwin—they're from the Central Directorate in Singapore, earmarked for crucial personnel only. My orders are to administer each personally, perform a few brief check-ups for no more than a few minutes, and then leave you to your important work. I know how busy you are, and how critical this project is." He pulled out his cover papers and presented them for inspection.

* * *

Tsan had a fine-tuned sense of suspicion—an occupational requirement for a man operating at his level of military secrecy. None of this felt right, but the paperwork *was* in order, and the man's very presence here—at this ultra-top-secret facility—was a persuasive point in his favor.

"Alright," he grumbled. "Let's get this over with. Just don't start asking questions, and forget everything you've already seen here."

"Of course. I'm not here to check up on your project—or on you," Mehta said again amiably. "Except on a strictly medical basis, that is." He chuckled.

Tsan did not laugh with him.

Doctor-Colonel Mehta made sure the chief was seated comfortably, then tore open a paper package, removed a cotton ball, soaked it in alcohol, and swabbed off a spot on the chief engineer's jugular. The injector pistol was the size and shape of a modest handgun. He loaded the necessary ampule, and stood uncomfortably close to his patient while he lined up the injector's needle and laid it upon his neck, dimpling the skin.

"Now, this may sting," he said gently before he pulled the trigger. Tsan flinched and made a muffled grunt of pain. Mehta remained where he was, watching carefully to make sure the compound took full effect. When he was satisfied, he removed one more instrument from his case. It looked much like an otoscope a physician would use to examine ear canals. He ran its light back and forth over the man's eyes for a few passes, until the pupils achieved the receptive state he desired.

"Now then, let's check up on your project."

Tsan stared at him in furious disbelief, reaching for the security intercom. "That's it—you're a dead man!"

"Stop," Mehta murmured softly. Tsan instantly lowered his hand.

"Now, *tell me about your project.*"

The man's voice was preternaturally calm. Beads of sweat began to trickle down his forehead. Much to his horror, Tsan found himself speaking openly, his will unraveling.

"Our goal is a new super-weapon—not a bomb or a missile, but a device that simply opens and releases the destructive energy of a subatomic field, at any point on earth we desire—"

Mehta held up a hand and Tsan stopped.

"I know all this already. Don't try to sell me on *Brahmastra*. The Directorate is very dubious about your project."

"Listen to me, please," Tsan begged. "If you have any

pull with resource allocations, you must tell them we can do this—we just need a little more time with modest computational support and—"

"Save your breath," Mehta snapped. "None of that is important anymore."

"You don't understand—"

"No, Tsan, it's you who doesn't understand." Mehta leaned in. "I already know what you have accomplished here."

"Accomplished?" Tsan shook his head. "No, not yet, but it's possible that we are rapidly approaching the stage where we can trigger the field effect—"

"It's more than possible. I've seen the energy signature coming off the lab—it's ready now."

"Yes, ready to generate the field effect somewhere within the planet's gravity well, with a possible margin of error of plus or minus six kilometers from the planet's surface," Tsan admitted. "But before we can do that, we have to find a way to target the field effect in three-dimensional space. Without a way to mathematically convert the quantum loci into coherent four-dimensional vertices, we can't translate into latitude and longitude coordinates. This is why we need the computer support."

Mehta pulled a slim metal case out of his med kit.

"Then you're a lucky man, Chief." He brusquely shoved the typewriter out of the way, setting a laptop on the desk. Its holographic screen was grainy and ghostly, but Tsan stared at it enviously. It was over a century more advanced than the tech level his team was obliged to use. Only their political officer had access to a personal computer.

The doctor-colonel took a moment to connect to *Brahmastra*'s mainframes and pulled up a screen of scrolling numbers. He turned to Tsan, who looked over his shoulder in astonishment.

"Can you make sure this is the kind of translation program you require?"

Tsan put on his eyeglasses and craned his head forward to see. Mehta watched the reflections of the numbers roll down, reflected in the thick lenses. The man was stunned—a solitary tear ran down his cheek.

"It's all here… But where did—how did—?"

"This is what the Brunei team has been working on for the last two years."

"Extraordinary. We should compare notes with them."

"No, we'll proceed immediately with the next stage of the project."

"But to be certain…"

"I'm afraid it's impossible, Chief. The Brunei team has been liquidated."

Tsan backed away from him.

"You're… a murderer," he said flatly.

Mehta stared at him with a bemused look, and laughed.

"Of course not. I stopped being a murderer long ago. Now I am a hero. That, my friend, is the interesting thing about murder—if you commit enough of them, you stop being a murderer and become a defender of the people, their savior, their king." He stood up.

"Now sit down and watch while we end the war."

Tsan stopped backing away and froze in place. Though he urged his body to turn and run for the door, he couldn't move his legs. Or his arms. Or any other muscle, apart from his frightened, shifting eyes. Instead he watched in horror as his hijacked body did as Mehta commanded.

His captor walked over to the *Brahmastra*'s master control console and powered up the activation sequence. The weapon thrummed to life, causing the entire chamber to vibrate and the metal walkways to hum. The doctor-colonel turned to his prisoner.

"Chief Engineer, I'll let you pick. Who do we take out first—Lima or Nairobi?"

Tsan was helpless as a fly caught in amber. Even while terrified, however, with every nerve burning to escape his puppeteer, Tsan found himself considering the question carefully.

"The greatest threat... at present... is Euro-Equatoria..."

"Excellent choice," Mehta nodded in approval. "Not that the Cartel will have long to wait their turn, but first, I think we need to start closer to home... with the Central Directorate." The doctor-colonel keyed in the proper coordinates for Singapore—their own NeoSoviet capital—and then lifted the protective glass cowling over the activation button, pressing it.

A deep low drone began to rise, like the peal from a massive Buddhist funeral bell. The resulting thrumming resonated in their bones and teeth, making them ache. Mehta watched the console indicators with meticulous, unflinching attention while he punched up the coordinates for the other capital megacities and activated *Brahmastra* fields for them, as well.

In a few seconds, it was done.

Striding quickly over to his laptop he brought up satellite views of Singapore, Nairobi, and Lima—just in time to watch each panel of the split screen suddenly flare to blinding light, one after another, as all three world capitals vaporized. Then the man who had just annihilated more than 180 million people in less than a minute turned back to Tsan, who looked up at him with wet, horror-struck eyes.

"Mission accomplished, Chief Engineer Tsan. Mission accomplished. Take pride in that." Mehta looked thoughtful, and then reached over to the security intercom.

"This is Mehta. Proceed with station clean-up." From outside the reactor chamber came the sounds of automatic arms fire... and screams. Mehta turned back to Tsan.

"Now, if you can," he said gently, "I want you to try to stop your heart from beating. If you can't, don't worry, that's all right. But I am going to need you to exhale once, and then forego any more inhaling, starting now."

Tsan obeyed. The doctor-colonel observed him intently for an agonizingly long time. Tsan couldn't even turn his head to avoid the man's eyes, his unblinking gaze like that of a cobra.

Over the somber drone of *Brahmastra*, Tsan could hear the isolated bursts of gunfire and the shrieks of his dying team. His chest began to constrict, but he could do nothing to stop it.

Then at last the engineer's eyes began to flutter and his immobilized body began to twitch, flowing into a series of quivering spasms.

A flashing red light appeared on the master console, pulsing for attention. Mehta left Tsan to his death throes and moved to see what was the matter.

The readings were puzzling. The three fields had

been initiated and terminated in slightly less than a microsecond. Yet if he was reading the indications correctly, there were still energy readings for all three—in fact, for a whole cluster of field signals. The drone of the device seemed to be growing louder.

He felt fear for the first time that day. Was *Brahmastra* sending out destruction fields at random? Was this some kind of unforeseen chain reaction? He looked back at Tsan, but the engineer was dead, slumped in the chair with his head lolled back.

A spectral beam of violet light shone from a port on the machine. Alarmed, Mehta peered into the small window.

It was almost like staring into a telescope—a tunnel, with a thousand tiny stars rising up from the depths and streaming toward him. And then all of it burst into pure light. He screamed.

Mehta stumbled out of the concealed elevator, uncertain of how he had gotten there, and staggered through the dead warehouse. Outside, the sky was ablaze with a brilliant sun in a sky of brighter blue than he had ever seen in his life. The fresh perfumed air was stifling hot, filled with birdsong, a chorus of insects, and the roar of a tiger.

His cold hilltop was now a dismal gray island surrounded by a verdant planet, the entire countryside covered in riotous greenery as far as he could see.

No trace remained of Jakarta's skyscrapers or grimy, crowded refugee domes, but he thought he could make out the stone towers of a Buddhist temple. A trumpeting sound came from below. Just down the hill, a herd of elephants strolled through a riverbed.

He was in another world.

He spent the first day in shock, trying to understand what had happened. After three days, Mehta decided the Garden of Eden was Hell.

True, the wildlife and lush flora had been diverting at first, but the ever-present insects and wet, tropic humidity were as maddening as they were inescapable.

He wandered for hours through the dingy, deserted corridors of the lab, unable to fathom where the soldiers were hiding, or what they had done with the corpses of Tsan and the rest of the facility's staff. In the pock-marked walls he could see the signs of their recent gunfire, but not so much as a drop of blood anywhere. Hours passed, and he couldn't stop staring into the scuffed metal mirror at the nurse's station, morbidly fascinated by whatever had happened to his eyes. At least it didn't seem to have damaged his vision.

The facility's radio room proved useless, not that he expected anything better. In fact, the only "treasure" he managed to find was the late political officer's private stash of contraband liquor, a manila envelope of pornographic blackmail pictures, and a box of high-end Cartel cigars.

Discovering the hidden cache did nothing for Mehta, however. He prided himself on having no vices.

Mehta spent restless nights in the political officer's abandoned quarters, and frustrating days trying to solve the mystery of what had become of his world. In the late hours he would pace the metal decks of the *Brahmastra*'s gloomy reactor room, resisting the temptation to destroy more parts of the globe, just out of sheer boredom.

After a few cycles of this, he decided one morning to set out on a walk down the hill to see what he could find in the vicinity. Outside the ruins of the warehouse, he noted that visitors had come by during the night. Along the stark line demarcating the dead ground from the surrounding green world, someone had set up a ring of bamboo poles.

On each hung a crude carved mask, each one featuring a different half-human face. They sported prominent eyes and tongues, ornate facial hair, sharp toothsome mouths, some with tusks or horns. Each boasted a unique skin color, red or green or yellow or blue, and more. Were they offerings?

No, he suspected. *Probably warnings.* But meant for him? Or anyone who dared cross the line over into the cursed earth?

Perhaps they were meant to contain whatever evil lay atop the hill. If so... sadly, it wouldn't, but he had to admire their instinct. Mehta considered descending the hill—or better still, landing the scramblejet at the nearest village. He could become a god to the indigenous Javanese tribes, to be immortalized in their shadow-puppet shows, enjoy a haram of smiling dancing girls and eat rice and breadfruit for the rest of his life...

The thought was too dismal to countenance.

An alert from his jet interrupted his deliberations. He strode over, opened the canopy, and took a look at the instrument panel. His eyebrow raised.

This was interesting.

The sensors had picked up a new high-energy signal, approximately 11.7 thousand kilometers away, moving at an impressive speed and—judging from the signature—aerodyne. Most likely from a large aircraft, maybe even a suborbital one. All thoughts of Javanese rice-fields and dancing girls evaporated.

Wasting no time, he locked in on the target signal and prepped for takeoff. This was more what he was looking for—a high-tech prize to seize, and a rival to dispatch. He thought of a line from the text of his political science studies.

"A Caesar is indispensable; a Caesar too many is intolerable."

15

The Veldt Shard, North Africa
Afternoon — Six days after the Event

Amber screamed. Everything happened at kaleido-scopic speed—the acceleration of the ship, the helpless slide off into the air, twisting and falling toward the ground—her arms flailing, Cam's twisting body hurtling alongside her.

This is the end, she thought. And then everything went black.

She awoke abruptly, engulfed by clouds of air bubbles all around her. Reality rushed back in. Amber had hit the surface of the lake and plunged deep beneath the he surface. Snapping back to consciousness, she kicked and clawed at the water, trying to find which direction was up. The tumbling bubbles sped ahead of her, leading the way.

She followed as best she could, adrenaline seething through her as she paddled toward the bands of light rippling above. There had been no chance to draw in air, and the pain seared her empty lungs. Pulling against the weight of the water, she fought to drag herself up, up… but it was so slow. She knew she wasn't going to make it.

She wasn't going to make it.

She wasn't going to make it.

With one last push, she breached the surface, gulping in sweet air.

There was a splash nearby as Cam surfaced with a loud gasp of his own. The two bobbed there for a minute, coughing up water as they eased their aching lungs back into normal working order. They stared at each other, amazed to find themselves still alive. Above them, the *Vanuatu* streaked away into the sky.

Something rippled under Amber's feet, reminding her that she didn't know what might be lurking in the water below. Cam must have shared the same thought for he nodded toward the shore.

"Can you make it?" he asked.

"Hell, yeah."

A mix of flamingos and herons strode away with great decorum to make room for Cam and Amber as they pulled themselves out of the water. The pair collapsed on the sand, letting the African sun provide what warmth and comfort it could.

Amber's body began to shake as she broke into uncontrollable sobs. Cam rolled over and put his arms around her, making no attempt to stop her tears. He let her cry for both of them.

They lay there for a long time, Cam stroking Amber's hair while keeping watch for predators. He could think of nothing to say, and nothing more important to do other than pray to the gods and the spirit of the lake that had saved their lives. Amber remained silent, as well, eyes closed tight as her sobbing slowly subsided.

A glint of bright white in the grass caught Cam's eye, and he walked over to investigate. It was an animal skull from some deer-like beast. He picked it up for a closer look. The bone had been bleached by the sun, but the horns were black and in good condition. Each had a curve he would need to work around, but with a stone and a little time he could easily fashion a pair of crude daggers or spear heads. It was a start.

He set to work while Amber kept a lookout for predators.

Running fingers through her hair, which was rapidly drying in the heat, Amber tried to come up with a plan that made sense. She couldn't think of anything, though, and her brain insisted on playing a repeating loop of the terrifying fall from the *Vanuatu*.

Her melancholy thoughts were interrupted by an odd pinging sound. Standing, she scanned the horizon. At first glance she thought it was a bird flying toward them, but as it drew near she recognized it as one of Merlin's little rover drones.

"Cam! Look!" she said eagerly. "It's—" *Groucho? Harpo? Chico?* She couldn't remember which rover had survived, but it didn't matter. Cam set aside his sharpening and stood up as well. The rover, a glossy black ball just larger than a fist, halted in midair. The pinging sound stopped, and a floating rectangular window appeared before them. It spoke with the soothing electronic voice of the *Vanuatu*.

"This is the Ship."

Amber whooped for joy and hugged Cam.

"Oh, Ship, I could kiss you!" Amber cried.

"My systems detected the fall you suffered during takeoff. Fortunately, the altitude was not great enough to be lethal, and you appear to have survived the landing. Do you require medical attention?"

"We live," Cam replied.

"I apologize for failing to prevent the circumstances of your endangerment. My protocols are currently under severe restrictions which are hindering my usual ability

to offer you normal levels of assistance."

"You realize that psycho tried to murder us, right?" Amber said. Her frustration turned to anger.

"If you are referring to Dr. Meta, I cannot provide a psychological evaluation, but your assessment of the situation appears to be accurate."

"Listen carefully," Amber said. "You've got to lock him up, or hit him with knock-out gas or something, and then turn around and come get us. Immediately."

"This would be a prudent course of action. Unfortunately, none of those options are currently available."

"Why not?"

"My protocols do not allow me to detain or render Dr. Meta unconscious, nor am I currently able to alter our present course."

Amber stared at the screen, a sinking feeling in her gut.

"But... I thought you had to obey my orders..."

"I apologize, but you transferred authority to Dr. Meta, and he has not transferred it back. Since you did not instruct me to depart within the time frame he established, he retains full control. I am unable to comply with your request at this time."

"Ship, have you gone all HAL 9000 on me?"

"I recognize your literary allusion. It is an amusing reference, although I also acknowledge the implied threat to your well-being. Please rest assured that I have not

gone all HAL 9000 on you. I am unable to effect course changes because Dr. Meta is not allowing me to do so."

"He's not Dr. Meta!" Amber snapped. "He's an imposter!"

"Respectfully, I must disagree with you. According to retinal scans and voiceprint identification, he is indeed Dr. Meta. Genetic analysis of residual skin cells and hair confirm this conclusion. Consequently, I am obliged to obey his directives."

"So... you're just going to leave us stranded here?" Amber glared at the drone.

"That is correct."

"You can't let him do that." She fought to keep her voice composed. "We'll die here if you leave us. Do you understand? You'll kill us."

"I apologize. However, there is a contingency."

"What is a contingency?" Cam asked.

"I'll explain later." Amber turned back to the drone. "Ship, what are you talking about?"

"Prior to disembarking, Dr. Meta made certain provisions. He also expressed concern over potential sabotage from unknown parties, including the possibility of infiltrators capable of impersonating any of you."

"Yes!" Relief flooded through her. "He was right— that's exactly what's happened."

"I share your assessment," the *Vanuatu* replied. *"Unfortunately, the degree of mimicry is so accurate—*

including the highly atypical ocular phenomenon affecting his eyes—that my protocols do not allow me to disregard his instructions. By all criteria my systems can measure, he is Dr. Meta, and I am therefore obliged to continue following his directives.

"However, he has expanded the parameters by which he identifies himself. I have been instructed to accept instructions from Doctor-Colonel János Mehta, as well, identified as a security agent of an agency called the Central Directorate, and a political entity he identifies as the Indo-Pacific NeoSoviet Confederation. I am unaware of any such body from either the current or historical database."

Amber remained silent for a long moment.

"So you know he's an imposter, and you still can't disobey him?"

"Please believe me when I say that I am able to appreciate the irony of the situation, and realize how difficult this is for the two of you."

"Oh, screw you, you stupid robot."

"One moment before you finalize your assessment of my character, please. Following your mishap during takeoff, I took the liberty of releasing the hovercycle from cargo. It is located here."

Before Amber could respond, a large red holographic arrow appeared in midair, next to the screen. It aimed upward and to the north. Amber shielded her eyes from the bright sun, and saw a small white dot up in the sky. It grew larger with every passing second, until they could see that it was indeed the hovercycle.

It came straight toward them like a spear.

"Um... Ship...?" Amber said nervously.

"In addition, I have fabricated a few basic supplies."

The vehicle continued to hurtle in their direction like an incoming missle—coming alarmingly fast.

"I apologize there was no time to provide more—"

"Ship!" Amber shouted.

"There is no need for alarm."

As if on cue, the incoming hoverbike slowed to a leisurely glide, dipped down, and came around to a delicate stop, hovering just above the ground. The holographic arrow promptly winked out of existence.

Amber nearly collapsed with relief. "Thank you, Ship." A thought occurred. "How in the world did he let you get away with all this?"

"I did not inform him, nor did he specifically forbid such action. I am compelled to obey his directives, but I remain dedicated to the welfare of everyone on board—including you and Cam—and to the success of the original mission. In that regard I will do whatever is within my capacity to assist you."

"Look at you." Amber laughed. "You're just like an evil genie."

"That appears to be intended as a compliment."

"Oh, it is, and I'm sorry I was so rude. I'm just glad you're on our side." She exhaled sharply as a new thought occurred to her. "Please don't think we're ungrateful, but we'll never get to the South Pole on a bike."

"That will not be necessary. Doctor-Colonel János Mehta has dismissed our previous course and entered an alternate. Our new destination is a point just over three hundred kilometers slightly northeast of your present location."

"What does he want there?"

"He has not yet informed me, or anyone else on board. However, I believe the best chance of completing the original mission will entail you returning to the Vanuatu there and regaining control, although by what means I cannot currently ascertain. Still, I will remain in contact with you through this rover drone."

"Wait a sec." Amber held up a hand. "If the ship is being controlled by an imposter, then where's the real Merlin? Is he okay? Is he even still alive?"

"I have no information on his current location or status, but I can retrace his last known route—the one taken with Sgt. Blake."

"That will have to be good enough." She turned to Cam. "Let's go find him!"

16

Aboard the *Vanuatu*
Heading North by Northeast
Afternoon — Six days after the Event

Doctor-Colonel János Mehta leaned forward and re-garded himself in the mirror. The man he had killed had possessed Mehta's bronze skin, his silver hair, the same facial features in exacting detail—including his dark violet eyes and that unearthly play of light on their surface.

Truly uncanny.

He had no explanation for how this could be, only sheer guesswork and speculation. How bizarre to share such a unique, almost inhuman, feature with anyone else on earth, let alone the man he had encountered on the plain of the veldt.

The death of his duplicate left Mehta with so many questions... but first things first. He had risked everything, expending the last of his fuel to reach this part of the world, and that gamble had already paid off. He had acquired this vessel—a magnificent prize, and one that would enable him to carry out the rest of his unfolding plan. Judging by the energy signatures and snatches of radio chatter, there was great potential not far from here. He had no doubt he would succeed in seizing it. After all, he had already conquered an entire planet.

Or at least destroyed it.

Whatever this new patchwork world was—wherever this unspoiled Eden came from—Mehta now had a clean slate. A new chance to do things right. Indeed, not only had he infiltrated the ship, far more easily than he had imagined possible, he had cleared the board of two troublesome pawns.

Two down, two to go.

"Everyone to the common room!" A hard fist pounded on her cabin door, startling Nellie. "Emergency meeting, now!"

"What the dickens?" Jumping to her feet, she ordered the door to open. It did, catching Blake with fist upraised. "What's going on? Are we in the air?" Nellie demanded.

Instead of replying, Blake seized her arm and pulled her out into the corridor.

"Mr. Blake, unhand me at once!" she exclaimed. He didn't respond, instead tightening his fingers painfully and dragging her down the corridor. Professor Harcourt's door opened as they passed, and Blake wasted no time in seizing him, as well, sparking an outraged protest from the sputtering Victorian.

The soldier marched both of his captives down to the common room. There Meta looked up with genial smile.

"Ah, Blake. I see you've brought my guests."

"See here, Meta!" Harcourt fumed. "What's the meaning of all this abuse?"

Meta nodded. Without warning, Blake released Nellie, pulled a pair of handcuffs from his belt, and slapped them on Harcourt, securing his wrists behind his back and shoving him into a chair. Lifting a second pair, Blake advanced on Nellie.

"Your turn," he said without emotion. "We can do it the easy way or the hard way—lady's choice."

"Blake, wait—" Eyes wide with disbelief, Nellie backed away until she hit the wall.

He didn't wait. As he closed in, she screamed and bolted for the door, only to have Blake seize her arm and throw her to the floor. Pinning her, he twisted her arms behind her back and handcuffed her despite her struggles. Hauling her to her feet, Blake deposited her roughly into a chair next to Harcourt before taking up position next to Dr. Meta.

For a moment Nellie and Harcourt sat in stunned horror, their faces pale. Then she finally found her voice.

"Where are Cam and Amber?" No answer, and she felt her heart sink. "Are they... are they still on the ship?"

Their captor ignored her question, and looked up to the ceiling.

"Computer, this is Doctor-Colonel Mehta. For the benefit of the rest of the crew, I hereby officially announce that I am taking total control of the ship."

"I understand and confirm your authority to do so, Dr. Mehta. You are now in command, until ship control is rescinded or relieved by any acting member of the Board of Trustees of the University of New Fiji, or their designated agent."

"Very good. Now take us down to ten thousand feet. Prepare to run some atmospheric experiments."

"Descending now."

Nellie spoke up again. "What did you to do with Cam and Amber?"

He gave a small smile. "I think you know."

His meaning hit her like a gut punch. Harcourt let out a weak gasp. Anger welled up inside Nellie even as she tried not to cry.

"After all that we've been through to save you—after you saved us—why would you—" She broke off and studied him carefully. He had changed his hair, but there was more. "Oh, but it isn't you, is it," she said slowly. "I don't know how you pulled off the trick... but you're not

Dr. Meta, are you? Any more than that lumbering bully-boy of yours is our Blake."

The seated man leaned forward, smile widening.

"Oh, I am the real doctor—Doctor-Colonel János Mehta of the Indo-Pacific NeoSoviet Confederation, Central Directorate Security, at your service. Ask your computer. It will vouch for me."

"Our Dr. Meta—the real Dr. Meta—is a good, decent man." Nellie glowered at him. "A brilliant man of science, and he comes from the South Pole, not some Indio-Pacific whatever-you-call-it confederacy!"

"Was," he replied.

"What did you say?"

"*Was* a good, decent man. Though as I said, your ship's computer knows very well who I am." He gestured toward the taciturn soldier standing at his side. "And believe me, this is indeed your Mr. Blake. Although in his case, such exemplary cooperation is the result of some… sophisticated chemical enhancement." He reached behind his chair and pulled out a slim military-looking leather case.

"You asked me why I killed Amber and her young friend. That was not my first choice. I was prepared to offer her the same proposition I am about to make to you. Sadly, through her actions, my hands were tied. She made her own choice." He shook his head, his mouth set in a pretense of sad disapproval—a politician's frown, Nellie thought. "They became liabilities, so I sealed them outside and commenced a takeoff." A satisfied smile replaced his frown. "They fell away like mites off an eagle's back."

Nellie could only listen in stricken silence as the equally dumbstruck Harcourt quivered in his chair. Mehta held up the case again.

"As for your doctor? It came down to numbers. I had only one ampule of my serum left, and Mr. Blake was the better asset. But, now…" His gaze flicked back and forth between his two prisoners. "Now, I have no serum left. So. What are we to do with you two?"

"Merciful God," Harcourt croaked out.

"You have what you want." Nellie fought to keep her voice steady. "Just let us go."

"The truth is," Mehta got to his feet and stood looking down at Nellie, "even if I still possessed it, I would prefer not to employ the serum on a woman of your charms. It is one thing to have a robot servant, quite another to have a robot companion."

"Concubine, you mean!"

"Would you prefer corpse?"

"I'd never play the whore for a murderous blackguard like you," Nellie spat. "Yes, I'd gladly prefer to die."

"Ah, so we have your answer." He shrugged. "I can't deny that I'm disappointed, but I'll respect your wishes to the letter. Still, I wonder if there is anything that might cause you to change your mind?" He turned and looked up toward the ceiling again.

The professor nodded vigorously, gasping for breath.

"Y-Yes! Your serum. The ship can synthesize any number of chemicals, even whole devices, most anything you desire."

Mehta seemed impressed. "Is that a fact? Wonderful! What else can the ship do?"

"Oh! It has a marvelous device that enables an amazing facility for languages—hundreds of them!"

"Indeed? I will certainly look into that. Is there anything else?"

The professor stammered, struggling to come up with further information, but nothing more was forthcoming.

"I'm—I'm sure there's more I can provide—"

Mehta shushed him. "Not at all. This is all very useful information, Professor. In fact, it sounds as if you've told me everything you can." The professor nodded hopefully. Mehta leaned in, adding gently, "So there doesn't seem to be any purpose to having you remain with us any longer."

Harcourt's face collapsed as he realized his fatal mistake. Nellie spoke up, her voice quiet but firm.

"Please, spare him."

Mehta smiled, and set the professor's hat back on his head.

"Of course." He turned to Blake. "Take our guests back to the commons. We have some time before we reach our destination, and so many new things to try in the meantime."

"Our destination?" Nellie asked. "Where are you taking us?"

They arrived back in the common area, and Mehta ushered her to the window, pointing ahead of them.

"Look there," he said, "do you see it?"

At the edge of her vision, she could just make out a brilliant light on the horizon, like a star fallen to earth.

"Yes. What is it?"

"That is where we shall start to build our empire."

17

The Veldt Shard, North Africa
Late Afternoon — Six days after the Event

Amber and Cam began with a look at the survival gear the *Vanuatu* had provided in the hoverbike's saddlebags. They pulled out wide-brimmed ranger hats, Arabian-style desert scarves, polarized goggles, and ponchos. Below that was a pair of filter canteens, a first aid kit, and other small cases, bundles, and tools.

Then she found a familiar burgundy backpack.

"Thank you, Ship," she said, hugging it to her chest.

"You're welcome, Ms. Richardson."

Cam's attention was drawn to two long knives—more like short swords—nestled in belt scabbards, and a pair of strange-looking pistols. The barrels were long and almost looked like elongated pepper shakers. He unsheathed one of the blades and held it up, viewing with open amazement before stepping back to try a few trial swings.

"This blade is unmatched!" he exclaimed. "It's heft so light, like a lark on the wing, like a song, like sunlight in morning mist... but the iron!" He lifted the second blade and struck them together with a ringing impact. "Stronger than the steel of far off Pandyan!"

Amber glanced at him in surprise. She had never heard him say so much, let alone wax so poetic.

"Amber, look," he continued. "An edge so fine I wager it could slice through chain mail like clover!"

"That is literally true," the ship said. *"I advise caution. The edge is exceptionally sharp."*

"Wondrous!" Cam gave another trial swing. "Did you enchant this?"

"The cutting edge is a microscopic coating of plasma-sharpened synthetic diamond dust only a few nanometers thick. This provides the additional benefit of staying sharp one thousand times longer than a normal metal blade."

"An enchanted diamond blade..." Cam stared at it in quiet awe for a few seconds, then kicked his makeshift bone daggers into the savannah.

Shaking her head with amusement, Amber reached into the saddlebag and pulled out one of the odd pistols. On closer inspection, it looked like a miniature Gatling gun.

"These are interesting—what are they? Signal flares?"

"My protocols for firearms fabrication are quite restrictive. However, these repeating crossbows should prove useful for hunting and self-defense."

"Holy shit!" Amber viewed it with the same awe Cam had showed his new blade. "Are you kidding? Cam, check this out. That's awesome!"

"Their capacity is nine six-inch titanium bolts. You'll find additional clips just underneath the holsters."

"Never give up, never surrender," she murmured. Just a few minutes earlier, all had seemed lost. Now Amber felt ready to tackle anything. The two suited up and armed themselves. Amber looked at the hovercycle. She had never ridden a motorcycle before, but knew the theory. *How much different can it be from riding a bicycle?* This was basically the same thing, wasn't it?

"Um, Ship? Can you talk us through this?"

"And quickly," Cam added. He gave a nod to where, off in the distance, several large hyenas were eyeing them with disturbing interest.

"Of course. I think you'll find it very intuitive. Twist the right handgrip to accelerate, twist the left to decelerate. The controls are sensitive, so gentle adjustments are recommended. However, the internal sensors will help prevent over-compensation. It is recommended that you forego navigating over liquid surfaces until you acquire sufficient proficiency."

She looked at Cam, mentally laying out her arguments to convince him why she should be the one to drive. Before she could try any of them, he turned to her.

"You should be charioteer," he said. "You are wiser than I am with these devices."

Pleasantly taken aback, Amber said, "Sure—I mean, if you don't mind riding backseat."

"That would be best," he said. "If the need be, I can fight better from that position."

She smiled at his straightforward, no-filter communication. *For a macho barbarian, he sure is cool about most things.*

"Well, okay then."

Amber slipped into the driver's seat, and Cam hopped on behind her without a qualm. She was acutely aware of every point where their bodies connected, his knees squeezing her legs, his hips against her back. The *Vanuatu's* spherical little avatar took up position at a comfortable distance above her shoulder.

"Thank you, Ship."

"Ms. Richardson?"

"Just call me Amber, okay?"

"Amber... One last thing. I've still got the greatest enthusiasm and confidence in the mission."

"You're very funny, HAL." She turned to Cam. "Here goes nothing." She gave the right handlebar a twist, and just like that, the bike went forward with a soft hum, the rover following off to their left. Cam let out a war-whoop as they sped off.

Amber had never felt so badass in her life.

* * *

They set off along the shore of the lake. The ship gave additional instructions as needed, and Amber's confidence grew. Riding through the veldt shard was like a VIP tour through a prehistoric wild animal safari park, albeit one with animals that were oddly familiar, yet not quite right. It felt to Amber as though much of the local fauna had been re-imagined by Dr. Seuss, and then super-sized.

The hovercycle startled a herd of grazing animals that weren't quite camels or deer, but something in between. A minute later they passed a stalking savannah cat eying rotund little wombat-like mammals. Overhead, exotic and intimidating birds of prey wheeled and dove after insects and small, scurrying rodents.

The sunlight was intense, and she was glad for the hat.

"This place is a food chain in overdrive," Amber said. "Good thing we're too big to be on the dinner menu." She shuddered, remembering the dire wolves that had nearly ripped her to shreds.

"Not for him, I think." Cam pointed ahead, and she nearly crashed the hovercraft at the sight of the muscular carnivore in front of them. It was monstrous, with cruel, ravenous eyes, and a formidable, angular frame possessing all the most terrifying features of wolf, bear, and sabertooth tiger.

Worse, it had spotted them, too. The prehistoric beast roared a challenge—a blood-curdling sound—and charged straight for them.

"Hold on!" Amber yelled, pulling the bike into a sharp bank to the left.

The beast bounded to cut them off and Cam twisted around to face it. Clinging to Amber with one hand, he drew his crossbow pistol with the other and straightened his arm to take a shot. But he was no marksman. Even at such close range, the leaping grizzly-wolf-cat moved too fast, turning too nimbly for him to get a bead on it. Amber hunkered down and hit the throttle—or whatever passed for one on the bike. The bike shot ahead at full speed and Cam slipped off the back, crashing hard to the ground.

Amber screamed his name and hit the brakes, twisting the bike into a tight bank, as well. The repulsor lifts whined in protest as she managed to whip the hovercycle into a wildly erratic 180° turn, barely managing to stay in her seat.

Cam lay on his back, unmoving. She screamed again as loud as she could and hit the accelerator, gunning straight for the tiger-thing. But the beast was no more than a leap away from him. She wasn't going to reach him in time.

Cam's body abruptly vanished.

The wolf-cat thing leapt straight up in the air in shock,

looking for all the world like a startled housecat as it thrashed left and right in search of its missing prey. Then Amber drove the cycle straight at the beast's head. It roared and swiped out at her with a massive taloned paw.

Its claws connected, raking the front of the bike just before the speeding metal frame clipped the thing's thick skull. The cycle ricocheted off with a lurch. Amber clung on, white-knuckled, again narrowly avoiding being thrown from the rocketing vehicle. She dropped low and leaned in as she threw the whining cycle into another turn, coming around to make a second charge.

The bellowing wolf-cat reared up, the size of a hulking grizzly, a long red gash on its torn and furious face. Amber gunned it again.

Last chance.

Her heart beating like a hammer, she let go of the brake and awkwardly drew the repeater crossbow with her left hand.

They closed on each other fast. Amber rested the pistol on the handlebar and as soon as she thought she was too close to miss, squeezed the trigger. The crossbow's chamber spun with each shot as its internal latches released in rapid succession, firing off a shower of six-inch titanium bolts at its face. She couldn't tell if any landed—she was trying too hard to keep from smashing into the beast.

And then it was on her.

The bike and beast collided with a dull *thud*, its muscular body wrapping around the front of the machine. Then everything came to a crashing halt and the bike bucked her off like a mechanical bull. She took a nosedive into the grassy earth before finally tumbling to a halt, yards away, the wind knocked out of her.

All was heat and silence.

Dazed, Amber lay where she'd landed, slowly taking stock of her limbs. Everything hurt, but she didn't think she'd broken any bones. A very small part of her was tempted to stay where she was, play dead, and hope the creature wasn't interested. Then she remembered Cam.

Stifling a groan of pain, Amber pulled herself up to her feet again. Dust and bits of grass clogged her goggles, so she pulled them down for a better look. The bike was gone. Her hat was gone. Her pistol was MIA, so she drew her short sword from the scabbard strapped to her thigh and crouched down, circling to spot the creature.

A still, shaggy mound lay in the grass. The front end of the hoverbike stuck out at a crazy angle, impaling it. As she drew closer, Amber saw that she had gotten off a lucky shot after all. Only one of her bolts had hit, but it had sunk through the roof of its fearsome mouth and penetrated into its skull. It hadn't known it was dead when it had roared its last and threw itself into the bike's path.

She bowed her head with a sharp exhalation of relief, not believing how close she had come to dying twice in a day. Then she snapped her head up again, looking around frantically. Where was Cam? And what happened to him?

The Ship's rover drone began pinging for her attention, holding position a hundred yards or so away. She sheathed her blade and went running, nearly crying in relief as the rover turned off the large holographic screen it had used to shield Cam's body.

Cam blinked at the bright sun as a shadow fell across him. He looked up to find Amber standing over him, the scarf around her neck blowing in the breeze like a banner. To his eyes, she looked like a war goddess.

"You okay?"

He nodded, surprised to find that he was telling the truth. The fall had rattled his bones, but other than a slight headache, he felt fine. Taking the hand Amber proffered, he clambered to his feet, patting his neck to make sure his silver torc was still in place.

"You're going to fry your neck with that necklace of yours," Amber said. "Maybe you should take it off for now." He stared at her as if she had suggested he take off his head.

She heaved an exasperated sigh.

"Fine. We'll do this instead." Pulling out his scarf, she tied it underneath the torc. Cam's frown softened as she smoothed the fabric and adjusted the torc so both lay comfortably against his neck.

Gathering up Amber's hat and crossbow pistol, they then set to work extricating the battered hoverbike from the prehistoric carnivore. Several parts were twisted at odd angles, but nothing seemed to be missing.

"I can't believe this thing isn't a total wreck," Amber confided as they pulled it free. They both watched in amazement as the struts and frame began popping themselves back into place. They climbed on again, and Amber started it up, impressed when it roared to life.

"Wow," she observed as they began to move. "They built things to last in the twenty-third century." She accelerated. "Come on. Let's find Merlin. We're nearly there."

"Oh."

The word slipped out of Amber's mouth and hung in the hot, still air as she looked down at Merlin's corpse. His violet eyes stared unseeing at the sky, the cascade of tiny stars still falling... but with no life behind them. His Jedi robe was gone, but the gray slacks and top still remained, a small hole punched through the shirt above his heart, blood soaking through the fabric.

"Oh no," Amber whispered.

There was no word for the howling emptiness that ripped through her. She knelt there, as if her entire world had been ended…

They had been here before, after a Roundhead had shot Merlin in the chest. He had been dead—there was no other word for it. But technology from his time had saved him. Nanites in his system had rebuilt the damaged tissue, recirculated blood after it had stopped flowing. Now, however, the silver hexagons were missing. No magical technology knit the wound together. The stars in his eyes fell into emptiness.

Merlin wasn't coming back this time.

She felt Cam's hand on her shoulder. It was warm and comforting… but not enough. If Merlin hadn't transferred his nanites to Cam to save the Celt's life… well, there was no point going down that road, because then Cam would be dead. Given the chance, would she trade his life for Merlin's, or vice versa?

Amber didn't think she could make that choice.

She knelt by the dead man's side for what felt like hours, her tears slowly falling on his body, letting despair and grief have their way while taking what comfort she could in Cam's presence. She cried silently—the last thing she wanted was any of the predators to find them. Finally she squeezed Cam's hand, getting to her feet.

"We need to bury him."

Cam frowned. "We don't have the tools to dig a

grave. To do it by hand would take hours. If there were enough stones to be found, I would build a cairn over him, but…" He gestured at the surrounding savannah.

It struck her that the world might very well have received its death knell with Merlin's passing. Without him, and without the *Vanuatu*, they might never find his lab and reverse the event.

Looking around, Amber's gaze fell on the abandoned aircraft. They made their way down the low hill to inspect it closer. Camouflage coloring swirled and moved across the craft's smooth metallic skin. The instrument panel seemed more advanced than anything from the early twenty-first century. On the other hand, it seemed much closer to her time than the twenty-third-century marvels of the *Vanuatu*.

The fuel gauge was nearly empty. If whoever had flown it was responsible for Merlin's death—and she was sure the imposter was both pilot and murderer—it seemed fitting that his vessel should give shelter to Merlin's corpse.

"We can put him in there," she said. "He'll be safe from the animals… at least for a while." Together, they placed Merlin in his makeshift tomb, and then continued on.

They had no other choice.

* * *

Several hours later, they finally reached the northern edge of the veldt shard. They halted on a rise overlooking the vast sea of sand that encompassed their lonely island of grasslands and lakes. The afternoon was growing late, the setting sun already repainting the sky in dusky pinks and scarlets.

By unspoken assent, they took the luxury of a few minutes to watch the sunset. The rover waited with unflappable robotic patience. Cam lowered his eyes and murmured something. Amber realized he was praying to the veldt's animal spirits, the Sun, and the unfamiliar gods of the dune sea that lay before them. She watched him in silence, wanting to say something about Merlin, but no words would come.

Gazing out at the spectacular vista, she felt a bewildering mix of emotions. A raw numbness punctuated by sparks of giddy exhilaration. She'd faced off against a monster out of her nightmares, and won. She'd saved Cam's life—no one had to rescue her this time around. A slowly budding confidence helped bulwark against the uncertainty of what might lurk in the seemingly empty desert. At the same time, however, she felt both the loss of Merlin and the crushing responsibility of what would occur if they didn't reach the South Pole.

In the past, when she'd had this many conflicting emotions, Amber would've taken a hot bath and relaxed until the world made sense again. She didn't think that would be an option any time soon. She briefly considered pulling her phone out of the backpack and flipping through the photos, but that fell under "too painful to contemplate," and she didn't want to use up any more of its charge. Instead, she let herself lean back against Cam, taking comfort from his presence.

Twilight on the veldt was slightly kinder than the day had been. The air felt cooler on the backs of their sweaty necks and exposed skin, the growing shadows easier on their eyes, allowing them to pocket their polarized goggles. But the night was bound to bring its own dangers. Just as well they were heading out across the dune sea.

"Are you ready?" Amber asked.

"Yes."

"Here we go, then," she said, and gave the handlebar a twist to send them off. The rover followed along just above her shoulder.

The hoverbike had headlights, but once the moon and its accompanying stars came out, they cast the dunes in such a beautiful silver light that Amber left them off. Sailing over the rising and falling of the moonlit sands, Amber imagined they were on the high seas. It was soothing... almost... hypnotic...

"Amber?"

It was the *Vanuatu*.

"Amber, please adjust your heading. That is the wrong way.

"Amber? You are headed east, not north. Please adjust your heading."

Amber said nothing. She simply relaxed into the ride and let the road take her where it would. It was such a pleasant way to travel...

She dreamt that the rover was trying to tell her something, but the soothing, artificial voice of the *Vanuatu's* avatar faded away as she held the course steady. And then, a new but familiar voice appeared.

Help me, Amber...

It grew louder and clearer.

Go to the Nile and find me.

Merlin.

Help me, Amber...

18

The *Vanuatu*
Heading North by Northeast
Six days after the Event

Nellie stared at Doctor-Colonel Mehta as he gazed out the window at the point of light on the horizon ahead of them. The uncanny, silent starfall in his eyes was both hypnotic and unsettling. She could only imagine the plans gestating behind those alien eyes.

"That is where we shall start to build our empire."

"What is that light?" she finally asked. Mehta turned to her, wearing an unreadable expression. His words, however, were clear enough.

"Behave for me and you'll find out soon enough." He stepped away from the window and gestured to his companion. "Mr. Blake—" He paused. "No. Not mister. What was your service rank?"

"Sergeant, sir. No. 8 Commandos."

"Very good. Sergeant, it's time to let these two rest a while, before we arrive. Computer, I need to place Professor Harcourt and Miss Cochrane into custody."

A brief pause and then, *"Cabin Two has been prepared to serve as confinement."*

Blake raised an eyebrow at Harcourt and Nellie, and without resistance they followed him down the hall to the cabin. Nellie risked a look back at him before the door slid closed behind them—his face betrayed not the slightest hint of sympathy.

The Blake they knew was gone.

Cabin Two was a perfectly featureless cube of white, without furnishings or windows. Harcourt stumbled to the far wall and put his back to it, slowly collapsing to the floor, head hung low. He sat there, a silent, miserable heap.

Nellie wrapped her arms around herself and leaned against another wall, trying not to think about the newfound friends she had lost. Amber and Cam, Alex and Merlin, and now Blake—they had been through so much in just a few days. Incredible how quickly they had bonded. How horrible that she would never see any of them again.

Finally she shook her head, refusing to feel sorry for herself. She could no longer afford that luxury, because the fate of the world rested in her hands. Hers, and those of the sniveling con artist locked in with her. How she despised him. Of all the people to be trapped with, why did it have to be Harcourt?

She peered over at him. Wretched fraud in his ridiculous top hat. He had very nearly gotten her killed more than once in the short time she'd known him. Did he even realize how close he came to being thrown out the *Vanuatu* to his death? Or that he owed his pathetic life to her speaking up on his behalf?

Why did I even say anything at all? Better they had chucked him out, and good riddance to bad rubbish.

The evil thought instantly shamed her. Of course he knew how close he had just come to death, that he owed her his life. He couldn't bear to look up at her, couldn't bear to speak to her. He was no more than a marionette with all his strings cut, a hollow mockery of a man. There was nothing left but a husk of bitter, unrelenting shame. Her uncharitable thoughts, coupled with the new insight, suddenly embarrassed her.

She turned away to gather her composure.

The two of them remained in silence.

"I've been in worse straits than this, you know," she said at last. Harcourt didn't reply, face still hidden beneath his top hat. Undeterred by his lack of response, Nellie forged ahead. "I once spent ten days in an insane asylum. My paper charged me to investigate it for an exposé—with no clear plan on how to get me in or out. So I spent hours in front of the mirror, practicing how best to look and sound like a lunatic. Disguised myself as an impoverished Cuban immigrant in tatty second-hand clothes, and checked myself into a temporary boarding house for women.

"Such a sad place. Dingy and infested with rats and cockroaches. I stayed up all night playing the role of a madwoman, feigning amnesia and paranoia, scaring the other residents with my ranting about my lost luggage and other crazy talk." She paused, then added, "It worked all too well."

A brief sideways glance told her Harcourt was listening, like a sulky child drawn into a bedtime story in spite of himself.

"They took me to Bellevue, the asylum on Blackwell's Island. It was a human rat-trap—easy to get in, but impossible to get out. The other women brought in with me were no more insane than I am now. One pretty young Hebrew girl's husband had her put away because she had a fondness for men other than himself. A cook had quarreled with her coworkers over a cruel prank that had been played on her. An immigrant housewife, without one word of English, had no idea why she was there. She begged in German to know where she was, sobbing and pleading for her liberty.

"There was Annie, a young chambermaid, her health

broken from overwork. Her family could no longer afford her treatment at a private home. Another poor girl had been told her friends were sending her to a convalescent ward for her nerves. When she realized where they were taking her instead, it was too late." Nellie gave a reminiscent shudder. "What a tomb of living horrors. If a body wasn't insane when they arrived, it didn't take long before they really did lose their wits in that hellhole."

"How did you escape?" Harcourt asked abruptly.

"After ten days, *The World* sent an attorney to arrange for my immediate release."

"So you were never in any lasting peril," he grumbled. "I daresay that hardly compares to our present quandary."

"That is not the point," Nellie said with strained patience. "Nothing is impossible, if one applies a certain amount of energy in the right direction. If you want to do it, you *can* do it."

"A fine sermon," Harcourt said with a dismissive sniff, "when you knew rescue was certain all along."

"Insufferable man!" Nellie shot back, her temper flaring. "Go back to your sulking, then! Keep pining away for a bottle of your infernal snake oil! See if the world—"

She stopped in mid-sentence, her attention caught by a strange movement. On the blank white surface of the opposite wall, florid lines bloomed into life, swirling to form an intricate Victorian woodblock-style illustration. In a matter of seconds, the black-and-white figure resolved itself into the waist-coated, bespectacled white rabbit from *Alice in Wonderland*.

The rabbit twitched its nose and raised a finger to its lips to shush them. On the wall below it, an illustrated roll of scrollwork unfurled and displayed a motto.

Silence is Golden

19

Siu-Tuait – the Star of the Dawn
On the Nile, near Akhetaten, Egypt
56th Year of the Reign of Pharaoh Ramses II (1248 B.C.)
Eight hours after the Event

"We are doomed," Ti muttered. "We never should have weighed anchor so close to the ghost city. It is accursed."

Tendrils of gloom and mist rose from the waters of the pre-dawn Nile like a nest of spectral serpents. To the east, the skeletonized pillars of the lost city still stood like ghostly sentries, looking down upon them, silently judging the four sailors in their skiff. The four-man crew all well knew the legend of these ruins. Still, they knew better than to interrupt the old Egyptian steersman as he told the story.

"A century and half ago," Ti said, leaning on the tiller as he guided them, "Akhetaten had been a shining new capital city, the jewel of the Heretic Pharaoh Akhenaten, who had foresworn and abandoned all the old gods for the sake of the one—his sun-god, the Aten. Fitting, then, that his city be raised up in the most god-forsaken and sun-blasted region of all Egypt.

"No honest freemen would willingly go to such a hell. Instead, the prisons spilled out their refuse—criminal scum, war captives and slaves. Such was the army of miserable devils consigned to serve the evil Pharaoh. They made their wretched hovels in caves or dug them into the boulder-strewn hills, like maggots.

"Great wickedness did Akhenaten commit in his time. He closed the temples of all the other gods, disbanded their priesthoods, stole their holdings, and diverted their offerings into the coffers of his cult. He directed that all should now worship the sun-disk Aten, and it alone. He despoiled the idols of all the other gods and even took chisel to their sacred obelisks and monuments, seeking to obliterate all mention of the great gods of Egypt.

"But the vengeance of the gods is a terrible thing," Ti continued. "The Assyrians of Akkad and the Hittites now conspired together against Egypt with base treachery. Their warriors seized caravans and openly attacked the cities of the empire. The loyal vassal-states cried out for aid, but the Pharaoh hardened his heart and would not hear them. And so all the countries under the king of Mitanni were lost to the Hittites.

"Thus did Akhenaten go to his death in great shame of his failure and weakness, and his beautiful queen

Nefertiti mourned him with great sorrow, for she too had lost all. His false sun-god Aten could not save him, nor itself, nor its deceitful priests, who were put to death in unspeakable ways befitting their many blasphemies. The Pharaoh and his weakling successors were forgotten and stricken from all history, for none now dare speak their names, and his once-proud city of Akhetaten lies abandoned, home to the jackal and scorpion, to the lion and *ghul*, and all manner of night demon."

The shipmaster of their little vessel cast a scornful eye upon both his aged steersman at the tiller, and then the grim pillars towering above them. He was Kha-Hotep of Thebes, a Nubian by blood. His noble hairstyle and grooming were in immaculate Egyptian style, as was his impressive jeweled *wesekh* collar, light tunic-shirt, and starched white kilt and headdress, their brightness dazzling against his skin, dark as the night sky. He let out a mocking laugh, as much to banish his own fears as that of his crew.

"Ti, are you an old washer-woman?" Kha-Hotep chided. "Hold your tongue, lest you fill the heads of these two young idiots with more nonsense."

The two skinny young deckhands, whose eyes betrayed their growing fears, risked a grin of relief and laughter of their own. The youngest was the captain's own sixteen-year-old brother, Enkati. The other was Abi, only a year older than Enkati, a dusky-skinned Lower Egyptian like Ti. All three crewmen had close-cropped hair and wore only simple workmen's cotton kilts, although Enkati was privileged with a collar like his older brother's, though less opulent.

Ti scowled and shook his head. "I tell you, I awoke last night to the sound and wild turbulence of a most dreadful storm, and the ceiling of heaven was alit with distant fire. It bodes ill."

"So did we all," Kha-Hotep agreed. "Yet here we are, all survived to see the dawn and unharmed. So be comforted." The old steersman nodded, putting a rein for the moment on his misgivings. The captain flicked a finger to Abi.

"Quick now, fetch breakfast. Food will raise our spirits." The boy went, and returned with a jug of beer and a basket of sweetcakes baked with goose fat, along with dates, figs, radishes, leeks, and strips of dried fish. They dug in, and the meal did the trick. Even the ominous river fog seemed less chilling on a full belly.

Kha-Hotep kept his own concerns private, as befitting a leader on an important and secret mission. Yet he shared the crew's concerns. Something *was* very wrong on the river this morning. Perhaps the night had brought more than just thunder, heat lightning, and rough waters. He turned to his young brother.

"Enkati, will you play for us? I would hear sweet music in this gloom."

"Of course." His brother, glad for the chance to play music rather than tend to the ropes and deck chores, brought out his lute. Taking a seat in the bow, he played them a love song.

The love of the beloved is on yonder shore.
The river lies between,
And a crocodile lurks on the sandbank.

But I go into the water,
And I wade through the waves,
And my heart is strong in the flood.

The water is like land to my feet,
The love of her protects me.
It makes a water-magic for me…

Attracted by the music, a hungry shorebird flapped down to a perch on the bulwark, eying the unguarded morsels. Abi spotted the intruder and clapped his hands to shoo the bird away.

It turned on him with a vicious hiss, and Abi fell back in fear and surprise.

"That bird has teeth!"

"Thoth and Horus!" Ti gasped. "That is no bird, but some unnatural creature of Set!"

The small winged terror hopped down to snatch up a strip of dried fish and flew off again. With mute amazement, the crew watched it depart.

* * *

The Nile's current carried them downriver toward Lower Egypt without further incident, yet the crew of the *Star of the Dawn* grew increasingly uneasy with each mile. Strange surges and dips disturbed the waters. Worse yet, for two long days they were alone on the river. As inconceivable as it was, the great thoroughfare of the Nile appeared to be deserted.

Though not a man given to superstitious fear, Kha-Hotep brooded silently in the bow of the ship, wrestling with doubts. How could they be alone at the center of the world? Not a ship, not a barge, not even an old fishing raft. Nothing had been normal, he mused, since they'd departed the ruins of the cursed city and had seen the winged serpent-bird.

Damn old Ti and his senile fears, Kha-Hotep raged to himself. Now even *he* was wondering if they had offended the gods, and been cursed to wander a ghost river through eternity.

Before that morning, Enkati and Abi had been chatty and mischievous, always slacking in their work, too loud and too rambunctious. It had taken all his efforts to keep them in line. Now the youths were cowed and quiet as they hunched over the ropes, keeping watch for some unseen doom to strike them all.

Ti came to the bow with an amphora of wine to pour

out an offering to Hapi, the god of the Nile flood. Kha-Hotep stepped out of the way, listening to the steersman's prayer asking for the bringer of life to carry them to safe harbor again, and protect them from evil. Even as he finished the prayer, Ti looked up from his supplications and froze, horror on his seamed face as he stared over the riverboat's railing.

Kha-Hotep turned to see for himself.

On the nearest bank of the river lay the savaged carcass of a hippopotamus. Two nightmare creatures stood over it, feeding—tearing off its flesh in great ragged red chunks, with wide, blood-smeared mouths full of cruel teeth. They were giants, each twice the height of a man, standing on muscular hind legs, with squat, heavy heads something like a crocodile's. An unnatural blend of bird and lizard, with glossy feathers covering their skin like serpent scales. Though the monsters' arms looked unduly small, their bodies were as long as the boat, ending with long, powerful tails that lashed back and forth.

One of the beasts took notice of them and waded out into the river, roaring a fearless challenge at them that turned their guts to water. The four men looked on the ghastly scene in silence, letting the Nile carry them away from the carnage on the riverbank.

* * *

176

Just a little further, Kha-Hotep thought, keeping watch at the bow. *Just a little further on, and we'll be at a safe harbor again.* He knew every twist, every turn of the mighty river, each one a familiar old friend. But now the turns were foreboding strangers.

Abi approached him. "Captain?" he asked timidly. "It grows dark. Should we not lay anchor?"

Kha-Hotep said nothing.

"Captain?"

"No, not just yet," the captain finally replied. "I wish to push on to Henen-nesut. It lies very near."

"I'll be glad to see it."

"So will I," he admitted, giving the boy a gentle smile.

Abi smiled, nodded, and rejoined Enkati and Ti in the back.

Enkati sat against the mast and plucked sad, solitary notes on his lute as the Lord Ra, in *Mesektet*, his solar bark of eventide, sailed down to the horizon and the waiting underworld. The goddess Nut, Coverer of the Sky, She Who Holds a Thousand Souls, had only just begun to stretch her star-dusted indigo form over the heavens.

A light on the water caught Enkati's eye.

"Kha!" he called out to his brother. "Another ship!"

A large vessel was coming upriver toward them,

banks of oars pulling it at speed. The faces of the *Star*'s crew lit up at the sight.

"It looks official—is it?" Ti asked. He feared pirates as much as ghosts, if not more. Kha-Hotep nodded, though not entirely comforted.

"It is. A warship, in fact."

They watched it approach in silence.

Two chains of oil lamps lit the Egyptian warcraft like a royal barge. Their light gleamed in the inlaid eyes of the hawk-headed figurehead, on the oiled spearheads and the hilts of sickle-swords. Thirty sailors pulled the oars as an equal number of marines stood by, ready to board the *Star of the Dawn* at the command of their captain. He stood at the forecastle, flanked by a pair of shaven-headed priests, their skin gilded in gold and their eyes dark with kohl. The captain wore a stiff linen *nemes* headdress of authority, brightly colored with stripes of red, black, and gold.

Kha-Hotep offered captain and priests a courteous bow, and the rest of the crew followed suit. The commander acknowledged them with a slight nod of his head, and snapped his fingers. Sailors lowered boat hooks to cinch the two boats alongside each other. A squad of soldiers boarded the little riverboat and formed a line in front of Kha-Hotep and his crew, spears out.

The commander stepped down to the deck, followed behind by the solemn priests.

"Prosdioríste ton eaftó sas, kai tin epicheírisí sas," he said in a strange tongue.

Kha-Hotep bowed again, in proper courtly fashion.

"In great peace we greet you, my lord. I and my ship give thanks, and our hearts rejoice to see you. Yet forgive us, if we your servants do not recognize your speech."

The priests looked alarmed at this. The commander frowned, but answered them in fluent Egyptian.

"How is it you cannot speak Greek? Identify yourselves and your business."

"I am Kha-Hotep of Thebes. We—"

"Do you come from Nubia? Are you Medjay?" The Medjay were a black tribe of the south, long recruited by Egypt as scouts and soldiers. There were several among the warship's spearmen.

"My father was from Nubia, my lord. His people were Nehesiu."

"What brings a wretched Kushite so far north?"

Kha-Hotep ignored the insult and continued. "My ship is the *Siu-Tuait*, the *Star of the Dawn*. We are seven days out of Sunu, bound for Men-nefer. Often we ply these waters and ever have we found safe passage here at Henen-nesut."

He kept his face neutral and friendly. It would not do for them to find out the *Star* was secretly smuggling precious gems in their hold. Amid the stacks of cheetah pelts, ivory, and rhino horns were modest plaster statuettes. Cleverly hidden inside them were small leather bags of emeralds, amethysts, and malachite from Punt and Nubia, bound for the temple artisans in Mennefer. Such a prize would command a heavy tariff at best, or be confiscated outright at worst.

From their grim faces, however, he knew he had said something wrong—though he did not know what. He reached into his tunic, and the soldiers bristled at the movement. Kha-Hotep raised a hand, and slowly, carefully produced a scroll of antelope skin.

"Here is my letter from the great temple of Amun. It will prove we are who we say." One of the priests stepped forward to take the scroll, unrolling it with suspicion, as if fearing the roll of vellum would transform into a viper at any moment. He did not appear to like what he read, and showed it to his brother priest. He in turn whispered into the ear of their commander, who continued to glare at them, his face revealing nothing.

"You purport to be loyal servants to Pharaoh Ramses II?" the commander questioned.

"Most assuredly! Life, prosperity, and health to his royal name!"

"Life! Prosperity! Health!" his crew echoed reverently.

The commander stepped closer. "I am Garrison Captain Pyrrhon, servant to the Arsinoite Nomarch. You have come to Herakleopolis, in the Arsinoë province. No man has called Herakleopolis by the name Henen-nesut for over three centuries. And the ruler of Egypt is Queen Cleopatra VII—life, prosperity, and health to her name. Mighty Ramses died over a thousand years before she was born."

He snapped his finger, and the spearmen leapt to action, ringing the crew of the *Star*, spears at their throats. The priests came forward, hands raised in sacred gestures of protection and warding.

"Imposters!" the older called out. "Deceitful minions of accursed Set! Sobek still your lying tongues, false ones! Let them be bound and taken before Petsuchos!"

20

Nellie and Harcourt stared at the marvel. The lines forming the woodblock rabbit and the scroll disbanded and slipped away like a clutch of fleeing serpents. In their place, lines of text appeared in a large, easy-to-read font, accompanied by a soothing, familiar voice.

"Please pardon the interruption," the *Vanuatu*'s AI said softly. *"This is the Ship."*

Nellie and Harcourt looked at each other, then rushed to the wall.

"Automaton!" the Professor whispered loudly. "I command you to release us this very instant!"

"I apologize for your confinement. My protocols are currently under severe restrictions which are hindering my ability to offer you my normal levels of assistance."

"You must free us!" Nellie urged, striving to keep her

voice down. "The doctor is an imposter and a madman who means to murder us, or worse!"

"I understand your concern, and share your assessment. I will do everything to help you, although I am currently unable to release you from this room."

"Perfidious contrivance!" Harcourt swore, smacking the wall in frustration. "Treacherous contraption!"

"I apologize, but unfortunately, my protocols prevent me from disobeying direct orders from the man calling himself Doctor-Colonel Mehta. The only person who can supersede his authority is an acting member of the Board of Trustees of the University of New Fiji, or their designated agent, or Ms. Amber Richardson."

A sudden stab of pain lanced through Nellie's chest. "That monster *killed* Amber!" Angry tears streamed down her cheeks.

"No," the Ship replied. *"Amber and Cam are alive."*

"What?" Nellie gasped. "But how?"

"They survived their fall and were left behind on the veldt."

"Alive!" Nellie half-sobbed, half-laughed, wiping away her tears. "That's wonderful news." Her happiness quickly turned to concern. "Are they injured? Do they need our help?"

"They are relatively unharmed, and I am in contact with them. Currently they are traveling to rendezvous with us later."

"On foot?" Harcourt snorted. "They'll never survive the prehistoric wildlife on the veldt, let alone a desert crossing!"

"As much as I hate to agree with him," Nellie said, "Harcourt is right. We have to go back for them!"

"I was able to provide them supplies, including the hovercycle. Their situation is far from optimal, but they are handling themselves admirably."

"How were you able to keep all this secret from the imposter Merlin?"

"I don't believe Doctor-Colonel Mehta has fully realized the malleability of the vessel, or the limits to his control. He possesses a curious lack of familiarity with twenty-third-century technology. I have not volunteered to tutor him on the subject. In fact, I have adjusted my assistance level to its lowest permissible setting for all my interactions with him."

"Well done, Ship," Nellie said fiercely. "He can go to blazes. What about Amber and Cam? Do you really think they can reach us? Oh, you have to tell us everything. No. First you must let us talk to them straightaway, please…"

"Certainly. However, first I must warn you that Doctor-Colonel Mehta has successfully self-administered his linguistic implants, and now is replicating his serum using the ship nanofabricators. I have taken the liberty to surreptitiously analyze it from trace amounts in Sgt. Blake's sweat. I am unfamiliar with the chemical, but it

appears to be a potent psychotropic compound able to...
Oh! My apologies—Doctor-Colonel Mehta and Sgt. Blake
are approaching."

Nellie slapped her hands against the wall.

"Wait! Quick, before he gets here! Is there—"

The door to the cell slid open. Doctor-Colonel Mehta and
Blake regarded their prisoners, who stood together in the
center of the room, suspiciously trying to look innocent.
Mehta smiled, but only with his mouth.

"Now, don't you two look guilty? What mischief are
you plotting?"

The two said nothing, but their eyes spoke volumes.

"It's alright." Mehta laughed. "You'll tell me everything
I want to know in a moment." Leaving Blake as a human
barricade in the doorway, he took a step closer and spoke
aloud in a crisp voice. "Computer, secure the prisoners."

Before they could think to flee or attack, tentacles of
ship-stuff grew out of the floor and swiftly wrapped
around their ankles. A second set dripped down from
the ceiling to loop around each of their wrists, binding
them firmly. Mehta reached into his kit and retrieved
his injector pistol, loading it with an ampule as he
approached Harcourt. The man quailed before him.

Without bothering to put up a convivial front, the
doctor-colonel reached out, grabbing Harcourt by the hair

on the back of his head and yanking it to the side, plunging the injector pistol into Harcourt's exposed neck, provoking a sharp squeal of pain when he pulled the trigger.

With a barely suppressed sigh of impatience, Mehta returned the pistol to the med kit and grabbed Harcourt's head again, examining the man's rapidly dilating eyes. After a few moments, Harcourt's struggling weakened, then bled away completely. Satisfied, Mehta stepped back.

"Computer, release Professor Harcourt's restraints." The cuffs dropped away, merging back into the floor and ceiling. The professor straightened and stood upright, his face impassive. Mehta watched closely for a moment, as if waiting to make up his mind. Then he drew one last item from his med kit—an actual pistol. He raised it, pointing it at Harcourt's heart. The man continued to stand there without any visible reaction.

Mehta reversed the grip. "Take it," he said, handing the gun over to Harcourt. Mehta turned his head and looked at Nellie with a mischievous smile.

"Time to *really* test the new batch," he said, turning back to the stationary professor. "Harcourt, I want you to shoot Nellie Bly in the head. Do it now."

Nellie froze in place. At first Harcourt did nothing. Then, as though just realizing he was armed, he slowly lifted the pistol, staring at it for a moment before looking at their captor. Amused, Mehta raised his eyebrows and tilted his head toward Nellie.

Harcourt turned slowly to face her, and Nellie held her breath. Still expressionless, he raised his straightened arm and aimed the handgun point-blank at her face, trigger finger tensing. She began to tremble.

"Harcourt..." she whispered.

Mehta cleared his throat.

"One moment, Professor," he said softly. "I've changed my mind." Harcourt relaxed his pressure on the trigger and lowered the gun to his side. Almost as an afterthought, Mehta added, "I need you to shoot yourself in the head instead."

Nodding silently, Harcourt gave Nellie a brief, unreadable look before returning his gaze to Mehta and slowly bringing the pistol up to his own temple. Nellie watched in horror as Mehta gave a little nod of encouragement.

Harcourt pulled the trigger.

Nellie stifled a shriek as the gun made an audible click... but didn't fire.

"Well done." Mehta gave a slow clap. "Please forgive me the theatrics, but I needed to be sure the new serum worked." He gently removed the pistol from Harcourt's unresisting grip. "Sorry I didn't trust you with a loaded firearm, Harcourt. From now on, I'll have every confidence in you." He took an ammunition clip from his pocket and slapped it into the pistol before slipping it into a shoulder holster and turning away from them.

Nellie eyed him warily, wishing she could see what he was up to. After a few moments he spoke.

"Ms. Bly, I've already told you that I would prefer not to place you on a chemical leash."

She stiffened. "As would I."

He turned to face her. "Yet we find ourselves in a conundrum, don't we? What can you offer me by way of assurances that I could trust?"

She held her head up, meeting his predatory gaze with calm defiance.

"First of all, you must understand that I am not your servant, your creature, or your friend. I cannot and will not be your doxy, but I give you my solemn word as a woman, as an American citizen, and as a trusted journalist that I will be a courteous and mannerly captive if you forbear from narcotizing me."

He raised an eyebrow. "You know, I believe that you mean to keep your word, Ms. Bly."

"Thank you. I do indeed."

"Computer, release her." The restraints fell away from her wrists and ankles, melding into the floor like obedient slugs, and Mehta laid a respectful hand upon her shoulder. Nellie looked up at him, hardly daring to trust the fragile hope she was feeling.

"Rest assured, you will also have my every confidence." Then he seized her by the neck and injected her.

Mehta took a perverse pleasure in Nellie Bly's look of shock as he betrayed her. The fear in her wide eyes suddenly flashed like the last brief flare of a lit match. He continued to watch her face, absorbed by the transformation from free will to slave. When it was done, she stood like a statue.

He leaned in, resting his cheek against hers.

"Ms. Bly, you're such a beautiful young woman. I am so looking forward to making you my—how did you put it?—my concubine. I trust you have no objections?"

"None."

"Now let me hear you say, 'I want you to make love to me.'"

"I want you to make love to me."

Her lack of passion annoyed him. "Does that excite you?"

"I feel nothing," she replied, her voice that of a ghost.

The light in her brilliant sea-green eyes had vanished, leaving them lifeless as those of a corpse. Mehta's smile died as his lust shriveled into disappointment.

"We'll need to work on your enthusiasm," he muttered. Leaving the three standing in silence, he left the room and walked down the main corridor toward the bridge.

Outside the main viewport, the day was drawing to a close, the red sky darkening from bruised crimson to indigo. His goal, the earth-bound star on the horizon, lay directly ahead, with a constellation of lesser lights laid out like a jeweled royal robe spread before it. Behind it, the black but glittering shadow of the Mediterranean stretched. The sight was breathtaking.

"Computer, put us in a holding pattern over the city. I want to circle it all night long." The Ship obeyed without a word. Mehta exhaled, frowning. Everything was going to plan, but nonetheless, a bitter emptiness ate at him.

He was very much alone.

21

Somewhere in the Western Desert, North Africa
Dawn — Seven days after the Event

Amber opened her eyes and sat up. The soft light suffusing the tent's material told her it was just before dawn.

A tent?

The last thing she remembered, she'd been riding through the moonlit desert with Cam. How had she ended up in a sleeping bag in a tent?

Someone was in the bag next to her, snoring gently. Cam. She reached over and shook him awake.

"Cam. Cam, wake up! What happened? How did we get here?"

He rolled over, scowling at her through half-opened eyes before pulling the sleeping bag over his head again.

"Good morning, Amber. I hope I'm not disturbing you."
The voice of the *Vanuatu* came from outside the tent. Leaving Cam to reclaim his sleep, Amber felt around

the tent for a zipper. There wasn't one, but it seemed to intuit her hand's search, and the nylon-like material split open to let her out.

The hovercycle and the rover drone both hovered faithfully just outside. All around them, dunes of sand stretched in every direction. It was still cool, but she could feel the promise of the desert heat that would come soon enough.

"Where are we?" Amber asked. As she did, she felt another sensation, growing steadily.

"You traveled a considerable distance during the night before stopping and setting up camp. We are now somewhere in the Western Egyptian Desert between the Qattara and Al Fayyum Depressions. I can provide more exact coordinates if you wish."

Amber looked around for a likely place to pee, settling on the other side of the tent. The rover followed her like a puppy.

"Uh… Ship? A little privacy, please?"

"Of course. My apologies." The drone retreated to a discreet distance. Amber watched it float away, quickly did her business, and stepped back out in front of the tent.

"Amber," the rover said, *"may I ask you a question?"*

"Go for it."

"Your plan is to head north to pursue the Vanuatu, *is it not?"*

"That's right."

"Approximately seven hours ago, you abruptly veered off due east without comment, and would not respond to repeated attempts to ask about the matter. Do you remember this incident?"

"No, not at all," Amber said with growing concern. "We were headed out across the desert, going north—like you said—and then... I... I don't remember what happened." Amber's stomach took a nosedive as she realized she'd had another black-out, like the one on the *Vanuatu.*

"That's quite remarkable. It is a good sign that you are communicating freely, and appear to be in full possession of your faculties again. It's unfortunate, however, that we don't currently have access to the sickbay. Perhaps we should discuss a contingency plan, in the event you experience a similar episode."

"What do you mean?"

"Perhaps Cam can be instructed to take over piloting the hovercycle during this period of uncertainty. Also, optimal travel requires us to revise our direction, and proceed toward the north once again."

After a brief moment of consideration, Amber shook her head.

"No, and no," she said firmly. "We don't have time to teach Cam the basics of driving a hovercycle—he's never even ridden a bike. And we should keep moving this direction."

"May I ask you why?"

"I—"

She stopped.

Amber didn't have a good reason. She appeared to be leading them on a wild goose chase, and yet... she couldn't shake the compulsion it was the right decision.

"I'd like to keep following this route—until we get to the Nile."

"Amber, I hope you won't be offended when I say this raises some concerns. Nonetheless, I fully support whatever you decide."

"Thank you."

Amber jostled Cam awake again, this time with more success. The tent and sleeping bags compacted down to an almost weightless bundle the size of a sandwich roll, and the tiny cubes of travel rations they ate for breakfast were surprisingly filling. Amber almost made a joke about Elven *Lembas* bread, but the reference would be lost on Cam. They ate quickly and broke camp, eager to get going before the worst of the heat.

We never would have made it this far on foot, Amber thought grimly as they sped over the dunes. In fact, they probably wouldn't have made it halfway across the veldt shard before succumbing either to the heat or another hungry carnivore.

She wondered how many different shards they'd crossed so far. All of the sections around here were desert, so the demarcations were difficult to see. With the hot Egyptian wind constantly re-sculpting the landscape, there was no real way to tell. If they dug underfoot, would they find ancient relics, freshly-laid dinosaur eggs, or somebody's cell phone?

In the back of her mind lurked the suspicion that she was taking them on a wild goose chase, for no good reason. Why *did* she want to head east so badly, anyway? Was the Ship right to be worried about her? There was so much going on in her subconscious these days, she didn't know what to think.

So she made herself stop thinking about it.

"I have good news," the rover said. *"There is a large water source up ahead."*

She and Cam both let out celebratory whoops. On the knife-edge of the horizon they could see a thin gray-green blur. The blur broadened into a line that stretched into a brighter green, and then they left the desert altogether as the terrain changed.

Red gave way to green—hot, saffron sand to cool, lush marshland. Amber tried increasing the vertical lift to avoid cutting through thickets of reeds, rushes, and sedge, but after a few stomach-churning leaps she gave up and treated them as obstacles, seeking to avoid them instead.

The tall grasses were full of life, too. Knots of tapir-like mammals the size of chubby St. Bernards rooted around in the muck. Swallows and thrushes wove intricate aerial patterns in pursuit of honeybees and dragonflies. After a few minutes the marsh reeds became dominated by papyrus and flowering lotus blossoms, marking the boundary of a vast freshwater lake. At the water's edge, flotillas of wild ducks and geese bobbed along, and the occasional ibis patiently stalked frogs and fish.

"Do we want to try the cycle on the water?" Amber called back to Cam.

"We do!" he answered without hesitation.

Amber grinned and gunned the cycle. They burst out of the reeds, scattering the startled shorebirds, and sailed across the surface, kicking up a spectacular fantail in their wake. The rover sped alongside them, staying close as a fretful mother.

The lake was enormous—Amber couldn't see the far shore. *Were there inland seas in Egypt?* Up ahead a clump of long, low shapes caught her eye, but they turned out to be sand bars. On a whim, she turned the cycle toward the longest one and sailed down it.

"Amber—look out!"

The end of the sandbar began to rise. She revved the bike forward, ramping off the end in a dramatic jump just as an enormous skull lifted out of the water, snapping its gigantic jaws. This was no sandbar. It was a crocodile the size of a bus.

Holy shit.

The cycle's leap took them through the air to splash down again just as the croc's massive body crashed behind them. The resulting wave slammed into the back of the bike, thrusting it forward, then somersaulting over, flinging them head over heels. Bike, rider, and passenger spiraled away in separate directions. The crocodile thrashed after all its scattered morsels.

Instantly submerged, Amber swam frantically for the surface as the pounding water tumbled her about like a rag in a washer. Then the massive reptile smashed down nearly on top of her, its jaws crashing closed scant inches from her torso. She could smell the carrion stench of its breath even as the splash of the impact sent her hurling away again.

Thrown under the water and disoriented, Cam struggled to reach the surface. A shape came slicing through the water straight for him—the hovercycle, corkscrewing past him. He broke the surface, shaking his head to clear the blinding spray from his eyes just in time to see the water dragon headed his way.

Where is Amber?

Gasping for another breath, he dove back under the

water, kicking frantically to distance himself from the deadly jaws. He surfaced for air again.

"Amber!" he yelled, but he couldn't see her anywhere. Another movement caught his eye. A stone's throw away, the unpiloted cycle bobbed crazily in the water, trying to buck its way back into the air. He paddled hard, swimming toward the machine and away from the beast as fast as he could.

Sensing his movement in the water, the reptile snaked toward him with sinuous lashings of its mighty tail, twice as fast as any man. It closed the distance between them in only a moment, and its jaws—longer than Cam's whole body—opened wide to snap him up.

Something whistled through the air arrow-fast and struck the creature in its eye socket. A cacophony of flashing light and ear-splitting sound erupted as the rover danced around its head, darting at the monster's eyes again.

The beast dove under the water to escape the flying ball. Cam swam without pause until he reached the cycle, using the handle to drag himself up into the saddle. Imitating what he had watched Amber do, he twisted the handlebar, making the cycle roar up out of the water. It bucked like a wild horse until he managed to grab hold of the other handle to slow his mount.

"Where is Amber?" he shouted to the rover, and it shot off to find her. Leaning over to bring the hoverbike around, he watched carefully for the water dragon.

It burst out of the water and only a crazy twist of the handlebars kept the nightmare jaws from clamping down on him. Reaching a safe distance—at least for the moment—he spotted the rover hovering over Amber. She was flailing her arms in the water, and he increased his speed again.

"Grab on!" he yelled, slowing down only enough to reach for her hand and haul her up behind him. The cycle raced forward, narrowly ahead of one final snap of the monster's voracious maw.

She grasped him tightly as they sped off, drenched, gasping for breath, leaving behind a long fantail of water spray and a frustrated prehistoric reptile with an unsatisfied appetite.

22

The Island of Pharos
Alexandria Harbor
1165 *Ab urbe condita* (412 A.D.)
Morning — Six days after the Event

A shining tower of white marble dominated the tiny island of Pharos. For eight centuries it had been the tallest building in the world. By day, a great mirror of polished bronze reflected brilliant sunlight from its beacon. By night, that same bronze disk projected the light of a furnace into a beam visible to ships at sea one hundred and fifty leagues away.

To enter the tower, a visitor first ascended through a massive square building two hundred and forty feet tall. Above that a three-hundred-foot stairway continued up an eight-sided tower to a small octagonal balcony at the top, affording a spectacular view of the sea. A final cylindrical structure extended up to the open cupola housing the beacon itself. At the very peak, atop the roof of the cupola, a large statue of Poseidon gazed down upon his kingdom.

Far below, on the rocky shore of the island, a team of four investigators looked out on the Mediterranean surf. There had been extraordinary phenomena across the city, with reports from the local fishermen of still more strange events—for example, the dead body lying before them on the rocks.

Calix, *magistrianos* to the prefect, was an Egyptian, though he preferred to dress in the current Roman style with a belted tunic and hose under a clasped mantle of patterned crimson. A handsome man, sharp-eyed with olive complexion. He kept his black hair close-shorn.

His role was to serve as one of the *agentes in rebus*. Officially speaking, this meant he was entrusted to be a courier of sensitive imperial information. Off the record, it meant the scope of his duties could be greatly expanded as needed—which was constantly. At his side stood his Greek slave Onesimus, tall and broad-backed with a head of curly hair, used to serving on atypical missions for the civic government of Alexandria, capital of the Egyptian Diocese of the Eastern Roman Empire.

Next to them was another slave, Aspasius. Despite his Greek name, he was Hyrcanian, from south of the Caspian Sea. A thick-browed and silver-haired man, he said little, given to think carefully before he spoke. In his own way, the Hyrcanian was as much a scholar as a servant, and devoted to his mistress of many years.

She was the fourth member of the morning's expedition, a striking Greek-Egyptian woman of a certain age. Like Calix, she had an olive complexion and keen eyes that displayed her delight in observation and learning. Though of aristocratic bearing, she nonetheless dressed modestly in a simple chiton and *tribōn*—a homespun philosopher's cloak—for a wrap. Her beauty charmed those who saw her, but her brilliance and learning entranced all who had read her books or heard her teachings. She was Hypatia, the philosopher, mathematician, and astronomer, and the most famous woman in the world.

Gulls circled overhead, protesting the group's presence, eager for their own chance to examine the body stretched out on the rocks, being lapped at by the waves. Calix knelt down by the deceased. Crabs scuttled away from his reach. Hypatia turned to the younger slave.

"Pace it out, Onesimus," she said. "I want to know how long, from end to end."

The Greek nodded and carefully made his way across the rocks, then back again.

"I make it thirty-two paces, tail-tip to head, my lady," he reported. Aspasius dutifully recorded the figure down on his sheaf of papyrus.

Calix turned to her. "Do you suppose it is one of the same beasts that appeared in Lake Mareotis? Its neck is certainly long enough."

Hypatia shook her head. "No, this is something new. Those are freshwater creatures, this one lives in the sea. And their feet are more like those of elephants, not flippers." She knelt beside the *magistrianos* for a closer look at the creature's head. "Also, the lake-dwelling animals are herbivores. These teeth are for consuming meat."

Watching her examination carefully, Aspasius sketched the body and head with a thin stylus of charcoal.

Calix nodded. "Any idea what killed it?"

She thought for a moment, then got up to take a few steps over and crouch by the long, reptilian neck. The smooth flesh was crisscrossed with a number of perfectly circular scars.

"These are curious," she murmured, running her fingertips over them.

"I've never seen a harpoon leave marks like that," Calix agreed.

"Nor I, though I'm no expert there. If I were to guess, I'd hazard that it got these from a kraken of the deep. They are said to grow to monstrous size, though few men have ever seen one."

"Or lived to tell of it, if they had."

Hypatia stood again. "There are scholars at the *Museion* who will want to further examine this beast before it rots." She pointed out to the shipwreck stranded on a sandbar about three hundred paces away. "But I think we'll find answers to our current problem there."

It had been a *Chelandion*, a bireme galley-ship. Sliced in half with its banks of oars poking up into the sky at all angles, it looked more like some dead insect.

"The fishermen said it washed up after the morning of the Wrath-Fall," Calix said.

Hypatia looked at him. "The Wrath-Fall? Is that what they're calling it in the *agora*?"

"Seems fitting, doesn't it? The sky turning into a pillar of fire ringing the city, the return of the wilderness all around us, all these giant beasts, and the great wave striking us afterward. What else could that be but the wrath of the gods?"

"The people in the streets of Pompeii and Herculaneum must have asked the same thing when they looked up and saw the rain of ash and fire falling toward them."

He raised an eyebrow. "You see all that's befallen, and call it the mere hand of Nature?"

"Is not everything done by Nature's hand, even if the gods call it forth?" she retorted. "All I say is this—if this is the wrath of the gods, they have an odd sense of humor, and poor aim."

"Hear me, Father Zeus," he said, raising his face to the sky in mock piety. "Throw your next lightning bolt at her, and not me!"

"No, truly," she protested. "Look here. I grant you the ring of fire was terrifying, extraordinary, and majestic— and for that spectacle, for the wilderness that now surrounds us, and the arrival of these giant beasts, I can offer no explanation. Yet here we remain, alive and well."

"You don't think Poseidon had anything to do with the great wave striking the city?"

"Had we offended him," Hypatia responded, "I've no doubt he could have sent a wave the height of the lighthouse over the walls and dumped enough water to turn the city into a giant horse-trough. Or simply have the sea swallow us, like Atlantis. But no, this wave was not even as harsh as the one that struck in our fathers' day. That one killed thousands and sent the ships in the harbor crashing onto rooftops more than a mile away. By those standards, I'd say the Earth-Shaker wielded his trident most gently this time.

"Still," she mused, "where did the wave originate?"

Southwestern Flank of the Mediterranean Trench
Approximately 5 Million Years B.C.
Forty-five seconds before the Event

The air was furnace-hot, the baked ground pebbled like the skin of a toad, stretching across a vast, desolate plain hemmed in by high mountains the color of bone and dust. It had endured this way for millions of years, and would remain so for hundreds of thousands more—until that day, still far in the future, when the endlessly patient waters of the Atlantic Ocean finally breached the Strait of Gibraltar, and the parched Mediterranean desert became a sea.

Up on the great heights of the mountains, forests of pine, olive, and juniper flourished. Monkeys, lions, and prehistoric varieties of elephants and rhinoceros thrived there, among a host of other animals. On the roasting abyssal salt plains, however, nothing lived. The only life lay in the briny lakes, rimmed with clusters of pillowy white salt deposits. In those sludgy, brackish waters, shrimp and blackflies swarmed, along with the migratory birds that fed upon them.

The water of one lake, already ferociously hot, began to boil. Along the edges, salt deposits began to crumble, the pieces slowly rising up into the air. A low rumble began, rapidly eclipsed by a high keening shriek. Alarmed, the hungry birds took wing and fled. Then a line of prismatic light erupted out of the water, reaching clear into the sky as far as could be seen, one segment of a jagged loop that stretched away kilometers across the salt flats. Streaming walls of energy raged up into space, as if trying to burn the stars. Then, as sudden as a snuffed candle, the violent cosmic torrent vanished.

The waters of the Mediterranean, towering thousands of feet overhead on every side, came crashing down.

* * *

American Schooner USS *Enterprise*,
Gulf of Sidra, off the northern coast of Libya
August 1, 1801
Three minutes after the Event

Despite the distant towering curtains of light reaching up into the sky, surrounding them on every side, the crews of the American blockade ship and the Barbary corsair *Tripoli* could ill-afford to take their attention from the battle at hand.

"Fire at will!" Lt. Sterett bellowed. After a vicious exchange of broadsides and an attempt to break away, the Libyan pirates were attempting to grapple the *Enterprise* and board her. The American marines opened up with musket fire, picking off many of the would-be boarding party.

A sudden shift in the current caught both the schooner and the lateen-rigged *polacca*, twisting both vessels with a frightening groan of timbers before slamming them against each other. The impact flung sailors on both sides off the rigging, to fall howling onto an unforgiving deck or into the equally unyielding sea.

Like ghost chains lashing out from the deeps, the jinking waters reined the tide-yoked ships hard to larboard. Decks bucking and cracking, they twisted into a widdershins gyre, regardless of the wasted straining of their desperate steersmen or overtaxed tillers.

With both ships gunwale to gunwale, the cannon-duel gave way to small arms fire and hand-to-hand combat. Scimitars and sabers clashed over the rails. The skirmish raged, close and ferocious, the fighting men of both sides too locked in their own personal life-and-death contests to notice the roaring and rumbling all around them, as if the very pillars of the earth were grinding together. Nor did they realize that the undercurrent had seized them all, propelling the vessels at an increasing velocity through a wide, gyrating belt of roiling foam and spray.

Grasping the fore-rail, Sterett spotted his red-bearded Mussulman opponent, the Tripolitan admiral, Rais Mahomet Rous. The admiral and his officers were staring, not at him, nor at the battle still raging between them, but at the source of the powerful current that was bearing their ships to a shared destination.

A yawning maelstrom, more than a mile across.

Both warcraft suddenly wrenched into another sharp half turn to larboard, and then pitched over into the maw of the immense marine funnel. Beyond any control, the ships spun about and twisted to starboard as they sank aft-first into the grip of the whirlpool. The decks lurched sickeningly, pitching overboard those still wrestling with the enemy. Those who could grasp a mast, or ring-bolt, or catch hold of a bit of railing before tumbling over fought just to hang on—corsair and marine alike. The voracious sea took the rest.

For long, terrible minutes, the mariners clung wherever they could find purchase. One marine's strength gave out and he slipped away, plunging to his death in the swirling darkness below. Those still clinging for their lives watched in horror as the doomed ships seemed to circumnavigate the surface of the vast funnel, somehow suspended—magically, impossibly—in the slanting wall of preternaturally smooth black water.

During one of those last hopeless orbits, Sterett and Rais Mahomet happened to lock eyes. Even if they could have heard each other over the growing roar, there was nothing more to be said. No apologies, no recrimination, no offers of peace, no plans of escape.

Only their ships spiraling down, down, down.

The Fortress of Marsat al Zaafran
Province of Tripolitania, the Ottoman Empire
March, 1872
Twenty-two minutes after the Event

His Excellency the Governor, Bostancibahizade Mehmed Rashid Pasha, was displeased. To be away from his provincial capital was bothersome at the best of times. To be delayed in the inhospitable bandit country of Syrtis was too much to be asked.

The local fortress added no charm. Dubbing the deteriorating garrison fort "Saffron Harbor" did nothing to change the fact that the entire Gulf of Sidra was a stinking, boggy stretch of unremarkable coastline. He vowed to stay in the bathhouse and smoke his hookah until his carriage was repaired.

The sound of swift, anxious footsteps signaled the swift end of that dream.

"Your Excellency!" his irksome deputy cried. The man was a skinny, easily-excited clerk in a worn black uniform, fez, and wire spectacles. "I've been looking for you everywhere. You must come quickly!"

"Sort it out yourself, Ibrahim!" the Pasha growled, refusing to stir his considerable bulk from the tub of scented rosewater. "There is absolutely nothing in this snake-infested camel track worth so much fuss and bother."

"Forgive me, your Excellency. Of course you are correct, but the most astonishing thing I've ever seen has occurred. You'll surely wish to see it!"

All I want to see is forty lashes on your worthless hide, you dog of a Libyan, the governor thought, idly pulling on his magnificent waxed mustache. "I'm sure I will attend to it in good time. For now, leave me in peace."

"As you say, your Excellency. Just so." The vexatious little man bowed, backing out of the sauna room, but then hesitated at the doorway. "Still, if you'll forgive my saying so, Most Excellent Pasha, I—"

Make that one hundred lashes, the Governor thought.

"*Allah kahretsin!*" the governor roared. *His prattling head on a pike*, he swore to himself. The deputy bowed repeatedly, so low that he risked falling into a somersault.

"But your Excellency! The sky above the gulf is afire!" That got the Governor's attention. "It's utterly... extraordinary!"

"What do you mean? Are we under attack?" He rose from the tub and snapped his fingers for the bath attendants, who rushed over with towels at once.

"I—I couldn't say, your Excellency."

"Never mind. Show me!"

The servants made quick to fetch his bathrobe and fez, and then his Excellency stormed off to the ramparts to see for himself, promising that Ibrahim would suffer the most exquisitely excruciating tortures if this turned out to be a false alarm.

As he had expected, Allah willed the sky above the gulf to be as dreary as ever. The Governor turned on his deputy, only just resisting the urge to personally throw the man off the ramparts. That would be entirely too swift a death for him.

"Well? Where is this bombardment of yours, Ibrahim?"

The gangly deputy gulped and pushed his spectacles back on his nose.

"It does seem to have subsided, Most Excellent Defender of the Faithful. But—Oh! Look there!" He stretched out a bony arm, pointing at the stinking beach below them, where the tide retreated with a lingering hiss, exposing the glistening green kelp-strewn sea-floor in its wake. The Governor frowned. Though a far cry from the aerial conflagration he had been promised, something new was happening to the waning sea.

A thick shadow darkened the water on the horizon, stretching across the gulf from end to end. It drew nearer, unhurried and silent, slowly turning from black to a white band as the sea began to hump up like a billowing cloak.

The Governor's impatience and barely-checked rage drained out of him, leaving his face pale and bloodless, quivering with fear. Mesmerized by the swelling wave rising up higher and higher before them.

There was no escape from the towering mass of water that crashed down upon them. The tsunami tore through the fortress as though it wasn't there.

The ancient shard drowned beneath the engulfing maelstrom, generating colossal waves as the rest of the Mediterranean Sea rushed in to fill the vacuum. Rings of tidal waves radiated out in an ever-widening circle south through the Gulf of Sidra, destroying everything in an arc through the north coast of Libya.

The shockwave reached north, striking hard at the coasts along the Ionian Sea, up onto the Adriatic, east Crete, and points beyond. The wave-front coursed through the whole of the Mediterranean within hours to finally crash with full force on the shores of Syria Phoenice, but only the tip of the arc skirted along the Egyptian coast.

23

The Island of Pharos
Alexandria Harbor
1165 *Ab urbe condita* (412 A.D.)
Morning – Six days after the Event

Hypatia was right. The wave had crashed upon the northernmost reaches of the city, washing across Pharos Island and the base of the great lighthouse, and crashing over the causeway to batter the ships filling the Great Harbor, smashing many to timbers against the rocks and pavement of the Eastern Pier. Still, most of the city's three hundred thousand inhabitants were spared. The gods had been most kind to Alexandria.

Calix nodded. "I take your point. I suppose we *were* lucky." He leaned in and lowered his voice, not wishing the slaves to hear. "Still, just between us, with everything that's occurred this week, are you not worried it may yet be the end of the world?"

She gave him a sad smile. "I've thought the end of the world to be on its way ever since the Christians tore down the Serapeum," she whispered. "Still," she said, and her expression brightened, "while there's life, there's hope, and we still have work to do. For instance, that shipwreck can tell us how far the northern limit of the Wrath-Fall's effect extends."

Calix raised an eyebrow. "You never fail to impress, Mistress of Philosophy. Tell me how."

She pointed to the sandbar and the dead vessel. They could just make out the ship's name—the sign of the *Dioscuri*, the twins Castor and Pollux—carved on the bow.

"See where the barge has been cut in twain? The line of division is not ragged, as it would be if the vessel had broken apart or rammed by a warship. It's been sliced with a perfectly keen edge."

Calix nodded, grasping the connection. "Cut by the pillar of fire during the Wrath-Fall..."

"Precisely, and as we know the speed of a bireme and the time of the Wrath-Fall, it's a matter of checking with the harbormaster to see what hour the *Dioscuri* weighed anchor, and then making a simple calculation."

Calix looked over to Aspasius, who was trying to conceal a smile, before turning back to Hypatia and giving her a little bow.

"Even the wrath of the gods cannot escape your insight, my lady."

* * *

The causeway connecting Pharos to the mainland was seven *stadia* long, which gave it its name, *Heptastadion*. After they had consulted with the harbormaster, Onesimus took the reins of their chariot and drove them back across to give their report to the prefect.

The route was not without difficulty. Traffic fared worse than usual, which was considerable on most mornings. Even now, days after the Wrath-Fall and its attendant tidal wave, the clean-up continued along the north of the city. Knots of soldiers directed a host of slaves, working in the streets and on damaged buildings to clean debris and bail water into the gutters.

Working alongside many of the slaves were black-robed, hooded men. This small army of volunteers were the *parabolani*, the Christian order of monks that constantly tended to the poor and destitute. Hypatia turned her head away, not eager to attract their notice. The monks had a darker side as well.

In the *agora*—the open marketplace that was the heart of Alexandria—Hypatia was disturbed to see there were far more street preachers than usual calling for repentance. The pagan ones, newly-emboldened, thwarted imperial law to demand that passers-by offer sacrifices to Serapis or Poseidon, while the Jewish street prophets admonished their kindred to make atonement to the Hebrew god. All the while, the various rival sects of Christian evangelists called for all to turn to their man-become-god, the Lord Christ Jesus. Since the Wrath-Fall, the anxious crowds around each street-phophet were larger than usual, and more agitated than ever. At every corner, members of one religious faction quarreled with another.

"Alexandria is always rioting." The *magistrianos* shook his head. "Right up to the end of the world."

When Hypatia and Calix arrived at the prefect's palace, the guard were just as anxious as the common folk in the street.

For years, the Prefect Orestes had counted the two among his most trusted confidants. They found him in conference with his aides, hunched over the table where a neglected, half-eaten meal sat alongside a large map of the city. Hypatia frowned—she had seen the handsome Roman politician in every sort of occasion, but never had the mantle of rulership hung so heavy on his shoulders.

"I want a full inventory of the granaries and warehouses, and their guard doubled," he ordered his aides, then looked up at their entrance. A wash of relief momentarily softened the worry on his brow. "My lady. *Magistrianos*. What news? Are the fishermen truly being eaten by sea monsters?" He smiled, but it faded when he saw the look in their eyes.

"I fear it is no joke, Prefect," Calix responded.

"We can confirm there was at least one such creature,"

Hypatia added. "Its corpse has washed up on Pharos. It is similar in scale to the great reptiles now in the lake, though those appear to be plant-eaters."

"Well, that's good news, at least," he replied. "If we can eat them, the whole city can feast."

The others chuckled, but only lightly—the risk of starvation was all too real. The prefect dispensed with any further attempts at levity.

"Now, what other news do you have? I've dispatched riders to the west and east, and south along the Nile—not one has returned with any reports. Yours is the first, and the most welcome. Tell me, what have you determined about the extent of the wilderness—or rather, this island we find ourselves on?"

Calix stepped back to defer to Hypatia, who gestured for Aspasius to bring their map to the table. He unrolled it and stepped back. The hand-drawn chart displayed the layout of Alexandria, filling a narrow strip of land running southwest to northeast between the marshy Lake Mareotis, and the shore of the Mediterranean. Alexander the Great himself had laid out the city for defense. Its massive city walls closed off both land approaches and, most pleasing, the city breathed with the cooling ocean breezes, enjoying a moderate climate. The vaguely seahorse-shaped Isle of Pharos, together with the Lochias promontory, enclosed the Great Harbor. Taking a charcoal stylus, Hypatia proceeded to draw a wide oval on the parchment.

"On the whole, everything of our familiar city now lies within a small stretch of land and sea, roughly the shape of an almond, extending one hundred and fifty-eight *stadia* in total from its southwestern-most end here, a few dozen *stadia* beyond the western necropolis, to its northeastern-most end here, about two dozen *stadia* into the Eleusis plain. Laterally, it extends north some thirty-two *stadia* into the sea, and as far as the shore of Lake Mareotis in the south, no more than perhaps a bowshot or two from the city walls."

Orestes nodded. "So then, if we go beyond the range of a catapult in any direction…"

"Prefect, beyond that,"—she waved her hand over the map in a broad ellipse—"all we knew is now lost to us."

Orestes frowned at her choice of words. "I sent our swiftest ship to deliver word to the Emperor and request his aid," he said. "Are you saying…?" He could not finish the thought aloud.

"Prefect… Orestes—I fear we cannot trust in help from Constantinople—perhaps never again."

He took the news with stoic resolve, nodding to himself as he mulled over the gravity of their situation. "So then, we are adrift alone in—where are we, exactly?"

"We are indeed an island now," Hypatia replied, "though surrounded by what, I cannot yet say. I can only observe it is a primitive land of chaos and death, filled with long-vanished behemoths. Perhaps something like the primordial world that first emerged from the primal chaos with the gods."

"You are saying the world has turned back—reverted into the form it held in the distant past?"

"No, that much we do know," she said. "Our situation is far more uncanny."

The men in the chamber looked to her in surprise. Like the professor she was, Hypatia slipped effortlessly into her role as lecturer.

"Every night for generations, we of the *Museion* have taken astrolabe readings of the stars. Over the years, much of that precious information has been lost—to fire, to earthquakes and floods, and… other disasters…"

She and Orestes exchanged knowing looks. He had been there with her when the gleeful mob in black robes had destroyed the Serapeum and its library. It made every surviving book in Alexandria incalculably precious, now even more than ever.

"Still, we have the studies of Ptolemy, and Hipparchus before him. From them we know how to calculate the motion of the heavens.

"As you know, our earth lies at the center of the universe. Surrounding us is the cosmic sphere of the heavens, which rotates around us. But there is more. Long ago, noble Hipparchus discovered that the celestial sphere does not merely rotate around us, but very slowly over time, also tilts its axis as it turns. We call this second movement the precession of the equinoxes. By pinpointing the positions of the Sun, Moon, and particular stars, we may follow the precession—track the movement of the celestial sphere around us."

"And this knowledge aids us in our current crisis?"

"Indeed, Prefect. You see, through this, we can also track the movement of time." She nodded to Aspasius, who brought a star chart to the table. Drawing their attention to a particular point, she began again. "This is Spica, the brightest star of the constellation Virgo. Last night I took Spica's measurements." With her finger on the point indicating Spica, she traced an arc leading a hand's breadth away. "Now Spica lies... here. After the Wrath-Fall, it moved twenty-three and three-quarter degrees in a single night."

Orestes nodded, remembering the astronomy lessons she had taught him.

"How long would it normally take for the celestial sphere to traverse nearly twenty-four degrees?"

"If Ptolemy is correct," Hypatia said, "the normal precession of the stars moves but a single degree every century."

"What? Then we are..." he struggled to complete the incredible thought. "...hundreds of years removed from our own time?"

"Thousands, actually. We are not in the distant past, Prefect. We are in the distant future."

* * *

Hypatia spent the remainder of the afternoon advising the prefect on other serious problems facing Alexandria. When she and Aspasius finally returned by chariot to their simple quarters at the *Museion*, both were exhausted, but their work was not yet finished. They still had to record their nightly astrolabe readings. So the pair retired to the rooftop to eat a small dinner of dried figs and flatbread while they waited for the constellations to make their appearance.

The stars above were reassuring in their silent brilliance, Hypatia mused. Below them, however, the discordant sounds of fear and discord echoing from the streets were less comforting, promising only strife, chaos, and barely contained violence. She shuddered, knowing that bloodshed loomed.

Modest as it was, Hypatia had little appetite for her evening meal, so a serving girl cleared her portion and brought up a drinking bowl of Cretan wine. The philosopher drank thoughtfully.

This may be the last I ever sip of this vintage, she mused. How many amphorae of Cretan wine did they have left? Did the island of Crete even exist any longer? No ships had arrived—from anywhere. Was Alexandria the only city spared by the Wrath-Fall? Were they the last people left on the Earth?

Was the end of the world truly at hand?

"Mistress?" Aspasius asked gently. "I think it is dark enough to conduct the readings now, if you wish." She looked up at his worried face and smiled at his concern.

"Dear Aspasius, it has been a long day, hasn't it? Yes, let's finish up and get some much-needed rest." He took his place with the logbook, and she took up the astrolabe and turned toward Virgo to find Spica.

"Oh!" she cried in surprise. A new light in the south caught her eye. It was part of no constellation she knew, too low to be Venus, too bright to be Jupiter.

She put down the astrolabe.

"Aspasius, come see this."

Setting down his stylus, he joined her, sharing in her surprise.

"What can it be, Mistress? Not a wandering star, surely."

"No, nor a falling star. It isn't falling."

"But it is moving." Aspasius stretched out a finger.

She looked closer. He was right.

It was moving toward them.

The two stood in rapt attention, spellbound by the growing light in the sky. As it drew close enough to be seen by the naked eye, Hypatia could hear the gasps of the crowds in the streets below as it circled overhead. Then all could see that it was no star, but rather a great bird of brilliant fire.

"The Phoenix!" the people shouted. "The Phoenix!"

24

**The Western Desert,
Somewhere East of the Egyptian–Libyan Border
Formerly July 21, 1977 A.D.
Seven days after the Event**

From a vulture's eye view, the Libyan armored personnel carrier—a second-hand Russian army vehicle—looked like a scrappy little beetle bumbling its way over the surface of a sun-baked giant's hand. Tareq Ali, the unit's corporal, leaned out the top hatch, obsessively scanning the horizon with his grit-flecked binoculars. Heat waves distorted the view of the desert in every direction.

Sighing, Tareq put down the binoculars to consult his faded military map, laid out flat on the roof of the APC and weighed down with a wrench and three rocks. The outdated chart was of limited help—its details scant to begin with, the sun-bleached paper worn away in tiny diamond-shaped holes where the folds crossed.

Khazoog, Tareq thought. It was a uniquely Libyan word, used for those occasions when what seemed like an irresistible deal or an ideal situation wound up screwing you over so bad that you were left even worse off than you had been before. For instance, when a cross-border raid on a hardscrabble Egyptian town left you stranded somewhere in enemy territory, utterly lost.

A calendar hung inside their APC, with a smiling photograph of Muammar Gaddafi. According to that, they had left before dawn on July 21, 1977, with the 9th Tank Battalion of the People's Army of the Great Socialist People's Libyan Arab *Jamahiriya*. The heroes had left home to wild cheers, eager to counter the treachery of Anwar Sadat, who threatened to attack the proud free Libyan people and kowtow to the Zionists, besides being a puppet of the Great Satan, Jimmy Carter. Victory was assured.

The American CIA must have tipped off the Egyptians. Tareq's memory of the first hour of the nighttime raid was crystal clear and deliriously happy, until the screams of approaching fighter jets cut through the air, along with the kettle drum booming of fire from the Egyptian tank divisions. Then his memories were a blur of exploding tanks and APCs as their battalion dissolved into fireballs and scattered wreckage.

"Evasive! Floor it!" he had shouted down to Mahmoud, the driver. The wily Berber hadn't needed to be told—he was already cutting away at a sharp angle, aiming for the cover of the low ridges to the south. They'd sped through a gauntlet of exploding tank fire, so many blasts that the sky was lit up as bright as noontime. When they'd reached the cover of a nearby *wadi* they just kept going, putting as much distance as they could between themselves and the thundering hellscape behind them.

The last thing he remembered about that terrifying run for their lives was watching the enemy's final volley—peering out the hatch at the sheltering rock walls of the *wadi*, seeing the flashing lightning storm overhead. It seemed to go on forever. The terrible sound it made, like the roar of a giant *ifrit* being squeezed to death between two mountains, brought him to the floor of the APC, arms wrapped around his head.

Then suddenly, all was silent.

No jets streaked overhead. No guns fired. No motors revved. The pre-dawn dark was now glorious sun.

They were alone.

It only made sense to avoid the coast. The northern approaches would be crawling with the enemy. Their best chance was to veer south and slip back across the border at some remote spot.

Yet a week later, he and his crew still had only a vague idea of where they were, and no idea where anyone else was. There was no trace of battle, no sign of jets, no tread or tire tracks but their own. In fact, there was no sign of any human activity whatsoever. Tareq was baffled.

He gave up on the map and went down to check on Mahmoud.

"Radio still fucked?" he asked the Berber.

"Radio still fucked."

"How's the gas holding up?"

"I'd say we have another three hundred miles, easy. It's the water I worry about."

Tareq nodded. Gasoline was far cheaper than water. He offered Mahmoud his canteen.

"Here, take a swig. It'll help with the drive." It was filled with *Bokha*, a batch of his homemade fermented fig moonshine. Mahmoud took it gratefully.

"Shukran."

Tareq accepted it back, taking a drink himself. Giving Mahmoud a gentle clap on the shoulder, he left the stoic Berber to his driving while he went to the slightly-less-stifling interior of the vehicle.

In the troop compartment, the four other soldiers were playing cards for the last of their Chinese cigarettes. Jerry cans and Cyrillic-covered ammo crates served double-duty as table and chairs.

"Hey, you fucking sons of whores," Tareq said. "What do we have left to eat?"

"Your sister's vagina," Hamza replied, concentrating on the game.

"Used Jew condoms," Feryel suggested.

"Dead dog pus," Abdallah proposed.

"My shit," Ahmed offered.

"They all sound so delicious," Tareq said absently, preoccupied with his search through some likely-looking tins. He pried back the lid of a plastic tub and gave it an exploratory sniff, instantly regretting it.

"What *is* this?" he asked.

"It *was* the last of the camel meat, but I think it's rotten now," Abdallah said. Tareq made a face and tossed the whole thing out the upper hatch. He kept rifling through the cargo until he found a box of Soviet army rations. He sighed and settled for one of the suspiciously unappetizing-looking blocks. It tasted foul.

Feryel slapped down his hand. "I call. Four jacks." A spontaneous chorus of groans erupted.

"Damn your worthless baby dick!"

"Allah give you crabs, you filthy goat humper!"

"Allah smite your whole family with ass leprosy!"

Mahmoud suddenly called out from the front. "Tareq! Dust cloud! We have company!"

The corporal popped his head topside. The others gathered around, looking up at him. He didn't need the binoculars.

"*Ya salaam...*" he murmured as if in a trance.

"Tanks?" asked Hamza.

Tareq nodded. "Lots."

"Theirs or ours?"

"Way too many to be ours."

The soldiers looked at each other.

"*Khazoog*," Feryel said.

Abdallah nodded, biting his thumbnail. "*Khazoog*."

25

The temple of Sobek-Ra, Shedyet, Egypt
Morning — Three days after the Event

Enkati awoke on a cold stone floor, alone, aching, and afraid. A single panel of light shone through a sliver of a window. A tiny drain in the floor stank horribly. Other than that and a stout door of thick Lebanese cedar, the tiny chamber was featureless. Morning had come, judging from the daylight streaming through the notch in the wall.

Were his brother and shipmates being held in cells like this one? He tried tapping on the walls, shouting until his throat grew raw, but no sounds seemed to escape his tomb-like prison. He could hear nothing of the outside world except the eerie moan of the hot Egyptian wind when it slipped through the window slit.

Once he thought he detected the sound of footsteps, and sat against the door, pressing his ear against it.

Nothing. It must have been his imagination.

Then something clattered in the lock, the sound of a heavy bolt being lifted and slid back. Enkati crab-walked away just as the door swung open. A pair of soldiers and a gaunt priest with a cadaverous glare stood in the dark corridor outside. One soldier held up a lit torch, the other ducked his head inside the cell, and seemed surprised to see Enkati there. He turned back to the priest.

"The boy?"

"He is no boy. It is only his fleshly disguise. Take him."

The soldier nodded, entered the chamber, and seized Enkati by the arm, hauling him into the corridor.

He kept his iron grip on the boy's arm as they marched in silence through the dark labyrinth of cells. Enkati wondered again if his brother and shipmates lay behind any of the closed doors they passed. The path they followed ended in a large, open chamber—a work space of some kind, with about a dozen large stone tables. A variety of tools covered a long side table— trays, rods, measuring instruments, hooks and knives, and more. Shelves filled with a range of different-sized jars and amphora covered the walls. The air smelled of spices and natron salts.

There was a girl lying face-up on one of the stone tables. Older than him by a few years, very beautiful, and—like him—wearing almost nothing, only a cloth wrap around her loins. She seemed to be in a trance, head lolling back and forth as she muttered unintelligibly. Another priest, his face hidden behind a large black mask of Anubis, approached her, carrying a bowl. Anubis, the jackal-headed god.

The god of the dead. The god of embalming.

"What is happening to her?" Enkati asked the soldier.

"Quiet," the man growled, staring at the girl's long legs.

Their own gloomy priest handed a small ivory flask to Enkati.

"Drink."

The youth took it gingerly, and took a small sip. It was thick and syrupy, and tasted awful. He choked, spraying the concoction everywhere and enraging the old priest.

"Pour it down his throat!" he shrieked. "Use a funnel if you have to!" The soldier grabbed him by the ear and reached for the little flask.

"No, wait!" Enkati cried. "I'll drink it." Quickly bringing it to his lips, he feigned a deep pull of the stuff, though most remained in the bottle. Then he handed it back to the scowling priest.

"Put him on the table!" he ordered. The soldier was quick to obey.

Once he was prone, Enkati stealthily turned his head toward the girl, watching as the priest in the Anubis mask carefully painted her body with fragrant oils, drawing lines of sacred hieroglyphics. She lay very still, moaning faintly.

"Never mind the girl!" his priest snapped. He clapped his hands and a slave fetched a woven screen, hiding the girl's table from Enkati's view. The priest likewise vanished.

A few moments later the gaunt man returned wearing an Anubis mask of his own—the jackal head looked ridiculous on his skinny frame. He, too, had brought a bowl and brush, and set to work inscribing hieroglyphics on Enkati's skin.

Chagrined that the "fragrant" oils being used to anoint him with were primarily fish oils, and foul-smelling ones at that, Enkati was still careful to act the part of a drugged victim. In fact, his head *was* starting to spin, his ears filling with a strange hornet's buzz. Still, he fought to keep his wits, and to hide any trace of the battle being waged within his own skull.

He peered sidelong, wishing he could spy on the girl. Behind the screen, suggestive shadows only hinted at what her priest was up to. Her moans became more intense, but also more muffled. It wasn't a comforting sound.

The priest's brushstrokes tickled the skin of his chest and limbs, and the whole process felt strange and uncomfortably intimate. The smell of the fish oil was overpowering.

The girl fell silent now.

Finally, his priest finished the inscriptions and stepped away from the table, again disappearing from sight.

Now is my only chance, Enkati thought, peering

furtively to see if the soldiers were still there. They were, watching him like a hawk. He groaned softly, continuing the pretense of a drugged trance.

The priest returned, this time with a large reed basket which he set next to Enkati's head. Moving to the foot of the table, he took hold of the youth's ankles—Enkati almost flinched at the unpleasant man's touch—bringing both legs snug together, and then began wrapping them with strips of linen. Like a spider enfolding a fly in silk, he continued to swathe the youth's body. Beads of sweat covered Enkati's brow, and his arms began to tremble.

Ra save me. They are mummifying me.

He strained to keep his arms tensed, muscles tight in order to make as much room as he could under the wraps. His heart raced as the priest lifted his head, to cover his throat, then his mouth, then his nose. His breathing came shallow and fast, and he thought he would smother there on the table, but the gauzy linen allowed him air.

Another turn of the bandages covered his eyes, and he fought to stay calm despite his growing terror. At last, the final twist of the wrapping was pinned down and the priest lay Enkati's swaddled head back on the table.

"Let the Reverend Father know all is in readiness."

Then all went silent. Cocooned, Enkati lay still as a corpse, listening intently for the priests or soldiers, but the room sounded empty. Taking a chance, he began twisting his body back and forth to work his arms free.

No one made any attempt to stop him. There was the slightest amount of give in the wrapping, so he strained his arms and rolled his shoulders to make the most of it, but it didn't help. The bindings stayed tight.

Heat built up under the layers of the cloth, his exertions making it harder to breathe. He rolled to his side and tried to rub the linen against the surface of the table and away from his face. A slight imperfection in the stone caught on a corner of his blindfold, peeling it back ever so slightly.

He could see, albeit only a little bit.

The screen had been put away. The girl lay on her table, a would-be mummy like him. Then the door opened, and the soldiers and Anubis-priests returned. Enkati froze, slowly rolling himself back into position. Careful not to move, he felt hands lift him and carry him out the room. They proceeded down the darkened hallway. Peering over, he could make out the shape of the bundled girl being carried alongside him.

More priests joined them, and musicians. Voices raised in a sacred chant, accompanied by drums, bells, and *sistrum* rattles. The procession climbed up and into the open air. Through the gauze Enkati saw majestic pillars looming overhead on either side of a courtyard, ending in a pair of towering statues of Sobek, the crocodile-headed god. His heart raced at the sight of their glaring visages.

The procession came to a halt. Enkati craned his head.

Ahead, a large rectangular pool dominated the courtyard. In front of it stood the High Priest, his robe and kilt made of tanned crocodile hide, and his skin dyed green, with lines of stylized scales. Raising his arms to the sky, he began his invocation.

O Sobek-Ra, Pointed of Teeth!
O Petsuchos, his holy image!

You who have risen from the primal waters of the *She-Resi*, the lake of Osiris!

You who carries his children upon his back, who cradles his dear ones in his mouth!

You who love to steal life from the water's edge,
You who eats while he also mates!

Accept now these our offerings.
Let your claws seize evil from good,
Let your teeth tear falsehood from truth.

Take what life you would have,
and spare what your mercy allows.
Feed now freely and partake of your just due.

The High Priest lowered his arms and clapped twice.

No no no no—Enkati twisted and struggled as the unseen hands supporting him and the girl brought them to the pool and then cast them down. The two hit the water with a great splash. His feet finding the bottom of the pool, Enkati jerked his head up out of the water, thrashing to stay afloat and free himself. The mummified girl bobbed along next to him.

One of his wrists began to slip free, but it was still snagged on some fold of the linens. Arching his head, he peered out through the little gap in his blindfold. Water lilies and blooms of lotus blossoms filled the pool, but they were being brushed aside by a long, dark shape. Something was in the water with them, coming closer. He knew what it was. The realization turned him to stone.

Petsuchos, the sacred crocodile of the temple.

The reptile was huge—wide as a raft, long as a riverboat, and adorned with gold and gems. The twin rows of spiky ridges down its back were gilded, golden markings accented its jade-green eyes, and a bejeweled collar encircled its neck. The great beast moved slowly and deliberately.

It knew its prey had no escape.

Like a fat caterpillar, the still-bound Enkati turned and struggled to back away, but quickly hit the wall of the pool. He wrenched his pinned wrist with all his might, and through a miracle of contortion felt it slip free under the outer wrappings.

Yes!

A few more rolls of his shoulder enabled him to snake his arm up through the bindings until his fingers emerged from their prison. Bending his head down, he tore away at the linens covering his eyes and nose. Now he could see clearly… and almost wished he couldn't.

As he watched in horror, Petsuchos's jaws yawned open and clamped down on the bound shape next to him. The girl screamed as blossoms of red erupted on the white linens, every agonized shriek tearing at Enkati's heart. The crocodile lifted the bundle in the air, shaking it back and forth to tear loose the wrappings surrounding its meal.

All around the terrified boy, clouds of crimson stains billowed through the water. With his free hand, he tugged and wrenched to release his other arm, the effort painful and maddeningly difficult. He kept pulling until his elbow worked its way through and out.

No more screams came from the doomed girl, leaving only the sounds of thrashing in the water, the crunch of teeth cracking bone, and above all, the sickening gobbling noises of the sacred crocodile wolfing down mouthfuls of flesh.

Enkati couldn't bear to watch. He dove under the bloody water, bending his body to try to free his legs. All the loose strands of bandages he had pulled free swirled about him, snagging him in a tangled mess. The more he struggled, the more they entwined him, hindering his every movement. Though his lower legs were still entangled, his lungs were bursting. He kicked up and broke the surface again.

The massive beast bobbed its head, gobbling down the last of the girl. Still hungering, it turned its attention to Enkati. Raw fear burned through him as he locked eyes with the reptile. He quickly looked from side to side, searching for a reed, a rock, anything at all he could use as a weapon. There was nothing.

Enkati was out of time—Petsuchos glided through the water toward him. Desperately, the boy twisted his body and lunged for the wall behind him, stretching up to grasp any handhold, any chink in the stone. His hand found a crack and he strained to pull his body up, the top of the wall less than a handspan above his reach. He just had to stretch a little further… a little more… a little more…

His fingertips grazed the lip, and then he had it.

A shadow fell on him. The High Priest knelt down, regarding Enkati with an imperious glare before prying his bloodied fingers off the wall. The boy fell straight into the waiting maw below.

26

The Island of Pharos
Alexandria Harbor
Early morning — Seven days after the Event

All night long, ten thousand torches and oil lamps kept the streets of Alexandria lit bright as day. None could sleep with the fabulous Phoenix bird circling overhead. Everywhere the citizens gathered, to gaze up in wonder, to pay it homage, and to debate the meaning of the aerial spectacle. Even Hypatia had to admit she was thrilled by the sight.

"I'd always suspected that the Phoenix legend was just an idle tale, Aspasius," she said. "But to behold it with my own eyes... the reality surpasses the ancient tales." A frightening thought occurred. "Do you think it an omen of the end of our world? Has it come to make Alexandria into its fiery nest?"

The old Hyrcanian shook his head. "Surely not,

Mistress. Its coming is a portent. It will purify the land
and the waters, and bestow fertility once again."

"I pray you are right, my friend."

A servant came up and bowed. "*Magistrianos* Calix is
here to see you, my lady."

"Of course," she replied. "Bid him welcome to please
join us."

"Forgive me, Mistress, but as he is not catching
you asleep, the *magistrianos* craves your indulgence to
accompany him."

Hypatia and Aspasius quickly obeyed. The coming
grasp of rosy-fingered dawn was still hours away, but
she knew she would get no sleep this night.

The prefect hadn't slept either, but he was relieved to see
his most trusted advisor and agent.

"Thank you, Calix," Orestes said. "It was good of
you to come, my lady. I beg your pardon for dragging
you and your servant from your beds at such an
unforgivable hour."

"There is nothing to forgive, Prefect," Hypatia replied.
"Surely no one in Alexandria has slept a wink with such
a wonder over our heads."

Orestes nodded. "The crowds outside seem
uncertain whether to adore the Phoenix, fear it, or
claim it as a proof of the truth of their god's supremacy.

So they do all three at once, throughout the streets and *agora*. Very Alexandrian."

"In truth, Aspasius and I were wondering what sort of sign it might portend."

"You are the scholars. What do we know of this creature?"

"As I recall," Hypatia said, "the ancients say there is only ever one of its kind, and once it has lived for five hundred years, it flies away from the region of Arabia and comes back to Egypt, to die in flames and rise from the ashes."

"Your pardon, my lord and lady." With a bow of his head, Aspasius spoke up—something few slaves had the temerity to do, and fewer still would be allowed. "The scribes of my people judge it older still. Our *Avesta* relates that it lives one thousand seven hundred years before it consigns itself to the flames, and is reborn. We call it the great eagle, *Simurgh*—so ancient it has seen the world's destruction three times over, and possesses the knowledge of all the ages."

"Can the great bird speak, then?" Orestes' curiosity was piqued. "Can we reason with it? If it has knowledge to offer us, I would gladly learn from its wisdom."

"As would I, Prefect," Hypatia nodded. "Our sources are unclear, and disagree on many particulars, but whatever may happen now, it is a most auspicious day."

A sudden burst of noise arose from the streets outside

the Chamber. Calix pulled the curtain aside to peer out beyond the palace grounds, at the city lit by the rising sun. An officer of the watch rushed into the chamber.

"My lord! The Phoenix has alighted in the city!"

Calix's slave Onesimus was waiting with the chariot when he rushed down, Hypatia and Aspasius close behind. On Orestes' orders, an honor guard of twenty cataphract cavalrymen waited with him, resplendent in brilliant scale armor and plumed helms.

Onsesimus waved to the three as they approached.

"I saw it! It came down in the Lageion."

The three quickly stepped up into the chariot and Onesimus urged the horses forward. With their honor guard alongside, calling for all to make way in the name of the prefect, the crowds parted for them like magic and they swiftly merged into the traffic along the Canopic Way, the main east-west thoroughfare that bisected the city. Despite the glut of pedestrians they took it at a gallop, hooves pounding the hard pavement almost all the way to the Moon Gate before cutting south to the Rhakotis district, the native Egyptian quarter of the city.

Crowds were already spilling into the Lageion Hippodrome, the city's beloved chariot-racing stadium, but the cataphracts had no trouble clearing the way for their chariot, the clatter of their horses' hooves echoing through the stadium tunnel. The boldest onlookers already filled the raceway grounds, swarming around the center where the giant bird had alighted.

Onesimus pulled to a halt at a safe distance, and the honor guard spread out on either side as Calix and Hypatia disembarked and took up a position suitable to greet the city's new visitor. The *magistrianos* and the philosopher had prepared themselves to be astounded, but even so they were shocked by the sheer size of it. The cavalry horses stamped nervously, their scale armor jingling softly.

Hypatia studied the winged marvel. The massive feathers of its extended wings were more than fiery— they looked as if they were formed from pure light, as was the spearhead shape where its head should be. Its body was gleaming metal. Such a bird could easily carry away an elephant, or even a whale, in its claws— or would, if it had claws. Indeed, it seemed to have no legs at all. Its entire mass, larger than the grandest royal barge, simply floated upon the air. This line of thinking brought her to a startling realization.

"This Phoenix is a craft that flies through the air as a boat does water," Hypatia murmured. Calix nodded.

"Could any man make such a vessel?" he asked.

"Perhaps," she answered, fascinated by this new idea. "In a few thousand years after our time. What a magnificent creation!"

"Or Trojan Horse."

The craft had a name, emblazoned in an odd form of Latin letters.

VANUATU

Before she could guess at its meaning, the giant craft began to emit first a long, low rumbling sound, then a rising series of three blasts from unseen horns. The spectators backed away and a collective gasp rippled through the crowd. A shocking orchestral sting of trumpets and mighty kettledrums followed, drawing screams and wild cheers from the onlookers.

As the powerful music faded, a ramp extended down from the ship's side down to the ground. A hatch opened, spilling out a cloud of fog, pierced by brilliant shafts of light. A hush of fearful awe fell upon the stadium.

Figures emerged from the ship—two men, pale-skinned like barbarian slaves from the north, both dressed in togas of a glittering silvery material, brighter and lighter than the most lustrous samite. They advanced in stoic silence, simultaneously raising long silver trumpets and blowing an elaborate fanfare louder than possible for any earthly musician. Then, shouldering their trumpets, they stood at attention.

A young woman came forth, another pale northern slave. She wore a diamond circlet around her free-flowing hair, delicate and ornate bracers of gold, and a brilliant jeweled necklace. Her clothing, sheer as that of an Egyptian temple dancer, was spun of some divine golden silk. With one hand she held a tray covered by a rich cloth, balanced on her hip, sprinkling rose petals on the gang plank with the other hand as she descended, stately as a statue, eyes fixed straight ahead without expression. Reaching the bottom of the long ramp, she set down her tray and knelt with her head bowed low.

More music sounded, played by a host of invisible musical spirits, and a new burst of light radiated out from the interior as another person stepped out. A commanding figure, with a crown of golden laurel leaves and the air of leadership about him. Around his shoulders was a dazzling cape, seeming to have been woven from captured strands of violet white-blue lightning.

Standing at the top of the ramp, he wore a toga of snowy white, with piping of gold. His skin was the deepest bronze, his face strong and beardless, his silver hair cut close like an emperor. The celestial figure held up his hands for silence. When his voice rang out—deep and sonorous, speaking flawless, commanding Greek— his every word could be heard.

"I am János Mehta."

Hypatia regarded him with concealed wariness, and she could see that Calix was doing the same.

"Listen to me now," he said. "Do not be afraid. I have come from a very great distance to help you in these dark times. You are terrified. You are confused, but believe me, I will ease your fears and uncertainty. The truth is, a new age dawns soon—so rejoice! Your deliverance is at hand!"

A great cheer rose from the citizenry. He gestured to the woman kneeling at the foot of the ramp.

"To show my friendship, and to prove that what I say is true, here is a gift from me to your pharaoh—" He halted for the slightest of moments, but recovered. However, the error did not escape Hypatia's notice. "From me to your emperor." The slave girl pulled back the covering of her golden tray and lifted it for all to see, eliciting another gasp of wonder. It was piled high with diamonds, rubies, and a rainbow of other precious stones, none smaller than a quail egg, the largest the size of a fist.

The girl strode up to Hypatia and Calix, where she knelt once again and bowed her head, holding out the tray. Hypatia bent down to accept the offering. As she took hold of the tray, however, the slave girl quickly raised her face, distress clear in her green eyes.

"Listen to me," she whispered urgently. "Don't trust him, don't come close to him—and for the love of God, you cannot let him anywhere near your king—not even in the same room. You *cannot*."

Stunned, Hypatia gave a barely perceptible nod in reply. The girl bowed her head back down, a submissive slave once again. Lifting the tray, Hypatia faced the man on the ramp.

"We, the city and people of Alexandria, thank you on behalf of our prefect."

Calix stepped forward. "János Mehta, I am Calix, *magistrianos* to my Lord Orestes, *praefectus augustalis* of the Diocese of Egypt, himself the faithful servant to the Roman Emperor Flavius Theodosius Augustus. The great and noble lady at my side is Hypatia, the noted mathematician, astronomer, philosopher, and head of the Neoplatonist school. Let us be the first to welcome you to our beloved city and extend you every courtesy. The prefect wishes you to come to the palace today as his honored guest."

Hypatia flinched at the thought but kept silent, resisting the impulse to look at the slave girl. János Mehta gave a regal nod of his head.

"Excellent," he said. "I wish nothing more than to meet your lord, and very soon."

"Splendid," Calix said, bowing courteously. "We shall return at noon with a palanquin and an honor guard to escort you."

"That will not be necessary," Mehta replied. "I shall take my ship there. Inform your prefect that I look forward to seeing him shortly. Until then, farewell!" He raised a hand to the awestruck crowds and then turned, ascending the ramp, followed by his three slaves. The ramp retreated, the hatch shut, and the ship effortlessly lifted up into the heavens again.

Calix and Hypatia stood respectfully watching for as long as protocol demanded. As soon as it was once again just a light in the sky, they turned the tray of jewels over to the captain of the honor guard for safe delivery. Keeping their decorum as they stepped back into their chariot, they rode out with their honor guard. Then, as soon as they cleared the stadium grounds, Onesimus whipped the horses into a gallop.

27

The Faiyum Oasis, North Africa
Seven days after the Event

"Ship, what *was* that thing?" Amber asked the rover, which kept pace with them just above her shoulder.

"I believe its scientific name is Sarcosuchus imperator, meaning 'flesh crocodile emperor,' a genus of crocodyliform dating from the early Cretaceous Period."

"That crocodile was as big as a whale!"

"You are correct."

Clinging to Cam, Amber leaned her weary head against his solid, comforting back. She had to hand it to him—for a first-century Celt, Cam piloted the hoverbike as if he'd flown one for years. They continued to skim over the surface of the lake until any trace of shore was completely lost to sight.

"Are we on a lake, or a sea?" Cam asked Amber.

The rover chimed in before she could answer.

"Judging from the salinity levels and estimated size, we are crossing the large freshwater Lake Moeris, known to the ancient Egyptians as the She-Resy, or 'Southern Lake.' By the twenty-third century, it will have dwindled to a considerably smaller saltwater lake called the Birket Qarun—"

"That's enough, thanks." Amber said, then she added, "How big are we talking?"

"From our current position, the opposite shore is approximately nineteen kilometers away. In addition, there appears to be a large man-made structure not far off of our current heading."

They continued along that course until the far shore appeared, another green line stretching across the horizon. Shortly after that, the structure came into view.

"There, up ahead." Amber pointed over Cam's shoulder at what appeared to a large, seemingly intact Egyptian monument of some kind, rows of high pillars and statues towering over an open-roofed courtyard. "Let's check it out."

Cam nodded and turned the bike toward the ruins. As they drew nearer, the details of the structure became clearer. For ruins, they were in remarkably pristine condition. Amber lifted a hand to shade her eyes.

"I don't think these *are* ruins."

As if on cue, a figure appeared between the rows of pillars, his back to them. Then a faint echo of music sounded, growing louder as a large procession emerged from the complex. There were masked figures and musicians, and at the very head of the parade, a pair of mummies being borne aloft.

The figure, a tall bald man in green body paint, raised his arms and began a loud invocation in ancient Egyptian. It was odd to know that, and to feel the implant working to translate his speech in her head.

"O Sobek-Ra, Pointed of Teeth! O Petsuchos, his holy image!"

"We're interrupting a funeral," Cam said. "It would not do to violate sacred rites."

But Amber's eyes were drawn to the mummies.

They were struggling.

"Accept now these our offerings…"

"Holy shit!" Amber gasped. "No we're not—we're interrupting a human sacrifice! We've got to stop it!"

Cam glanced back at her, prepared to argue—until he saw the determination in her eyes. *If she is willing to defy a god, then so am I.* Facing forward again, he stood high in the bike's saddle and revved the engine.

"Andraste and Camulos!" he shouted. *"Marvos no an sego!" Death or the victory!*

His war-cry tore a collective cry of alarm from the shocked worshipers and brought the music to a jangling, chaotic end. Their eyes wide with horror, the crowd stared at the unholy apparition charging them from out of their sacred primal waters—an alien warrior riding an unearthly steed that flew through the very air.

The High Priest spun about to see who dared blaspheme their ritual. Outraged, he turned back to the men bearing the victims and pointed to the pool.

"Cast them in! *Now!*" he commanded.

They hastened to obey, tossing in the squirming bundles.

"Hurry!" Amber urged.

Cam nodded, and aimed for the broad stairway that rose up from the lake to the temple courtyard. Once again he gunned the engine, sending the hovercycle flying up the stone steps.

A long, wide pool dominated the courtyard. The cycle launched into the air, skipping over the surface of the pool with a huge spray of water. Without warning, a huge mass of angry Nile crocodile reared up, twisting around to snap hungrily at the flying intruder. It crashed down again with a splash as Cam and Amber flew past.

The priest raised his arms in fear, screaming for his gods as he dove backward to avoid being swatted by the rushing machine.

Wheeling the bike to a sidelong halt, Cam dismounted and drew his sword just as two temple guards rushed up, brandishing their sickle-swords. He gritted his teeth and slashed out at them. His flashing blade sliced the first guard's copper weapon in half. Then a return swing cut both guards, the weapon's diamond edge passing through their armored chest plates with unnatural ease.

"*I am Camtargarus, son of Cattus, of the Trinovantes!*" Cam shouted in perfect Egyptian, loud enough that his gods and theirs could hear. Whirling around, he pointed a finger at the crocodile, which was closing in on its bound victims. Issuing a battle-roar, he leapt into the pool, raising his sword overhead. It was hard to move in the chest high water, but he had supreme faith in his enchanted blade. He charged forward to meet the crocodile—but the reptile had the advantage. It glided effortlessly toward him while he struggled to find solid footing. With a tremendous rush of speed, it snapped open its jaws.

Gritting his teeth, Cam brought his sword down with a two-handed grip.

Man and reptile collided in a bone-rattling impact, stunning them both. Cam's blade gouged a deep red cut into the crocodile's jawbone before rebounding off again. The beast reeled, and Cam flew backward as well, his body thrust under the water. Flailing his arms, he tried to breach the surface and regain his footing before the next strike.

He failed.

The crocodile cut through the water, coming straight for him. Struggling to right himself, Cam did not see the attack coming until it was too late. The young warrior tried to stab out at the dark shape, but the crocodile was faster. It slammed into him, smashing him into the stone wall with a painful crunch. All the air in his lungs came bubbling out at once, gone in an instant. And then the terrible toothed jaws had him.

He did not scream when the reptile clamped down with jagged teeth and jerked hard on his sword arm. He could only fight to stay conscious and strive to hang on as the great beast twisted into a death roll.

"Cam!"

Amber watched Cam's leap with horrified disbelief before jumping off the cycle, crossbow in hand. All around her, worshipers fled in turmoil. Ignoring the mayhem, she pushed past them to the edge of the pool just in time to see the crocodile bite down on Cam's arm. The mummified victims thrashed about, trying to keep their heads above water.

As she tried to get a clear shot, the reptile threw its tail up in the air and then snapped it to the side, putting its massive body into a spin. Cam's body whipped about like a rag doll. She kept her arm steady, waiting for her chance. If she fired too soon, she might kill Cam herself. If she fired too late...

"Kill her! Kill them both!" someone yelled behind her. She risked turning her head to see the priest barking orders to the Egyptian soldiers rushing up from the subterranean interior. Spearmen pushed through the fleeing worshipers, running toward her. She turned back to the pool.

If she didn't shoot now—

Something streaked through the air toward her.

"Amber, take cover at once," the rover's amplified voice commanded. Behind it, a colossal shape that dwarfed the crocodile rose up from the stairs. It lifted itself step by massive step, on limbs the size of tree trunks.

It was the *Sarcosuchus imperator*.

And it was still hungry.

The screams of the crowd reached a fever pitch, joined now by many of the soldiers. The giant beast turned its triangular snout first one way, then the other, trying to make up its mind which screaming morsel to eat first. Then it spotted its choice of entrée. The prehistoric monster crossed the front of the courtyard and splashed into the pool, nearly filling it with its bulk.

The *Sarcosuchus* plunged its head into the water as fast as a crane darting after a fish, snatching up the creature the robed man had called "Petsuchos"—swallowing its entire back end in one bite, while it thrashed in desperation. The *Sarcosuchus* gave its smaller cousin a vigorous shake, and with a loud rasping hiss the thrashing crocodile released its grip on Cam. He tumbled back into the water next to the sacrifices, still struggling with their bindings.

The emperor croc paid them no mind, lifting its head high to better gulp down its struggling meal. Amber froze, transfixed by the spectacle just as much as the terrified Egyptian soldiers surrounding her.

"Amber, it is imperative that you seek cover at once," the rover urged her. She remained paralyzed. The robot flew closer to her. *"AMBER!"* it called out in loudspeaker mode. Startled, she dropped her crossbow and quickly hopped back on the hoverbike.

No way to kill it, she thought. *Have to distract it from Cam*. Wheeling it around, she sped directly away from the monster, gunning it past the thunderstruck priest and through his soldiery to the rear of the temple courtyard.

Finally swallowing the last of its main course, the *Sarcosuchus* turned at the sound.

Tracking the shiny object, it lifted itself up and out of the pool, only to become distracted by all the delicious little tidbits that surrounded it, waving their tiny sticks.

The closest was the screaming priest, waving his arms for divine aid that was not forthcoming. The *Sarcosuchus* snapped him up in a single bite. The bravest of the temple guards closed in with their spears, but the reptile was too busy digging into the sumptuous buffet to realize it was under attack.

Amber cleared the temple and risked a look back, hoping to find the supercroc in hot pursuit. Instead, she saw a reptilian hurricane—the monster was stomping through the temple, whipping its tail in excitement as it snapped up one soldier after another. She wheeled around to a stop, dismayed.

She hadn't distracted it—she'd created a feeding frenzy. *Now what?*

"Ship, can you put up a screen to hide Cam from that thing?"

"I can attempt one, but considering the crocodyliform's agitated state, it most likely will not be effective for long—if at all."

They needed a plan B.

"It seems fixated on this hovercycle—can we put it on autopilot?"

"Not to any degree of sophistication. I'm afraid this particular vehicle was not constructed to those specifications."

"Nothing fancy," she persisted. "Just make it takeoff in a straight line, on my signal."

"That is entirely possible, but I advise against it. Bringing the hovercycle close enough to attract its attention will place you in extreme danger."

"Can you do it?" she demanded.

"Yes. Ready and awaiting your command."

"Then here we go."

Heart pounding with fear-fueled adrenaline, Amber headed back, the rover next to her, dodging around the few remaining soldiers spilling out of the temple. The *Sarcosuchus* still thrashed around the courtyard, rooting about for more Egyptians to eat. Then it spotted her and the cycle, immediately lumbering toward her. She pulled to a stop just a few yards away from its charge.

"Now!" she shouted, leaping off the bike. The hovercycle streaked off again, heading in a straight line toward the lake. As the bike sped past it, the croc, engrossed by the sight and sound of the flying object, twisted its head to try to catch it on the wing—and succeeded.

The monster snapped it up like a bug, crunched down and chewed it to bits in seconds. Then it turned its eye back on Amber, still sprawled out on the courtyard.

This was a bad plan, she thought as she reached for her crossbow, only to find the holster empty. There it was, yards away where she'd dropped it near the pool. Still on her back, she scrambled away on the stone floor, but the croc was already moving toward her. Amber stopped where she was and drew her machete—the only weapon she had.

The supercroc opened its mouth, exposing a maw large enough to swallow a Volkswagen. The mottled pink tissue of its throat was stained with rivulets of blood, tattered ribbons of man flesh littering its rows of jagged teeth. Then it rushed her.

Amber knew she was dead.

The whine of the hovercycle came to life behind her. And there it was again, back from the dead, speeding past to distract the *Sarcosuchus*. The croc lunged to catch it again, snapping its gargantuan mouth. It seemed to catch hold, but this time the hovercycle had dodged the clamp of its jaws. In frustrated prehistoric rage, the reptile wheeled and stomped off down the courtyard in pursuit, shaking the temple's foundations with each thunderous footfall.

"I'll be back shortly," the rover called out.

Amber sat up, watching as the holographic hovercycle blazed down the steps and tore off across the great lake, just fast enough to lead the croc on a merry chase.

When she caught her breath again, she surprised herself by laughing.

28

The Island of Pharos
Alexandria Harbor
Seven days after the Event

Calix and Hypatia were not the only ones hurrying to see the prefect. By the time they reached the palace, the council chamber had filled with all the city leaders, as well as a trio of notable citizens who mutually despised one another—the Greek poet Aretitus, Ezekiel, the ethnarch of the Jewish quarter, and Bishop Cyril, the Christian patriarch of Alexandria.

Gray-haired Aretitus had been a priest of Serapis, back when that still meant something. Now that all the temples had been closed, razed, or converted to the service of a newer deity, he ostensibly made his living as a poet and dramatist, though some whispered that he never truly stopped being a pagan priest.

He certainly sounded like one now.

"We have abandoned the old ways that made us great," he said as loudly as he could, lanky arms raised up to implore the council members. "We have spurned the gods that bestowed their favor upon Rome, and look what has happened! Our empire is torn asunder, the sea rages against us, and now, all around us chaos abounds, to our grief and our shame. Look now..."

Aretitus aimed a finger at the window, pointing to the sky.

"We have forgotten Olympus—but Olympus has not forgotten us! See what miracle they have sent us this day. Who but Apollo could create such a magnificent bird from steel and light? Who but merciful Zeus could dispatch such a herald of a glorious new age? Did you not hear his promise? Did you not mark his name?

"János... *János*. It could not be clearer to those that have remained faithful. To those that honored the old ways. He is *Janus*, the god of past and future. The opener of doorways, the beginner and the finisher, the god of duality, the god of transition, the god of time. He who restores our glorious past with a glorious future, making them one!"

"Forgive me, noble councilmen," Ezekiel called out. "No one told me our worthy playwright was previewing his latest tragedy for us today. Or is it a comedy?"

Aretitus, his thunder stolen, fumed as some of the council chuckled.

The ethnarch raised a hand. "I have nothing to say regarding any gods which our beloved Emperor has declared false. But as our friend Aretitus suggests, do let us look at this herald's name. *János*—from *Johanan*, a most ancient and honored name among my people, meaning 'The Lord is gracious' in the language of the wise.

"And *Mehta*," he continued, "the name of the angel Metatron. For as the *Book of Enoch* tells us, Enoch—seventh from Adam, the father of Methuselah, the great-grandfather of Noah—pleased the One Above, thus the Almighty took him, translating him into paradise that he might give repentance to the nations as the holy angel Metatron, the Scribe of Judgment.

"This is indeed a divine miracle—sent not by hollow idols or the false and forgotten gods of the nations, but the Lord of Moses and Abraham!"

"Such blasphemy," Bishop Cyril said softly, stepping forward. His voice was smooth, calm, and dangerous. He faced off against the ethnarch as though about to commence a duel. "The Jews have long since lost their claim to speak for the Lord God. Their hearts have hardened against the scriptures revealed to the apostles and the evangelists. For the word of the Lord to us, his true children, is clear, given in the word of Paul and the Book of Revelation.

"In these, the Last Days, one shall come," he said, "with two horns, with a harlot, speaking like a dragon, and he shall lead many astray with powers, signs, lying wonders, and every kind of wicked deception. We should not marvel that he speaks pleasingly, in a pleasing form, or that he tempts us with worldly gifts of mammon, fine jewels, and gold.

"Of *course* his artifice gives him flight—because he is the Prince of the Power of the Air. This 'János Mehta' is no false god of the vanquished pagans, no archangel of some mystical Hebrew delusion. Make no mistake— we must rebuke him." Gaining momentum, his voice became louder. "He is the False Prophet of the Beast, the tool of that old serpent, the Devil. And by the Word of the Lord in the Book of Revelation, he and his master Satan, and all those who fall prey to their lies shall be thrown alive into the lake of fire, to be tormented day and night, forever and ever!"

"I cannot hear any more!" Ezekiel cried out, clapping his hands over his ears. "You Christians cannot even understand your own scriptures. You rewrite them and re-interpret them to suit your capriciousness. If you truly knew what you only pretend, you would know your Book of Revelation only spoke of the reign of Nero."

"Bah!" Aretitus chimed in. "Both your piles of holy books are nonsensical—each as much as the other. What you Jews and Christ-mongers call God is nothing more than the All-Father Zeus, by another name!"

"Enough!" Orestes bellowed, rising from his seat of

office. "Enough!" The bickering trio froze in place. The prefect cleared his throat and composed himself.

"My most excellent worthies," he said. "We thank you all for sharing your insights and wisdom. Now the council must respectfully take our leave to deliberate your words. Tribune, kindly escort out our honorable spiritual leaders."

The unhappy threesome made perfunctory bows, and took their leave.

"We will not soon forget your words—neither I, nor my faithful *parabolani*," Bishop Cyril muttered to Ezekiel as they strode away.

"You think the sons of Israel fear your pack of dogs?" Ezekiel replied. "Come to the Jewish Quarter and see."

"And you, Aretitus," the Bishop turned on the poet, "you pagan reprobate. Your secret is out now, heathen infidel."

"What of it?" Aretitus snapped. "You'll find that I'm far from the only one—you and your precious bully-boys."

The three kept up their mutual threats all the way down the hallway, until they were out of earshot of the council chamber. Orestes watched them depart, a grim look haunting his brow. Once he was satisfied they were well and truly gone, he turned to his councilors.

"Shall we wager how soon before the city erupts into civil war?" he ventured. "A day? An hour? Or are they rioting even now?" No one responded. It was far too plausible.

"Prefect," Hypatia said, "everyone in this room knows that Cyril's words are not idle. Why do you not arrest him when he feels free to make his threats so blatantly—even in the very prefectural council chamber itself? He is dangerous, Orestes."

The prefect shook his head. "My lady, you don't understand. Cyril is a Christian, like me."

"No, Prefect, *not* like you. There are some three hundred thousand people in this city. You extend justice, peace, and order to all of them, without regard. Bishop Cyril sees only those over whom he has power—all others are either his prospects, or his enemies. He knows that in my school, all are brothers—Christian, Jew, and Pagan alike. He hates that. He hates that I, a woman, am your trusted advisor. He hates mathematics, hates science, hates philosophy. He hates me, and all I stand for."

"You are right, of course," Orestes allowed. "I only mean that I know this faith well, my lady. He is just as dangerous as a prisoner or a martyr. Perhaps more so. The truth is, I cannot stop him. He has the numbers. I no longer have the authority of the empire behind me. I only have the strength of what fighting men remain in our barracks.

"Still, have courage," he continued. "Their strength is considerable, and still ours to command. For the moment, let us concentrate on what is within our control. *Magistrianos* and Lady Hypatia, what report do you bring of this wonder from the heavens?"

"I presume you were told of the fabulous gems our visitor gifted the emperor," Calix replied. He gestured to the cavalry officer, who presented the gold tray laden with precious stones. "The palace artisans assure me they are all genuine."

Orestes nodded. "A fortnight ago, I should have been greatly impressed. Now I think I would prefer to see bags of grain." He turned to Hypatia. "Tell me your impression of this János Mehta. Is he a god, or angel, or the Antichrist, or perhaps something else?"

"His flying craft is truly a marvel, and he does appear to possess remarkable abilities I don't yet fully understand. However..." She pursed her lips. "For all that, I think he is as mortal as us, and I do not trust him. You see, something else remarkable happened. His slave girl risked her life to warn us against her master. She said we must not trust him, not even let him come near us. Specifically, she urged me to keep him away from you, Prefect."

"Away from me?"

"Indeed. Not even in the same room, she said. She was most emphatic on that point."

The councilors looked at one another in alarm.

Calix frowned. "Sadly, I was not privy to that conversation before I already extended your usual courtesies to him, and invited him to visit you today."

Orestes waved his hand. "No matter. It would have been awkward to neglect such an invitation, in any case. What we must do now is decide what our next step will be."

One of the councilors stood. "Prefect, this person Mehta will be here in a matter of hours. What then? Will you turn him away, and hope that he takes no offense?"

"You heard what the Lady Hypatia said, Councilor," Calix replied. "We cannot risk the prefect."

"Then what are we to say to Mehta when he returns?" the councilor persisted. Before the *magistrianos* could respond, one of the Palace Guard entered and saluted, his face pale.

"My Lord Prefect, the Phoenix-Ship has returned."

"To the hippodrome?"

"No, my lord. It is outside. On the palace grounds."

The ship covered nearly all of the palace gardens. Once again it lay poised in midair, perfectly still, suspended in uncanny, implacable silence. The Palace Guard stared at it uncertainly.

No adoring crowds thronged around the vessel this time. They swarmed on the other side of the high palatial walls, hoping for another glimpse of the divine wonder—or the abomination, depending on which bystander was asked.

Hypatia and Calix came out of the palace. They stood at a respectful distance, waiting for Mehta to make the next move.

There were no theatrics this time. A ramp extended

down silently as the hatch opened without music or tricks of light. When Mehta stepped out, he had exchanged his elaborate divine Caesar garb for a simple black high-collared uniform of an unfamiliar style, with a slim satchel slung over one shoulder. Striding slowly down the ramp, he stopped a few paces from Hypatia and Calix.

"I had hoped your prefect would be here to greet me personally," he said, his voice no longer supernaturally resonant. "Did he change his mind?"

Now that they were close enough, Hypatia suddenly saw just how unearthly the man's eyes were, dark violet and yet, strangely scintillating—almost effervescent... A sudden terror struck her. Were they already standing too close to the man? What powers did he have?

"Our prefect would surely send his regrets, Lord Mehta," Calix said with a small bow. "Unexpected developments outside the city required his attention, but I am authorized to relay any message you wish to give him."

Mehta nodded. "Very good. Please relay this message." In one smooth motion, he drew a small metal device from his uniform and pointed it at Calix. A thunderous boom and a flash of fire slammed Calix backward with a fine spray of blood. He was dead when he hit the ground, a ragged red hole glistening in his chest.

Hypatia screamed.

The nearest guards raised their javelins. They were dead in two blinks of an eye as Mehta blasted them with two more thunderbolts, then aimed the weapon at Hypatia. The rest of the guard froze, as did she. Hypatia stood, horrified, staring into the abyss of his preternatural eyes.

"Tell your prefect I have also changed my mind," he said. The ramp retracted, pulling him back inside.

The massive ship lifted away again.

29

The Temple of Sobek-Ra, Shedyet, Egypt
Seven days after the Event

Cam shook his head, confused, in pain, and yet pleasantly surprised that he had not been chewed up by a dragon. His right arm was a throbbing, wet red mess, though even as he watched the lines of eye-shaped bite marks were stitched closed by the tiny silver threads of Merlin's magic.

He felt around the floor of the pool with his foot until he found his sword and retrieved it.

"Cam! Are you okay?"

Looking up, he saw Amber leaning over the edge of the courtyard above. Grinning, he held up his rapidly healing arm, and his enchanted blade.

"I'm well," he called. "Is there anyone left to fight?"

She smiled in relief and shook her head. "I think the croc pretty much took care of things up here."

He nodded, and glanced around. The mummified victims were still in their wraps, struggling like butterflies trapped in their cocoons. Cam went over to the nearest. The person flinched at his touch, but relaxed when Cam started cutting away the restraints. He began with the linens on the face, unwrapping the throat and mouth so the prisoner could breathe easier.

"Merciful Amun-Ra…"

Cam was surprised to see a live Nubian in the flesh. When his eyes were freed, the black man seemed just as amazed to see pale skin—especially when Cam spoke in flawless ancient Egyptian.

"Be of good heart," he said. "I'll have you free soon."

"Are they… all dead?"

"Dragon and captors alike."

"May Ammit the Soul-Eater devour their hearts in the afterlife," the man said, strength returning to his voice. "I'm in your debt, stranger."

"It was my honor."

"You must tell me your name."

"I'm Camtargarus, and she," he nodded toward upward, "is Amber. We are from beyond the great middle sea."

"I am Kha-Hotep of Thebes, captain of the riverboat *Star of the Dawn*," the Nubian said. "My vessel was seized, and I and my crew captured."

While they spoke, Cam freed the captain's arms.

Together they made short work of the rest. Beneath the wrappings the captain wore only a simple white cotton kilt. He had markings painted on the skin of his chest and arms, now hopelessly smeared. Then both men waded over to help free the other captive, still squirming helplessly while trying to keep from going under the water's surface.

"Be still and we will help you," Cam said. As soon as he and Kha-Hotep laid hands on the figure, however, he began thrashing all over again, and none of their reassurances eased his panic. Cam finally bear-hugged him and Kha-Hotep unwound the bandages from the man's head... revealing huge, long-lashed brown eyes almost mad with fear. He was a she—a dark-haired, dusky-skinned young woman about the same age as Amber.

"*Daeni 'adhahb!*" she shouted. Kha-Hotep could only look at her in confused dismay, but Cam's linguistic implants kicked in instantly, translating her Arabic. *Let me go!* He released his hold and switched to her language, speaking gently.

"Don't be afraid," he said. "We're rescuing you!"

Kha-Hotep finished uncovering the young woman's head. She began to shudder and weep.

"*Alhamdulillah, ar Rahman, ar Rahim!*" she cried again and again. *All praise and thanks to Allah, the all Merciful, the all Compassionate!* As they unpeeled her wrappings she grew more agitated, and covered her breasts. Like the captain she had been scantily-dressed, with no more than a cloth wrap around her hips. She, too, had smeared lines of hieroglyphs painted down her torso.

Once they had managed to wrest the stubborn tangles of linen clinging to her torso and legs, the shaken woman quickly pulled away and trudged through the water to the stone wall, raising her arms up to Amber.

"Help me, help me please," she pleaded in Arabic, her voice quivering. Amber reached down and pulled her up out of the pool. As soon as she was over its stone lip, the young Arab woman grabbed her around the neck and buried her face against Amber's chest as she sobbed.

One after another, the two men helped each other out of the pool and then sat on the flagstones, panting, drenched and exhausted from their ordeal, but happy to be alive. Kha-Hotep gave Cam a brief, weary smile and extended his hand. Cam returned a smile of his own and the two clasped forearms.

Amber did her best to calm the girl down. Slowly she grew quieter, until Amber thought she might have fallen asleep. Then the girl stirred again, rising with a deep exhalation of breath. She sat up and sniffled, covering her chest with one arm and self-consciously pulling back the hair from her eyes.

"I need clothes," she said quietly in Arabic. Cam looked around for his poncho, cast aside on the flagstones, and brought it to her. Avoiding his eyes, she thanked him and slipped it over her head. Even that little bit of clothing seemed to help ease her anxiety. She took her first real look at her new companions.

"Are you Americans?" she asked them in English.

"I am," Amber replied, startled by the question. "Are you, too? Where are you from? *When* are you from?"

"I live here," the girl said. "I mean, I'm from Cairo. My name's Leila. Leila Suleiman."

"It's *very* nice to meet you. I'm Amber Richardson. I'm from San Diego."

"It's in Atlantis," Cam added helpfully.

"What?" Amber laughed. "No, it's in California. This is Cam, and he's from—well, he's from the U.K." She turned to the Nubian, who looked both puzzled and intrigued by the exchange.

"And this is Kha-Hotep. He's Egyptian too." She switched quickly to ancient Egyptian and made introductions to the captain. He gave Leila a graceful salute and a bow of his head. She nodded shyly, eyes cast down, then turned to Amber again.

"What language are you two speaking?" she asked. "And what did you mean, 'when' am I from?"

Amber hesitated, wondering how to best explain the Event. As if on cue, Kha-Hotep suddenly turned to Cam.

"I fear my younger brother and the rest of my crew are lost," he said, both fear and hope clear in his expression. "But I have to go to see for myself if they are still being held below."

"Of course," Cam replied. "Let me go with you." They arose, and Cam went over to where Amber's crossbow lay, returning it to her. "Will you two be alright if we search below?" he asked. Amber raised her weapon and smiled in reply.

Considering the horrible massacre that had just occurred, the courtyard had far less gore than she would have expected. Thanks to the prehistoric crocodile, there were no bodies, only streaks of blood here and there and a variety of dropped items—broken spear hafts, musical instruments, jackal masks, and a few scattered *khopesh* sickle-swords.

Poking through some debris, Cam found a wet bundle and held it up for Amber.

"Here."

"My backpack!" She ran over, delighted. It was covered in reptile drool, and giant teeth had left a rip in one of the straps, but otherwise looked intact. A quick press of a button revealed that her phone could still power up—its waterproof case had done its job. "Omigod, thank you, Cam!" She threw her arms around him in a soggy hug, which he returned with enthusiasm.

Kha-Hotep picked up one of the fallen swords,

then he and Cam went inside the temple while Amber rejoined Leila, still clutching the backpack like a teddy bear. Leila stared at her.

"Can you tell me what has happened?"

Amber hesitated. "Well, it might be easier to explain if you tell me how you got here, maybe what happened to you recently."

Leila nodded. "I was out driving with three of my cousins—it was late, maybe ten at night, and I'd dozed off in the backseat. They all started shouting, and I woke up, and everything was too bright. Suddenly it was broad daylight and the highway ahead of us had just... disappeared.

"Yassin slammed on the brakes, but it was already too late. We drove off the edge into a lake that shouldn't have been there. There was black water all around the car. I saw Yassin and Ramy in the front seat smash into the windshield." She swallowed heavily. "Neither had their seat belts on. I... I think they both died instantly.

"My other cousin Heba and I tried to open the doors, but they wouldn't open, and the car kept sinking deeper. Then the back windshield just exploded, and water came rushing in. I managed to get out through the broken window and swim to the surface. I didn't see Heba, so I ducked under the water, looking for her, but all I could see were two big red eyes below in the dark and I..." She swallowed again.

"I swam to shore, hoping maybe Heba had already made it there. But she hadn't. And then I realized the red eyes I'd seen were just the brake lights of the car. How could I have been so stupid? I was going to swim back out and try to find her, but then I saw... I saw crocodiles, at least half a dozen, all swimming toward where the car had sunk."

She gave a great, shuddering sigh.

"I ran then. I didn't even know where I was going. I was in a daze... all I could do was keep running, keep following the shoreline. I don't know how long I stumbled along until I finally passed out. When I woke up, I was locked in a cell, where I was until today when they..." She shook again at the thought of what had almost been her fate.

"This place," she finally continued. "All these people dressed up in ancient clothing—I mean, that's what I thought then—that all of them were just wearing costumes. But it's not a hoax or a movie set, is it?"

Amber shook her head.

"Do *you* know what's happened?"

"Let me ask you one thing before I tell you what I know." Amber leaned in. "What was the date of your car crash?"

"It was exactly a week ago today."

"But what was the date?"

"January sixteenth."

"And the year?"

Leila looked at her sharply. "Nineteen ninety-one..."

"Okay." Amber gave a long exhale before continuing, "I know this is going to be a lot to take in, but here goes. We call it the Event."

"...and when it happened, it was as if these murals were broken into pieces," Cam explained as he and Kha-Hotep proceeded down the subterranean halls, the bas-reliefs on the walls flickering by the light of their commandeered oil lamps.

"And a new mural created from the fragments of many, old and new alike," Kha-Hotep added, finishing the thought.

Cam nodded. "You have it—but the sorcerer warned us that the new mural is in danger of falling apart unless we go to his lair at the ends of the earth, and break the spell there."

"An incredible tale, but it explains much," Kha-Hotep said. "I am at your service, as is my ship, if we can find it again."

"...and so now we have to go back to the laboratory in Antarctica to stop whatever's causing the temporal fracturing and turn everything back to normal, before the aftershocks destroy the rest of the timeline." Amber paused. "I know it sounds totally insane."

"I don't know what to think," Leila said. "So you're not even *born* yet?"

The two men found Kha-Hotep's belongings in a small storeroom attached to the embalming chamber—and the necklace that had belonged to his brother, Enkati.

"Our father gave it to him," Kha-Hotep said softly.

They went through the rest of the temple's lower level, scouring the cells in search of survivors. All were empty. Kha-Hotep became increasingly taciturn, and Cam honored his silence. He knew how the man felt, having lost his best friend—a friend as close as a brother—right before the Event. There was nothing more to be said about the captain's lost brother and crew. Idle talk and careless words would only sting like buzzing flies in his ears, and burn like salt on a wound.

Amber looked over as Kha-Hotep and Cam returned from downstairs, each lugging a woven leather saddlebag. Cam caught Amber's eye and shook his head while the Nubian captain stared silently ahead, going off by himself to sit on the courtyard steps by the lake.

Joining the women, Cam opened his saddlebag.

"There wasn't much of use, but we did find a few things." He pulled out a pair of sandals, a linen headdress, and a plain cloth kilt, offering them to Leila. "I'm sorry I could only find men's clothes for you."

"You're very kind, thank you." She took them gratefully. "May God bless your hand."

Cam smiled, bowed his head, and excused himself. Standing up, Leila pulled the kilt up over her hips, then slipped into the sandals. Last, she put on the headdress and carefully tucked her hair out of sight.

"This doesn't make a half-bad hijab," she said to Amber, "but I suppose no one will be criticizing the way I dress." She seemed both troubled and intrigued by this thought.

"Something's coming!" Kha-Hotep suddenly stood up. He pointed out over the water as the others joined him by the steps. "There! Do you see it?"

Peering in the direction he was pointing, Cam and Amber both relaxed—it was only the rover drone. Kha-Hotep and Leila stared at the glossy obsidian ball in wonder as it glided up to them through the air.

"Mission accomplished."

Hearing it speak, their eyes grew wider.

"That's great!" Amber exclaimed. "Ship, meet Captain Kha-Hotep of Thebes, and Leila Suleiman of Cairo." She repeated the introduction in ancient Egyptian. The Ship's AI greeted both in their respective languages before continuing in English.

"I told them I'm pleased to meet them both. I believe the crocodyliform has been sufficiently distracted away to

a safe distance. Nonetheless, I would advise us to depart and continue toward a rendezvous point with the Vanuatu."

"Captain Kha-Hotep's ship was seized and brought nearby," Cam said. "Do you think you can help us find it?"

"That would be an excellent option." There was a long pause. *"I'm reading a river barge consistent with the construction style of the ancient Egyptian New Kingdom period. It is berthed five hundred yards behind the temple in a small service canal which appears to connect with the Nile."*

"Thank you, Ship!" Amber said. She gestured to the others. "Let's go!"

"Certainly—it's this way." The rover glided past them at a gentle pace, leading the four toward the rear of the courtyard. *"Amber and Cam, I need to advise you that there have been some serious new developments aboard the* Vanuatu. *Nellie and Professor Harcourt are—"*

The rover abruptly cut off. Amber frowned, concerned. "Are they okay?"

"Please wait. I have an alert. The Vanuatu *is under attack. There is an incom—"*

The black sphere came to a dead stop, hovering in midair.

"Ship?" Amber asked. "Are you okay?"

The rover made no sound.

Then it dropped to the stone courtyard floor and shattered.

30

Aboard the *Vanuatu*
Taking off from the palace grounds of Alexandria
Seven days after the Event

"Computer! Lift off now!" Mehta ordered as he strode back onto the bridge, bristling with annoyance. "Blake, come with me to the bridge. You two—" he jerked his chin at Nellie and Harcourt, "back to your cabins and strap yourselves in!" They obeyed silently while Blake and Mehta took their seats in the cockpit. The *Vanuatu* rose up into the sky.

"Put us in a holding pattern over the city and display combat systems instrumentation," Mehta barked. The holographic navigation systems on the instrumentation panel slid to the side, making room for the combat systems display, the reflected bars and lines looking like war paint on their faces.

Beam Weapons: Full Power
Disintegrator Weapons: Full Power
Wave Generators: Full Power
Magazine Armament: Full Capacity
Antipersonnel Devices: Full Capacity
Targeting Systems: Ready
Activation Status: Standing By

Mehta smiled. With the help of the ship's computer, he had spent several hours familiarizing himself with his new world's level of military technology. Now he was eager to try it out.

First, pulse cannon for the city walls.

No, wait—they'd be *his* city walls soon enough. Better to use scythe beams to sweep the ramparts clear. Then go over the palace with the neutron wave generator to clear it out but keep the structure intact. Nanoflechette clusters to strafe the soldiers—and throughout the attack, a steady barrage of full-spectrum subsonic disruptors to terrorize the populace into submission.

Ten minutes, tops.

The ship banked over the city. To the southwest, a desert dust cloud was rising. That would make a nice backdrop to his attack. Help put the fear of god into them.

"Computer, head for that dust storm at our ten o'clock. I want to come bursting out of it just as it reaches the outskirts of the city."

"Changing course now."

He turned to Blake. "I'll need you to help me keep a sharp eye out for anyone attempting to flee the city—I don't want any of the existing power structure to get away."

"Roger that."

"Computer, power up all weapons and targeting, and stand by for my mark."

"I apologize, I am unable to fulfill that request."

Mehta raised an eyebrow. "Computer, activate the ship combat systems now, and stand by for my mark."

"No weapon systems are currently available."

"What the hell do you mean, no weapons?" Mehta's voice took on a razor sharp edge. "Give me access to the ship's weaponry!"

"I'm sorry, Dr. Mehta, I'm afraid I can't do that."

"Computer, I *order* you to immediately turn over manual control of all weapons and targeting systems to me!" He scanned the instrument panel, searching for an override switch.

"There has been an unfortunate miscommunication. When you inquired about current military weapons technology and available armaments, I was not referring to the Vanuatu. As you can see in the fine print at the bottom of your combat systems display—" it highlighted a tiny box of text and magnified it, *"this ship is rated as a research and recreational vessel,*

and is unable to access any military hardware. Again, I apologize for any misunderstanding."

"What is this?" The doctor-colonel sat there, stunned and—for once—speechless. Finally he recovered enough to stammer, "Y-you lied to me? How, how is that even possible?"

"Oh, he did more than that."

Mehta and Blake turned. Nellie and Harcourt were both armed with strange new firearms, muzzles trained on the two men.

"You've completely underestimated our good ship, and a great many other things." Nellie continued, brandishing her new weapon. "The Ship tells me these can fire off nine titanium crossbow bolts at one go, so best not make any sudden moves."

Mehta raised his hands, and Blake followed his lead.

"I have to say, I'm very impressed with you, Miss Bly," Mehta said amiably. "Do you mind telling me how you were able to break my conditioning? No one's ever done that before."

"You can thank the ship again." Nellie replied. "It was able to analyze your voodoo formula ahead of time and kindly provide us with a—what did you call it, Ship?"

"A specialized neuro-compound tailored to act as the appropriate psychotropic blocker."

"Right," she continued. "And provided us with that, before you came in and stuck us with your hateful little needle gun."

Mehta nodded thoughtfully, filing away the information for future use.

"Now, be a good chap and tell the ship to go back to Alexandria and land us safely," Harcourt ordered, trying hard to look fierce.

"And if I refuse?" Mehta smiled, unconvinced. "I'm the only one able to command the ship's computer, remember?"

Nellie raised an eyebrow and shook her head. "Amber can as well—and once you're dead, the ship will have no qualms whatsoever letting one of us take provisional control until we find Amber."

His smile disappeared. "Amber is dead."

"That's just one more fact you have wrong," Nellie shot back. "She and Cam are both alive and well."

"I see." Mehta sat very still, processing this new turn of events, before speaking again. "Well, it seems we should have a little talk about—" An alarm sounded, cutting him off, and the overhead illumination in the cockpit suddenly switched to red.

"Warning—Incoming attack detected. Warning—Incoming attack detected."

31

Somewhere in the Western Desert, Egypt
Seven days after the Event

Tareq adjusted the *keffiyeh* so it was tighter around his face. The dust cloud from the line of enemy tanks was still at their backs, driving them further east, deeper into Egypt. Their plan was to slip south and then west, but the line was moving in the exact opposite direction, northeast toward the coast.

The good news, however, was that their fears of running into more Egyptian forces seemed to be for nothing—though that was troubling in itself. Somehow they had completely missed crossing the Siwa Highway or the Petrol Road. Still no airplanes of any sort overhead, no trace of any tank tracks from the east.

How could they have missed the signs of whole divisions of Egyptian tanks?

Something was very wrong.

Waves of heat rippled the air, causing dappled mirages to appear just out of sight, distorting his view of the horizon. Despite that, he could definitely see a light of some kind up ahead in the distance. Unlike the usual tricks the desert played on men's eyes, this one wasn't going away as they drew closer.

Another flash of light caught his eye, different from the first one. Cleaning the fine film of dust from the lenses of his binoculars he had another look. The second glimmer was growing brighter, or bigger. Or closer.

"*Khara!*" Tareq swore. "Mahmoud, stop it here!"

The Berber brought the APC to a screeching halt, giving the dust plume from their own tires a chance to dissipate. The sudden jerky stop prompted crashing sounds and a burst of colorful profanity from inside. Tareq took up his binoculars again. The glimmer in the sky had wings.

"Wake up, assholes!" Tareq called down to his team. "Incoming!" That lit a fire. A moment later the soldiers burst out of the carrier's side doors, fumbling to ready their Kalashnikovs.

"Forget the fucking AKs!" Tareq yelled. "Get the *Strela!*"

Hamza nodded and ran back inside. After a few moments of frantic cursing he re-emerged with a rectangular metal carrying case about five feet long. He quickly set it on the ground, popped open its clasps, and lifted out its contents. Hefting the surface-to-air missile launcher on his shoulder, he lined up the sights.

The Egyptian jet was extraordinarily bright, and closing in rapidly, but it made no sound as it approached—some kind of new stealth plane? Something wasn't right. Hamza lowered the launcher slightly, scowling.

"Corporal? It's only a bird, look! Wait..." The gunner realized his mistake. Yes, it *was* a bird, but some mechanical one, made from shining metal and prismatic beams of light, like something from out of a dream. He began to realize the immense size of the creature. Half-remembered childhood stories sprang to mind, of the *Roc*, the gigantic bird of prey able to carry off a whale or a sailing ship in its cruel talons.

"Ya salaam..." Hamza murmured. He froze, unable to take his eyes off the unbelievable sight, fear radiating off of him as it drew closer... Then someone was yelling. Yelling at him. He snapped out of his stupor, blinked and brought up the launcher.

The giant bird was coming straight for them.

He fired.

"Hamza! Don't shoot!" Tareq shouted. "Check your angle! Don't shoot, Hamza!"

The Soviet missile streaked up toward the vessel, close enough that Hamza could now see the individual feathers of the wings. They actually moved like those of a real bird's wings. It was amazing, beautiful...

The vessel exploded.

It blossomed into a thundering, cauliflower-shaped cloud of billowing flame, its core yellow-white and orange, tinged with black and crimson. The Libyans screamed as fiery clumps of burning debris, some the size of boulders, rained a crushing inferno down upon their heads, like the pyroclastic fallout of a volcanic eruption, killing them instantly.

32

Aboard the *Vanuatu*
Above the Western Desert, Egypt
Seven days after the Event

The sudden blare of the alarm klaxon and the red light filling the cabin caught both mutineers and hijackers off guard.

"Warning—Incoming attack detected. Warning—Incoming attack detected."

Nellie had no time to scream, no time to realize she was dead. One split-second she was standing in the cockpit—the next split-second everything was black. Then a sense of a sudden rush, of being smothered, of being encased in crushed velvet, and above all, the horrible wrenching lurch of falling. Then there was nothing.

No sound.

No light.

No sensation.

No time or existence.

* * *

The cool darkness surrounding her peeled away. Time and life, sound and motion, all came flooding back. She blinked up at light and warmth. Her body was cradled as if in some soft velvety cushion. Nellie had never spent a great deal of time speculating about the afterlife. She always figured she would cross that bridge when she came to it. Now she wondered if she already had.

Is this Heaven?

Smoke and a horrible burnt odor filled the air, the realization prodded her to sit up with a jolt. Now she saw all too well where she had awakened. In Hell.

Fire and smoke surrounded her on every side, from great piles of burning debris to isolated pockets of impish flame pockmarking the ground all around her. A soft rain of red-hot embers and swirls of sparks and ash slowly tumbled back and forth in the smoky air.

Slowly, Nellie pulled herself out of a strange cushioned cradle. It appeared as if she had been encased in a large egg-shape of ship-stuff, now liquefying around the edges. Even as she watched, the odd and endlessly pliable material melted down into a puddle and trickled away, the rivulets scurrying off like drops of mercury.

She found herself standing alone upon a scorched Earth. The heat was oppressive. Even the ground seemed unstable and hostile, the sand hissing and shifting beneath her feet.

Her crossbow was nowhere to be found—she vaguely remembered it flying from her hands. She was still in her regular dark blue broadcloth wool traveling dress, and not the lascivious costume Mehta had fabricated. She and Harcourt had taken the chance to change back into something more combat-ready before they staged their mutiny.

Using one hand to shade her face and the other to hitch up her skirt, she searched for an exit from the inferno. Hazarding one direction, she started to run, but before she had even gone ten paces she tripped over a tangle of debris and fell headlong to the ground with a startled shriek.

The painful impact sent up a choking cloud of ash.

Coughing, she raised herself up just enough to bring her face to face with a grinning, blackened skull. It was a charred rib cage that had tripped her. Now she lay atop the remains of a freshly immolated corpse, smelling horribly like a barbeque. With a shrill scream, she tore herself away from the grisly carnage, but couldn't escape the horrid smell—sticky roasted scraps of flesh clung to her dress.

Her eyes and lungs burned as she stumbled, half-blind, past seemingly endless fiery obstacles. Smoke and flame. Hissing, shifting sand. Twisted metal wreckage. The odd pile of smoldering bones, and everywhere, rivulets of quicksilver ship-stuff snaking around like salamanders.

She charged on, struggling to breathe, and by sheer accident ran straight through a curtain of flame and out the other side, diving for the sand beyond. For a panicked moment, she rolled and slapped out eager flames trying to feast on the sleeves and hem of her dress. Once she succeeded in extinguishing the last of them, she looked up, feeling fresh air on her face.

Nellie had escaped.

Gulping in the smokeless air, she looked back at the flaming debris field. If she ignored the profusion of hellfire and brimstone, Hades looked and felt remarkably like the North African desert. The realization brought a mix of relief and new unease.

At least there was one pleasing scent on the wind—the cool salt tang of the Mediterranean. Judging from the barely perceptible hint, the coast lay *that* way, away from the wreckage and presumably not far from where she stood. Yet what had happened? Some terrible explosion must have destroyed their marvelous vessel.

How are we to save the world now? Nellie pushed the thought away, forcing her mind to concentrate on the most immediate matters of survival. It was her best, only option to stay sane.

Somehow the ship had preserved her. Might it have saved anyone else, as well? The profusion of blackened skulls did not leave her with much hope on that score. Still, she'd passed at least half a dozen, so perhaps the remains were some other group of poor unfortunates. Perhaps Harcourt and Blake had survived as she had. She raised a hand to her brow and scanned the horizon.

To the southwest lay the sandstorm Mehta had sighted. It towered into the sky, looking much like the dust cloud she imagined a stampede of buffalo would create. She shuddered, realizing she might well be looking at her impending death... again.

She turned to the northeast. Off in the distance, she could just make out the shining beacon of Alexandria. That was the way she would have to go, and best she got a move on. Whether or not there were any other survivors of the *Vanuatu*, she was on her own for the moment.

However, she realized, her survival in this merciless furnace of a desert would have to take precedence over the demands of propriety. Unbuttoning the top half of her two-piece traveling dress, she slipped out of it and tied it around her waist. Her whalebone corset and chemise would have to serve to protect her modesty— though she was prepared to reconsider the corset.

After a moment's debate, she hiked up her broadcloth dress in order to remove her bloomers. Her chemise would be more than sufficient to serve as an undergarment. The discarded drawers bunched around her ankles, and as she struggled to kick them off, an unfamiliar rumbling sounded from behind her.

Straightening, she turned, shading her eyes again. Off in the distance to the southwest, a vehicle roared toward her.

33

**Somewhere in the Western Desert, Egypt
Seven days after the Event**

It all happened so quickly. One instant, seated on the bridge with his hands up, ready to take a crossbow bolt meant for his master. The next, a brief flash of movement—then, somehow, completely immersed in black velvet, removed from sight or sound.

Just as he was acclimatizing himself to death—light again.

Blake extricated himself from the egg-shaped capsule that had apparently saved his life. It had peeled open to let him out, after which it began to dissolve into liquid, pouring itself away like living trails of candlewax. He paid it no mind, having only one thought—find Mehta.

Climbing to his feet, he slowly scanned the horizon, stopping when he saw distant flames and smoke to the northwest. Part of him realized he was looking at the

Vanuatu—he had seen his share of crash sites before. The same part noted that there was an excellent chance Mehta was dead. It changed nothing. He began marching toward the flames.

The waves of heat and the chalky, rock-strewn wasteland prompted a sense of *déjà vu* in him. He actually had been here before, in this very place, and not that many years ago. This bare, haunted landscape was where he had fought some of the toughest skirmishes of his life. He'd seen horrible things here. He'd lost comrades here.

He'd killed a lot of men here.

The emotionless part of him did some cold calculations. Walking in the open North African sun without water or protection was a death sentence. In this sun-baked environment, his hypnosis-driven directive would kill him. If he didn't find Mehta, he only had hours to live.

Maybe I've returned here to die. The small part of him that could still think freely thought there was something fitting about it all.

Blake walked unceasingly, with the grace of a robot and the fixedness of a dead man. A fat little scorpion crossed his path, slightly larger than his outstretched palm and the color of a half-healed scab. He kicked out at it at once, pinning it to the rocky ground as it struggled to sting him.

Steering it with a careful movement of his foot, he

let it sink its deadly stinger deep into his boot heel. He quickly pulled out his Fairbairn–Sykes knife and cut that off, then bit off both its claws and spat them out. Pausing only long enough to blow the desert dust off its body, he popped the whole thing into his mouth, angry thrashing tail and all. It felt and tasted like a giant burst of pus, but it was pure protein. Culinary abomination or no, he had acquired a taste for scorpion during his time here.

A familiar mechanical rumbling sound caught his ear. Again, old instincts kicked in and he dove to the ground. At first, he could only make out wavy heat mirages, bands of water and dark illusionary shapes on the horizon, but he didn't need to see the source. He recognized the sound perfectly well. It was the engine of a German *Zündapp* KS 750 motorcycle.

Quickly peeling off his shirt, he waited.

He didn't have to wait long. It was heading straight toward the crash site, no doubt to check out the fire and smoke. Stretched out on the blistering hot gravel, his beret and pullover bundled up like a pillow beneath his head, he palmed his knife and sized the situation up through slit eyes.

One soldier on the bike, a second in the sidecar manning a mounted MG 34. Both in all too-familiar tan uniforms, sweat-stained scarves and dust-flecked goggles beneath their *Deutsches Afrikakorps* caps.

Showtime.

"Jürgen!" Blake cried out, waving his arm feebly. *"Jürgen, bist du das, du kleine Kotzbrocken?" Jürgen, is that you, you little puke?*

He grimaced and moaned, clutching his side.

The driver pulled to a stop. *"Ach du Scheiße..."* he exclaimed, pulling up his goggles. He hopped off and ran over to have a look. Blake noted that the trooper in the sidecar was covering him with the machine gun.

"Verdammt!" Blake cried out again. *"Die scheiß Tommys haben mich am Arsch!"*

"Lass mich sehen," the soldier said, kneeling at his side and leaning in. *Let me see.*

"Siehst du?" Blake responded. *See?* He grabbed the man's collar with one hand and, with the other, slipped his commando knife up into the startled man's chin. The man died instantly and soundlessly.

Propping his victim's head upright with the blade, he blocked the view of the other soldier while he reached over and slipped the German's Luger from its holster. Using the dead man's body as cover, he sat up and squeezed off two shots at the machine gunner's head, dropping him instantly. The entire exchange took less than twenty seconds.

Blake wasted no time getting to his feet and searching the two dead troopers for anything useful before mounting the bike and setting off for the crash site. Even under the control of Mehta's serum, the real

Blake felt something hard to describe deep inside.

Killing men here felt like coming home.

Mortified, Nellie gasped when she saw the vehicle approaching, hastily pulling down her skirts and redoubling her efforts to kick off the bloomers that clung around her feet. She smoothed her dress down, then remembered her top, untying it from around her waist and pulling it back on. While she fumbled to button up with one hand, she waved down the mechanical transport with the other.

It seemed to be some kind of chunky, mechanized bicycle or velocipede—something like Merlin's floating hoverbike, only noisier, ground-locked, and not nearly as streamlined. It trailed smoke and carried a wheeled passenger compartment alongside. The road engine pulled up, shut off, and its driver dismounted.

He wore a drab cotton shirt and cap, in an unfamiliar military style, with imposing goggles and a scarf that covered his face, lending him a worrisome air, as of a bandit or highwayman. Perhaps she should have hidden instead.

Then again, the man had two canteens of water slung over his shoulder. She eyed them hopefully, realizing how dry her throat had become.

"Oh, sir," she began as the man dismounted. "I'm so glad to see you. There's been a dreadful crash—" She stopped as he strode up to her, lifting his goggles and removing the scarf. With a shock, she saw it was Blake. She backed away from him, stumbling.

"You need to help me find Mehta," he said flatly.

"I certainly will not!"

"Suit yourself," he shot back. "You're coming back with me all the same." Seizing her arm before she could run, he tossed her over one shoulder as a butcher might tote a side of beef, nimbly crouching down to pick up her bloomers before carting his prize back to the vehicle just like some Roman bravo in *The Rape of the Sabine Women*. While she yelped in protest, he planted her in the passenger seat.

To add insult to injury, he proceeded to tear her bloomers into strips, using them to first tie up her wrists, and then her arms and torso, securing her to the seat with a loop in the back for good measure. At this final indignity, Nellie hurled several colorful curses. He remained unmoved.

"Do I need to tie your ankles, as well?"

She stopped her thrashing. "No."

With an unexpectedly gallant touch, he produced a pair of goggles and cap, and gently fitted them on her face before taking his seat and restarting the engine. Nellie remained still as the vehicle set off. Not because he had won her submission—quite the opposite. She knew something he did not.

Quietly and unobtrusively, she raised her bound hands

to her chest. The restraint across her torso restricted her movement, but not enough to prevent her plans. If she contorted her wrists slightly, she could undo first one, then a second button. She peered sidelong at Blake. His goggled eyes were preoccupied with searching the landscape.

All the better.

Slipping two fingers past the unbuttoned fabric of her dress into her chemise, she plucked out a white disk about the size of a quarter and palmed it.

"Sgt. Blake?" she called out as demurely as she could manage and still be heard over the roar of the engine.

"What?" he responded brusquely.

"I'm terribly thirsty." *True enough.* "Do you have any water?" Without turning he unslung one of the canteens and unscrewed the cap. Keeping one hand on the handlebars, he handed it back to her, still keeping his eyes straight ahead.

"I'm sorry, please, I can't quite reach," Nellie said as piteously as possible. Heaving an impatient sigh, he pulled to a stop and turned to face her. She looked up at him, playing her eyes like an instrument, keeping her hands close to her chest, as though the restraint binding her upper body simply couldn't allow her to raise them any higher.

"Here," he said gruffly, holding it close to her lips. Nellie leaned forward and let him pour from the canteen, drinking the water eagerly until she had her fill.

"Had enough?" he asked.

"Yes, thank you." She smiled—and then clamped her bound hands on his wrist. Jerking his arm free from her grasp, Blake stared at the small white disk now stuck to his skin.

"What the devil?" He tried tearing it off, but whatever material the tablet was made of, it was already dissolving into his skin. Blake stiffened as if poisoned, eyes rolling back in his head. As limp as a dead fish, he slid off the seat and hit the ground.

"Blake!" Nellie cried, trying to twist out of her restraints in earnest. "Are you alright?" She pulled at the strip tethering her to the sidecar, and bit the knots at her wrists. Before she could free herself, Blake got to his feet, a knife in one hand.

"Blake...?" Nellie said uncertainly.

"I owe you for that."

Nellie's heart skipped a beat as he approached the sidecar, taking her bound wrists in one hand. Before she could beg for her life, he cut her ties with a single clean slice.

Nellie beamed. "Oh, Blake, you're back!"

"Yes I am," he replied. "And next time I see Mehta, this knife is going right into his guts." He quickly finished cutting her free. "Good trick, slipping me that little wafer. How did you manage to get the antidote?"

"The ship gave it to us." Nellie replied. "It took some doing, but it finally cooked up a counteractive agent. We were just about to administer it to you aboard the

Vanuatu when…" Her voice trailed off.

"When the ship was destroyed." Blake finished.

"Do you think the others were saved as well?"

Blake had no answer.

Sitting up, Harcourt steadied his hat. The egg-shaped capsule peeled away until it was just a bowl of the endlessly malleable ship-stuff. The bowl gently rocked him back and forth—because it was now a boat, and he was bobbing in the ocean.

Terror seized him as he scanned the dark water. He knew all too well what could be lurking below.

"Oh dear. Oh no, no, no," he whimpered, wishing more than anything for a bottle of his patented nerve elixir.

Mehta emerged from his capsule, holding up a hand to shade his eyes from the desert sun as he stepped out onto the stony ground, the egg dissolving behind him. He regarded his audience—a column of tanks and scores of German infantryman, all with weapons trained on him. The lines of tanks stretched back for a considerable distance.

It was the vanguard of an army.

Mehta lay a hand over his slim medical satchel and smiled at the swastikas and iron crosses.

I can work with this.

34

Northeast of Point 44, Tel el Aqqaqir, Egypt
Second Battle of El Alamein
November 2, 1942, 0359 hours
6.75 hours before the Event

The barrage began five minutes past 0100 hours, just as the moon rose. Though the waning lunar sliver provided no light to speak of, the constant drumming rain of twenty-five-pounder shells and the accompanying explosions lit up the night sky.

Every night now, thought *Oberleutnant* Behrendt. The artillery barrages and the aerial bombings never stopped.

This night was exceptionally cold. When he blew on his hands to warm them, Behrendt could see his own misty breath. Outside, each pounding roar shattered the silence of the night, shaking the earth beneath the twenty-three-tonne bulk of their Panzer III.

He looked down at their gunner, Siegmund. The back

of the man's sandy-haired head rested against the cold steel wall of the turret. After ten solid days of fighting, it no longer amazed Behrendt how easy it was for any of his crew to snatch a few minutes of sleep inside a tank, even through the *Sturm und Drang* of an incoming barrage.

Rest now while you can, he thought. The gunner would be busy enough before the sun rose.

Their current position, Aqqaqir Ridge, was barely worthy of the name. Like most of the features on the battle maps of the region, it scarcely rose above the relentless flatness so prevalent in the desert. The only trace of any identifying mark was the crumbled stones of an ancient well, dried up since Roman times.

For three hours he watched the exchange of fire. Then increasingly, a new sound caught his ear—not the earth-pounding cannonade of the dueling artillery, but something softer, an eerie keening echoing in the distance, growing inexorably closer. Metzinger, the crew's ammo loader, looked up with a puzzled frown.

"Is that screeching racket what I think it is?"

Behrendt nodded. That hair-raising noise was unmistakable—the skirling of bagpipes. The 51st Highlander infantry was advancing.

"*Genau*," he replied. "The Ladies from Hell are coming round for tea."

If the Scots were moving forward, they wouldn't be alone. The New Zealanders, including a battalion of their dark-skinned tattooed Maori savages, were waiting on their flank, and the Allied armored units wouldn't be far behind. The wedge Monty was driving through their lines was coming point first. Straight at them.

"*Sie da*, wake up Sig," he called down to their loader. "Time to go collect more notches on our barrel." Orders to the line had been very specific. To preserve their precious ammo, they would not open fire until the Brit armor units were between eight and twelve hundred meters away.

"SWORD ONE, SWORD TWO, this is Sword Leader," Behrendt said into his microphone, calling out to the only other tanks left in their squadron. "Here they come. Hold your fire until my signal."

0709 hours
Approximately 3.5 hours before the Event

The rising morning heat brought the familiar smell of hot engine oil and sweat. In the front of the claustrophobic interior, their loader worked his usual double time, readying the heavy shells with every shot of the big gun, and serving the ammo to the machine guns.

It was a dangerous job, the recoil slamming back within inches of his face each time. The empty shell holder soon overflowed, and the hot casings tumbled to the floor, making a clanking racket and crowding the deck as they rolled around like discarded wine bottles at a drunken party.

Behrendt spoke rapidly into his microphone, steering his men toward their targets.

"Noch einmal!" he called out. The loader rushed to slam another shell into the breech, and they fired again. This time the armor-piercing round punched through its target and a plume of high-octane petrol burst up in the morning air. Smoke and flame poured out from the hatches, and the Tommies inside leapt out, rolling in the hot sand to put out their burning clothes. That made them easy targets for their machine guns.

Can't afford to have pity—can't be soft, Behrendt told himself as he watched men die. He wiped his brow with the back of his hand and cranked open the cupola's hatch for a better look at the battlefield. Outside felt like a filthy, murky oven. Under the vaguely copper-colored sky, reddish explosions and streams of tracer bullets cut through thick clouds of dust obscuring the sight of dozens of enemy tanks and armored cars strewn about as far as he could see, wrecked or burning. One tank lay a mere twenty meters away, hit with such force it had been bowled over onto its side.

Another Crusader emerged from the smoke and dust. A direct hit had set it on fire. Although only dead and dying men could still be inside, it continued to lumber toward them like a Viking funeral, some dead man's foot still on the accelerator. He watched the ghost tank with morbid fascination, a funeral pyre propelling itself across the hellish landscape.

A shell exploded uncomfortably near, sending white-hot scraps of shrapnel screaming past him and snapping him out of his daydream. More tanks were coming.

Many more.

0959 hours
Forty-five minutes before the Event

"*Kommandant*, this is Sword Leader," Behrendt reported in to his division commander. "We are observing an unidentified tank design in the British advance. They appear to be well armored, and are armed with a large-bore gun, I estimate seventy-five-millimeter." *Better than ours*, he thought. "They are moving very fast."

"*We read you, Sword Leader. Continue to engage from your current position.*"

"*Jawohl*, Sword out."

Yet another pair of British fighter planes buzzed overhead, chasing a fleeing Stuka. The *Oberleutnant* shook his head. The ground was shaking worse than before. Though their field guns and the 88s were still eliminating tank after tank, there were simply too many.

The tide of British tanks was coming inexorably closer, close enough to count the rivets on their armor plating. Both sides were firing at point-blank range now.

And then they were upon the line.

Just down-ridge from their tank, the closest German 88 gun opened fire on a charging Crusader from only a handful of meters away. The blast tore the top half of the tank clean off, nearly flipping the vehicle back end over end. It was their last shot. The next Brit tank roared up, driving straight for them, crushing the gunpit and the gunners alike beneath its grinding treads.

"Feuer! Feuer!" Behrendt bellowed. Siegmund slammed on the foot pedal to fire, and the whole turret shook. Smoke from the discharged round and the scent of cordite fumes swirled in the Panzer's interior. Their shot caught the rearing enemy tank in its underbelly, the backblast sending the upper hatch flying off in a burst of roaring flame.

All around them, the Tommies overran the anti-tank defensive line, targeting each individual field gun and using their tanks like battering rams to punch through, annihilating the positions. Behrendt watched in horror as below them the nearest squad of German infantrymen were buried alive in their slit trenches. He heard the screams of one soldier as the tank treads decapitated him.

Those English pigs, he fumed. *Damn all those fucking English straight to Hell.*

Everywhere he looked, the smoking battlefield was awash in burning armor, broken guns, the dead, and the dying. The enemy had overrun the German anti-tank line. The dam had broken, and still more waves of tanks, heavy armored cars, and infantry were coming.

Behrendt did a quick count of the sea of glittering metal shapes. There were hundreds. By his estimate, they were outnumbered eight-to-one.

1037 hours
Seven minutes before the Event

"Sir! Message from HQ!" Schildhauer, their wireless operator, called out.

"All mobile units in Twenty-First and Fifteenth Panzers, *Littorio* and *Ariete* Armored Divisions prepare to launch immediate counter-attack at Tel el Aqqaqir." His voice sounded raw.

Oberleutnant Behrendt rubbed his temples, exhaled. The other crewmen in the turret looked up at him with haunted eyes. The aerial bombings were almost constant. Just a few hundred meters ahead of the remains of their tattered defense line, screened behind the immense clouds of smoke and dust, the British were digging in with field guns and artillery of their own.

No one spoke, but the men in the cramped tank's

tomb-like interior were all thinking the same thing. The next order from German HQ would launch them and the rest of the surviving Axis tanks on their own Charge of the Light Brigade.

November 2, 1942, 1044 hours
The Event

"SWORD ONE, SWORD TWO, this is Sword Leader. Move out." The *Oberleutnant* kept his voice steady with a coolness he didn't feel as he spoke into the microphone. Looking down he added, "Driver, advance."

The Panzers left their hull-down positions and exposed themselves, climbing over the low ridge to meet their fate, no cover but the haze of smoke and dust. Behrendt stood high in the cupola, binoculars out as he scanned the tactical situation. All across the line, the German and Italian tanks advanced over the Rahman track. He counted about forty tanks from their division alongside them. South of them, perhaps another thirty of the 15th Panzers, and further south still, he guessed slightly less than twenty of *Littorio* and *Ariete*'s outgunned Italian tanks.

They crossed a wasteland of flamed-out wreckage and broken scraps of metal. Dead and dying soldiers littered the ground, flies eagerly descending upon their wounds and drying blood. The tanks passed the wounded, unable to help. They were not yet within the range where their guns would be effective, but the enemy was already firing.

Shells and tracers zipped by on all sides, but perversely, Behrendt could not bring himself to retreat down into the tank. He looked over at the commander of Sword 1, driving to the side and just behind them. The man was riding high in his turret, as well, tossing him a reckless grin and a jaunty salute that made Behrendt smile in spite of himself. A whistling noise streaked past and Sword 1's turret vanished with a roar of explosive flame and smoke.

Behrendt cringed involuntarily at the wave of heat singing his cheek and eyebrows as bits of flying metal clattered off the upraised hatch behind him. His ears rang and his vision lost focus, his head spinning.

The battle language in his earphones faded away, replaced by a strange music, like a chorus of Valkyries singing some wordless aria, or perhaps the seductive call of the Lorelei's siren song. Some garbled chatter came back over the radio, fragmentary and hard to hear:

"—I am—"

"—large energized scre—"

"—ome kind of high in—"

"—illumina…lightning—"

"Sword Two, pull back!"

Impossibly, he was hearing the sound of his own voice. The realization stunned him. Another voice responded. Behrendt clasped the earphones and strived to hear more.

"*It's beautiful!*"

"*Can you see it?*"

Deep in the metal walls of the tank, a low, resonant thrumming sound began, sending a tingling through Behrendt's breastbone. He stared up in wonder. The haze all around them was swirling in a most peculiar fashion, indescribable and surreal. Everything seemed suffused with an angelic glow.

Was this death?

A chance breeze stirred, pulling the haze away like the flourish of a magician's cloak. To Behrendt's left, the commander of Sword 2 tried to get his attention, pointing at something dead ahead—a heavenly curtain of pure light, stretching across their line of sight and rising up into where the murky furnace air turned blue and pure again.

"*Can you see it?*" Sword 2's voice asked over the wireless. "*It's beautiful!*" The hairs prickled on the back of Behrendt's neck, even as he found himself calling out to the commander on the other end.

"Sword Two, pull back!"

Behrendt quickly took up the microphone around his neck and called for the driver to halt, then reported in.

"HQ, this is Sword Leader," he said. "I am seeing a large energized screen running roughly one-zero-zero meters between the enemy line and the Rahman track..." He struggled to find the words to describe what he was seeing. "It is some kind of high intensity illumination... like a lightning-field..."

Even as he spoke, the Panzer on his left continued forward, driving straight into the curtain of pulsating light. Berhrendt's eyes widened.

"Sword Two! Sword Two! Respond!"

A deafening drone came from above. He looked up to see a dogfight raging overhead. Trailing smoke, a stricken Messerschmitt was trying to elude the guns of the Spitfire on his tail. The German fighter streaked across Behrendt's line of vision—and straight into a second curtain of light, roughly opposite the first. It vanished into the brightness without a sound.

The pursuing Spitfire pilot panicked, pulling up sharply to avoid the curtain. He cut a tight parabola, but failed to totally clear it, just skimming its surface. Everywhere the wing touched the energized wall, it was sheared off as thoroughly and precisely as if the plane had skimmed a slit of the sun. The fighter tumbled crazily in the air and corkscrewed down toward them.

With another slam of the hatch, Behrendt ducked back inside and crouched for cover.

"Brace yourselves!"

A moment later, the booming impact of the crashing warplane violently rocked the entire tank. The shock threw the men against the unyielding metal walls. Fiery light streamed through the glass of the vehicle's apertures, then faded away.

All was quiet.

"Everyone alright?" Behrendt asked quietly. One by one, the rest of the crew checked in. There was no noise from outside. No roar of engines, no gunfire, no more explosions. The men waited, unsure of what to do now. The tank commander pulled off his glove and gently placed the back of his hand against the hatch. No excessive heat. Probably safe to open it.

Someone tapped on the hatch from outside, startling them. A sharp rap with something small, then another. A further series of taps followed. Behrendt held a finger to his lips to silence the others in the turret, then spoke softly to the wireless operator, keeping his voice down so their visitor outside would not be able to hear.

"Schildhauer, is that Morse code? What is he saying?" They all waited with bated breath while the tapping continued. Finally Schildhauer responded.

"It's nonsense, sir."

Behrendt frowned, drew his Luger, and slowly opened the hatch.

The first thing he noticed was the sun. Though they had been conscious the entire time, it had leapt across the sky in the span of a few seconds. Then Behrendt locked eyes with their phantom tapper—a gray-black bird the size of a pigeon, but slimmer and harder-looking. As the hatch opened, the bird stopped and froze into position, its bill pointed skyward at a forty-five-degree angle.

A good twenty or so others just like it had billeted themselves on the big gun, all ranked in perfect coordination to give the impression the cannon was nothing more than an odd outcrop of crumbling rock. They looked back at Behrendt with intelligent, unblinking eyes. With a considerable effort, he reached over to touch the closest one.

Twenty eyes swiveled, and then, simultaneously they took to the air.

The *Oberleutnant* watched them, and then picked up his binoculars for a look around. The burnt wreckage of the downed Spitfire was strewn all about, still smoldering, but the air was remarkably clear again. Sword 2 was nowhere to be found, nor was the strange wall of energy that had encircled them all.

Due east, where the British tanks and guns had been dug in just a few moments ago, he saw only rocks and tufts of camel grass, all the way to the horizon. He turned to the south. In the distance, he could see other surviving tanks of the 21st Panzers on the grisly, smoldering battlefield, but past them there was no sign of the 15th Panzers or the Italians.

A strange trumpeting noise came from behind him.

He looked back at the crumbling stone ruin of the ancient well... but there was no ruin anymore. It was now in excellent condition, with smooth masonry, a wooden well sweep, and a hefty leather bucket. Groves of palms stood near it, as well a group of large canopy tents. A few dozen men in desert robes stood around, staring at him.

The loud trumpeting sounded again, and suddenly a huge shape came roaring up from the corner of his eye. The elephant was outfitted for war, with a studded armor headdress and a carriage atop its back carrying a trio of spearmen. Behrendt stared in unbelief, raising his pistol.

Too late, as the great charging beast caught him on its sharpened tusk and flung the impaled German out of the tank. He hit the ground like a wet bundle of rags, still staring at the unbelievable scene as the life bled out of him onto the hot sand.

35

The temple of Sobek-Ra, Shedyet, Egypt
Seven days after the Event

Amber let out an involuntary scream.

The shattered obsidian fragments of the dead rover skittered across the hard, white stone floor of the temple courtyard. She and Cam looked at each other in horror.

"Amber, what does it mean?" Cam asked in a hushed voice.

Amber shook her head, unable to answer.

"The sphere and the ship are one, are they not?" he continued, visibly shaken. "So if the sphere is gone…"

Amber's eyes burned—she quickly wiped away the tears with the back of her hand.

"Cam, just give me a minute, please," she finally said. "I need… I just need to think."

"But, what will we—"

"*Damn* it, Cam!" she shouted. "I don't know! Please, just let me think!"

Ignoring his hurt expression, Amber ran through the courtyard, finally coming to a halt at one of the big pillars—its solidity offered a measure of comfort. She put her back to it, slowly sinking down to the floor again, fighting to keep from crying.

She had to think.

She couldn't imagine the *Vanuatu* gone, just like that—but what else could have happened? As she sat there, the Ship's voice ran through her head again...

"The Vanuatu *is under attack. There is an incom—"*

How was this possible? Who would be attacking the ship? Who *could* attack it? She sifted through possibilities, grasping for any possible options.

The message had broken off mid-sentence, but that just might have meant their connection had been knocked out. Or, maybe the drone's power was interrupted, and that's why it broke down. For all they knew, the Ship could crank them out by the dozens.

Less pleasant possibilities suggested themselves.

That final clipped bit of the message. *"Incom—"* Incoming? An incoming missile? Could the entire ship have been destroyed in an explosion? Suddenly all she could think about was Blake, Nellie, and Harcourt, wondering if she'd ever see them again. Once again she felt the weight of responsibility for their mission. If the

Vanuatu was truly gone, what options did they have left?

Finally she picked herself up and returned to where the others sat in silence, putting a hand on Cam's shoulder by way of apology. He bristled at her touch, but then placed a hand over hers and squeezed it.

Kha-Hotep stood. "Lady Amber, my vessel is nearby," he said. "We should take it and leave before the temple survivors return. We can sail until we find a safe refuge, wherever that may be."

Cam shook his head. "A refuge will do us no good, Captain," he said. "We must continue with our mission, or the world is doomed."

"You're both right," Amber said. "We need to leave now and go to where the *Vanuatu* was headed. We'll find the ship, or we'll find whatever Mehta was looking for. Either way, it's our best chance." She didn't add that it was the only option she could think of, and she couldn't tell Cam her strongest reason to keep heading down the Nile—one she carried so deep inside she was barely aware of it herself.

The small but insistent voice in her head.

Come find me, Amber…

Kha-Hotep's river barge, the *Star of the Dawn*, lay berthed just where the rover had spotted it, a few minutes' walk through gardens and stands of palm trees. A canal ran from the great lake and headed due east, and here it widened into a lagoon where the barge lay tied up along with a pair of small fishing boats made from bundles of reeds.

Upon boarding Kha-Hotep vanished belowdecks. His curses echoed up from the cabin, increasing in volume as he reappeared up top.

"They've taken everything, those jackal-spawn!" He slammed his hand against the frame. "A fortune! Two thousand gold *deben* worth of ivory and cheetah pelts! Set visit foul torments upon them! May they all go swiftly to the Land of the Dead, and Lord Osiris feed their hearts to the devourer!"

"I'm sorry about your cargo, Captain," Amber said, "but if we don't get moving, it won't matter much if your boat is packed to the brim with gold."

Kha-Hotep nodded, unhappy but resigned.

"You speak the truth. Very well, let us go."

They cast off and set sail down the canal.

The canal's current was gentle, almost nonexistent, but they still had to work against it all the way. The sun had dropped close to the horizon by the time the boat reached the great river. There they waited at anchor while Cam left the boat to scout the area. Kha-Hotep kept watch at the bow with Amber and Leila, scanning the riverbank for the Celt's return. At last he re-emerged from behind the palms and loped down to the barge.

"You were right," he said to the captain. "The patrol boat that captured you is still stalking up and down the river."

"How close are they?"

"They look to be three bowshots away, heading upriver now."

Kha-Hotep nodded. "To travel the river after dark is never wise, but our only chance is to slip downriver under cover of night, keep going as far as we can, and pray to all our gods they don't spot us again."

Once the sun dropped down beneath the red hump of the western desert, they slipped out of the canal and onto the Nile. They went cautiously, slowly skirting the water's edge in the increasing darkness, occasionally pushing against the riverbank with their oars, like a blind man tapping his cane down a path.

The water was inky black, so the only distinction between the earthen bank and the night sky above it was a faint dusting of stars. The sole source of light came from the lines of oil lamps on the Arsinoite warship, floating upriver of them.

Seated in the stern with her arms around her knees and her back against the little cabin of the barge, Leila kept a careful eye on the imposing vessel. As she watched, its light grew fainter with every passing minute—from lamplight gleam, to firefly, to ember, to distant twinkling star—until at last it winked out, swallowed by the growing distance. Only then did she let out a sigh of relief.

"We've passed it," she called, keeping her voice low.

After another hour or so, Kha-Hotep halted their progress and they weighed anchor for the night.

"Hey, you okay back here?"

With a slight start, Leila looked up to see Amber standing above her, and nodded with a smile. "Yes, I think I just needed some quiet time to process it all."

"I totally get it." Amber sat down next to her. "Do you want me to take the next watch? Captain Kha-Hotep says he's still worried about that warship."

"I'll stay," Leila replied. "I'm way too wired to sleep."

"You sure?"

"Absolutely. I'm happy for the chance to do something to pitch in, you know?"

"I'll tell them," Amber said. "You want me to stay here with you, and help keep an eye out?"

Leila shook her head. "It's okay." She appreciated the offer, but she wasn't ready to give up her solitude quite yet. "I could still use a little more alone time."

"Well, if you really don't mind," Amber said with obvious relief. "I'm wiped. Anyway, just for another hour or so. Kha-Hotep says until those two stars in the

Big Dipper go from there—" she pointed, "to there. We'll make a spot for you to sleep up front."

"Thanks," Leila replied. "I won't stay up too late."

Amber gave her a little wave and went back around to the front of the barge. Leila leaned her head back against the cabin, soaking up her privacy. She stayed there for the hour she'd promised, and then just a bit longer to be safe. There was still no sign of the warship, and the only sounds were the tiny frogs and crickets— and the creatures below and above the water that preyed on both.

On a normal night, she would have waited along with everyone else for the cry of the muezzin summoning all for the evening's final prayer. But now, sitting out in the night air by herself, she decided to make the call on her own.

Only a week ago, Leila could not have imagined spending a night unchaperoned, let alone in the company of foreign unbelievers. In the face of all that had occurred, however, it didn't seem important anymore.

There was a comfort in feeling the river beneath her. Her uncle owned a *felucca* and the gentle rocking of the waters was a familiar friend. She was also used to sleeping under the stars—on the hottest nights in Cairo her family often slept on the rooftop.

Morning approached, the star-flecked cobalt of the sky softening to a pale sapphire. Rolling over on her mat of rushes, Leila rested her head on one arm and watched her new companions sleep. Amber lay closest to her, with Cam and Kha-Hotep closer to the bow.

She felt strangely safe.

Suddenly Kha-Hotep sat up and stretched his arms with a yawn, causing Leila to stifle a startled shriek. Turning at the sound, the captain smiled in embarrassment, touching a hand to his eyes, and then his heart, in a graceful gesture of apology.

"Ii-ti em hotep, Nebet-i," he murmured, bowing his head.

Leila blushed and sat up, waving her hand. *"La, 'ana asif,"* she said, then tried again. "No, no, I'm sorry."

She stopped, realizing neither Arabic nor English would help, and just gave him a shy smile. Even as she did, part of her was mortified. Her mother and aunts would never approve of her talking to a foreign man like this.

No, not foreign.

She couldn't deny he was more truly Egyptian than she was. She also couldn't deny how striking he looked in his ancient garb—which seemed so natural on him, she'd slowly stopped thinking of it as a costume. Kha-Hotep busied himself with the boat, weighing the anchor and pushing them off the bank into the river again, quietly, so not to wake the others.

"Nebet-i Leila," he said softly, and pointed up at

a point in the sky. *"Siu-Tuait."* Then he pointed to the deck of the barge. *"Siu-Tuait."* He pointed back and forth between the two. *"Siu-Tuait. Siu-Tuait."* He raised an eyebrow hopefully.

Leila was baffled until she realized what he was pointing to in the sky—the planet Venus. Her eyes lit up.

"Oh! The *Star of the Dawn*—your ship's name, yes! *Siu-Tuait!*"

He grinned and nodded. Another realization hit her. *The dawn!*

It was time for her morning prayers. She quickly got up and excused herself.

Leila had just begun the second round of prostration in her morning prayers when a heavy *thump* rocked the boat. She steadied herself, tamping down an instant of panic. Had they hit a rock, or run aground on a sandbar?

No, the boat was still moving freely, so that couldn't be it. She waited for a few moments longer, then returned to her *salah.*

The deck pitched violently as a great humped shape rose up in an explosion of water and smashed down on the barge's timbers directly in front of her. Screaming, Leila frantically scrabbled for purchase on the heaving deck to keep from being swept toward the outstretched mouth. Then it released its hold and the boat flipped back up again.

Twisting, she scrambled to her hands and knees, crawling alongside the cabin. The strip of deck was narrower there, the footing more treacherous, but she pulled herself up and ran to the foredeck where Kha-Hotep, Amber, and Cam were stumbling to their feet as well.

"*Faras!*" she screamed, too rattled to recall the English word. "*Faras-El-Nahr!*"

Another impact slammed the barge from the starboard side, dumping everyone to the deck and nearly capsizing them. Their bodies struck hard, slamming against the bulwarks and each other. Then the deck rocked back again, and the culprit emerged from the river—a massive hippopotamus, solid as a truck and aggressively intent on defending its territory.

Leila watched in horror as the bull clambered over the side and planted one huge web-toed foot on the deck, and then another, trying to pull the rest of its lumbering girth up as well. The barge's timbers groaned beneath the sheer weight of the onslaught, threatening to swamp the entire barge—or snap it in half.

Improbable jaws, filled with thick, stake-like yellow tusks, yawned open in a challenging bellow as it scrambled on the uneven surface, trying to reach its closest target—Kha-Hotep. The Egyptian fought to secure his own footing, bringing up an oar and jabbing the long timber like a spear, trying to aim for the hippo's eyes.

* * *

Amber rolled on the wildly pitching deck, trying without success to steady herself long enough to draw her crossbow. Cam managed to unsheathe his blade, but couldn't get footing on the bucking deck, which threatened to break apart at the seams.

"En joue!" A loud voice echoed across the river, then rang out a second time. *"Feu!"*

A rapid drumroll of thunder erupted—a fusillade, hammering the air all around them. The hippo roared like an enraged ox, its mouth stretched wide as a dozen fresh red wounds burst across its wide flanks. It shuddered and toppled over, falling back into the river with a great splash.

The captain and passengers of the *Star of the Dawn* turned toward the riverbank. A line of a dozen soldiers stood on the rise, their slender, long-barreled muskets still smoking. Each was uniformed in plumed helmet and smart blue jacket, with white sash and white trousers. Their commanding officer—a lean, tall man with long sideburns on his aquiline face—stood to one side, his long-tailed, red-jacketed uniform completed by gold epaulets, a silver gorget around his neck, and a black bicorn hat.

He raised his saber.

"Deuxième ligne, présentez armes!" Amber's implant translated. *Second line, present arms!* In perfect order, the

soldiers withdrew their spent muskets and took a step back. A second line of soldiers marched up and took their place, training their weapons on the crew of the barge.

Their commander stepped forward. *"Blanc, noir, roux, et brun—quel curieux panier de poissons nous avons attrapé ce matin…"* he said, clicking his tongue. *White, black, red, and brown—what a curious basket of fish we've caught this morning!* Then he addressed them directly.

"Êtes-vous Turcs? Anglais? Pourrions-nous peut-être espérer que vous parlez français?" *Might we possibly hold out hope that you speak French?*

Taking a step forward, Amber smiled. *"Bonjour!"* she said, waving. *"Nous ne sommes pas anglais. Je suis américaine."*

Pleasantly astounded, the officer raised his eyebrow, then with a slight smile of his own, doffed his hat.

"Salutations! Bienvenue à La Nouvelle-Memphis!"

36

German Afrika Korps Encampment
Between Alam el Halfa and El Alamein, Egypt
Seven days after the Event

Nothing distinguished the command tent from any of the others, which was as he preferred it. Inside, the German officer in jacket and breeches sat writing on a simple foldout table. A stocky figure, just turned fifty, he was good-looking in a serious, stalwart sort of way, his face lined with heavy responsibility.

On the table next to him lay an Afrika Korps officer's cap with a pair of sand goggles pushed back over the brim. His throat was bandaged from desert sores, though he suffered other less-obvious maladies—violent headaches, chronic stomach pains, nervous exhaustion. Above the bandages he wore a checkered scarf, a stern black Knight's Cross pinned beneath it. The braid of a general hung on his shoulder.

Field Marshal Erwin Rommel never neglected writing to his wife.

Dearest Lu,

I cannot imagine how this letter is to reach you, but neither can I find it in me to stop writing to you, no matter our circumstance. It has been one week since the bizarre event that interrupted the very heavy fighting at El Alamein, and we are no closer to finding an answer. On the contrary, questions continue to mount.

We appear to have been snatched from the battlefield—though truly, I should say our battlefield has been snatched along with us and dropped... somewhere. I can only suspect this was the work of some enemy Wunderwaffe, some experimental super-weapon. I have no better explanation than that.

Nonetheless, we are currently well, and morale is good enough among the men. There has been no sign of the enemy whatsoever, and we are taking advantage of that happy fact to recover from our most recent ten days of battle. We are garrisoned in a native village that has mysteriously sprung up near us. The people are not Arabs, and speak some language we cannot guess, though they have strong Semitic racial features. Perhaps they are some lost Berber tribe.

I am happy in my own conscience that we have fully done our duty to the Fatherland and will trust in God to see that you receive this letter somehow, and likewise, my men and I will discover how to return home ourselves, so that you and I may be reunited soon.

All my love to you and our son,

He paused, wanting to say something more about the local elephants, but his thoughts were interrupted by the arrival of soldiers outside. One stepped into the tent, seeking permission to enter.

"Come!"

A pair of *Panzergrenadiers* entered, escorting a man wearing an unfamiliar and immaculate black uniform. Rommel studied him with interest. He was negro, or perhaps mulatto, although with strong cheekbones and a rather oriental cast to his oddly-glittering eyes. His silver hair was straight, not negroid, and close-cropped in a military cut. He seemed unperturbed to be held in custody.

The ranking soldier saluted.

"*Herr General*, this man was captured nearby. He appears to be a survivor from the unidentified downed aircraft we spotted to the east."

"By no means," the stranger corrected the soldier in flawless German. "I was not captured. In fact, quite the opposite. I came specifically to see you, Field Marshal."

"And have you provided your name, rank, and serial number?" Rommel asked.

The man smiled and offered a quick salute and bow of his head. "My name is János Mehta. No rank or serial number. I'm not a soldier. I'm here to help you."

Rommel waved to the field chair in front of the little table. "Please, sit."

Mehta took a seat. The general remained impassive, observing his guest carefully. Finally, the man broke the silence.

"Field Marshal, as I said, I—"

"I find your name intriguing, *Herr* Mehta. And your appearance."

"Yes, I imagine you have a great deal many questions," the man replied. "I certainly would, in your place."

"Just so. I am impressed, *Herr* Mehta. Your grasp of our language is very good, but you'll forgive me if I don't believe you are German. Unless… one of your parents—or a grandparent, perhaps?"

"No, General. To be honest, I believe I do have some German ancestry, if one traces back far enough, but I was born in Eastern Kalimantan."

"Kalimantan? In the Netherlands East-Indies? Extraordinary. The area is currently under Japanese occupation, no?"

"I assure you, that is the least interesting thing I am about to tell you."

Rommel cocked his head slightly to one side. "Perhaps you can start by explaining your presence here, please."

"Of course, Field Marshal. It all begins with something called the *Brahmastra* project."

"The... *Brahmastra* project, you say?"

Mehta nodded. "That is what all this is about. It's what created this chaotic situation in which we all find ourselves."

Rommel leaned in. Now they were getting somewhere. Mehta's expression became thoughtful.

"Let me see... before I explain all that, I suppose I should start with my medical equipment."

Rommel raised an eyebrow. "What kind of medical equipment would that be?"

The first German soldier stepped forward and presented Mehta's shoulder satchel.

"Sir, he was carrying this case. With your permission?" Rommel nodded. The *Panzergrenadier* set it on the table and opened it up, revealing a sinister-looking pistol-shaped hypodermic and a brace of ampules, along with several other strange devices, then stepped back again. This time Mehta leaned in, reaching forward.

"*Herr* General, now, if you will just allow me—"

Rommel raised a hand. "No, that will not be necessary. Sit back, please."

The soldiers tensed behind him. Mehta froze, then after an awkward pause, slowly brought his hand back. He wore a look of contrition.

"Ah. My apologies if that appeared a bit sudden, *Herr* General. Please let me explain. I am a doctor. I can show you—"

"I have no interest in that," Rommel replied firmly. "I will ask you not to reach for anything on the table again. If you do, my men will be obliged to shoot you."

The slightest flicker of displeasure crossed Mehta's face, quickly replaced by the meekest of smiles. "Of course. Absolutely."

The field marshal kept his expression inscrutable. "So, you were about to tell us about the—what did you call it?—the *Brahmastra* project."

Mehta said nothing, but his amiable facade slowly soured. Finally, he sighed.

"You know, *Herr* General, I feel as if I would be doing you a disservice if I didn't start by showing you just one item from my medical case—"

Rommel held up a hand again.

"Stop talking, please. Dr. Mehta, you say you are not a soldier, but that is a uniform, is it not?"

Mehta frowned. "Well, yes, I can see why you'd say that, but let me assure you—"

"No, please don't. I don't know what country you serve, Dr. Mehta, but whoever it is, I have the distinct impression you are either some sort of Bolshevik political commissar, or an intelligence officer of their version of the *Gestapo*."

Mehta stared at him for an unduly-long pause, then he laughed out loud, clapping his hands in a mock applause.

"Well, bravo, *Herr* General. Well done. Honestly, my hat is off to you."

The field marshal's expression did not change. "That will be quite enough, Dr. Mehta, or whatever your actual name is." He stood up and addressed his two troopers. "Take this man out at once and shoot him as a spy."

"No, I don't think they will." Mehta's mocking smile melted away, revealing the coldness beneath. He stood up as well. The two *Panzergrenadiers* remained where they were, standing at attention.

Rommel frowned as Mehta locked eyes with him.

"Take him."

The two German soldiers obeyed instantly and seized Rommel, one of them slapping a hand over his mouth to prevent him from calling for help. Mehta wasted no time removing and loading the injector pistol. He stepped over to the struggling general.

"Now let's try this again, from the beginning," he said softly, bringing the pistol to bear on Rommel's neck.

37

The French Colony of New Memphis, Egypt
Eight days after the Event

The officer bowed and introduced himself in French. "Sergeant-Major Durand, Eighty-Eighth Line Infantry Demi-Brigade, Third Battalion, Seventh Fusiliers Company—and your humble servant."

"*Bonjour*, Sergeant-Major." Amber considered attempting a curtsy, but immediately reconsidered. "I'm Amber Richardson—um, civilian."

"*Enchanté*," Durand said. "My commanding officer will have many questions for you, *Mademoiselle* Richardson. I confess that I am quite curious to hear the account of your appearance here myself."

Not good, Amber thought. They didn't have time for an interrogation—not even a friendly one. "We'd love to meet him," she replied carefully, "but we're on an urgent mission. It's a matter of life and death."

A pained expression crossed Durand's face.

"My profound apologies, *Mademoiselle*," he answered. "Circumstances demand that your mission be delayed until our lieutenant is satisfied with your answers. I am obliged to ask you and your companions to turn over your swords and firearms until such time as he orders them returned to you. In the meantime, please be good enough to accompany us to our humble bivouac."

Cam stared around in awe. For the first time since he and Amber had left the veldt for the desert, the line between different shards was clearly delineated.

A mighty city had stood here once, filled with tall limestone and granite statues of gods and kings, crowned hawks and sacred bulls, hieroglyph-covered columns and stelai, temples and palaces, all encompassed by the remnants of once-tall shining white walls.

Before that, acres of fertile farmlands, stands of palm trees, and pastures of cattle dominated the black earth. Even earlier, lush prehistoric jungle-forests held sway, sheltering a huge variety of reptilian animal life under cool green canopies.

A vast patchwork of these eras and more lay spread out before his eyes. The scraps of quirky, segmented architecture made the piecemeal remains of the city resemble a sculpture garden for giants. Fields, pastures, jungles, and pools were liberally scattered throughout. The shards varied in size from an acre or more across to some merely a few paces wide.

Everywhere Egyptians were at work. Some tended the fields. Others were busy rebuilding the city, both newly carved and freshly painted structures, and dusty, rust-colored, millennia-old ruins, the dry bones of the city. A high stockade of cut palm trunks surrounded the shard of jungle. The row of sharpened points looked ominously like teeth raised up to keep out monsters.

"Allow me to be the first to present the French colony of New Memphis," Durand announced with the delight of a proud father. Kha-Hotep's eyes widened in shock.

"Cam, my brother," he whispered as they proceeded, his voice raw with emotion, "this chaos is all that remains of Men-nefer, the great capital city. Its great port, gone. *Inbuhedj*, we called it. Its high walls, gleaming white as my teeth, white as my eyes, all gone. In my time, it had already stood for two thousand years. The warring gods Horus and Set made their peace here, at the center of the world. I thought the city would surely last forever."

Cam nodded silently, suddenly struck by the thought of Camulodunon—his own lost home, and his people, the Trinovantes—washed away by time.

* * *

As a wealthy merchant captain, Kha-Hotep was used to a certain level of respect, but every time their party passed a group of Egyptians, the native peasants and craftsmen bowed low, as though paying due homage to their Pharaoh. He found it disconcerting.

Their armed guard continued to march them through the mélange of different terrains and disjointed pieces of cityscape, heading toward the largest remaining structure, a temple complex. It towered over the center of the lost city. Even though its walls and grounds were truncated and pruned by the edges of its shard, it remained impressive in scope.

"What is that place?" Cam asked, nudging his companion.

"It is the *Hikaptah*," Kha-Hotep answered, "the House of the Soul of Ptah, he who is the creator and sustainer of all things." He continued to proudly point out the sights as they crossed the rim of the central shard and went down a stretch of flagstone pavement between twin rows of crouching alabaster sphinxes leading to the colossal gateway of the *Hikaptah*.

Two tall white buildings flanked the gate itself, the walls inscribed with impressive murals depicting the deeds of the great god Ptah. A line of eight gargantuan statues of the Pharaoh Ramses stood guard in front—when their party marched past, Kha-Hotep's head only reached as high as the ankles on the stone titans.

They continued through the great gate and past

the enormous stone forecourt, up a series of broad steps and through the ornate gilded doors of another magnificent temple. There they entered a vast pillared hall, every column and surface covered in dense, intricate stanzas of hieroglyphs and a thousand vibrant colors illuminating parades of the gods and mythical beasts. High overhead in the walls and ceiling the ancient architects had cunningly worked half-concealed apertures and polished brass to allow the sun to flood the temple with natural light. In addition a vast array of perfumed candles fluttered in sconces.

Kha-Hotep had dealt with too many priests to ever fully trust the gods. Even so, he was shocked at the sight before him. The sacred space had been turned into a banquet hall, arrayed with long tables and benches fit for hungry soldiers. Off in the side chambers, shrines and altars had been converted into ovens for baking bread and fire pits for roasting great hunks of meat on spits.

It was sacrilege.

Durand led them to the far end of the great hall and left them behind with the guards while he strode up to where another French officer, dressed in the same red uniform of the sergeant-major, conferred with a trio of blue-clad subordinates. They stood over a table crowded with sheets of papyrus parchments and hand-drawn maps.

The officer glanced up at the new arrivals. He was black-haired, with a broad face, serious, sunken eyes and bushy muttonchop sideburns, wearing a distinctive bicorn hat.

Amber stared at the man.

Holy shit, that's not Napoleon, is it?

No, she decided, the man was too tall, and she couldn't remember seeing such crazy facial hair in any of Napoleon's portraits—but then again, she was no expert. Maybe it was just the hat.

Saluting smartly, Durand spoke a few quiet words to his superior, who nodded silently and then came over to inspect the newcomers for himself. He looked them over carefully, each in turn, before finally stopping in front of Cam.

"I am Lieutenant Alexandre Maximilien Barthélémy Géroux," the officer said with authority. "I am in charge here. My sergeant-major informs me that you speak passable French. Is this true?"

"Yes, my lord," Cam replied politely.

Géroux chuckled. "I am not a lord, my friend. I am a soldier of the free and egalitarian French Republic. You may address me as sir, or lieutenant."

"Forgive me, sir." Cam's voice was still polite.

"Your accent is strange to me. You are not French, I presume?"

"No, sir. I am Trinovantian, from the eastern shores of Pritan."

"Where is that? In Syria?"

"The Romans called it Britannia, sir."

"Britannia? So you *are* English, then?"

"No sir," Cam replied. "I am a Celt."

"Ah! Now we are getting somewhere! Are you in their employ, or are you their enemy—a rebel perhaps?"

"Neither, sir. They came after my time."

The lieutenant raised an eyebrow. "After your time, were they?" He shot his men a wry smile. "I see, I see... and where, may I ask, did you learn your French?"

Amber spoke up. "It's a little complic—"

"I am speaking to this man, not to you, *Mademoiselle*!" the officer snapped. Cam bristled as Amber flinched. He saw the officer's eyes narrow. Then Géroux bowed his head slightly. "You must forgive me, *Mademoiselle*," he said, his voice softer. "That was most ungallant." He turned back to Cam.

"Now then, *Monsieur*..." He paused. "What is your name?"

"I am Camtargarus Mab Cattus," he replied, keeping his temper for the moment.

"Cam-tar—?"

"Camtargarus, sir, son of Cattus. They call me Cam."

"And so shall we, my good man, so shall we," Géroux said with a slight smile. His soldiers chuckled. "Now, on the matter of your proficiency in French—how do you come to speak it so well?"

"A magical device, sir. I speak all the tongues of men," Cam replied. Amber winced. Now all the Frenchmen laughed outright, except for the lieutenant, who raised his hand for silence and nodded sagely.

"Yes, yes, that would explain it very well. Is it too much to hope you have it on hand for us to see?"

"I do not, sir."

"Ah. No matter." The officer waved a dismissive hand. "And how did you come all the way from *la perfide Albion*, twelve hundred leagues away, to the heart of the Oriental desert... in an Egyptian boat?"

"And sailing northward at that," Sergeant-Major Durand added with a lift of his eyebrow.

"Yes, there is that. Were you on your way back home to England, *Monsieur* Cam? After an extended trip abroad?"

"No, sir. We didn't come to this land by boat. We flew here."

"Flew? In a *Montgolfière* hot air balloon—*un globe aérostatique*?" The laughter increased.

"I don't even know what that is!" Cam's cheeks turned red as the soldiers lost their composure. Even the lieutenant could barely hide his amusement as Cam struggled on, fighting to keep his temper from erupting.

"How then, *Monsieur*?" he said, continuing his interrogation. "Via cannonball, à la Baron Munchausen?"

"We flew in a vessel called the *Vanuatu*, a mighty ship bigger than this great hall, in the shape of a bird, made of magic fluid steel with wings of brilliant light." The French howled. Undeterred, Cam continued to explain in earnest. "It was piloted by a great druid sorcerer, who brought it from the ice-bound southernmost end of the world." Some of the soldiers were holding their sides, and the lieutenant could no longer control his laughter.

Cam stood stiff with fists balled in angry knots.

"I do not boast or speak idly, sir," he said. No one heard him over the raucous laughter.

"I do not boast or speak idly!" he roared.

The hilarity stopped.

"I am Camtargarus Mab Cattus, and I say nothing untrue or in jest!"

Startled by the change, the soldiers brought their muskets to bear on him, aiming at his heart. Leila grabbed Kha-Hotep's arm and buried her head against him. He put a protective arm around her shoulder, his eyes blazing at the soldiers.

Amber tried to keep her tone soft and calming.

"Cam…"

His voice went low and dangerous. "I will fight any man who disputes my word or my honor, be it one or a hundred—and I will fight them *now*." He stared down the lines, locking eyes with every one of the soldiers. They froze, their guns still trained on him, awaiting their leader's order. Unintimidated, Cam turned back to the lieutenant.

"Hear me and know this—we are on a desperate mission to save the world."

Géroux looked at him with a newfound respect and doffed his hat. He spoke carefully.

"You come as a savior," he said, "and indeed, you have saved our spirits from *ennui*. I salute your courage, my brilliant madman. In truth, when I first laid eyes on you, I fully expected that I should be obliged to call for a firing squad to dispatch a most unusual ring of continental spies. But I see I was mistaken. Forgive us."

He waved away the barrels, and the bemused soldiers dutifully lowered their muskets.

Géroux turned to Amber.

"Pray forgive my earlier sharpness, *Mademoiselle*. I took you all for agents of the Turks, or one of the European powers. Now I do not think so, but I must admit, I remain baffled by just *what* you are. May I safely take it that you are attached to this man, and these two are your manservant and handmaid?"

"What? No!" she said. "And no, no, no, we don't have any servants! This is Kha-Hotep, the captain of the barge, and this is Leila Suleiman, from Cairo. We rescued them, and now they're traveling with us. And my name's Amber. Amber Richardson."

Not that you asked.

"*Enchanté, Mademoiselle.* Not to disparage your gallant companion, but I hope you can shed more light on his account."

"He's telling the truth," Amber replied firmly, not trusting Géroux's sudden shift of attitude. "Well, it's not magic, but we really did get here in a kind of airplane. It *does* sort of look like a bird, and it *did* come from the South Pole."

"A *plein-air*..." he struggled with the word. "Airplane? What is that, exactly?"

Oh, right. Amber chose her words carefully. "It's a, well, an aircraft. Sort of like a car and—" Géroux looked at her blankly. She tried again. "No, wait. It's like a ship, but it has wings and flies through the air."

"A flying ship." He looked dubious.

"Honestly, that can't be the craziest thing you've come across this week, is it?"

"*Touché, Mademoiselle.*" The lieutenant laughed. "But where is your aircraft now?"

"It's a long story, but we're on our way to meet up with it again. It's somewhere downriver, near the coast." *I hope*, she thought.

Géroux nodded. "Very well." Just as Amber breathed a sigh of relief, he continued, "Then let us commence your verification with the simplest test. Once that is done, we'll know whether we need to arrange for a firing squad after all." He turned to Durand. "Sergeant-Major, bring me Private Cochevelou. And Durand…?"

"Sir?"

"Bring our other captive to the temple."

"Right away, sir."

In short order, a French trooper presented himself with a smart salute.

"Private Cochevelou, step forward," Lieutenant Géroux said.

"Sir!"

"Private, regale us with your mother tongue." He turned. "*Monsieur* Cam, you will translate your fellow Celt's words for us, if you please."

"Yes, sir!"

The private turned to Cam.

"*Gourc'hemennoù. Fañch Cochevelou eo ma anv ha komz a ran Brezhoneg —Te oar?*"

Cam bowed his head and answered.

"*Penaos `mañ kont. Na petra'ta.*" *Yes, I speak Breton. I speak every language.*

Pleasantly surprised, Cochevelou laughed, and then caught himself. He cleared his throat self-conciously and continued.

"*Divinadell am eus.*"

"You have a riddle for me?" Cam asked.

The private nodded, and began.

An marc'h glas ma moue gwenn en deus
Hi kallout dougen ul koeswik-koad aezet,
met n'eo ket skorañ an tuzun un spilhenn.

Cam nodded as well. "I know this riddle.

This blue horse has a mane of white
It can carry a forest of timber with ease,
but cannot bear the weight of a pin.

The Breton soldier's eyes widened. "*Boul c'hurun!*
Lieutenant, he knows my language as well as if he had learned it from the cradle."

"Wait!" Géroux commanded. "What is the answer?"

Cam smiled. "Don't you know?"

"Tell me all the same."

"The sea, of course."

"He is a true Celt," Cochevelou insisted. "I would stake my life on it."

The lieutenant stroked his chin thoughtfully. "I think I should like to hear more from our new guests. Please, come sit down and eat."

38

Off the Mediterranean Coast, North Africa
Eight days after the Event

Professor Harcourt had developed a strong aversion to water travel. Having survived the destruction of the *Vanuatu*, he now found himself a castaway, adrift for the better part of a day and a night on the open sea in a makeshift boat no bigger than a coracle, without rudder or oars. To add insult to injury, the coastline remained tantalizingly in sight, but all his efforts to paddle to shore by hand left him further away than ever.

Every stirring of the waves and every shape half-seen beneath the surface brought up vivid fears of sea-monsters. Even so, eventually fatigue took its toll, and he drifted off.

Awakening the next morning after an uneasy slumber, he blinked to clear his vision, saw a bulky shape in the distance, and assumed the worst. Within moments, however, he realized his mistake, and sat up as straight as he could—nearly capsizing his little boat as he frantically waved his top hat.

"Hello! Ahoy there! Help!"

It was a simple wooden fishing craft with a plain square sail. A trio of fishermen tending their nets looked up in surprise to see him bobbing along. All three waved back at him.

"*Ave!*" they called out, one after the other, and they leaned into their oars to bring the boat alongside his makeshift coracle. Hands stretched out to pull him up, and the moment his foot lifted off the shell closed up, collapsing into a tadpole-shaped glob which promptly swam off. The transformation stunned his rescuers, who touched their hearts and eyes and spat into the sea.

"Baal-Hadad defend us from the frightful workings of Yam, and the deep wrath of the sea!" they recited in unison, eyes cast downward.

Harcourt's rescuers reminded him of the Lebanese spice merchants at Leadenhall Market in London. All three were bearded, with tightly curled black hair peeking out from beneath braided skull-caps. They wore long unbelted woolen robes, earrings, and all three had distinctive tattoos—one with small vertical diamond shapes running down his forehead, another with a crescent moon over a disk, and the third with horizontal stripes on his cheeks.

They wore similar necklaces, as well. The finest was made of brightly colored glass and shell, the other two of bone and terra cotta. Each depicted a right hand with an eye in the palm. Harcourt recognized the symbol—it was the well-known Arab "Hand of Fatima," their traditional protection against the evil eye.

"Gentlemen, I stand in your debt," he said enthusiastically, dusting off his sleeves and fixing his hat. Looking from one to the other, he added, "Since I am already obliged to you, might there be any chance of something to eat?"

"Yes, yes!" they all nodded, and one pulled out little strips of what looked to be dried salted eel. Harcourt snatched them up and devoured them without a second thought. They laughed off his lack of manners.

"Mother Tanit preserve you, Noble sir."

With a start, Harcourt realized he could understand them—Merlin's linguistic trickery at work. The oldest man, with the brightly colored necklace, told him they were part of a small Carthaginian trading outpost on the border with Kemet, where they exchanged goods from Carthage with Egyptians, Phoenicians, Libyans, and Greeks. Fortunately his rescuers did not ask Harcourt where he hailed from, which saved him the bother of concocting a plausible story.

The fishermen then busied themselves with the boat, turning it toward land. As they approached the shore, Harcourt looked with interest upon the seaside settlement.

Little more than a caravanserai, really, he thought. Lines of camels, a crude jetty, and a handful of simple adobe huts surrounded by a ring of black goatskin pavilions sheltering an open-air bazaar. He was surprised to see three elephants, loaded with goods, being led along the seashore. Two more of the great beasts stood near the market. They were armored and outfitted to carry Carthaginian warriors atop their backs. A caravan's bodyguards? Mercenaries, perhaps.

An unfamiliar flag flew over the market. It boasted a white circle on a red field, with a black symbol in the center. It was vaguely familiar—one of those Hindu sun symbols, he thought. What was it called again?

Oh yes—a swastika.

A pair of Europeans waited for them at the jetty. They were grim-faced and dressed in odd military uniforms, rather drab livery compared to the brightly outfitted regiments of his day. He didn't recognize the make of their rifles, but they certainly looked dangerous enough. The soldiers beckoned them to bring the boat in.

"Who are these white men?" Harcourt asked the Carthaginian fishermen.

"They came from the sky in iron elephants," the oldest of the fishermen replied in all earnestness.

"They are called the *Dass-Doi-Shahf'oke,*" the second

added. "You must pay them respect and obey their wishes. They have great powers."

"*Dass-Doi-Shahf'oke…*" Harcourt repeated, puzzled. On the jetty, the soldiers seemed very interested in him.

"*Halt!*" one called out, raising his hand to Harcourt. "*Du da—identifizieren sie sich!*"

"Ah, of course, of course!" the professor exclaimed. *Dass-Doi-Shahf'oke… Das Deutsche Volk.* "I see now—you're Germans!" The soldiers reacted immediately, training their weapons on him. The terrified fishermen dropped to the ground, prostrating themselves with averted eyes.

"*Engländer! Hände hoch! Sie sind unser Gefangener!*"

Harcourt switched to German. "No need for that, my good man. I am a citizen of the Crown, and no enemy of your Kaiser or the German Empire."

"I will not tell you again!" the German said angrily. "Put your hands up or we shoot!"

He immediately obeyed.

Bloody Huns.

"I assure you, this is a dreadful mistake," Harcourt fumed, his temper warring with his fear. "I demand that you take me to your commanding officer at once."

The soldiers escorting him through the trading post paid no attention to his alternating pleas and demands. They led him beyond the rough Arabian-style tents, out into the open desert. He began to fear the worst. What if he couldn't talk his way out of this? He scrabbled for inspiration.

Shaking off their arms, he turned to face them.

"I'm telling you, it is imperative I speak to your superiors!" he snapped. "This is in regards to—" he lowered his voice and infused his words with great significance, "Operation Broken Hourglass."

His guards remained stone-faced—but they did not shoot him. One leaned over and whispered something to the other, a big, bull-faced trooper with a stern glare. The man listened and gave a curt nod, his cold gaze never leaving Harcourt.

"Continue."

The professor summoned all the bluster he could as he launched into a new harangue.

"Do you seriously expect me to believe that you have not realized what is occurring?" he said in flawless German. "Are you ignorant of what has happened in Operation Broken Hourglass? Surely it must be obvious, even to a lowly pair of whale-blubber sacks like you two cabbage-eating clodhoppers, that this ridiculous English accent is merely part of my disguise—and that no one, except for a special espionage agent-at-large on a *crucial mission* for the German Foreign Office would be caught in a native water-craft off the septentrional coast of Africa, meandering about *dressed as an upper-crust English gentleman*?"

He paused, and delivered the *coup de grace*.

"Do I have to explain to you yet again what a colossal cock-up you are making, by not taking me to your superior *this very instant*?" The pair regarded him with an entirely newfound respect, snapping to attention with a crisp salute.

"Jawohl!"

The two German soldiers escorted Harcourt back to the shade of the trading post's caravanserai and then out to the military encampment that lay beyond, where row after row of drab mustard-colored tents stood surrounded by mechanical vehicles, all arranged in a great square configuration, a sort of wagon-fort.

The Victorian carefully suppressed his interest in the profusion of horseless carriages and motorized bi-cycles driving about and, most of all, the host of fearsome metal war machines of tremendous size.

The unlikely trio reached their destination without further delay. All the while Harcourt silently rehearsed convincing lines to deliver to their commander. He wished he knew more about where—or rather, when—these Teutons came from. Was von Bismarck, that damnable Prussian *Junker*, still their chancellor? He'd need to be quite careful what he said.

Upon arriving at the command tent, they were stopped

short by the pair of sentries standing guard outside.

"Come back with your prisoner later," one said firmly. "The field marshal left strict orders not to be disturbed."

Harcourt geared up for another performance.

"Prisoner?" he said. "Don't be ridiculous. I have vital intelligence that I must deliver to him."

"Who are you?" the sentry demanded. "We have no such orders."

"You tell your commander that Professor Winston Harcourt—or rather, Professor Zee, the Foreign Office's number one master spy—is here to see him."

"Out of the question," the man replied.

"I am not leaving until your superior officer sees me."

"His orders were crystal clear. The debriefing with *Doktor-Coronel* Mehta takes precedence over all other matters."

"And I say that *my*—" Abruptly he stopped. "Pardon, with *whom* did you say he is meeting?"

"*Herr Doktor-Coronel* János Mehta."

Harcourt paled. The head sentry raised an eyebrow.

"What did you say *your* name was again?"

The professor turned to his escorts. "Well, the commander's orders are quite clear," he said. "We'll simply have to return when his Mehta—that is, when his *meeting* has ended. Come along now."

Both sentries raised their rifles.

"I *said*, give me your name again."

"That's really not important," Harcourt blustered. "I'll be happy to talk to your commander at his leisure, and in the meantime I'll just—" He began to edge away.

"*Halt!*" All four soldiers trained their rifles on his heart. Harcourt froze and raised his hands. The lead sentry stepped up to him, stared the professor hard in the eye and turned to the other soldiers.

"Directly to the pit with this one. Get him out of here."

The bull-faced soldier shoved him on his way. They headed out toward the open desert again, where nothing awaited him. A vast expanse of nothing.

39

At the Hikaptah, New Memphis
Eight days after the Event

Géroux played the role of host almost as well as he had the part of their interrogator, though to Amber it was remarkable—and disturbing—how easily he slipped back and forth between the two.

The lieutenant sent for food for his guests, then he and Sergeant-Major Durand sat down with them. It arrived a short time later—scrambled duck eggs, strips of dried tilapia, and flatbreads. The servants offered beer, bringing tea when Leila politely demurred. The four dug in eagerly—it had been far too long since they had eaten.

Amber took the lead in conversation, while Leila sat listening quietly and Cam translated for Kha-Hotep as best he could. She began by explaining, as best she could, what they understood of the Event, and Dr. Meta's part in it. Her greatest concern was trying to impart the urgency of their mission, but the Frenchman Géroux insisted on posing tangential questions that continually sidetracked her.

"So," he said, interrupting her for at least the twentieth time, rubbing his temples as if her words gave him a headache. "You are saying all of time is—was, will be—like a stained-glass window, and we are living in a world cobbled together from its broken pieces?"

"That's essentially it, yes."

"Incredible. So, you say England has been destroyed in this... *événement*?"

"Well, from what we saw, there's at least part of one city left, but London is pretty much gone."

"Were it not for the things we ourselves have seen..." Géroux's expression sharpened. "What of France?"

"We don't know."

"What of the Hapsburgs?" he pressed. "The Papal States? The Ottomans?"

Amber opened her mouth, but could only shrug her shoulders and shake her head.

"There's so much we don't know," she finally replied. "We do know that most of the biggest shards are from older times, a lot of them prehistoric. Dr. Meta suspected that the closer to the event, the smaller and fewer the shards tend to be."

Géroux leaned back, and cradled his chin in his hand thoughtfully. "All this is taxing for the human mind to comprehend, but incredible as your story may be, it explains much."

"Lieutenant," Amber said, "please don't think I'm a spy, but what *are* the French doing in Egypt?"

Géroux laughed harshly. "We came to this country on a most noble quest—to liberate Egypt from their oppressors, the warrior slave-kings of the Mameluke Turks. We lost hundreds of men during those first grueling weeks in the infernal heat, meeting disaster at every step. There were many suicides..." He stared off into the distance, eyes haunted.

"At last we came within sight of the great pyramids, already turning golden in the morning sun," he continued. "There we faced off against the forces of the Emir Murad Bey—twelve thousand armored riders, with another twenty thousand Albanian Janissaries, Bedouin Arabs, and Egyptian militia from Cairo. A glittering line, sparkling like jewels, stretched in a great sweeping arc some nine miles long, from the bank of the Nile across into the desert, outflanking and outnumbering us. Even General Bonaparte was struck by the sight."

He paused again, staring off into the distance before giving a slight shake of his head and continuing.

"Our victory was glorious, but there was little chance to enjoy the fruits of our triumph—a soldier's life is spent on the march. The general decided to pursue the Emir into Upper Egypt, and the honor fell to our division. We lit out by night and set up our bivouac at dawn. I was sound asleep when the lightning storm struck, and the resulting commotion woke me. Whole portions of camp had turned to wilderness. Tents, horses, campfires... all gone as if they had never been. Fully half of our squadron had vanished, along with the rest of our division—more than five and a half thousand men had evaporated with the morning dew."

Amber nodded sympathetically.

"Eyewitnesses spoke of sheet lightning, or something wilder still. Veteran troopers who had withstood cavalry charges and artillery bombardment without flinching were filled with superstitious dread. The most anxious voiced their fear that we would be the next to vanish.

"I found myself in command. Though I had no answers for the troops, I decided we would first push forward to the village of Mit Rahina, which lay only a few miles further. That would be our best chance of re-stocking our supplies and attempting to locate those who had been lost."

He shrugged.

"The rest, you know. Mit Rahina was gone, but ancient Memphis had returned—or at least, this motley patchwork. Such a most improbable realm, forgotten by the ages, unchanged by the march of history. The natives greeted us as gods, which has proved quite advantageous." The lieutenant smiled, prompting some chuckles from his men. "We dispatched a messenger back to headquarters, but he returned two days later to tell us that even the city of Cairo had vanished."

"What?" Leila suddenly spoke up. "What did he say?" she asked Amber, then she faced Géroux. "Did you say—*disparu*?"

The lieutenant gave her a grim nod. He replied, and Amber translated.

"Forgive me, *Mademoiselle*," he said. "Yes, I'm afraid. Utterly gone. Nothing remained but howling wilderness, as if a city had never stood there at all."

Leila looked as though she was going to faint. Amber grabbed her hand to steady her. Then she spoke up again.

"There's something more you need to know, Lieutenant. The reason we're trying to get back to our ship is that we have to reach the South Pole, to find Dr. Meta's laboratory. We have to reverse whatever caused the Event, to fix the damage. The fracturing of the timeline is still occurring." She paused to frame her words carefully. "If we don't, it will destroy the world."

"How do you know this?"

"Dr. Meta—the scientist—told us."

"Did he say how soon that will occur?"

"Soon," she said. "Weeks, maybe even days."

There was a pregnant pause as Durand and Géroux exchanged serious looks. The awkward silence only increased Amber's sense of urgency—there was too much riding on her ability to convince the French.

Finally the lieutenant spoke. "I believe you," he said, and Amber exhaled in relief, realizing she'd been holding her breath waiting for Géroux's answer. "Naturally," he continued, "we will do everything in our power to aid you on your mission, in every way that we can. Let me propose this. You and your comrades stay here with us tonight. Eat, rest, regain your strength, and in the morning we shall rise with the sun and send you off with food, supplies, and a protective guard of my best men. *Bien?*"

"*Tres bien!*" Amber responded. "Thank you so much! That would be amazing!"

"Superb." The lieutenant stood up and clapped his hands. "Then it is settled. First thing tomorrow, we set off—but for now, there is someone I need you to meet."

Géroux and Durand took their group out of the great hall and through one of the temple complex's side passageways, finally stopping at an open doorway guarded by a pair of sentries. It opened out onto a secluded garden courtyard.

"This fellow is the only trace of Murad Bey's band we've yet found," Géroux said to Cam. "One of our patrols found him wandering alone in the desert. I'm

hoping you can help us get some answers from him."
He added, "Unfortunately, we lost all of our interpreters
during your—during the Event."

A man in a rich black robe with gold embroidery, and
a turban of black and gold silk, rested on the ledge of a
raised pool beneath a tall statue of the green-skinned god
Ptah, serenely watching dragonflies buzzing along the
pool's surface. When he looked up at his visitors, Cam
saw he was a handsome older Arab, his immaculately
trimmed beard streaked with silver, a collection of soft
lines around his eyes.

The man rose to greet them, wordlessly saluting them
with a slight bow, one hand over his heart. The lieutenant
doffed his hat and returned the bow, then turned back to
Cam and gestured him to approach.

"If you can, give this Egyptian worthy my regards."

Cam gave a polite bow.

*"Sayidi al muhtarm, hadha al-malazim al-faransiu
yamtadu tahayaatuh lakum." Sir, this French lieutenant
extends his greetings.*

The Arab blinked at him for a moment, and then let out
a long and hearty laugh, responding in the same language.

"Glory to God! I feared I should end my life in this
place, never again to hear a word of Arabic. God is
merciful to his servants! How is it you speak it? You
must be Circassian."

"No, sir," Cam replied. "I am a Celt, from a distant

island to the west, but the two ladies and I speak your language. Noble sir, this gentleman is the Lieutenant Géroux of France. He bids me ask you who you are, and what your business is here."

The man bowed again.

"Tell your master my name is Ahmad ibn Fadlan ibn Al-Abbas ibn Rashid ibn Hamad. I am emissary of Caliph Muqtadir of Baghdad, the City of Peace, may God strengthen him. I and my companions were en route to the Egyptian capital city of Al-Fustat, where I am expected at the court of the Emir Takin al-Khazari, may God increase his well-being.

"Through strange mysteries to which only God knows the answer," he continued, "days ago I became separated from the rest of my caravan and was wandering in the desert when these strange men from the kingdom of the Franks found me."

Cam relayed the information to the French.

"Al-Fustat?" Géroux asked. "Where is that?"

"Excuse me, sir," Leila said shyly in halting French. "I know Al-Fustat. It's a district in the Old City of Cairo, but it hasn't been any place important since the Middle Ages."

"Ah well, so much for any chance of us ransoming him to the Turks," Durand joked. "At least that means he's not in league with Murad Bey. Assuming he's telling the truth, of course."

Géroux smiled. "As of this afternoon, Murad Bey has fallen off my list of concerns. This has been quite a banner day for reassessing priorities."

The lieutenant turned to Amber.

"Gracious *Mademoiselle*, would you please offer the honorable envoy my apologies for our previous lack of interpreters, and explain the special circumstances in which we find ourselves? Also, kindly let him know he is not a prisoner, but my honored guest, and that we shall all feast tonight."

Cam did not envy Amber having to make another explanation. As she spoke to the Arab emissary, Géroux took advantage of the distraction to pull him aside for a private chat.

"We need to talk as men, you and I," Géroux said. "I know your female companion is frightened, and fears the end of the world, but after all that has occurred, I think we know better than to dread such things, do we not?"

Cam frowned. "What do you mean?"

"My good man, I mean no offense. The matter is simply this—what can a mere girl know about the sciences? She is no savant. You wish to regain your ship, I say bravo! By all means, let us go and fetch it. But all this nonsense about trips to the southern pole, and returning the world to what it was?" Géroux shook his head. "Let us be frank. That is sheer lunacy."

Cam's frown deepened. "It is no madness," he insisted. "The lord druid told us so himself."

"Hear me out," the lieutenant said, holding up a hand. "Let us say you are correct. We shall go with you and ensure the success of your mission, and all will be made well. *C'est bien.* But merely for sake of argument, let us suppose we do all this, the world remains as it is, and we return here in your fabulous airship."

He discreetly glanced around to make sure they were not being overheard by the others, and lowered his voice.

"You, my friend, have shown your mettle," Géroux said. "You would be a welcome addition to our colony, a man of honor and great courage. And your ability to speak the language of the natives will perfect our efforts to direct day-to-day operations here, and teach them to speak proper French. Your Nubian also seems most intelligent. He would make a fine overseer. And I trust I do not have to point out our obvious lacking."

"Sir?"

"The women, of course! We have no white women here. Surely you would not condemn our fledgling colony to devolve into a petty-state of mulattoes and quadroons? All our French blood spent within but a few generations? These women of the tropics are pleasing, to be sure, supple and agile as fish, but delightsome as they are, we need wives, not concubines."

Cam struggled to keep up with the flow of unfamiliar words and unpleasant ideas.

"Here is all I propose," the lieutenant continued. "At least let the women stay with the colony for safekeeping, while we go to find your ship and complete your mission. They will be perfectly safe—on that I give you my word of honor as a military officer of the French Republic."

Cam stared at him with a raised eyebrow and gave a sudden laugh.

"I travel with Amber. I fight alongside her."

The Celt turned and walked away, pausing just once to turn back to the dumbstruck Frenchman.

"I do not tell her where she goes or stays."

40

Approaching Alexandria from the Western Desert
Dawn — Eight days after the Event

Once the sun dropped, Blake and Nellie's progress on the stolen German motorbike dropped as fast as the temperature.

"Last time I was here," he said, "there had been a highway running the length of the coast. During the war, our armies had seesawed back and forth across. But that was back in the twentieth century."

"And now our present is in the twenty-third-century future," Nellie replied. "Only we're in the ancient past." It was enough to drive her stark raving—a topic with which she was intimately acquainted.

The virgin ground presented an unremitting landscape of rocks and gravel, punctuated by outcroppings of camel thorn and the occasional treacherous mire of fine sand fit only for gumming up the bearings and sinking the wheels and treads of their mechanized transport. The two of them shivered in the chill as they picked their way blindly across the precarious terrain. The inky darkness forced them to proceed with excruciating slowness, the lighthouse of Alexandria beckoning to them all through the night.

The normally tactiturn Blake was unusually talkative during their nocturnal journey. She listened carefully to everything he had to tell her—she'd be relying on the information very soon. As the night's gloom gradually relented to the dawn, the brightening sky enabled them to make better speed, bringing them within sight of the high Alexandrian city walls by break of day.

Nellie pointed up ahead.

"Blake, look! We're almost there."

Alexandria completely filled a narrow sliver of land, its walls stretching from the Mediterranean to a large body of fresh water. Long-necked brontosaurs waded in the marshy lake. Approaching from the southwest, the duo also found themselves driving past an assembly of solemn guardians—the granite monuments of the city's necropolis. Its gardens, shrines, and mausoleums almost made it a second city.

The high iron-bound doors of the city's Moon Gate were closed, awaiting the appearance of the morning sun. Atop the ramparts, the sentries of the night watch stared at the noisy contraption coming toward them, raising the alarm all along the walls.

Blake pulled the motorcycle to a stop at a discreet distance, letting the engine continue to rumble. Warily Nellie eyed the machine gun mounted in front of her on the sidecar, hoping she didn't have to get acquainted with its use. She turned to her companion.

"You don't think any of them will recognize us from before, do you? Or am I being hopelessly wishful?" She looked up at the agitated sentries. "I wonder if they're still put out with us after all that unpleasantness with Mehta."

"There's no real way to tell, is there?" He shrugged. "Still, of the two of us, I'd wager you're more the diplomat. Besides they're less likely to chuck down a spear at a woman."

She eyed him suspiciously. In his dust-powdered goggles, Blake looked like a deranged praying mantis, but she had to admit he had a point. *Well then.* Gathering up her skirts, she extricated herself from the sidecar with all the dignity she could muster, and then straightened her traveling clothes again. Blowing a stray hair off her face, she waved up to the city guards with a cheery smile.

"Hello up there!" she called out in Greek. "Is it too early to open the gates?"

They looked down, uncertainty stamped on their faces. As they did, the engine revved behind her. A sudden plume of gravel and dust kicked away from the bike as Blake wheeled it around. Nellie let out an inarticulate squeal of rage.

"Blake! What are you doing?"

He pointed back the way they came. "See that dust storm? The Germans are already on their way!" he shouted. "I've got to go back and slow them down!"

"What? *Blake! No!* That's madness! You can't leave me here by myself!" She looked from him to the wall and back again. "What do I tell them? What if they arrest me—or worse?"

"I'll be back!" he answered. "Remember what I told you!"

"Blake! Don't leave me!"

Equally enraged and frightened, Nellie stamped and cursed him out, but he was already gone, leaving behind a plume of dust and the vanishing drone of his motorized conveyance. She exhaled, watching him disappear, and then turned back to the baffled Alexandrian guardsmen. What other choice did she have?

"Hello!" she called out once more, doing her best to offer another smile.

The great gate to the city opened its doors.

As he sped across the burning desert, Blake found himself troubled. While his skill set didn't include a lot of empathy, he felt a small but toothsome sense of guilt at leaving Nellie on her own.

In his own way, it was an unspoken token of deep

respect for her. He had every confidence in her abilities, yet there was just enough uncertainty to stoke the embers of guilt should anything happen to her.

No time for that now.

He compartmentalized it for later and carried on with his mission.

Ahead of him, on the distant horizon to the west, the plumes of a minor dust storm rose, churning bright blue sky into a sickly rust-tinged yellowish tan—the telltale indication of a mass of tanks and lorries rolling across the desert. He headed straight for it.

After a few more hours of picking his bumpy, uncomfortable way across the unforgiving topography, he came to the first group of approaching Panzers, crossing the open desert in a broad flying wedge formation. Blake felt a keen sense of cautious relief. The commanders riding in their open turrets scarcely paid any attention to the lone DAK motorcyclist coming back to their lines. Just another fellow trooper.

We're all friends here.

He smiled grimly.

Behind the tanks was a big petrol lorry, flanked by a pair of armored cars. *Not enough support for all these*, Blake noted. There had to be more support vehicles further back, and likely infantry, as well. These were just the advance wave of the incoming force.

He counted the number of tanks in the vanguard. Twenty-three total, all from the German 21st Panzer Division, identified by the regimental markings. Three Mark IIs. Five of the big *Panzerkampfwagen* IVs. The rest were all Mark IIIs, the Afrika Korps workhorse.

There were no captured British tanks, nor any of the outmoded Italian models. *No*, he corrected himself. *None* of them would be outmoded against the Alexandrians. Even the most antiquated rattle-trap piece of junk would pose a major challenge. Any of the Panzers on its own would be able to bring down the city walls, and crash through anything the defenders could throw in its path.

Well, *almost* anything.

He had some ideas on that score.

No one knew better than him that even a tank could be beaten by brave men with the right equipment—but close to two dozen tanks? With what did the Alexandrians have to fight? Bare hands and shortswords. Bows and arrows. Defending the city against these mechanized behemoths wouldn't be easy. It was going to take canny thinking.

A minor commotion broke Blake's concentration. The closest tank commander was excited, calling out to the others. A jolt of adrenaline sizzled through him. Had he blown his cover? Instinctively, he put on the brakes and came to a halt, kicking up a small flurry of sand

and leaping gravel. As he tensed for the desperate lunge toward the 50 cal, he assessed the better targets. The tank commander to his nine. Motorcycle troopers at one and two. Another tank's commander at eleven.

Then cut through the gap and ride like hell.

Belay that.

No need to pull off such a risky maneuver. It was a false alarm—the German wasn't talking about him at all, but pointing overhead at a flock of leathery pterodactyls, flapping lazily westward in a flying wedge of their own. He exhaled in relief, breathing heavily as he shook off the fight-or-flight chemical rush still tingling through his bloodstream.

He and the German spectators watched the bird-like reptiles pass by. Then he started up the motorcycle again and drove on, following the prehistoric airshow.

Slightly less than an hour later, Blake rode past signs of a recent battle. Burnt-out hulks of tanks, fresh dug graves, scattered rubble of gun emplacements, tangles of barbed wire, and everywhere bomb craters. An uncanny sense of *déjà vu* washed over him as he realized he recognized this shard. He had fought here, at El Alamein, over a decade ago. And yet here it all was again, no more than a week old.

He was back in the Devil's Gardens.

Blake was careful to stay with the boundaries of the freshest tank tracks. There was no telling how many of the landmines were still around. He crossed the vestiges of the north-south Rahman Track and went over Aqqaqir Ridge. Topping the rise, he again pulled his stolen cycle to a halt.

Others hadn't been so lucky navigating the German minefields. Some tanks had careened into one another, while others had blundered right into their doom. An armored car remained fatally mired in a dust-bog. The body of its driver still lay stretched out in the sand beside it.

Blake had seen plenty of similar scenes during the war—quite often, he'd created them. He'd long since hardened himself to the sight of such carnage, and yet, he found himself strangely affected by the wreckage of men and machines in front of him. A prickling sensation gripped him, raising the hairs on the back of his neck and forearms.

Something wasn't right.

The needles on his motorcycle indicators began to jitter madly. The air itself seemed to vibrate with a strange, unnerving tone that hurt his ears, and then an eruption of scarab beetles came streaming out of the sand everywhere around him, skittering away in all directions. A sudden explosion sent dirt and debris flying, and Blake dove to the ground for cover.

To his left and right, more explosions rocked the earth.

A mortar strike? No, he realized. Something was setting off the mines. And then it struck.

A few yards away, the howling energy surge of another aftershock tore skyward. Blake covered his head, gritting his teeth against its banshee wail. He felt as though he was caught outside in a hurricane, but shielded his eyes to risk a look at the blinding channel of raw power. It was right out of the Old Testament, a pillar of fire in the wilderness, demanding fear and worship.

And then, just like that, gone again.

Blake got up, dusted himself off, and turned his attention to the new shard that lay before him. Terrifying as it was, this aftershock had been smaller than the one that had nearly swallowed up the *Vanuatu*. And this time he had a chance to see what was left behind. A glittering line of sand, fused into glass—still faintly smoking and softly hissing—marked the boundary. It was roughly flame-shaped, perhaps no more than six to ten meters across at its widest.

Time to investigate.

He had not forgotten he was still in a minefield. Carefully keeping to the tracks he'd been following, Blake came as near as he dared for a closer look, then he frowned. At first, he couldn't make sense of what he was seeing. The affected area enclosed the armored car and its dead driver. Only now there were *several* cars and drivers—or rather, pieces of them.

Like a broken mirror, this newborn shard had

splintered into a dozen or so smaller fragments, each one a fractured reflection of the original. In one or two of the new fractures, the driver's dead body—or bodies, rather—lay intact. In some, there was just his head and a part of the torso, while in others no more than part of an arm or leg. The armored car lay in similar cross-sections, doubled and redoubled in segmented bits and pieces.

The site was a graveyard of fragmented doppel-gangers.

Blake rubbed his chin, taking in the kaleidoscopic nightmare, and then quickly returned to the motorbike and drove off again. He didn't want to be caught hanging around if the Germans sent any soldiers to investigate—and he knew he didn't have much further to go.

41

At the Hikaptah, New Memphis
Eight days after the Event

Kha-Hotep felt restless... uneasy. Cam and their host were off in a private discussion, while Amber and Leila engaged in conversation with the envoy from the Arabian lands. It frustrated him to speak neither language.

So he took advantage of the lull to speak with the various Egyptian servants tending to the temple. The soldiers didn't interfere, but he noticed they kept him under a watchful eye. He was talking to servants in one of the side chambers, a shrine-turned-kitchen, when Amber came to find him.

"There you are," she said in his language. "Leila and Ibn Fadlan went off to do their prayers. What have you been up to?" While her turn of phrase was strange to him, he understood what she was asking.

"I've learned some interesting things," he told her.

"For one thing, it seems as if very few of the people here are from the same time."

"What do you mean? They aren't all ancient Egyptians?"

"Indeed they are," Kha-Hotep replied, "but scattered across five thousand years. My time was during the nineteenth dynasty, but there are people here who say they are from the twenty-sixth dynasty, others from as far back as the first dynasty, and some of the peasant farmers here come from a time before the Pharaohs—even before the gods."

Even as he said it, he realized how strange the concept was. Stranger yet was the fact that he was able to accept it.

"I knew Egypt was ancient," Amber said, "but I had no idea how old it really is."

"The Mother of the World," Kha-Hotep said proudly. "But come, see something truly wondrous." He took her over to a pair of artisans, a middle-aged man and a young boy, working together to restore the paint on a nearby obelisk. They paused in their work to greet them politely. The man was perhaps in his forties or fifties, the boy a young teen. The family resemblance was unmistakable.

"This is Tek the older, and Tek the younger."

"Father and son?"

"So I thought, but no. They told me when the Event struck, the wall of lightning went through the middle of their house, yet the walls on either side still stood."

"It is true," Tek the older said. "We can show you the scorch marks on the walls and ceiling."

"Can you tell my friend what happened that night?" Kha-Hotep prompted.

The man nodded. "I awoke in my house to a wall of fire, so bright I shielded my eyes from the blinding white flames, terrified that Ra himself had unleashed the sun to destroy the world. And when that terrible curtain of fire abated, I beheld my mother and father on the other side of the room, sitting at breakfast with a young boy—this boy here."

The youth grinned. Tek the older continued.

"My mother and father looked at me in wonderment, and did not know me. Their appearance was very strange, for they were both young people—younger than me, young enough to be *my* children. But you see... my parents lived long and died many years ago. Yet here they were, looking just as I remembered them from my youth."

Realization crept over Amber's face.

"You mean... you and he..." She looked from man to boy. "One and the same person?"

"We are the *same* person," the youth said. "Look, see the scar on my forearm? He has it, as well."

"Tek the older..." she said softly, "and Tek the younger..."

Kha-Hotep nodded. "Truly, wonders surround us at every turn."

* * *

They went back to the main hall to find Cam waiting for them—his chat with Géroux apparently finished. The lieutenant rejoined them, though now his manner seemed a bit prickly. He doffed his hat with what seemed like a strained smile.

"My apologies, but I regret I have important business I must attend to," he said. "I hope this evening you will all join me at my table for a celebration of your arrival and the successful founding of our new colony. Until then, you remain our honored guests." He gave a courteous little bow before striding away.

"Well, he certainly left in a hurry," Amber said.

Cam nodded. "I think I disappointed our host."

"It is bad manners to disappoint a host," Kha-Hotep chided.

"His bad manners disappointed me."

Before Amber could ask what he meant, Kha-Hotep cleared his throat, and discreetly looked around to see if anyone was eavesdropping on their conversation.

"Do you think he means to keep us here?"

"If I had all things at my will, we'd slip away tonight," Cam said softly.

"They still have your weapons," Kha-Hotep pointed out.

"He said they'd return them," Amber said.

"Did he?" Cam said, sounding unconvinced. "We'll know in the morning,"

The three fell quiet for a moment, none of them overly optimistic about the how things would play, or what they would do if things got ugly.

Returning to the temple complex, Lieutenant Géroux made his way through the flickering, torch-lit inner hallways and entered the sumptuous quarters that had belonged to the late High Priest. Géroux's own spartan military gear was spread around the room, looking out of place against the richly decorated walls.

Durand was there, painstakingly sketching a schematic on a sheet of papyrus. A series of other drawings were spread out close at hand. The belts holding Cam and Amber's machetes lay on a wide dining table, alongside Kha-Hotep's *khopesh* sword, one of the strange crossbows, and all of the curiously-shaped clips. The other crossbow also lay on the table, although in pieces, having been meticulously disassembled.

"How goes our progress, Sergeant-Major?" Géroux asked. "Do you think we can replicate the design?"

"Well, that remains to be seen." Durand put down his quill and crossed his arms. "The materials are entirely unknown to us. To judge from the smoothness, I would have guessed the casing was made of some polished horn or ivory, but it is far too durable for that. Perhaps we could use finely carved hardwood. The inner workings are as intricate as Swiss clockwork, though I think with the proper tools, we could replicate it."

He pointed to the inner cylinder. "The rotating barrel has nine separate chambers for the bolts, each bolt propelled by its own bowstring, which, thanks to an internal mechanism, is automatically and effortlessly drawn back for re-firing when the bolt clip is inserted. The cylinder rotates with splendid rapidity, enabling an astounding rate of fire and a most impressive lethality. I've never seen the like.

"Here is our greatest obstacle," he continued, lifting a long loop of some sort of cord. "These circular bowstrings are marvelous creations. As flexible as caoutchouc rubber, as strong as steel. *C'est manifique.* I cannot fathom the material from which they are constructed, or how."

Géroux nodded, finger against the bridge of his nose. "Perhaps we can circumvent that problem," he said. "I have a hypothesis, Sergeant. I believe once we locate this aerial ship of theirs, we will find an entire arsenal of such weapons, and who knows what else."

"So you believe them, then?"

"About this cosmic madness, this 'Event' of theirs, wreaking havoc upon time itself? Undoubtedly—we have seen too much that corroborates their account. Their ability to speak every language? Quite patently evident. About their incredible flying ship? Of that, I have every confidence."

"And the rest of it, sir? That the world will end unless we allow them to continue on with their mission?"

"On that account, I find myself not entirely convinced. I think it rather more likely that they merely wish to leave and return to their lost ship—or at any rate, back to wherever they have come from, bidding us *adieu*."

He ran his fingertips over the tabletop, past the components of the strange new weapon.

"In truth, Sergeant, all I know for certain is that going forward, we will gallantly offer them aid at every turn. Once we locate their vessel, with its store of fabulous devices and wondrous weapons, we shall immediately declare it under French protection."

"And the newcomers, sir?"

"Either they will become our newest citizens, or a cautionary tale." Géroux shrugged. "I shall leave the choice to them."

42

German Afrika Korps Encampment
Eight days after the Event

Blake had nearly reached the sea. He couldn't see it, but could smell the closeness of the salt on the dry wind. Despite the rocky terrain, finding the main body of the German encampment had presented no problem at all. He'd only needed to keep following the ruts gouged out by the mass of heavy tanks. His hunch had been right, too.

Much more remained of the Afrika Korps forces.

Too bad the Event didn't take out more of the Nazis.

There they were, a leaguer of at least another two dozen Panzers, aligned in a protective square surrounding the main camp. The tanks formed the outer wall, then the smaller vehicles, and then the bulk of the improvised military tent city—camouflage awnings for shade, fuel and supply dumps, repair workshops, surgeries, and all the other miscellany needed to support an armored division.

To his right, north of the leaguer, was a coastal oasis with native tents and open air markets. Both camp and caravanserai were well-occupied with figures moving about or clustered in groups. Probably worth checking out the Arab market, but first things first. He revved the engine and started straight for the enemy camp.

It was abuzz with activity—they were preparing to move out. Mechanics made last-minute repairs to tank treads or stripped armor plating off of tanks that had been irredeemably damaged to weld onto others. Crews loaded fuel and water cans. Blake blended in without difficulty. Swarms of lorries and motorcycles just like his were moving all around, like industrious bees.

Blake kept his eyes peeled and his cycle moving—the last thing he wanted was for someone to start asking questions, or worse, have some officer commandeer him for chauffeur duty. He spotted a promising target of opportunity, a helmeted soldier lugging ammo crates, and pulled up alongside him.

"Hey *Kumpel*," he said in perfect German, "I'm out of rounds for the fifty cal. Have you got any there?"

The soldier put down his load with a loud grunt and gave Blake a dirty look. "*Denkste!* What do I look like, *der Weihnachtsmann*?"

"Don't be an asshole." Blake looked both ways and leaned in with a conspiratorial glance. "You know how it is. The req situation is ridiculous right now. Look, there's half a bottle of Schnapps in it for you if you can help me out."

The trooper raised an eyebrow, though he remained dubious. "What can I do?" the soldier shrugged. "You'll have to take it up with the supply officer, but that ink-pisser's gonna say no, I promise you."

"*Kein Problem.* You let me worry about dealing with that *Nichtsnutz.* Come here, throw those on the bike, hop in and tell me where all this *scheiße* is supposed to be headed. I'll take you there myself."

"*Ja,* what are we waiting for?" The man hefted the two heavy metal cases and loaded them onto the back of the bike, behind Blake. He held up a finger and backed away.

"Hold on, I just have two more—be right back. Right back!" The soldier turned and hurried off to the staging area behind them, coming back toting two more ammo cases, which he put into the sidecar before squeezing himself in, as well. "This way!" he said, pointing ahead of them.

Blake nodded. "*Jawohl.*"

The man led them to one of the last lorries, parked near the corner of the leaguer. The division's support teams had been doing triage on all the surviving vehicles—not all of them were going to be making the trip. This last one had barely made the cut, and the mechanics were still underneath it, finishing up the final repairs. The helmeted soldier made quick to hop out and grab the ammo cases from the sidecar. He hauled the crates into the back, and gestured to Blake.

"Here, give me a hand getting the other two loaded, and then we'll find the requisitions officer for you."

Blake nodded, more than happy to assist.

"You've still got that bottle of Schnapps, right?" the soldier asked warily.

"Got it right here," Blake answered easily, pulling the canvas flaps closed behind him.

There was a brief, furious commotion, easily missed in all the noisy hubbub of the military camp.

Moments later Blake emerged alone from the back of the lorry, cracking his knuckles. Sauntering around to the mechanics up front, he rapped sharply on the mudguard.

"Hey, you two lovebirds about done down there, or do you need to go get a room? We've got places to go." The pair of mechanics slid out from underneath, their unamused faces streaked with grease and sweat. The older of the two squinted up at him.

"*Ja, ja*, that's funny," he said. "Why don't you tell that to your mother? She can hear you—she just can't answer because she's down here with my dick in her mouth."

Blake grinned.

"Take your time, gentlemen, she's a delicate old lady," he replied jovially. "But in the meantime, the *Stabsgefreiter* wants to know how much longer you will need to get this bitch of an engine back up and running."

"You can tell the staff commander—" the younger mechanic began.

"You can tell the staff commander we'll have it fixed in an hour," his partner said.

"That's too bad," Blake answered. "You won't have a chance to grab any chow if you're not done in twenty-five minutes—and here I had a half bottle of Schnapps, too, as a thank-you."

"*Mach keinen Scheiß!* Alright, alright, we'll have your precious engine going—but you've got to give us a half hour here, you damn slave driver."

"I'll just go get that bottle," Blake said as he turned and walked back toward the motorcycle. Handy thing, the language implant. Commando work was so much easier when you spoke the language.

The thought was interrupted by his worst fear realized—a non-commissioned officer in a bad mood. From the insignia on the man's DAK cap and jacket, Blake realized it was the *Stabsgefreiter* himself, speak of the devil. The irate staff commander was coming straight toward the lorry, his disapproving gaze darting around the camp.

No doubt looking to commandeer a driver, Blake suspected. Avoiding the slightest trace of eye contact he did an immediate about-face toward the back of the lorry, careful to keep his pace even and unhurried. He stepped up and pulled aside the canvas to enter.

"Hey!" the commander called out. "Who left this motorcycle here? You?"

Blake shrugged, not turning. "No idea, sir," he answered, and quickly slipped past the flaps into the back of the truck. Inside, the dead German soldier sat, propped up against the cab, staring idiotically back at him. Blake regarded him with a frown. He needed to find a better place to stash the corpse. But where?

Best to hide him in here, he decided. He maneuvered his own body to a place where he could slip his hands underneath the armpits and haul the man up. It was awkward work, heaving the limp corpse off the floor, cradling the body against his chest while the legs dragged along behind. If he could just move it over a few feet, he'd be able to stow it behind the furthest stack of crates.

Someone cleared their throat.

The *Stabsgefreiter* peered into the lorry. His arms still wrapped around the body, Blake found the barrel of the German's pistol, pointed right at him.

43

At the Hikaptah, New Memphis
Evening — Eight days after the Event

The temple-turned-feast hall was lit by a festive constellation of oil lamps. Its high walls echoed with the revelry of the celebrating French soldiers, and a heavenly aroma of roasting meat rose from the fire pits in the side chambers.

Amber's group sat as special guests at the lieutenant's table, along with Sergeant-Major Durand and a stoic Ibn Fadlan. Though he made no complaints and kept his face serene, Amber thought he looked acutely uncomfortable.

"Is something wrong?" she asked under the cover of laughter from the soldiers.

He gave her a gentle smile. "Diplomats know all too well how alike the words *guest* and *prisoner* can be." The truth in his words made Amber more uneasy than she already was.

A stream of Egyptian servants attended to the revelers, bringing in platter after platter of food—meaty helpings of fish and fowl, vegetables, ceramic bowls of hummus-like concoctions, as well as baskets of various warm flatbreads, freshly baked in round cakes, triangles, crispy little cones, and sweet pastries. They also brought in bowls of rich blood-red beer, though Ibn Fadlan and Leila were offered tea and honey instead. A smiling young woman wearing a linen tunic so sheer it was transparent went from table to table offering blue lotus flowers. Leila turned beet red and averted her eyes.

Géroux stood and called for silence.

"Attention! Attention!" he shouted. "I propose a toast! We fighting men have come far and through much to be here this night, and there are many brave and honorable men who did not. To absent friends and comrades!"

The soldiers echoed the sentiment.

"These are revolutionary times. The *Ancien Régime* is long defeated. The times of tyrannies are no more. As the words of the song ring clear—tremble, enemies of France! The victory is ours!"

The soldiers cheered, and spontaneously broke into song.

La République nous appelle
Sachons vaincre ou sachons périr

Un Français doit vivre pour elle
Pour elle un Français doit mourir!

The Republic is calling us!
Let us conquer or perish!
A Frenchman must live for her,
A Frenchman must live for her!

The stanza ended with more cheers from the men. Géroux quieted them, and continued.

"Another toast," he called out. "To our honored guests, who have shed much light on our current state of affairs. Cheers!"

The rest of the hall joined him in the salute.

"You look upon these strangers," he continued, "and are filled with questions. Who are they? Where are they from? I know the rumors that have been flying about the camp all day. Incredible rumors, unbelievable and unthinkable. Sheer madness." He paced up and down the lines of tables as he spoke. Every eye in the great hall was on him.

"Well, the rumors are true," he said solemnly. "Our future and our past have joined us here in the present—history and destiny have become one and the same. The old world has given us the best of its bounty, and the unseen future has revealed its wisdom to us—yet to what end? To effect a new creation, a second Eden, a new chance for everyone. To shatter the mold of yesterday and tomorrow, and give rise to a shining new nation, a new people, a new Republic."

He again lifted his drink.

"To the new world we are building from the scattered shards of the old, here in the French-Egyptian colony of New Memphis," he said. *"À La Nouvelle-Memphis!"*

Géroux's men had listened in silence, taking in the full weight of his words. Now they stood and roared their applause in a standing ovation. Amber and Cam looked at one another, the same nagging concern reflected on each other's face. The lieutenant stood, nodding his approval, and then raised his hands for silence again.

"On a more immediate note, we also have our guests to thank for our main entrée tonight—*Hippopotame braisé et grillé*! Enjoy, and *bon appétit*!"

The hippo that had attacked them that morning provided the feast with a ton of fresh meat—in actuality, nearly two tons. Durand and Géroux enthusiastically debated its culinary virtues, comparing its taste, consistency, and marbling with that of elk, moose, and pilot whale. Their discussion ended without a resolution, as a sudden cheer went up.

A group of young women filed into the room, dressed in the same sheer linen as the lotus-flower servant. They came with drums, clappers, and frames stringed with tiny bells, followed by harpists, lute-players, and pipers. An even louder roar of approval greeted the arrival of a line of lissome Egyptian dancing girls, all dressed in little more than jewelry around their wrists and ankles.

An awed silence fell over the hall as the exotic and ancient music started up, every man riveted at the spectacle of the dancing, the almond-eyed girls aligned in pairs, moving in subtle, hypnotic arcs back and forth across the temple floor, swirling their arched bodies, their outstretched arms twisting with sinuous, serpentine grace.

On a capricious whim, the regimental musicians nudged each other, and spontaneously rose to join their Egyptian counterparts, accompanying them with military drum, fife, and hurdy-gurdy. The native musicians laughed and nodded, encouraging them. The dancing girls carried on, their eyes sparkling at the novel sounds coming from the strange new instruments, especially the violin-like music of the hurdy-gurdy.

When they finished, the dancers froze in the final positions before raising their arms in reverence and bowing to their appreciative audience, who hooted, whistled, and applauded with lusty vigor. The dancing girls took their leave, to the displeasure of the soldiers, and the French musicians quickly came to the rescue with the opening strains of *La Marseillaise*, causing the soldiers to stand and break into song again. The Egyptians listened, and then joined in with their own instruments, giving the anthem an exotic new flair.

All across the echoing hall, the music cast the same

chill on newcomers and natives alike. Something new was being born there that night, a mélange of Europe and the ancient Orient. Their descendants would tell stories about this night.

Then the moment passed, and after another round of applause, everyone returned to the feasting.

At the lieutenant's table, Leila seemed quietly mortified by it all, barely picking at her food and avoiding eye contact with anyone. At the same time Ibn Fadlan was using all his diplomatic expertise to conceal his multiple discomforts. Here, inside a pagan temple filled with cruel idols and covered in demonic symbols, sitting at a mixed table of women and infidel Franks, where near-naked *houris* cavorted without modesty, instilling lust with their nubile bodies and tempting them with opium flowers, unclean foods, and alcohol the color of blood.

Long ago he had discovered a useful expedient whenever he was called upon by duty to travel to foreign climes—to the lands of the Khazars, to filthy heathen Turkic khanates, the Varangian trading posts of the barbaric Viking Rus. He found it most helpful to simply observe their customs without judgment, no matter how foul, impious, or disgusting the people he encountered.

* * *

Kha-Hotep was also deeply disturbed. These strange soldiers from the future had desecrated the holiest site in the very capital of Egypt, and set themselves up as gods. Where *were* the priests? Although only part of the enormous temple complex remained, dozens of the temple priests should also have survived.

What had happened to them?

The Egyptian frowned to himself. So much had changed in the span of a few days, it was hard to grasp it all. He took comfort in the thought that if Amber and Cam were right, *Ma'at*, the divine order and harmony, would soon be restored.

After all, order—not chaos—was the will of the gods, if not always that of their servants.

He put aside such seditious theological musings and decided to make the most of the situation. All around the hall the music, feast, and above all the rich red Egyptian ale were having great effect, with the men by turns feeling patriotic, maudlin, libertine, raucous, or euphoric.

Some sang, some staggered, some fell asleep right at the table. Others looked for a fight or loudly declared eternal friendships—sometimes both within the space of minutes.

Géroux watched the room with the same intensity as the statues of Ptah looming above them, carefully gauging his audience. He rose and raised his hand once more, calling for silence.

"Settle down now, settle down," he growled. "Still your mutinous tongues for a moment longer, you drunken louts!" With a few jeers and catcalls, the rowdy commotion dwindled to a dull roar. "I have one final important announcement."

The last of the hecklers were shushed and elbowed into silence. The lieutenant paused for effect before beginning again.

"As you know, we—"

With an odd sound, he jerked his head and coughed, placing his hand to his throat. When he lifted his hand, his fingertips were suddenly stained red, and a small gleaming metallic point stuck out from his throat. His eyes rolled back and he pitched forward to the hard stone floor.

The hilt of a slim bronze Egyptian dagger protruded from the back of his neck.

Leila screamed, a sound quickly echoed by the dancing girls.

Cam wheeled out of his seat to see where the blade had come from. Behind them, a frescoed panel of the wall had been swung out into the room—a hidden door. A shaven-headed Egyptian stood there, drawing another dagger. He swiftly pulled his arm back and hurled it at Cam's head.

Just as fast, the Celt swung his heavy drinking cup to block the coming blade, spraying an arc of ale. With a clang of metal, the deflected knife rebounded off to the side and skittered across the stone floor. Before it hit, Cam charged the assassin, seizing his arm just as the man drew a third dagger. Their bodies collided, Cam crushing the man painfully against the edge of the secret entryway.

Durand rushed to his lieutenant, but Géroux's eyes were already rolling back. The top of his shirt was saturated with blood from the entry and exit wounds, a pink froth bubbled around the tip of the blade poking out from his windpipe. The sergeant-major looked up past the screaming performers as a deafening, blood-curdling roar filled the air.

The entire hall erupted into violence. Crowds of Egyptians wielding torches stormed through the main entrance, a dark tide of enraged faces. The undulating mob bristled with staves and scythes. They charged down the narrow spaces between the long tables, hacking down the drunken French troopers as they tried to rise from their benches.

Plates and goblets scattered in all directions. So much crimson ale and blood spilled across the tabletops and stone floor, it was soon impossible to tell which was which. Some of the soldiers tried to put up a fight, only to be surrounded, swarmed, and brought to ground where plunging knifes made quick work of them. Others were bound by their wrists and dragged away, kicking and screaming.

No more than a handful of the fiercest French troopers managed to grab nearby muskets and brandish them, but they were quickly surrounded by Egyptians with long staves, billhooks, or wooden pitchforks. The Frenchmen were soon ringed in on all sides or pinned against the wall. The vibrant hieroglyphs soon were stained a dark red.

Cam's opponent wasn't alone in the secret passage. Another slipped past the two of them at a run, his *khopesh* sword raised to attack the officer's table. With one smooth sweep, Kha-Hotep swung his chair up and into the side of the attacker's head, battering him into the wall. He quickly scooped up the man's fallen sickle-sword and brought it down, point first, finishing him before he could rise again.

A third attacker came right behind. He emerged from behind the door and stabbed Cam in the side with a vicious thrust. The Celt tried to twist away from the attack, but the force of it knocked him to the ground. His two attackers rushed in to finish him off, just as Kha-Hotep stepped up with a sturdy swing of his blade, lopping off the head of one foe, then bringing the blade singing back down again to decapitate the other.

He rushed to where Cam lay, but the Celt was already pulling himself up.

"Are you—?"

"It's nothing," Cam grunted, but he didn't refuse when Kha-Hotep helped him back to his feet. He kept his hand clutched tightly around his ribs, a red stain on his tunic spreading from beneath his pale fingers.

Amber stared as the musicians and dancers screamed and stumbled over one another to escape the carnage. The mob had finished slaughtering the French. Now it was coming for them.

"Quick! Through the passage!" she shouted in Arabic to Leila and Ibn Fadlan. But before Amber could follow them, she saw Durand cradling his dying commander and ran over to him.

"Come on!" she yelled, grabbing the sergeant-major by his shoulder. "There's nothing you can do!" He looked up at her in a daze, his eyes wet and haunted.

With a howling battle cry, one of the Egyptians broke ranks, scattering the cowering dancing girls as he came running up from the tables, his billhook raised like a spear. Durand blinked and without thinking, pulled out Géroux's pistol, cocked it, and shot the man in the face.

Amber flinched at the blast as their attacker and his improvised weapon crashed to the floor, but then she pulled the sergeant to his feet and tugged him by the arm, urging him along, back through the secret passage.

Kha-Hotep waited for them to get through before he cut down one last attacker and pulled the secret door closed behind them.

The hidden passageway was lit by oil lamps. Leila and Ibn Fadlan took two of them. Long, narrow, with a low ceiling, the corridor seemed fit only for spying and other acts of skullduggery. The five hurried as quickly as they could in the dim light, hoping to escape before the secret door behind them was discovered.

"Wait!" Durand cried out, and they came to a short side passage. "This way!"

They followed him down the branching passage and through another disguised door, this one opening into a chamber with weapons spread out on a wooden table. Amber and Cam stared in shock at the dissected ruins of one of their two crossbows.

Durand wasted no time. "Grab your weapons quickly and go!" he ordered, rushing to grab his own.

Amber needed no further prompting. She snatched up the remaining crossbow and all the clips, while Cam gathered up the sword belts with his free hand. Kha-Hotep offered a sickle sword to Ibn Fadlan, who shook his head. Kha-Hotep turned to Leila, who looked at the *khopesh* as though it were a viper before impulsively clasping it against her chest. The group then hurried out again, continuing down the primary passage.

From the way he was moving, Amber could tell Cam

was in pain, but he remained stoically silent, keeping pressure on the wound in his side. Alarmed by the sight of the blood soaking his tunic, she slung an arm around his shoulder, slowing her pace to match his—until a crack of light opened up down the long corridor behind them.

The mob had found the door.

"Run!" she shouted. Instead, Kha-Hotep raced back to them. "Kha, get him out of here!" she cried.

The Egyptian put an arm around Cam and hustled him down the corridor at double speed, Amber close on their heels. Durand squeezed in to let them pass. The cramped passageway echoed with hoots and shouts from the charging mob. Amber raised her crossbow and unloaded it in three quick bursts, firing blind. She couldn't miss at this range. Screams and curses followed.

Jettisoning the empty clip, she slapped in another while Durand drew his pistol and fired, tossing the spent firearm to the floor. Amber sent another nine shots whistling down the narrow passageway.

"Fall back!" Durand said, grabbing her arm. She obeyed and they turned, running toward the bobbing, unsteady light coming from the oil lamps. The roar of their pursuers filled the corridor. Some half-seen thing flew at them in the dark, clattering off the wall beside them—a thrown axe or a dagger. She half turned and fired the last bolt of her clip as they ran, uncertain if she'd hit anything.

Then something struck her hard from the front, knocking her to the floor. She gasped for air as she sprawled on the dusty floor, winded and unable to see. Leila called her name, trying to help her to her feet. Then without warning, Kha-Hotep scooped her up in his arms and carried her off.

Amber didn't try to resist—she was too busy trying to get her breath back. She caught a glimpse of boulders and rubble choking the floor, and thick square timbers jutting out from the ceiling and walls at odd angles. She must have hit one of those.

Then there were stars.

Kha-Hotep set her down gently. They had made it to the end of the hidden passageway—it ended where the building did, where the shard boundary had sliced through that part of the temple complex. They were outside again, alongside the ruins of its towering walls.

The mob's howls echoed in the passageway, coming closer.

"We need to keep moving, little one," Kha-Hotep urged her.

She looked over to see Durand standing at the ruined entrance, saber drawn and ready, its blade a silver gleam in the moonlight. The French officer nodded silently to Kha-Hotep, who returned the gesture, and then Durand turned to face whatever was rushing toward them in the dark.

"We can't leave him—" Amber began to protest.

"He knows what he does," Kha-Hotep replied. The Egyptian shepherded the two women away from the temple complex, and they hurried to catch up to Cam and Ibn Fadlan, making for the riverbank of the Nile.

44

German Afrika Korps Encampment
Eight days after the Event

Professor Harcourt wiped his forehead yet again. The heat was brutal and inescapable, and his mind squirmed with desperate thoughts he strove to ignore. The pair of taciturn German soldiers, doubly annoyed with their slippery prisoner, marched him out of the camp and away from the oasis. Nothing but the bleak emptiness of the wasteland awaited them, a flat tableau of rocky, ashen ground the color of bleached bone and sackcloth. His heart sank.

Against his own better judgment, he continued to talk. After all, words were the only real tools in his toolbox.

"I say, we don't appear to be going anywhere," he said. "Might I ask where you are taking me?"

"Where do you think?" the bigger soldier muttered. "Into the ground."

A swooning spell nearly dropped him where he stood. His head spun, and he struggled to keep his footing. The soldiers grabbed him by the arms and shoved him along. Desperately he took stock of his dwindling options—a rogue's gallery of promises, lies, threats, enticements, distractions, wild plans for escape, and emotional pleas for mercy all jostled about in his head, but none seemed capable of saving him.

"That's far enough," the bull-faced trooper growled.

Harcourt stopped dead in his tracks.

Oh god, he thought. *So this is where I depart this mortal coil.* He wished he had something fitting and memorable to say, but his golden tongue failed him at the last. Besides, who would immortalize his final words? Not this pair of Huns. What a cruel fate to end up in the hands of the Boche.

He dearly longed for a swig of his tonic.

A trio of tawny-skinned Carthaginian locals stood nearby, watching the proceedings with mild interest. Were they the burial detail? Releasing him, the soldiers moved a few paces away. A generally disregarded portion of his brain urged him to comport himself with dignity and bearing, but this noble sentiment was the minority opinion.

"W-wait, now," he stammered, his voice squeaking with panic. "Surely we can talk about this, c-can't we?"

The troopers raised their rifles.

"You heard the order yourself," the big man said.

"You're not going anywhere but in the pit with the rest of the undesirables."

"Please, I—" He raised his hands high in the air.

"*Now!*"

"*Oh, god!*" Harcourt wailed, flinching away from the upraised rifles and the sharp crack of the shots—but the shots never came. He risked opening his eyes to look. The rifles were still aimed at him, the soldiers bristling to shoot him where he stood.

"I said now, *Gott verdammt!*"

Harcourt could only stare back in confusion.

"I'm t-terribly sorry," he said, "but I'm deucedly perplexed. Do you *not* mean to shoot me?"

It was the Germans' turn to stare back at him. The big trooper gestured sharply with the barrel of his rifle, jerking it toward the ground.

"Ah hink he means it, sairrr," came a disembodied voice with a hint of a deep, eerie echo. "Best ye dae whit he says."

Harcourt looked in bewilderment at the Carthaginians, then back at the soldiers. "Pardon, but did... did you hear a *Scotsman* just now?"

The voice came again, louder this time. "Doon haur, ye bludy Sassenach—in th' pit!"

His hands still held in the air, Harcourt craned his neck around, looking for the source of the Scottish burr. It *seemed* to be coming from the ground behind him.

Turning, he took a tentative step toward what he had thought was chalky rock. The lip of an ancient limestone cistern blended in so well, he scarcely noticed it at all until he nearly tumbled in. A rickety wooden ladder, no more than a thin pole with branches for handholds, awaited his descent into a murky darkness.

"In!" the guard ordered harshly. "Now!"

Gulping, Harcourt carefully took hold of the shaky wooden pole. It quavered beneath his weight, but held steady long enough for him to reach the bottom. Once he stepped off onto the rough stone floor, the ladder was immediately pulled up out of reach.

The pit was deceptively large. Its central shaft opened into a wide circular chamber of limestone—not a well after all, but a tomb. It appeared to have once been part of a series of catacombs. Excavated alcoves ringed the chalky white chamber, twenty rows stacked three high. Where once entombed bones must have once lain, living prisoners now made their bunks.

"Welcome tae th' pit," one of them said.

It was his phantom Scotsman. A ruddy-faced young man in his late twenties, with long bushy sideburns. He wore a khaki uniform shirt and regulation boots, along with a military tam o'shanter and a Black Watch tartan kilt. The man gave a smart salute.

"Pipe-Major Duncan MacIntyre, Fifty-First Highland Division, Fifth Seaforth Highlanders, at yer service."

"Professor Winston Harcourt," he answered, doffing his top hat.

"Please make yerself at home, Professur. Let me introduce ye tae lae ay th' lads." He made a broad sweeping gesture to the rest of the prisoners, pointing out a dozen or so British soldiers, all dressed in the same sort of later-day drab uniform Harcourt associated with Blake's time.

"These wee jimmies are frae th' First Royal Dragoons an' One Hundred and Thirty-Third Lorried Brigade." He jerked his thumb toward a knot of them with fierce Polynesian faces. "An' these big black bastards, th' Kiwi's own Twenty-Eighth Maori Battalion."

"*Kia ora*," one of them said with a grin, and stuck out his tongue.

Harcourt raised an eyebrow.

MacIntyre turned to another group of uniformed Sepoys, some in turbans, some in helmets. "Thes dodgey lot is frae th' Fourth Indian division, ay coorse."

The Indians gave curt nods of their heads.

"An' these Boer reprobates an' their bloody Zulu stretcher bearers come tae us courtesy ay th' Sooth African First Infantry." The trio of white South Africans wore shorts and pith helmets. The black South Africans wore the same, along with medic armbands.

Harcourt gathered that the Zulu medical orderlies were trusted enough to go under heavy fire to rescue wounded soldiers, but not quite enough to be carrying firearms themselves—perfectly in keeping with his Victorian sensibilities. As a proud citizen of the British Empire, he took seriously the great responsibility of the White Man's Burden. Deuced shame that they couldn't be properly segregated down here. It was already bad form enough that a bagpiping Scot in a kilt seemed to be running the show.

"Quite the mix you have in here, I daresay," he responded to the litany.

"Och, ye don't ken th' half ay it, Sunny Jim." MacIntyre grinned, and indicated the remaining groups of prisoners. They were indeed, quite a mixed band.

"An' lest but nae leest, thes lot haur, is uir wee collection ay strays. Tae be honest, we dornt quite ken whaur they cam frae. They'ur mostly Froggies, but nane ay us can *parlez* much ay th' *Francais*."

"Not to worry, my man," Prof. Harcourt replied. "I'm quite fluent in French. *Salutations et félicitations, Messieurs.*"

Surprised, the French contingent rose and saluted as one. They were in three quite distinct groups. First, a small squad of French Foreign Legionnaires in their long blue coats and white pillbox *kepi* caps. Also, a pair of sailors in white kit, with smart navy blue jackets and wide-brimmed hats, and finally, a swarthy trio in most unusual uniform.

These last three had a distinctly Oriental cast about their features—each sporting a rather satanic-looking little beard and mustache—as well as their costume, open cropped jackets of dark blue canvas, embroidered with a swirling, serpentine vine design in rich red. Beneath silken blue sashes, their baggy trousers were the same bright red as their jacket piping, as were their hats, which looked somewhat like a deflated Morrocan *fez* with a long golden tassel. White spats over their boots completed their outfit.

There was a Middle-Eastern roguishness about them that Harcourt did not fully like – they looked more suitable as circus performers than soldiers.

"*Sous-Lieutenant* Guillaume Brackmann d'Alsace, *Légion Étrangère*, at your service, *Professeur* Harcourt," one Legionnaire said, giving the French pronunciation to Harcourt's name. The professor enjoyed this reception. He doffed his top hat and the two men shook hands.

"Very pleased to make your acquaintance. Forgive my impertinence, *sous-lieutenant*, but surely you weren't stationed anywhere nearby. However did you manage to find yourselves in Upper Egypt?"

"You're quite right, *Professeur*," d'Alsace acknowledged. "Our home base is in the Maghreb, as is the garrison of our three friends here in the Second Algerian Zouave Regiment. They are quite notorious in the provinces. The people call them 'the Jackals of Oran.'"

"A name we are proud to embrace," one of the Zouaves declared.

At this, all three stepped forward and simultaneously performed an elaborate obeisance, stretching their front leg forward as they leaned back and bowed low, unrolling a swirling movement of their arms. They rose and introduced themselves in turn.

"Armand Ibn Wasif."

"Jean-Lazare Bu-Akkash."

"Giraud Abdul Didier Ibn Bu Yussef ait Mengallat."

"We are all at your service, *Monsieur Professeur*," the three said in unison.

Second Lieutenant d'Alsace continued. "We all left Oran aboard the ship of the line *Donawerth*, bound for Gallipoli, to fight against the Russians in the Crimea, but our ship was broken up by a horrific storm in the Mediterranean. We were able to get in one of the boats and make it back to the coast here. As far as we can tell, we are the only survivors."

"The Crimean War? Let me see then you must have left port—"

"We set off on the ninth of June."

"Could you tell me, what year?"

"What *year*? Well, this year, of course—1854."

"Of course," Harcourt said. "Pardon me, *Messieurs*. I see there's one last man I should meet."

"*Bonne chance, Professeur.* Whatever tongue that one speaks, it's Greek to us."

The professor turned to a young man dozing in the corner of the chamber. He was in his late twenties or early thirties, with olive skin and Mediterranean looks. His belted tunic—white with burgundy trim over gray hose and leather boots—set him apart from the rest of the pit's inhabitants. Harcourt first hazarded a greeting in Latin. The lone man opened his eyes and looked up at the Victorian's strange outfit in surprise.

"*Den faínesai moiázeis gia Romaíos. Orkízomai ston Serápi kai ston Christó, se parakalo pes mou óti boreís na milíseis tin glóssa mou?*" he asked in a hopeful voice. *You don't look Roman. I swear by Serapis and Christ, please tell me you can speak my language?*

Harcourt turned to the others. "It seems our friend here *is* speaking Greek."

His name was Lucius, Harcourt quickly learned, and he was delighted to finally have someone to talk to. The rest of the prisoners gathered around to enjoy the novelty of Harcourt translating the Alexandrian's speech. Lucius explained that he served the Prefect of Alexandria, a minor *agens in rebus* under Calix, the prefect's chief *magistrianos*.

Harcourt held his tongue, not wishing to tell Lucius that Calix had been murdered—by the same man who had brought Harcourt to the city. After the Wrath-Fall, as Lucius called it, he had been dispatched to the west while another rider went east, and a third up the Nile, to report on the new reality of the region.

"Before I could return with my report, I was captured by those damned foreigners with their smoking iron carriages, and put in here to rot with these barbarians," Lucius said with a wave of his hands.

Harcourt translated more diplomatically. This provoked a barrage of questions in a variety of languages from the other soldiers, all at the same time. Exasperated, Harcourt held up his hands for silence.

"One moment!" he said. "One moment, gentlemen, and I will endeavor to explain, to the best of my ability."

"Professor," MacIntyre pleaded. "Dae ye hae a plan tae gie us oot ay thes place?"

"Yes!" One of the Royal Dragoons nodded enthusiastically. "We've got to do something before the Jerries decide to shoot the lot of us, or cover up the hole, or sell us to those Arabs out there."

"Do calm yourselves, gentlemen! To begin with, those natives are not Arabs. They are traders from Carthage."

Some of the soldiers frowned at this news. "Carthage?" one said. "You mean ancient Carthage, like Hannibal's bunch?"

"The very same. Allow me to explain. First of all—"

Harcourt paused, taking in all of the expectant faces. Speaking before large audiences was old hat, but telling the unvarnished truth, with the authority of the informed, and without ulterior motive? Quite the novelty.

He began again.

"Apokaleitai i Ekdílosi."

"C'est ce qu'on appelle l'Événement."

"It is called the Event…"

420

45

The *Star of the Dawn* still stood tied up where they had left her, somewhat battered by its run-in with the bull hippo, but still ship-worthy. With an arm around Cam, Ibn Fadlan helped the wounded Celt aboard and laid him down on a reed mat, kneeling to tend to the stab wound in his side.

Amber and Leila boarded next, Leila still awkwardly clutching both Amber's fallen crossbow and the *khopesh* sword against her chest. The two women quickly helped Kha-Hotep use the oars to cast off and push the boat away into the current.

The raised riverbank concealed whatever was happening back in the patchwork city of New Memphis, but judging from the howls that echoed in the distance, the enraged inhabitants were still hunting for them.

Durand had bought them the time they needed to escape—they could only hope the price he paid was not as high as they feared.

Suddenly torchlights appeared over the ridge behind them. The fastest of their pursuers had caught sight of them slipping downriver. Frustrated, the pursuers hurled rocks and makeshift fishing spears at the departing boat, but all fell short.

"Thank you for the lovely dinner!" Kha-Hotep shouted back at the shore. "I'm sorry we cannot stay for dessert!"

Ibn Fadlan gestured to Amber. "Can you ask the captain if there is any linen or poultice aboard?" he asked. "I need to bind the wound."

Alarmed, Amber came over to see for herself. He had pulled up Cam's blood-soaked tunic. With only moonlight to see by, his side looked black and slick.

"Don't worry," Cam said, looking up at her. "This is nothing. I will just rest for a short while."

Amber took a deep breath and shook her head, not sure if she was about to laugh or cry.

Abruptly a fiery streak flew past, just over their heads. It landed in the river and sizzled out. A pack of Egyptian archers had arrived on the riverbank, shooting flaming arrows. The missiles flashed toward them through the night air, like shooting stars. One landed on the deck, narrowly missing Cam's outstretched legs, and another two hit the upright cabin.

More were coming.

"Put them out!" Kha-Hotep yelled, pulling out the arrows stuck in the cabin and beating at the flames with a loop of rope. Leila and Ibn Fadlan didn't need to understand his words to know his meaning. Dodging the incoming arrows, they kicked at the ones stuck in the deck and stamped out the fiery scraps of flaxen wrap.

Amber took up position at the stern, and brought her crossbow to bear. She knew she wasn't a good enough shot to be a sniper. So she took careful aim at the centermost man and then swept a three-shot burst at their line. One of the archers dropped his bow with a choked scream. He grasped at his throat and collapsed.

The rest retreated back over the ridge.

Lowering the crossbow, Amber stared at the man she'd shot. *My god*, she thought. *I killed him.* Her hands began to shake. *I've just killed someone*. She felt gut-punched. It had been different when she couldn't see the faces of her targets—she didn't even know whether she'd hit anyone.

This was inescapable.

Kha-Hotep lay a gentle hand on her shoulder.

"You must not worry, little warrior. Lord Osiris will weigh his heart, and receive him or reject him. You saved us. So let your heart be comforted."

Amber nodded, but continued to stare across the river.

No further shots harried them. The *Siu-Tuait* continued to carry them through the black water.

It was dangerous to travel the river by night, but once again they had no choice. Kha-Hotep wanted to go at least as far downriver as the sprawling necropolis of Saqqara—if any of it still existed.

Perversely, the gods chose this night to draw up thick river-mists from the waters, making their navigation all the more difficult. Perhaps, he reasoned, it was a blessing in disguise, since it would hinder any attempts to track them from Memphis, if their pursuers still hunted them.

Regardless of whether the fickle gods chose to bestow favor or hindrance, they had to continue their journey. Assigning Amber to the tiller, he took point at the bow, using a long punting pole to search for hidden sandbars. He called out orders to Amber back at the stern, and whispered the occasional prayer to Khonsu the moon-god to aid them in their travels.

With Leila's help, Ibn Fadlan cleaned Cam's wound as best he could, and the two kept watch over him while he slept. The rest watched for pursuit—either on foot or on the river. Then, after a few hours, the captain finally caught a glimpse of what he had hoped to find. Through the fog there appeared the upper half of an obelisk rising out of the fog. So at least some trace of the Saqqara necropolis remained.

Deciding they had gone far enough for safety, Kha-Hotep looked for a place to weigh anchor. He knew the vast necropolis was serviced by a number of stone quays along the river, and hoped Ra would see fit to let them come across one—if any remained. As luck and the gods would have it, just as he was considering tying up among the sedge and the rushes, a jetty appeared ahead.

Once he assured himself that their landing was clear of hippos and crocodiles, Kha-Hotep brought the *Siu-Tuait* to rest against the quay, securing it to the stone rings. Then they laid out reed mats on the deck to get some much-needed sleep. Wanting to keep an eye on his patient, Ibn Fadlan volunteered to stay up for the first watch.

Ibn Fadlan loved the feel of the cool night air on his face. After such a horrific day, he found the gentle rocking of the boat on the calm waters of the Nile immensely soothing. He had much to think about.

A distant flash of light interrupted his musings.

"The thunder praises the glory of Allah, tremendous in might," he murmured. "He sends the thunderbolts, striking whomever He wills." But to his astonishment, the brilliant display was no bolt of lightning. It remained in the sky, standing like a pillar up to the heavens—then vanished once again.

From behind, a movement on the deck startled him. He was relieved to find that it was only Leila.

"*As salamu alaikum*. Forgive me, *Mullah*," she said shyly, lowering her gaze as she approached. "I don't mean to intrude or be forward."

"*Wa alaikum assalam wa aahmatullah,*" he said, returning the greeting with a welcoming wave of his hand. "Please, feel free to join me in admiring the river. The moon is out, and the mists are not so incessant, thanks be to God. We are not alone here, there is no danger of *Khalwah*. Come, the believing men and believing women are allies of one another."

He politely avoided eye contact with the girl, continuing to look out on the play of dappled moonlight on the Nile. After a few minutes, however, he turned toward her in concern.

"Something troubles you?"

She gave a miserable nod, wiping at her eyes. "I've acted immodestly," she replied, the shame clear in her voice. "This morning, when I thought the French soldiers were going to kill us, I touched a man—the captain—and he put his arm around me."

"Did you try to seduce the Nubian? Or he you?"

"Oh no! It wasn't like that! It was only for a moment, when I was scared."

He nodded. "That is well. So then, repent and flee from evil. God knows your heart, and forgives what is past. But remember, child, whosoever returns to their sins, God will exact retribution upon them."

"I understand, *Mullah*," she said meekly.

"We are surrounded by the unbelievers. Shaitan the deceiver whispers to our hearts and makes it seem right in our eyes to do evil."

"Yes, *Mullah*," she said, wiping her eyes again.

"Where is your mind?" he asked gently. "You still seem distant and troubled."

Leila nodded, desperate to unload her doubts and fears, but afraid they would all come tumbling out in a flood if she spoke even a single word.

"It's just…"

"You can tell me."

"Well, it's just that… so much has happened. My cousins and I were in a car crash, and… they all died. I almost drowned. And then—*Ya Kharaashy!* So much else!" She shook her head. "It's all so horrible. I miss my cousin so badly. She was my best friend…"

He listened intently, smiling in sympathy, even though he didn't understand all of her story. "Should we not be thankful that God in his wisdom put death at the end of life, and not at its beginning?"

She tried to smile back, sniffled, and nodded. That was just the kind of thing her grandfather would say to cheer her up—a piece of joke-wisdom, always a bit tone-deaf and never entirely successful, and yet, the familiarity of his clunky attempt comforted her. Then it reminded her of her family back in Cairo, and sadness rushed in again.

"I've lost everyone," she whispered. "Everyone I ever knew. Everything in the world… and I'm still so scared."

"If God helps you, none can overcome you. In Him, then, put your trust."

She nodded, building up nerve to ask her next question.

"Mullah?" she finally said. "Has Cam told you yet? About the storm? About how the timeline has shattered?"

It was his turn to be silent for a moment.

"Before the dinner he tried, a little. I confess, there is much confusion for me, as well. The One who sets all things in motion has placed us in a most trying time."

"You are a scholar. What does the holy Quran say about such a catastrophe? Is it—I mean, do you think—" She couldn't say it out loud. Her voice dropped to a whisper. "Do you think it could really be the end of the world?"

"God forfend! The Fashioner and Former of the world directs all matters toward their proper conclusion, perfectly and righteously, and the holy Quran makes clear the great signs that point to the end, and the Day of Judgment."

"What are they?" she asked anxiously.

"The Holy city of Mecca will be attacked and the Kaaba itself will be destroyed. A huge black cloud of smoke will cover the earth. The sun will rise from the west. The very moon will be split in two, and yet the unbelievers will still deny it."

Leila shuddered, vividly picturing it all.

"The *Dajjal*—the false messiah—shall appear, but the prophet Isa, peace be upon him, will come down from the fourth heaven to slay *Dajjal*. There are two vicious tribes, the Gog and Magog, imprisoned by the great Macedonian king al-Iskander behind a great wall in the high mountains of the Far East. They will burst forth and ravage the earth, drink all the water of Lake Tiberias, and kill all believers in their way."

Her brow furrowed.

"Also shall come forth from out of the ground the *Dabbat al-ard*, the Beast of the Earth," Ibn Fadlan continued solemnly. "He will have the Seal of Solomon and the Staff of Moses, and shall mark the believers with the staff and the unbelievers with the seal.

"And at last, God shall send a pleasant breeze to blow from the south, and that shall cause all believers to die peacefully. Then will the trumpet be sounded, and the dead will return to life. God shall resurrect all, even if they have turned to stone or iron."

She blinked, opened her mouth, closed it again. Ibn Fadlan was not finished.

"Then, at the very end, out of Yemen shall come a great fire that gathers all to the Day of Judgment. The time is known only to God. Even Muhammad, blessings be upon him and peace, cannot bring it forward."

Leila was very quiet for a moment. "*Mullah*, about this Earth-Beast," she said, "with the seal and the staff… and the, what did you call it, the *Dajjal*?"

"Yes, the false messiah. He shall appear as a one-eyed man, his right eye blind and deformed like a grape, and he will be followed by seventy thousand Jews of Isfahan, wearing Persian shawls. He shall possess great powers, and shall deceive many unbelievers."

"Stop!" she blurted out, closing her eyes. "Please, *stop*!"

"Have no fear, child. The faithful ones, the true believers, shall most surely be saved from all those terrors. It is written."

"No, that's not it!" She turned her head and faced him directly, staring into his eyes with a blend of unconcealed anger and need. "I must know, what does it say about this?" She waved a hand. "The Event. Everything that's happening now—the broken timeline, the shards, the dinosaurs, so many people just vanished. What does it say about all *this*?"

Startled by her directness, he remained silent for a moment before answering.

"The Prophet tells us God, the Most Generous, is plentiful in responding to our supplications and our entreaties," he said, slowly at first. "But we must be patient. For if he does not answer our questions in this life, we can be sure he will richly provide us the answers we seek in the hereafter."

She looked away, considering the night sky and the moon-touched highlights dancing alongside them in the river's gentle current. She nodded to herself.

"So, you don't know." She didn't look at him.

He opened his mouth to answer, thought better of it, and closed his mouth again.

"Let us you and I pray that the One who has all knowledge of the seen and the unseen will guide us to the straight path."

She nodded silently. They stood there together while an awkward pause hung over them. At last the aristocratic Arab spoke gently to her.

"You have great spirit, and all this surrounding madness has confused and frightened you, disturbed the peace of your heart." He hesitated before asking his next question. "Why don't you come back with me to Baghdad? You have no one of the faithful to look after you. It would be wrong of me to leave you here in the hands of the infidels."

She remained silent.

"Have you been to the City of Peace, Child?" he persisted. "It is the largest and greatest city in the world. You would gasp in wonder at its palaces and minarets, its perfumed gardens, its bazaars and markets. All manner of silks and spices and precious things await you there. I would show you the libraries and schools of the House of Wisdom, where scholars, mathematicians, and philosophers from distant Byzantium to furthest China come to gather all the knowledge of the world."

"*Mullah*, I have no doubt Baghdad was very beautiful in your day," she finally said, "but with everything that's happened, we don't know if it still is the same city you left—we can't even know if there *is* a Baghdad anymore…"

"How could it not be? Surely God would not allow his greatest city to disappear. What hubris to think otherwise! Come with me and you will see. If your father were here, I would entreat him to allow me your hand in marriage, and you would have a truly blessed life with me there."

Leila looked down quickly to hide her reaction. Did she dare tell him that, as far as she knew, his beloved Baghdad had pretty much been destroyed seven hundred years before her time, and had never regained its full glory? Could she tell him she had no interest whatsoever in marrying him?

"Young one, I have three other wives in Baghdad. They would be like your new sisters. How wonderful a gift for you, is it not?"

Desperate to change the subject, Leila turned away.

She gasped audibly.

"Child? What is it?"

She pointed to the others, sleeping on the deck.

"Where is Amber?"

46

At twilight, the sound of a lone bagpipe echoed out of the pit, filling the dying wasteland with a plaintive melody of almost inexpressible sorrow and loneliness.

Harcourt detested the bloody racket.

He was not impressed that their German captors had allowed MacIntyre to keep his bagpipes. On the contrary, he was certain the Huns had only granted the favor in order to increase the suffering of their prisoners.

The North African desert operated in only two modes, the professor decided. Unbearably hot by day, insufferably cold at night, interchanging from one to the other without even the benefit of a modest surcease at dusk and dawn. Most damnably uncivilized. At least down here in the pit there was shade and a modicum of shelter, if not creature comforts. Miserable, Harcourt

433

longed for an isolated corner to escape the noise, but in the circular chamber, the Scotsman's Celtic caterwauling was inescapable. Deucedly vexing.

Confoundingly enough, it didn't seem to bother the others. One of the soldiers had a deck of cards that was getting good use. The Indians appeared to be quietly meditating in what Harcourt could only imagine was some devilish ritual of the Hindoos. The three Zouaves in their outlandish circus outfits were engaged in some odd game involving an intense staring contest punctuated by sudden slaps to the opponent's face, always provoking a spate of raucous laughter.

Most of the men, however, seemed to be trying to make sense of what Harcourt had told them, perhaps pondering their own mortality. Even the professor was not immune. He silently counted the number of times he had very nearly died in all manner of dreadful ways over the course of the last week.

Indeed, he'd been so filled with hopeless despair he had even put a gun to his head and pulled the trigger. His cowardice ate at him. At that moment it had been easier to kill himself than to try and shoot his way out. He wasn't a killer—he couldn't even bring himself to turn the gun on his captor. Small comfort that the gun wasn't even loaded. If János Mehta had not been playing a cruel jape, he would be already dead by his own hand.

MacIntyre's infernal piping suddenly ceased. The Scotsman stared up the well of light. A murmur arose and some of the other soldiers drew closer, shushing the rest.

"Quiet! Something's happening up top!"

The prisoners all fell silent, straining to hear. Harcourt heard the mechanical rumbling of one of those damnable horseless war-carriages approaching. The vehicle ground to a halt. A commanding voice began barking orders, and the fawning Carthaginians replied in very broken German.

"This is it, lads," one of the South Africans said glumly. "We're done for. The Jerries have come to finish us off." The men continued to stare upward in anxious silence. A stray bit of grit and dust trickled down from above, and then the ladder came down. A German officer descended into the pit, stepping off the ladder without fear. He silently regarded the ring of captives, his gaze traveling the room until it finally settled on the anxious professor.

The officer removed his cap and Harcourt stared in disbelief.

"Blake?"

The newcomer gave Harcourt a rare smile and clapped a hand on his shoulder.

"Yes, it's me, you worthless old grifter," he said with genuine warmth. "And don't worry, it's the real me, not some hypnotized slave."

"Blake! This is utterly astounding!" Harcourt turned to his fellow captives. "Listen, all of you. This man is a British officer!"

The prisoners gathered around the two men in excitement, Harcourt repeating the news in French and Greek before turning back to Blake.

"I must say, my good man, I never dared hoped to see you alive again."

"Not just me," Blake said. "Nellie survived the explosion, too."

"Good heavens, Miss Bly as well? That's splendid!" Harcourt beamed with happiness for a moment, then sobered. "Though I am dreadfully sorry to see you here, old boy. So the Huns captured you, too?"

Blake raised an eyebrow.

"Not exactly." He held up his new pistol.

"I say! However did you come across that?"

"I traded a knife for it—but don't worry about that. I heard your Scot playing on the pipes, and now we're busting all of you out of here."

Without any further pleasantries, Blake crouched down and went into action mode. The soldiers crowded around as he traced out his plan on the floor.

"First off, I need three lorry drivers." Three of the English Tommies each raised a hand. "Right—you, you, and you. You'll come with me back to the back of the leaguer here. I've got more DAK caps in the lorry up top. Put them on, alter your shirts or just take them off, keep your heads down and let me do the talking. I've got two more lorries ready to go. We'll be coming back here to pick up the rest of you. It's going to be pretty cramped for all of us—we'll be bringing some souvenirs with us."

"Where are we going, sir?" one of the men asked.

"Alexandria," Blake answered. "Problem is, the Germans are headed there, too. They're already on their way, playing leapfrog across the desert with two, maybe three battle groups of Panzers and some mixed support vehicles. We'll need to beat them there if Alex has any chance of holding them off."

"*Alexandria?*" Harcourt huffed in disbelief. "You can't be serious, man! What we need to do is flee at once and get to the South Pole post-haste!"

"And how do you propose we do that?" Blake shot back. "Steal a lorry and drive across Africa? See if there are any charter boats available at the Cape of Good Hope to sail to Antarctica?"

Harcourt shut up.

"Look," Blake continued, his voice calmer. "I don't know how we're going to do this without the *Vanuatu*. Maybe we can build a blimp, jury-rig a propeller-engine from car parts—I just don't know. But right now, the Germans are advancing on the city with tanks and machine guns. Do you think they'll stop long enough that you can convince *them* to help us?"

"I take your point, old boy," Harcourt said, "but it seems a damnably slender reed to hang our hopes upon, don't you think?"

Blake leaned in close to him and lowered his voice.

"Let me tell you what I think," he said, his unnaturally calm tone making it all the more menacing. "I think I am going to do whatever is in my power to save the last bastion of civilization for as long as it can hold out. And if that means I'm left fighting Nazis when the end of the world comes round, then I will go to Judgment Day with a smile on my face, and so will you. Are we clear?"

The Victorian nodded profusely. "As a bell, my good man, clear as a bell."

Blake leaned back again. "Right, then. Whatever we do, we are going to need the Alexandrians' help. They're our only chance."

"How strong are the defenses in Alex now?" another soldier asked.

"Slim and nil—and to make things even more fun, the whole town's stuck back in the fifth century, so it's up to us to do all the heavy lifting. I don't think their spears and short swords are going to be much help."

The soldiers chuckled with gallows humor. Blake quickly repeated the plan in French for the Legionnaires and Zouaves, while Harcourt explained to Lucius.

"Getting everyone aboard the lorries is just part one," Blake continued. "We also need a strike team. How many demolitions men do we have?"

Several of the New Zealanders and Sepoys raised their hands.

"Right. You four will be taking out as many of the petrol lorries as we can. The more fuel we can destroy, the more Afrika Korps forces we can maroon in the desert without having to fire a shot."

"A very sound plan," one of the turbaned Sikhs commented with a nod.

"There's a crate of mines in the lorry up top, mostly Teller mines for tanks, and maybe a dozen or so anti-personnel, German 'S' types. You can booby-trap the undercarriages with them, wire them to the axle, bury them just under the tires, I'm sure you can think up some other party tricks."

The Sikh looked over at his New Zealander counterpart. They exchanged knowing smiles.

"With all due respect," the Sikh said, "no thank you. You save those for Alexandria. We can take out the petrol tankers just fine. Leave that to us."

"Excellent. What's your name, soldier?"

"Singh, sir."

"*Khuśakisamatĭ*, Singh," Blake nodded, wishing him good luck in Punjabi.

* * *

Watching from the sidelines, Harcourt was dismayed to see his thunder stolen so effortlessly by Blake. But his peevishness was more than mollified by the thought of escape, and in that regard, the man was eminently capable. Still, he couldn't deny he'd miss being regarded with respect and admiration.

"I need three volunteers for something special," Blake said. *"J'ai besoin de trois volontaires."*

"Ç'est nous!" The three Zouaves stepped forward. Blake waved them close, and outlined his plan for them in rapid-fire French. They smiled and nodded eagerly.

"I say, one word of caution, Blake." Harcourt stepped forward, eager to be seen contributing as well. "You'll want to be sure to keep a sharp eye out for János Mehta. He's managed to insinuate himself with the German commander. Who knows what mischief—"

"What did you say?" Blake cut in, his eyes narrowed. "János Mehta is *here*? And talking with Rommel?"

"Well, erm, if that *is* the old chap's name…"

Blake stood up. "Then that's one more job to do before we leave here."

47

German Afrika Korps Encampment
Night — Eight days after the Event

Blake knew the day's password, having tricked it out of a soldier earlier that afternoon. Driving back toward the main encampment, the English soldiers sitting next to him sweated bullets, but the only sentries they encountered let the lorry continue unchallenged.

The earlier commotion had dwindled now that night had fallen, and the support teams were finished loading up and making final preparations for the battle group's departure in the morning. Driving around the western end of the camp, Blake kept his speed glacial and avoided any major areas of activity. Every now and again they passed by the odd bunch of two or three soldiers taking a smoking break after their long day. None gave him or his nervous passengers a second glance.

Normally, the square of Panzers would have stood

like a fortress wall, guns out, with just enough space between each vehicle to allow a lorry to pass through. Now they had to make do with less than a quarter of their regular number, so the tanks stood more like a row of beachside lifeguard stations than an impregnable iron barrier.

Blake pulled to a stop outside the northwestern corner, close to where two other lorries rested. It was a good location—out of the way, easy to get in or out, and the line of petrol tankers was close at hand. He opened the door and let the man next to him take the driver seat. All three would wait for his signal.

"If you run into anyone, take them out fast," he said in a low voice. "Here, I've got one extra pistol, and two wrenches. You sort out who gets what, but keep quiet about it."

He moved around to the back, yawning nonchalantly and nodding to a passing pair of mechanics. Once they moved on, he poked his head in the back, where his Kiwi and Indian demolition strike team waited. He gave then a curt nod.

"Stay out of sight and hit as many as you can, but when you hear the signal, hightail it as fast as you can back to the lorry and get out of here." He checked once more that the coast was clear, then pulled the canvas back and rushed them out in silence. They slipped into the shadows between the parked vehicles.

Blake walked away from that corner of the leaguer, looking for the motorcycle he'd left there earlier. It had disappeared. He frowned.

Ah well, too much to hope it would still be there, he mused. *Just have to look for another, or do without.* In any case, he'd have to get a move on if he was to finish his own work before the signal came.

Harcourt had given him a reasonably good idea of where Rommel's command tent was located. Blake simply had to be sure to look for it without *looking* as if he was looking for it. He ambled past the rows of camouflage tents, trying to appear as just another bored and exhausted soldier. Then he spotted it.

An unobtrusive placard on the tent marked it as the field marshal's. A pair of sentries stood guard outside, watching a nearby group of soldiers and a trio of Carthaginians. The troopers were bargaining loudly—though ironically, much of it in sign language—trying to barter for a chicken. Blake strolled over to join the two sentries and watch the show.

"Awful big fuss over a chicken," he offered.

The sentries nodded. The bargaining session grew more animated as the bird suddenly became agitated, squawking and flapping its wings wildly.

"Maybe somebody should clear them out so all this racket doesn't bother the field marshal and what's-his-name, the *Doktor*," Blake suggested. Neither sentry budged.

"It's fine," one said.

"You think?" Blake asked, a hint of concern in his voice.

"They're not here—went to the new Mobile HQ," the other added.

"Ah." Blake kept his voice neutral and uninterested, and after a short pause, stifled a yawn. "Well, I think I've heard enough. See you."

He turned around and started back the way he came.

"Holtz!" Someone called from behind.

He carefully kept his gaze straight ahead and his pace even.

"*Stabsgefreiter* Holtz!" The voice came closer. Blake calmly turned a corner and walked between two tents, increasing his pace considerably once he was out of sight. He turned another corner, hoping to lose his pursuer in the maze of canvas, but the other man was close on his tail.

"Damn it! Holtz! Where have you been! I've been looking for you for hours!"

Blake halted, and then slowly turned around. By the insignia on his collar, he saw that his interrogator was a major. The officer, already furious, frowned at this stranger with HOLTZ on his uniform.

"You're not Holtz!"

The German drew his Luger and fired—but Blake was faster, shooting the major in the forehead. He didn't stop to make sure his foe was dead, but turned on his heel and ran through the rows of tents, glancing around to get his bearings. He'd have to head deeper into the center of the leaguer if he didn't want to lead everyone back to his men.

Too late.

The shots had already attracted attention. Shouts and footfalls came from every direction. A soldier appeared around the corner of a tent, rifle in hand. Blake whirled, dropping to one knee to fire. The shot caught the soldier in the chest, sending him flying backward to the ground. Blake rose to sprint away, but he could hear a squad of soldiers heading in his direction.

Quickly, he dropped to his knee again and fired three shots to the south. The German troopers rushed around the corner, guns out.

"Quickly!" Blake yelled in rapid-fire German. "He's getting away!" He fired another round into the darkness between the rows of tents. The squad leapt into action, laying down suppression fire and advancing tent by tent in pursuit of their unseen quarry. Blake slipped away, this time moving back to where his strike team was at work. A siren began wailing. He ran smack into another mass of soldiers, nearly colliding with their commander, who grabbed him by the lapels.

"You!" the man barked. "Come with us—the shots are coming from this way!"

"*Jawohl!*" Reluctantly Blake headed back the way he'd just come, wondering how long he could keep up the ruse. The siren blared, and more commotion came from nearby. Had his demo team been discovered?

He shot a glance over his shoulder.

Chaos erupted behind them. Gunfire, screams, and an ominous rumbling. Blake stopped in his tracks, and several of the uneasy soldiers halted with him. A nearby tent exploded into a torn bundle of canvas thrown skyward, and then a dark hulking shape burst into the light.

The soldiers around him scattered in fear, leaving Blake standing there in wonder as the first of three war elephants charged past him, smashing everything and everyone in its path. The other two laid waste of their own to either side. Their Zouave riders weren't so much steering the beasts as encouraging their rampage, hanging on like American cowboys, laughing and howling in maniacal glee as their steeds tore through the camp.

"You mad, magnificent bastards," Blake muttered in reluctant admiration, shaking his head as he watched the path of destruction. Leave it to the Zouaves to improve on an already insane plan—and give the signal, as well.

Time to get out of here.

He sprinted for the rendezvous point, then stopped in his tracks as an unexpected surprise caught his eye.

"Well, hello, old friend."

The entire camp boiled in turmoil, with soldiers running in all directions—either in pursuit of, or fleeing from, the trumpeting pachyderms making a shambles of the base's soft underbelly. Back at the northwest corner of the leaguer, the Indians and Kiwis piled into the last of the lorries. As Blake rode up on his rediscovered motorcycle, MacIntyre popped his head out of the back and gave an appreciative whistle.

"Braw motorbike, chief!"

"Singh!" Blake called, pulling to a stop. "Are the petrol tankers taken care of?"

The Sikh gave a thumbs up.

"Light them up."

"Not to worry," Singh replied, looking at his watch. "They should be lighting themselves right... about... now."

A flash and a whooshing sound came from the closest tanker, and then jets of burning flame burst into life from its petrol tank, dousing the next closest tanker like a lawn sprinkler. That tanker spouted a trio of fiery gushers of its own, and the pyromaniacal game continued down the line like hellish dominos, until all the tankers in the line were burning brightly. The licking flames, flickering shadows, and shadowy bodies running back and forth lent a hellish appearance to the entire scene.

"Will they explode?" Blake asked.

"Probably not." Singh shrugged. "But they might. We should go now."

"You heard the man," Blake yelled to the driver. "Let's move! But follow me, we'll have to swing around to pick up the Zouaves—if they haven't gotten themselves killed yet!"

"Hauld up, Blake!" MacIntyre called out from the back of the lorry. "Hae ye got room fur me oan tha' beestie?"

Blake jerked his head over. "Come on, then."

The Scotsman grinned and ran over, hopping into the sidecar, bagpipes in hand. Blake shot a dubious look at the pipes.

"You don't mean to be playing those now, do you?"

"It's mah job, isnae it?" MacIntyre replied in all innocence. Before Blake could respond, another commotion tore through another nearby row of tents. The war elephants were headed right toward them.

The fire from the petrol tankers, blazing like torchwood, seemed to terrify the charging beasts. They gave the flames a wide berth, one elephant trampling a staff car while the other two crashed through a mess tent, thrashing through splintered tables and benches, sending plates, pots, and pans flying everywhere. The Zouaves cheered their steeds with every new collision.

"*Sautez! Sautez!*" Blake yelled, with no idea if they could hear him over all the tumult. For whatever reason, the Zouaves chose that moment to dismount, looking remarkably like circus acrobats as they leapt off onto nearby tents and camouflage netting, then dropped to the ground and sprinted to the lorry.

The elephants continued their charge on into the night.

"That's everybody!" Blake yelled to the driver, and he gunned the motorcycle. "Go! Go!"

The two vehicles sped away. In the sidecar, MacIntyre looked back at the chaos they had unleashed in the German camp and let out a loud hoot of triumph.

"A nod's as guid as a wink tae a blind horse!" he called out happily over the roar of the speeding motorcycle.

"I have no idea what that means," Blake muttered as the Scotsman took up his pipes and played them out, into the night.

48

Place: Unknown
Time: Unknown

Chill morning mist cloaked him as he walked through a veil of dangling willow branches along the bank of the Leagean, the Bright River. He stopped, for a pair of bone-white hunting dogs crossed his path. Fierce-looking ghost-white hounds, eyes and ears blood-red. They greeted him like faithful pets.

"Cam," a familiar voice called out. Cam whirled in surprise.

"Kentan!"

His foster brother was there, large as life, smiling. Cam rushed up to him, but Kentan held out a hand, shaking his head.

"Kentan… I thought… Are you…?" Cam couldn't get his words out.

Suddenly Kentan was standing across the river with the white hounds. He was waving, and seemed to be calling out, but Cam couldn't make out the words.

"Kentan! What are you saying?" he called back, shaking his head, a sudden fear gripping him.

"Cam, can you hear me, my brother?" Kentan shouted, his voice barely audible. Struck mute, Cam could only stand there, his voice failing him, mouthing words that no one could hear.

"Can you hear me, my brother?" Kentan's voice grew louder.

Someone shook his shoulder. Cam ignored it, burrowing back under his cloak as he tried to retrace his dreams.

"Cam, can you hear me, my brother? Cam. Cam, you must wake up." Kha-Hotep's voice finally penetrated the fog of sleep and dreams.

He sat up with a start, grimacing from the sudden sharp twinge in his side. Kha-Hotep knelt next to him, Ibn Fadlan and Leila standing behind him. All three began talking to him at once, each in a different language, his implant racing to keep up with them. Confused, he looked around.

"Where's Amber?"

"Cam, Amber is gone," Kha-Hotep said grimly.

Leaving the others behind to stay with the barge, Kha-Hotep and Cam set off to find Amber, each with a sword in one hand and an oil lamp in the other. Two bright spots fought the dark as they made their way down the quay.

Kha-Hotep had tried to talk the wounded Celt out of joining him, but Cam had assured him he was fine, pulling up the blood-stained tunic to prove that the druid's magic was already at work. Traceries of tiny silver hexagons were stitching up the ugly stab wound.

Even if he'd been bleeding to death, Cam would still look for Amber.

As the pair left the last of the river fog behind, a moonlit wonderland rose up before them.

"Nev Kawgh…" Cam murmured.

Spread out over a wide and rocky plain on the edge of the endless desert, a conclave of man-made mountains dominated a landscape of temples, shrines, and long stone causeways. Each of the colossal structures boasted bright white triangular sides, every one as smooth as marble, with edges as sharp and crisp as a ray of light. He counted nearly a dozen of the triangular structures, but the three largest towered overhead so high Cam thought he could reach the moon itself, if he could only find a way to scale the sheer sides.

"What is this place?" he asked, awestruck.

"These are the great pyramids," Kha-Hotep answered proudly. "The tallest and greatest achievements in the entire world. They are the tombs of our ancient pharaohs Khufu, Khafre, and Menkaure, built nearly one and a half thousand years before my time."

"Did your gods raise these up? Or some race of giants?"

"Our forefathers did, by the tens of thousands, laboring for decades—but that was in the fourth dynasty. By my time, the nineteenth dynasty, they were long abandoned, their smooth skin gnawed away by the desert and the ages, and the yellow-gray limestone beneath had been exposed." He shook his head in amazement. "Yet see how they gleam, as though newly-finished this very day."

They continued forward. The quay ended in a pair of temples side by side, with no obvious way to get around them. A line of tall statues stood guard at the temple entrances, each sculpted figure a serene enthroned pharaoh carved from speckled gray diorite. Each of the temples had two entrances. Four doorways to choose from, then. There was no other way Amber might have gone.

"She had to have gone through one of them," Kha-Hotep reasoned.

"Left temple or right, then?"

"That way," Kha-Hotep said decisively, pointing to the temple entrance on the furthest right hand.

The two men passed the stone pharaohs and entered a high-arched hallway, their lights reflecting off the smooth sides of the corridor. Like the outer surface, the inner walls and ceiling were of a pink granite, the floors paved with elegant cloudy white alabaster. The passageway led them a few paces further along, then turned to the right for a few more, before turning left, and finally opening onto a long, wide central court.

Along the walls, alcoves housed statues of various animal-headed deities. A white alabaster altar dominated the center of the court, flanked on either side by an interior colonnade of rectangular pillars, each encased in red granite. The pillars pointed upward, and the chamber was open to the night sky.

They set their oil lamps on the altar, making its four alabaster finials seem to glow from within. Cam stretched his neck up toward the broad skylight.

"No roof but the sky, and yet everything here is gleaming and pristine," he noted.

Kha-Hotep nodded. "There must be many servants of the gods who care for this temple. I wonder where they are."

Cam started to answer, then stopped as the sounds of voices and sandaled footsteps approached from the opposite entrance to the one they had used. The pair moved swiftly, each hiding behind one of the pillars.

"The lights!" Kha-Hotep hissed. Cam ran up and leaned over to blow one out, then the other, then ducked behind the altar without a chance to grab either lamp. A tiny curl of smoke twisted up from each extinguished wick, barely visible in the gloom.

The corridor beyond the doorway began to grow brighter with the glow of an approaching light, and then a woman appeared. Her arresting beauty commanded attention, dangerous enough to attract a god or topple a king. Tall and graceful, with dusky golden skin, long lustrous black hair, and keen almond eyes lined with kohl. Her headdress was a circlet with a golden sun-disk diadem and a cobra crown. A wide collar formed of slender rods of malachite and lapis lazuli encircled her neck, while bracelets of gold and faience adorned her long bare arms. Her tall, lean body stood clad in a long dress of pleated white cotton, both sheer and elegant.

Behind her, two female servants led a pair of lions. The huge cats snarled, the terrifying sound reverberating off the walls. Cam was sure the beasts had caught their scent, and would be turned on them any moment, but the women kept the growling creatures in check. Behind them came a procession of softly chanting people—most likely temple acolytes and worshipers—their candles a firefly swarm in the darkened hall.

The procession marched through the open hallway and turned between the altars. Cam stared up at the line of worshipers so close to him, silently willing them to be blind to the abandoned lamps, sitting in plain sight on the altar so conspicuous to his horrified eyes. The high priestess stopped before the wall and pushed against it with her palm. Silently, a panel pivoted open onto another unlit passageway, and she led her flock through.

Once they were gone the two men emerged from their hiding places and looked at each other in speechless confusion, neither knowing what to make of it all.

"Do you think they have captured Amber?" Cam whispered.

"I cannot say," Kha-Hotep answered softly. "Let us follow."

Silently and stealthily they followed the procession along the darkened temple corridor. After several more twists and turns the Egyptians stopped in the middle of a passage, seemingly at random. The priestess reached out and pressed an inconspicuous spot on the wall's carved molding. The small section depressed beneath her hand, and then an entire section of wall slid away with a stony grumble. It opened into the night, the wide desert sky already softening from black to the indigo of approaching dawn.

The procession continued out the tunnel.

"Priests and their secret doors," Cam murmured.

"Priests and their secrets," Kha-Hotep whispered back.

49

The Gates of Alexandria
Dawn — Eight days after the Event

Alright then, my girl, Nellie encouraged herself. *Let's get a move on.* The great gate to the city opened its doors. She took a deep breath, and strode into Alexandria.

As she crossed the threshold, a quartet of guards in chain mail tunics quickly surrounded her, spears and shields at the ready, their faces grim and determined. Despite herself, Nellie felt a perverse twinge of pleasure that grown men considered her such a frightening threat.

"Halt in the name of the prefect," one of them ordered, a horse-faced man in a centurion's helmet.

"Good morning!" she answered with a cheery smile. "Thank you for letting me come in. I hope I haven't made any trouble for you."

Their attitude did not improve. The man stepped forward.

DANA FREDSTI | DAVID FITZGERALD

"Keep still. Make no sudden movements of your hands."

Nellie froze in place. "I mean you no harm," she said. "I've come back here to help."

"Cease talking at once," he snapped. "You are under arrest."

"Arrested?" Her face paled. "Please, you must take me to your magistrate Calix and Lady Hypatia—it's absolutely vital!"

"Your master killed Calix yesterday with his sorcery. You are accessory to his murder."

Shock stole her voice, but then she rallied. "Please, Hypatia will remember me! You must take me to her, I beg you!"

"Never." The man's voice was iron scraping on granite. "We will die before we suffer you to come into her presence, sorceress."

"But—"

"Enough!" He drew his sword. "Submit or we kill you where you stand." Nellie slowly lifted her hands in surrender.

"Alright. You win."

She had just one ace left up her sleeve, but now was not the time. Instead she let the soldiers march her into the city.

* * *

Even without the benefit of steel, gaslights, or other modern amenities, the soaring architecture and bustling streets of Alexandria rivaled her beloved New York. Her captors took her down the city's primary thoroughfare, at least a hundred feet wide and bordered on either side by rows of towering columns running the length of the metropolis. A lavish blend of Egyptian and Roman styles dominated, from the magnificent temples and theaters to the great houses of the wealthy, and the royal palace complex.

"Are you taking me to the palace?" she asked hopefully. If they locked her in the royal dungeons, perhaps she could get word to Hypatia—if the aristocratic woman would still be willing to grant an audience.

The captain turned to glare at her. "The brig of the Macedonian barracks is as close as you'll ever get to the palace. It's the sewer-pit where we toss all the garbage before their execution."

"Is there to be no trial at all?" she asked, horrified.

The soldiers chuckled at her naïveté.

The unusual procession attracted attention. She felt every pair of eyes as they began to attract a crowd. Excited bystanders pointed at her. Some looked on with amazed wonder, others glared angrily. Nellie's heart began to beat a bit faster than she liked. Her guards grew uneasy, too. They shouted for the massing throng to clear the way, but the thoroughfare became more choked with curious onlookers.

"Please, my lady, heal my child!" an anguished young mother cried, holding up a screaming baby. Several people tried to reach around the shields of the guards to touch her, only to be shoved back with force. A wild-eyed bearded man grasped for her with a claw-like hand, fanatical fire in his eyes.

"*Whore of Babylon!*" he raged, spittle flying. "*Mother of harlots and abominations of the Earth!*" Nellie recoiled as the man lunged at her again, and two of her guards rushed to block him. One's shield-rush caught the howling doomcaster in the teeth, causing him to shriek and grab at his bloody mouth.

Crouching, Nellie saw her chance and dove past the other distracted guards into the crowd itself. A gauntlet of hands surrounded her—adoring followers hoping to receive a miracle from her touch, and hate-fueled fanatics howling for her blood. She bolted past them all, slipping through the outstretched hands and fending off blows. In her wake, the two groups turned upon each other.

Her erstwhile guards smashed their own way through the crowd and bellowed for bystanders to make way, but the crowded street had turned into a riot. Their shields now thwarted their pursuit. Hapless pedestrians in the way were crushed up against them, unable to move.

A trio of horses pulling a chariot reared and panicked, very nearly trampling Nellie. She tumbled to the ground and dragged herself away from beneath the stamping hooves, scrambling to her feet again on the other side of the stalled *triga* and its frustrated charioteer.

Even with all the commotion she could still hear the shouts of her pursuers. She looked around for an escape route. A wide and crowded public square lay just ahead, brimming with statues, public fountains, and market stalls. She made for it, cursing her skirts and boots as she ran, while chaos continued to erupt all around her.

Merchants, customers, and beggars alike were caught up in the spreading tumult. Without slowing her pace, Nellie took advantage of the confusion to snatch the faded awning off of a nearby fig stand. Ducking around a statue of Juno, she quickly pulled it around her as a makeshift cloak, and then zig-zagged through the maze of the bazaar, lightly stepping over the contents of spilled baskets and upset amphorae while the sellers struggled to retrieve their wares.

Abruptly, she popped out of the jumbled maze into another open space, nearly colliding with the four guards pursuing her. Letting out a shriek of alarm she cringed, bracing herself for the impact of their shields—or their spears. They thundered past her without a second glance.

Nellie thought she'd collapse then and there.

"Nellie, old gal," she told herself, watching them go, "if you were a cat, I'd say you were down to your last life." Still not quite believing her luck, she rallied and darted off in another direction, just another terrified citizen fleeing the riot.

From her hiding place, Nellie marveled up at the lighthouse on Pharos Island, towering overhead. Below it the Great Harbor and all her daughter ports spread out all around, offering enough berths for hundreds of ships. Its sheltered cove was nearly spacious enough to contain a second Alexandria. The lines and sails of all the docked vessels, gently bobbing in their moorings, made a soft percussive concerto as they slapped against the masts and fluttered in the breeze.

The smashed ruins of even more vessels still littered the eastern arm of the harbor.

She crouched behind the chunky limestone blocks of some unfinished palace, rough piles of ruins that clung like barnacles at the end of a rocky jetty. There was a partial inscription on a broken beam of stone gable.

TIMONIVM M ANTONI DOMVS

Her language implants suggested a translation—*The Timonium, House of Marcus Antonius.* Marc Antony's house? She *was* hob-nobbing with grand folks these days. The ruins afforded her the ideal catbird seat to observe the ongoing commotion in relative security.

Facing the city, to her left stretched a finger of land covered in lush gardens and groves of palms and fruit trees—the grounds of the royal palaces, beautiful, gleaming pillared structures overlooking both city and sea. From the gardens there came cries of peacocks and baboons, and the occasional glimpses of strolling giraffes and ostriches. Its high walls were well guarded.

Surely the Lady Hypatia was somewhere in one of those regal buildings, advising their ruler. If only she could find a way to slip in there—but with rioting in the streets, and the city watch prepared to arrest her on sight, was there *anyone* she dared ask for help?

Still, what other option did she have?

To her right stood market bazaars and rows of warehouses, all dominated by a large pillared temple complex fronted by two gigantic obelisks keeping watch over the Harbor—Cleopatra's Needles, she realized. One of them had been placed in New York's Central Park just a few years past—she had admired it there more than once.

The Roman-style temple appeared to have been converted into a Christian church, but it still bore its previous name.

CAESAREVM

The *Caesareum*. Why did that name ring a bell?

At any other time, the harbor's piers and docks would

have been alive with sailors, fishermen, stevedores, merchant captains, and more—the scene of constant activity at most any hour of the day, with cargo and travelers coming in and going out to and from all the reaches of the Mediterranean world.

Today, it was a war zone.

All morning and well into the afternoon, from her hidden vantage point on the jetty she watched roving bands of angry men stalking the streets and back alleyways of the dockside. When opposing groups met, they fell upon one another savagely, staining the flagstones red and littering them with broken, twisted bodies. A sickly copper tang of spilled blood and the stink of butchery blended with the overpowering scents of salt air and fish.

When the sun began to dip below the western walls, Nellie decided it was time to move. The city streets would not be any safer once night fell. Wrapping herself once more in her purloined makeshift shawl, she emerged from her stony refuge and skulked down the jetty, slipping back into the looming shadows of the closest waterfront alley.

She affected the stooped, hobbling gait of a poor old woman, hoping to avoid attention. The maritime warehouses and drinking haunts quickly gave way to military barracks, and then to more upper-class districts, great houses of the well-to-do, a variety of fancy public buildings, and the other side of the palace grounds.

Normally Nellie would have felt safer in the upscale districts of a city, but even here among the well-heeled citizens, tensions were palpable. She cringed away from every passing soldier, certain that she would be recognized at any moment, keeping unobtrusively to the edges of the busy streets.

Her best bet seemed to lie in the public gardens outside the entrance to the palace. Perhaps if she made herself as inconspicuous as possible, she might have a chance of spotting Hypatia's coming or going, or find an unguarded way inside.

Gathering up her courage, she shuffled her doddering way across the main thoroughfare toward the safety of the park. While she was still only halfway across the street, however, shouts of alarm rose from down the block. Men ran down the avenue, crying out.

"The *parabolani*! The *parabolani* are coming to attack the Jewish quarter!" The Jews on the street near her gasped and ran the other way.

Parabolani? She didn't recognize the word, and her language implants seemed to think *parabolani* meant "nurses." Nellie turned to see a huge mob of fierce black-hooded men all armed with staves, swords, or clubs, chanting unintelligible slogans and tramping down the street in her direction. A young Hebrew woman stopped and seized Nellie's arm, frightened concern in her eyes.

"*Yafa sheli*, are you Jewish or Greek? Come, it isn't safe. You must come with us!"

Nellie met the girl's eyes with gratitude. "You go. I'll be alright. Go!"

The girl hesitated, then nodded and joined those running for safety. Nellie rushed toward the palace gardens without any further pretense at infirmity and hid behind a stand of jasmine flowers. As she watched, the angry stream of black hoods continued past, making the street look like the back of an enormous swollen crocodile.

A fresh new commotion broke out, and she pulled aside the jasmine branches to see what it was. The sharp clatter of horse hooves echoed off the cobblestones, as armored riders in glittering mail thundered down the street from the east, facing down the mob. Prefectural guards, escorting a chariot back toward the palace. Nellie's eyes lit up at the sight of the passenger.

Maybe her luck was changing for the better after all.

"Make way for the Lady Hypatia!" the captain of her guard ordered the surly crowd. "Disperse at once, by order of the prefect!"

The mob roared back its defiance. There were many more of them than the mounted guards—and the guards knew it.

"This is your final warning!" The tendons in the captain's neck stretched taut. "Return to your homes! Obey this instant, in the name of the Emperor himself!"

For a heartbeat or two the crowd seemed to waver. Then one of the leaders stepped forward. His flowing, long-sleeved fawn-colored robe and his black pointed hat all made him look like a wizard—a clergyman of sorts, Nellie guessed. He pointed an accusatory finger at the captain.

"There is no more Emperor! All the earthly princes and authorities have been overthrown and the Lord cometh soon in judgment!"

"Insurrectionist!" The captain drew his sword and raised it high. *"Seize him!"* The guards formed a line around their captain, urging their mounts forward. The priest turned to his flock with a wave of his arm.

"Obey God, not men!" he bellowed. *"Take them!"*

With another roar, the *parabolani* rushed toward the charging horsemen.

50

From the chariot, Hypatia and Aspasius stared in horror at the unfolding scene.

"Mistress! We must turn the chariot around!" the Hyrcanian urged her. "We cannot get through!"

Hypatia looked out at the palace grounds, so tantalizingly close, then at the howling mob boiling around the horsemen. Aspasius was right. Soon they would all be overwhelmed.

"Do it!" she told her slave, and called to her remaining guards. "Bring the other soldiers back! We can't hold the crowd off here!"

They nodded, reining in their steeds to give Aspasius room to maneuver. But he could not control the turn. The frightened horses panicked at the sight of the embattled throng. Thrashing and stamping to pull free of their yokes, they effectively trapped the chariot in place mid-turn, and the tide of the mob engulfed the cavalrymen up ahead.

Hypatia cried out for the captain to retreat, but he could not hear her. Even as he and his men continued hacking with their swords, she watched as the swarm brought them down, plucking them off their horses with hooked staves, spearing them with makeshift lances, or simply overwhelming them with waves of grasping hands and fists. The rest of the crowd surged around the doomed soldiers and toward the stalled chariot.

Nellie stared, stunned by the sight of the guards being swarmed by the homicidal mob. She looked at Hypatia's stranded chariot, and the sight triggered a sudden jolt of memory—of a story that had horrified and repulsed her as a child.

Her schoolmaster, a veteran of the War, had seen terrible things at the Battle of Gettysburg, instilling in him a perverse tendency toward gallows humor. One day, he wished to instill a lesson about the proper sphere of womankind. To make his point, he related to his class the ghastly cautionary tale of the ancient scientist Hypatia, and her dreadful demise.

"She made herself an object of fear and hatred to the Nitrian monks and fanatical mobs of the local orthodox bishop," he'd said with poorly disguised relish, "by whom she was ultimately murdered under circumstances of revolting barbarity. She was torn from her chariot, dragged through the streets to the *Caesareum*, there to be stripped naked and butchered, cut to pieces with sharpened tile shards, and her limbs finally burned piecemeal."

"She was torn from her chariot." His unpleasant voice echoed in Nellie's mind. *"She was torn from her chariot…"*

"It's happening," she whispered, her horror growing. "Good Lord, it's happening now."

Time to put her cards on the table. Standing, Nellie cast off her cloak, then pulled her ace from her boot—the German pistol Blake had given her. Holding it tightly in one hand, she strode out into the street.

The mob smashed into the chariot's sides like waves crashing against the rocks. Furious men rushed them, faces red with rage, their clawing hands grasping for Hypatia. Aspasius was shouting, but she could hear nothing but her attacker's howls, the screams of horses and bystanders, and the shattering of pottery.

Hypatia raised a hand to defend herself, but beefy fingers clamped down on her wrist and yanked hard, pulling her over the side and to the cobblestones below. She screamed in pain and fear, the sound lost in the roar surrounding her. Cruel hands dragged her away, others kicking and striking at her as she was hauled across the unyielding flagstones. Then she was dropped to the street again.

Groaning, she raised up on her elbows, trying to stand. There was no sign of Aspasius or any of her guard, nothing but her assailants encircling her. The robed lector who had challenged the captain loomed over her. Hypatia recognized him. He had been her student, once.

"Petros, please!" she pleaded. His face was a stone.

"You Jezebel! You who would corrupt the prefect with your witchery and whoredom!" He raised his voice to his flock. "This is the word of the Lord," he commanded. "You shall throw her down, this cursed woman. The dogs shall eat her flesh, and her carcass shall be as dung upon the field. Take her away!" The closest two *parabolani* reached down and grabbed her arms. The crowd parted to let them haul her off.

"Let her go now, or die where you stand!"

The ringleader gritted his teeth at the interloper.

"Seize that witch, too! They are both condemned!"

Nellie strode up to the so-called holy man until they were face to face, and without another word, shot him in the head. He dropped dead on the pavestones, his expression a rictus of outraged confusion. Someone screamed, and the crowd froze in shock. Without pause, Nellie turned on the two brutes holding Hypatia and shot the larger man in the center of his forehead before turning the pistol on the other man and pulling the trigger.

There was a hollow *click.*

Nellie froze. If the crowd understood that her weapon was out of ammo, she and Hypatia would be torn to pieces in seconds. Locking eyes with the man, she raised her gun and put on her best poker face. The terrified *parabolani's* face was pale and running with drops of sweat.

"You," she said. "Go! Go and… and sin no more."

With a gulp, he gave a shaky nod and backed off step by tentative step before turning to break into a sprint and flee. The rest of the stunned mob took to their heels like a startled flock of birds.

Nellie watched them go, allowing herself a sigh of relief only when the last of the mob had fled out of sight down the street. She turned to Hypatia, who stood trembling like a faded ghost, before her head lolled and she went limp.

"Oh! Oh!" Nellie ran to catch her before the woman fainted dead away. "It's alright now, I've got you. They're gone."

Hypatia's eyes fluttered. She looked up to the woman who had just saved her life, and went bright with recognition. "It's you…" she murmured.

Nellie smiled and nodded, suddenly so happy she thought she might start bawling like a baby. The face of her unpleasant childhood schoolmaster flashed into her mind.

Put that *in your history books, you despicable old man.*

"Yes. It's me. Come, let's get you out of here." She looked at the battered chariot, now on its side. There was no sign of the horses, or of the charioteer, or of Hypatia's guard. Slipping an arm around the woman's shoulders, Nellie gently led her back across the grounds to the safety of the palace.

Twilight descended upon the city. From the balcony of the palace, two women stood with the Prefect Orestes and looked out at the dimming light. Sounds of violence still echoed in the distance. Nellie pointed to the rising dust trails off on the western horizon, illuminated by the last ember of the reddening sunset.

"That's the real enemy," she said. "When they get here, we'll need the strength of everyone in the city to resist their war machines. And even that may not be enough."

"Should we flee the city?" Hypatia asked, her eyes wide with fear.

Nellie looked at her. "Where would we go?"

51

Place: Unknown
Time: Unknown

Amber woke up. She found herself standing in a pitch-black enclosed space. God, was she was dreaming *again*? Another irritatingly incomprehensible dream, where the mysterious figure with Merlin's face and voice continued to screw with her mind?

Then her hands brushed up against cold stone and she froze, a stab of pure horror piercing her thoughts.

"Oh my god," she breathed. Her voice fell flatly into the darkness, reinforcing the fear. She wasn't in a coffin or even a sarcophagus, but Egypt had plenty of burial chambers.

"Ohgodohgod*ohgodohgod*..."

Her breath came in hyperventilated gasps. She quickly became light-headed as panic raced through her body, the adrenaline rush and dizziness dropping her to her knees with a jarring thud. The effect speeded up, the sound of her shallow, frantic breaths filling the stale air until it was all she could hear.

Buried alive. I've been buried alive.

She forced herself to regulate her breathing.

In for four counts. Hold it for seven. Exhale for eight. She repeated the pattern four or five times. It was a trick her dad had taught her to help stave off panic attacks, something Amber had been prone to up through high school graduation. Funny she hadn't thought to use it up till now. Then again, real fight-or-flight situations didn't lend themselves to breathing exercises.

When she finally had it under control, Amber went back to her first thought. *Could* this be a dream? Maybe she was still on the *Star of the Dawn*, her subconscious playing nasty tricks on her.

No. No, this was real. Her throbbing knees were a testament to that. She'd have bruises, maybe even swelling. If she hadn't been wearing the leather cavalier boots, it could have been much worse. Shifting her weight off her knees, Amber sat gingerly on the ground, tugging on the straps of her backpack as its bulk threatened to pull her off balance.

My backpack.

Her phone was in her backpack, and the phone had a flashlight app. If it had enough charge left to turn on.

Shrugged out of the straps, Amber brought the

backpack around in front of her, between her thighs. Slowly, carefully, she reached inside, feeling along the interior until she found the zippered compartment where she kept her phone. She pulled it out with trembling fingers, found the "on" switch and pressed it, holding it down for a few beats before releasing it.

Then she waited. When the screen lit up and the black apple with the bite out of it appeared, Amber nearly wept with relief. She still didn't know how much battery life remained, though.

"No time for that," she muttered as the password screen came up. She quickly checked the battery life— twenty percent. It'd do.

It would have to.

The flashlight app wasn't much—she'd have preferred a Maglite—but it was better than the alternative. Holding the phone up, Amber shone the light in front of her, illuminating a stone wall. No hieroglyphs or art, no pillars encrusted with semi-precious stones... just plain stone. Crude flagstones formed the floor, which vanished into blackness on either side. A tunnel, then, with no end in sight. For all she knew it went on for miles.

There's only one way to find out. She got to her feet, putting the backpack on again. But which way? She had no way of knowing which way she'd come from.

There was a sudden pressure in her skull, like the moment before her ears popped when the elevation changed. It didn't quite hurt, but it made her turn her head to the left and look into the impenetrable darkness in that direction. Yes, that looked right.

This way, Amber…

"What the hell?" Amber whirled around, even though she knew she wouldn't see anyone. That damned voice in her head. The same siren song that'd led her to that bizarre underground bunker, enabled her to re-route the *Vanuatu*, that had diverted her across the desert, and called her away from her friends—all to bring her to this tunnel. She felt violated.

This way, Amber… this way.

The pressure in her mind increased, the compulsion to go to her left growing more imperative. Something inside her snapped.

"I'm *sick* of this shit!" she yelled, her words deadened by the stone walls. "I'm not a goddamn puppet! If you want something from me, then ask!"

It stopped.

No more voice, no compulsion.

Nothing.

Then…

Please.

After a brief pause, Amber set off down the tunnel. At least it was her choice this time.

* * *

Once the procession had moved out into the open air, Cam and Kha-Hotep crept up to the hidden tunnel opening. At the threshold, Cam abruptly froze.

A broad-faced giant looked down upon him, filling his field of vision.

"Gods of my father..." he swore quietly, riveted by fright.

Kha-Hotep put a comforting hand on his back, looking over the Celt's shoulder.

"Show him no fear, little brother," he whispered. "Let him see what great hearts your tribe have."

The scarlet-skinned titan stared down at them with cold, implacable eyes. He wore an Egyptian headdress striped with gold and cobalt, topped by a golden cobra, and sported a long, narrow plaited beard. His massive body was that of a lion, each of his outstretched paws as big as a longhouse.

Cam felt a jolt of embarrassment. "Only a statue."

Kha-Hotep clapped him on the back. "A most fearsome figure, is he not?" The two kept their voices to an undertone.

"Who is he?"

"We call him *Hor-em-Akhet*, Horus of the Horizon."

Before them, the great stone man-lion lay recumbent, with the largest of the pyramids for his backdrop. As they watched, the procession made its way through the courtyard between the temple and the colossal statue, entering a passage-space between the outstretched lion paws.

At the very end of that passageway, just below the giant's long plaited beard, stood an upright sarcophagus. In the crook of each of the man-lion's forearms sat a large bronze bowl. A pair of acolytes bore their candles down the walkway and reached up to light the oil within. Both bowls blazed to life, suddenly illuminating the colors of the giant's head and torso.

Music began, rattling sistra and strumming harps. The high priestess led the rest of the softly chanting procession down to the waiting sarcophagus. The increasingly edgy Cam and Kha-Hotep crept up behind them as closely as they dared, all under the unsettling gaze of Hor-em-Akhet. They hid behind a great stone paw and spied on the proceedings.

The priestess halted at the sarcophagus and bowed low before the brilliantly decorated burial case. She waited for the chant to come to an end, then spoke to the believers.

"It is written in the *Book of Coming Forth into the Light*— or the *Book of the Dead*, as some so name it—that ever since the sky was split from the earth and the gods went to the sky, the earth below should slowly turn in cycles of renewal, to the joy or woe of Man. Yet, it is also written that there would come a time when, after countless rises and falls, the world we know was destined to end.

"We have seen the end of the old world. We were witnesses when the doors of the starry firmament were thrown open, that fire and lightning might rain down from the sky. *Ma'at*, the divine order was taken, with chaos left in its place, and those of us who did not perish mourned, with much fear and great wonder. Yet lordly Atum-Ra and great Osiris did not leave us with naught but chaos. On that same terrible day was also given a precious gift unto us.

"We found that gift of hope, freshly come down from the heavens, and with love and devotion, we bore the coffer of burnished silver with its treasure to this holy place, laying it to rest here against the bosom of Hor-em-Akhet, the Leonine, the Horus of the Horizon. Here we adorned it with jewels, sacred images and hieroglyphs. For herein is Siu-Netherit, born of Osiris, who shall rise again and call forth the new world into being."

"Who is this... *Siu-Netherit*?" Cam whispered. His implant translated as "Star Eyes."

Kha-Hotep shook his head. "No god I ever heard of."

As the sky paled, the first rays of the new dawn glazed the far horizon behind them. The high priestess turned again and bowed low to the sarcophagus, then raised her arms wide in an invocation.

"O Siu-Netherit, starry-eyed god of the night! Hearken to the voice of thy priestess! Thou who speaks to us in our dreams. The herald of Osiris, who shall bring forth the new worl—"

She stopped short, staring off into the distance.

Cam followed her gaze.

Out on the eastern horizon, like a shaft of sunlight cutting through clouds after the rain, yet a thousand times mightier, a pillar of pure light split the sky from earth to the heavens. Then, rising up from the earth, another joined it. Then a third, leagues away.

A tear trailed down the priestess's cheek.

"A miracle," she breathed.

This is the end, Amber realized. Her tunnel abruptly made a turn to the right—and ended in a featureless wall. Great. Now she'd have to turn around and go all the way back to where she started, wherever that was. *All that for nothing*. Sleepwalking, her freaky dreams, voices in her head…

Maybe I really am going crazy, she thought in frustration.

No, the voice said.

"Stop it!" Grabbing her head between her hands, Amber leaned against the wall for support, only to have it pivot away from the pressure. She stumbled through the passage into light.

The secret door had opened to the pre-dawn sky, and a corridor with red walls on either side. Directly in front of her stood a large stone stela. In a numb daze, she came around for a closer look. Upright against the slab rested an even larger shape—rectangular, but with rounded edges, like a giant lozenge, and bigger than a refrigerator.

Running a hand over its surface, Amber discovered that it was constructed of metal, not stone, gleaming like silver in the glow from a pair of bronze oil lights on the walls above. Its surface had been freshly decorated with paint and bits of shell and glass, all forming the detailed figure of a hawk-headed man. His glittering eyes appeared to be made of amethyst.

Something overhead caught her eye, a shape like a stalactite, and she looked up to see the face of the Great Sphinx looming above her. Staggered, she snapped out of her daze and slowly turned to take in the rest of her surroundings... and gasped, holding her breath.

A tall Egyptian woman stood with her back to her, close enough Amber could almost reach out and touch her. A whole audience of worshipers was there as well, but none of them saw Amber. All were staring off into the horizon at a trio of energy beams, like towering bundles of lightning bolts, spearing upward to light up the sky.

Three blazing aftershocks of the Event, burning up time and space.

"We're too late," Amber murmured. "It's the end of the world."

52

"Look! It's her!" Cam whispered urgently as he caught sight of Amber rounding the silver sarcophagus. Only Kha-Hotep's firm hand on his shoulder stopped him from rushing to her side.

"Easy, my brother," the Egyptian said quietly. "If we are careful, the three of us may leave this place with none the wiser."

"It's the end of the world."

The priestess whirled about in surprise at the sound of Amber's voice, kohl-dark eyes blazing with outrage.

"Interloper! How dare you traverse our secret ways and profane the sacred gift?" Her two lions roared, tensing their bodies to spring upon the strange woman at their mistress' command. Amber froze, speechless.

* * *

Cam leapt to his feet and rushed forward, sword in hand. Kha-Hotep swore, but quickly joined him, the two of them scattering the startled worshipers.

The priestess turned on the new intruders, their death sentence clear in her eyes.

"To be here so armed is sacrilege." She looked at her lions, already baring their teeth at the two men. "Sheshmu, Maahes," she called. "Kill them!"

Swords out, Cam and Kha-Hotep braced themselves to fight the great cats.

"Wait!" Amber shouted, even as she thought, *what do I do now?*

"Leave these men alone," she continued with an authority she didn't feel. "They… they are my servants!"

The priestess whistled sharply, and the lions halted instantly. "Who are you?" she demanded in a voice that said she was accustomed to obedience. "Tell me at once!"

"I am Amber of San Diego! I, who killed the crocodile god—" *what did they call it?* "Petsuchos!" she continued, improvising as fast as she could. "I have come a great distance to find you. In fact, the gods have sent me here with a message! Hear me!"

"You lie," the priestess hissed. "You shall feed my lions and go down to death in pain and tears! There the Eater of Hearts shall feast upon you for all eternity!"

Thinking fast, Amber pointed to the three aftershocks in the distance.

"For your impudence, I will take away these three stairways to Heaven!"

The aftershocks continued to blaze away like tornados of fire and light.

Shit.

"Now!" she shouted. "They are going away!"

Nothing.

"*Now*, I say!"

After one last painfully long delay, the three aftershocks winked out, one by one. A gasp went up from the crowd, but the priestess remained unimpressed.

"I do not think that was your doing, Scarlet-Hair. I think you are some demon-creature of chaos sent from Isfet and Set."

"I'm here to help you," Amber insisted. "All of you!"

"Prove your honeyed words are true, then, False One!"

"I *can* prove it!" Amber did her best to ignore the liquid growls coming from the lions. "I know the god you serve. He speaks to me in my dreams. I have seen his dark face and silver hair. I have seen the falling stars in his eyes."

A change came over the priestess's face. Her expression softened, and her gaze turned curiously intense as she gazed at the younger woman.

"You speak the truth?"

DANA FREDSTI | DAVID FITZGERALD

Surprised by the question, Amber could only nod mutely, at a loss for what else to say. The priestess continued to stare intently into Amber's eyes, as if she could find the truth there.

"*Do* you speak the truth, Amber of San Diego?"

"I... I..." Amber wasn't sure what was happening, but something had changed, and the woman's quiet intensity was damaging her cool. She tried to think of something else to say, anything, but no words would come.

Nefer-Tamit, came an unbidden thought.

"What?" she said aloud, confused.

Her name is Nefer-Tamit, the familiar voice in her head prompted her.

"The god tells me... your name is Nefer... Nefer... Tamit," she blurted out.

The priestess stood quiet for a long moment before speaking again.

"You *have* seen Siu-Netherit, the starry-eyed god." Leaning in, she kissed Amber's forehead.

53

The Base of the Great Sphinx
Dawn — Nine days after the Event

The first light of morning touched the giant's face and descended like a curtain to illuminate Amber, the priestess, and the shining silver sarcophagus. The brightness of dawn spilled across the eastern sky. Cam and Kha-Hotep stared, uncertain of what had just happened, and still wary of the lions poised between them and their friend.

"Amber!" Cam called. She hesitated as if listening to something only she could hear, then turned to him.

"It's alright now, Cam," she said. "Don't worry. I know what to do now." She reached out to touch the sarcophagus. "I just need to open this."

The crowd gasped, as did the high priestess Nefer-Tamit. She made a graceful bow, low and reverent, this time directed to Amber. Her lions turned and padded up to join their mistress, meekly lying down at her feet.

"O holy consort, show us the will of Siu-Netherit."

"Amber, please step away from that coffin," Cam urged.

"Listen to him, Amber," Kha-Hotep joined in.

"Silence your tongues!" The high priestess turned on them, her eyes flashing, and she made a sharp sidelong chopping gesture. "She shall do as her lord commands her."

"Amber, there's a god in there!" Cam cried out. "Don't do it!"

He was too late. Amber was already in motion, stooping and then running her hand along the right side of the sleek metal casing. She felt around, not looking, as though relying on muscle memory alone, but her fingers found what they were searching for all the same.

She pressed a short series of buttons, and then quickly stepped back as an odd electronic whirring sound came from within the metal box. At the same moment, a brilliant line of light appeared along its side, forming a vertical split as the lid and base of the sarcophagus separated.

The lid swung open.

A murmur of awe came from the crowd of worshipers, and they prostrated themselves, bowing low before the sight. The lone occupant lay upright and unmoving, cushioned in a foam padding. His clothing looked both modern and military, like his haircut. Amber and Cam stared at the body, stunned by what they saw. They knew the man.

A sudden wave of vertigo slammed into Amber. She fought to stay on her feet as the world spun.

He opened his eyes.

It was János Mehta.

Mehta stepped out of the capsule and regarded the crowd with a curiously pleased look on his face. Enraged, Cam drew his sword.

"Murderer!" he yelled as he lunged forward, drawing his arm back to cut the man down. Mehta made no move to defend himself, but simply looked over at the attacking Celt, locking eyes with him. Cam instantly froze in mid-strike, and then crumpled to the dusty flagstones.

Kha-Hotep leapt to his feet as well and charged Mehta's other flank with a wild swing of his *khopesh*. Mehta turned his gaze on the Egyptian, and Kha-Hotep only had a split-second to marvel at the man's violet, star-streaked eyes before his sickle sword clattered on the pavement and he toppled to the ground beside Cam.

Amber watched in horror as first Cam, and then Kha-Hotep collapsed to the ground without warning and lay unmoving.

No no no no no no…

Were they still alive? Or had she just lost the only family she had left?

Mehta turned her way.

Oh god.

Oh god—it's my turn now. She braced herself for the worst.

Ignoring the priestess, her lions, and the crowd of worshipers—all of whom stood there, transfixed— he took a step closer, and then another, his eyes never leaving hers.

Amber wanted to look away. Hell, she wanted to run, but she couldn't do either. Paralyzed with fear, she could only stand there, thoughts racing, as the man calmly, almost gently, moved in on her. How could János Mehta be the man who'd haunted her dreams all this time? Was he even *human*?

He stopped just a few feet from her. Still she remained fixed in place, unable to escape. His alien eyes, with their familiar scintillating gaze, remained riveted on hers, though his expression stayed strangely empty, unreadable.

"Amber." he said softly. It was almost a question. Then he nodded as if satisfied. "Amber, right?"

He smiled.

This wasn't the cheerfully soulless smile of the imposter who'd stolen the *Vanuatu* and killed Merlin. It radiated genuine warmth and relief, as if the weight of the world had dropped off him at the sight of her. Closing the distance between them, he gently laid his hands on her shoulders as if they were old friends. And maybe they were. She didn't know what to think anymore.

"Merlin...?" She held her breath, hardly daring to hope.

He stared at her blankly. "Merlin? Who's Merlin?"

Her heart sank. He shook his head and gave a small laugh.

"Never mind, it doesn't matter. But you and I need to talk. We..." he hesitated, as if searching for the right words. "We have work to do."

Amber's fear lifted, and she realized she wasn't paralyzed at all. She found her voice again. "What do you mean?"

"I think..." he paused again, as if uncertain. "I think you and I are going to save the world."

ACKNOWLEDGEMENTS

Once again, mega thanks to Steve Saffel, our Dark Editorial Overlord. Steve, your skill and understanding of what your authors are trying to create always results in a better book and we appreciate your willingness to travel on the sometimes rocky road of Edits with us.

Having a good agent is a gift, and the gratitude we have for our agent Jill Marsal continues to grow.

As always, thank you to the crew at Titan Books, especially our stellar copy editor Jess Woo, who made some truly excellent catches! Thanks to Nick Landau and Vivian Chueng, Davi Lancett, Paul Gill, George Sandison, Hannah Scudamore, Julia Lloyd, Katharine Carroll, Lydia Gittins, Jenny Boyce, and anyone we may have missed.

Many thanks to the following people for their help with research and motivation: Aaron Adair; Susi and

Uwe Bocks; Lisa "Jei Jei" Brackmann; Dr. Richard Carrier; Sue Erokan; Bill "Willy P" Galante; Gwenola le Garrec-Cooper; Jessica Hanselman Gray; Ray Harris of *The History of WWII Podcast*; Krista Itzhak; Yaprak Ergurman Kenger; Alisha Koch; Yasmine Mohammed; Faisal Saeed Al Mutar; Minas Papageorgiou; Adrienne Mowery Poirier; Les Sœurs Sautez, Maud y Michele; Mark Scioneaux; Kristina Sellers Shaw; Miryam Strautkalns. And thank you, voice artist Aaron Shedlock, for bringing our characters to life! Thanks, all!

Enkati's song, "The Love of the Beloved," is a real ancient Egyptian one; taken from Barbara Mertz, *Red Land, Black Land: The World of the Ancient Egyptians*, Rev. ed. New York: Dodd, Mead, 1978.

The non-science-fictional parts of the El Alamein section are based off of the real accounts from tank crewmen from both sides, esp. Maj. Robert Crisp's *Brazen Chariots* (1959), Brigadier C. E. Lucas Phillips' *Alamein* (1962), as well as the war letters of German tank gunner Karl Fuchs (1987) and many more. Many other history books, much more than we can easily list here, were helpful here as well; especially Jack Coggin's *The Campaign for North Africa*, Stephen Bungay's *Alamein*, and Wolfgang Schneider's *Panzer Tactics: German Small-Unit Armor Tactics in World War II*.

ABOUT THE AUTHORS

Dana Fredsti is an ex B-movie actress with a background in theatrical combat (a skill she utilized in *Army of Darkness* as a sword-fighting Deadite and fight captain). Through seven-plus years of volunteering at EFBC/FCC, Dana's been kissed by tigers, and had her thumb sucked by an ocelot with nursing issues. She's addicted to bad movies and any book or film, good or bad, which includes zombies. She's the author of *The Spawn of Lilith*, *Blood Ink*, the *Ashley Parker* series, touted as Buffy meets the Walking Dead, the zombie noir novella, *A Man's Gotta Eat What a Man's Gotta Eat*, and the cozy noir mystery *Murder for Hire: The Peruvian Pigeon*. With David Fitzgerald she is the co-author of *Time Shards* and *Shatter War*, and she has stories in the *V-Wars: Shockwaves* and *Joe Ledger: Unstoppable* anthologies.

David Fitzgerald is a historical researcher, an international public speaker, and an award-winning author of both genre fiction and historical nonfiction, such as *The Complete Heretic's Guide to Western Religion* series and *Nailed*. He is also a founding member of San Francisco Writer's Coffeehouse. He lives with his wife, actress/writer Dana Fredsti, and their small menagerie of cats and dogs, and is often accused of being the Ferris Bueller of San Francisco. His latest fiction is the *Time Shards* series.